MEMORY
AND MAGIC

D. M. BEUCLER

Text 2025 © D. M. Beucler
Cover 2025 © Tara Bush
Editorial Team: Francesca T Barbini, Shona Kinsella, Libby Schade
Typesetting: Francesca T Barbini, Libby Schade
First published by Luna Press Publishing, Edinburgh, 2025

A CIP catalogue record is available from the British Library

www.lunapresspublishing.com

ISBN-13: 978-1-915556-62-2

To Joshua, Darian and Nigel with all my love.

Contents

Chapter One

On the other side of the west gate was a third of Tamsin Saer's rent money. If she could pass through it. The dozen blue-coated guards who manned the checkpoint, fidgeting with their muskets, were supposed to keep the parolees from Kingsgate gaol within the confines of the Narrows, the outer ring of the three-walled city of Celdre. In practice the gate guard turned away a handful of people, more or less randomly, every day. On the other side of the wall the limestone facade would be polished, but here a layer of soot and grime stained everything a murky grey-brown. To the left of the arched, iron gateway hung a lone gibbet, its contents far from fresh. The sign swaying from the corpse's feet said, 'blood mage'.

Tamsin settled her willow laundry basket on her hip. At least the cold kept the smell down. Rent money, she reminded herself. Slush soaked into her turn leather shoes. They needed re-waxing, but at three copper pennies for the service, it was too dear. Winter was not releasing its hold easily this year; it was at the second week of Spring, yet almost a yard of snow had barricaded the streets only a few days before.

"We was nearly without wood," the Granny ahead of her complained. Tamsin noted bands of silk ribbon at the hem of the old woman's dress – badly dyed silk, the colours were already bleeding into the wool beneath it. The woman must have just come into some money then, or she'd know which vendors cheated the Narrows folk in the Merchants' Ring. Perhaps one of the Bluecoat agents sent to spy on the Narrows? Failing to secure an audience ahead of her, the old lady turned back to Tamsin.

"My John had to go out in the worst of it and buy coal from the upper docks and mark my words there will be another snowfall before the week's out."

Tamsin couldn't quite keep the scorn off her face. Coal, down here? That was sloppy. Shipping coal in was ten gold sovereigns a wagon load. Even Tamsin's landlord, the baker, burned wood, and during the worst of the storm when no one was buying bread, he'd let his ovens grow cold. Tamsin had burned through her own small supply of fuel waiting the storm out. Whoever this woman was, she had no friends here. Tamsin shifted a half step back. The woman noticed and her face pinched in at the cheeks.

The man ahead of them turned in his spot.

"Shut it. My sister lost her youngest to the cold, last storm." His voice had a familiar anger. The old woman snorted.

"Shouldn't have been so careless with the fuel then." She glared at the man.

Someone yelled "shut up," from the back of the line. There was a dangerous rumble of voices. One of the gate guards stepped out of his post, musket in hand. The crowd's anger compressed to a tiny mutter of fear. The woman tried to meet Tamsin's eyes, uncaring of the guards or the anger building around her. When she failed to get a second rise from the crowd, the woman fell silent and the line inched forward again.

As she edged closer to the royal blue coats of the guards Tamsin tensed. Her fingers beat out a frantic tattoo on her basket edge. She stilled them. The old woman passed through the great arch, under the gleaming brass of the cannon ports set into the wall, then it was her turn. Tamsin sucked in a deep breath and tried to smile.

"Name, occupation, and reason for entry?" the guard asked. He sounded bored. He accepted her work papers without glancing at them.

"Anna. I'm bringing fresh linens to the Emirya Theatre. I'm a laundress." Her voice stayed steady. She tried to keep her eyes on him. *Some of it was true*, she thought. The forged papers Lacey had given her changed only her name and age.

He dug down through her basket, rumpling the crisp folded linen shirts. Inwardly Tamsin seethed. Elspeth wouldn't be happy if his grease- and gunpowder-stained fingers left marks. The guard pressed down on the bottom of the basket, no doubt hoping she'd let it slip. She dug her fingers into the broken willow branches and set her jaw. He rolled his eyes, tossed her papers on top of it all, and waved her through.

Only a few steps to safety. The prisoner brand on her shoulder seemed to throb in time with her heartbeat.

She was a half a step from the far side when a different Bluecoat called out to her.

"A moment. I know your face," he said. His musket was no longer quite resting on his shoulder. Tamsin froze.

"I come through this gate twice a week. More when the Emirya's shows run close together." Gods, don't let him look through the papers again. Whoever Lacey had cadged the papers from had an eccentric view of spelling. She ran the Bluecoat's face through her memory. His tanned jaw was shaved now, he was older, but so was she. She pulled her battered straw bonnet down over her loose, dark curls. He frowned at her, then his companion leaned over and said something sharp and unintelligible

Annoyance crossed the first guard's face. Without looking at the second guard he pointed into the Merchants' Ring.

"Move it along then or we'll cite you for holding up the traffic."

Tamsin bobbed a curtsy while backing away. Despite the chill, a rivulet of sweat dripped down between her shoulder blades. She wormed her way into a cluster of people. *Blend*, she thought. Her heart was beating loudly enough they could probably still hear it back at the gate.

No one seemed to be following her. As soon as the gate was out of sight she ducked into a shop doorway.

That was far too close. After three years, she'd hoped people's memories would fade.

To be fair, they had, mostly. But the years hadn't brought quite enough scandal to bury a tale like the crown hanging a Cyprycian blood mage. It left only a light covering over her half-foreign daughter's release a year later.

The shopkeeper rapped sharply at the window. His glare said everything. No shabby patched skirt was going to buy his upcountry lace. Tamsin's cheeks grew hot. She turned away from the doorway.

Hackney coaches and wagons crowded the streets in the Merchants' Ring. Tamsin walked around them trying to keep her skirt out of the offal. The streets here were wide enough to hold a wooden sidewalk, but they charged a copper penny fee to use them.

The Emirya Theatre had been built at least a century prior and sat closer to the stockyard than was fashionable. Someone had tried to revive the crumbling building recently with a facade of bricks and plaster columns. Behind the theatre, no one bothered with artifice. Tamsin rapped on the stage door.

After a few minutes, Elspeth opened it. Her cap was askew on her head, and tendrils of greying brown hair threatened her vision at any moment. Pins lined her sleeve hems. How she managed to move without impaling herself, Tamsin didn't know.

"Tamsin, what's wrong? You look flushed." Elspeth stepped back and let her in the door.

"The guard knew my face."

Elspeth caught her meaning and her lips thinned. She glanced at the street before she waved Tamsin inside, to safety.

The backstage of the Emirya was a clutter of discarded set pieces, costume racks, and surly people pushing through the mess. Onstage someone was rehearsing an opera. Elspeth led Tamsin through the warren to a smaller room only slightly less cluttered.

"Now, what happened?" Elspeth said, shutting the door behind her. Her tone brooked no room for lies or evasions. For one dizzying moment, she reminded Tamsin of her mother. Tamsin closed her eyes until the feeling passed, and set the basket down, dislodging a heap of half sewn shirts over the worktable.

There was an order to Elspeth's workroom, but Tamsin hadn't quite grasped it. The work table was strewn with fabric cut offs, loose threads, and bits of beads and ribbons in distinct strata. The wine layer was from the last love tragedy, the black beads and threads from the Puppet master play over festival week.

"A gate guard knew my face," Tamsin said. "I think he was part of the battalion that brought us ... me here."

Concern etched fresh lines over Elspeth's face. She knew the full story.

"If it's become too much of a risk for you to bring the washing here..." she began.

"No!" Tamsin half shouted. "That is, I need the money. The Bakers are good people, but they've half dozen mouths to feed there, I can't rely on their charity." It had been over a year since she'd cured little Logan's pleurisy. Nothing made ill memories fade like good health. Baker could rent her room for twice the ten silver pennies she paid.

Tamsin took in a breath. "I can manage this. They rotate out the guards." If she said it enough, maybe she'd believe it. And perhaps someone would drop a dozen gold sovereigns in her lap, with silk gowns and a house in the country.

Elspeth looked dubious but she opened a drawer on her work table and brought out her purse. "You go back through the same gate." She dropped three silver pennies in Tamsin's palm.

"They don't check people going into the Narrows as much as those leaving it." Tamsin laughed bitterly. "Why would they?"

Elspeth flushed. It hadn't been long since she'd shaken the Narrows dust off her own sturdy boots. "I could make a disguise for you? Lighten your hair or some face paint? I had to turn a leading man's hair russet for The Dulator, and his hair was near the same shade as yours when I started." Her hand hovered over another drawer.

Tamsin shook her head. "I doubt it would make a difference. I'll just have to be more careful. Maybe risk the North gate."

"That one is closer to the gaol," Elspeth said. Her lips were pressed together in a long thin line again.

Tamsin ignored that and gathered her basket. "You've got a show to do. I best be getting back. Thank you, Elspeth."

"I've got another load of underthings for you in the hall." Her lips were still pressed in a tight line. "And the lead from Tattercoat spilled wine all down the front of her act one dress again. Silly cow. It's red wine, so I'm not expecting it to come out, but you've worked miracles before. I'll pay you two silver pennies if you can get it fit for the stage again."

"I've got something that might do for it," Tamsin said. Now that conversation was back on safer grounds she relaxed.

"I have a friend, Tamsin. He might sponsor you for papers out of the Narrows." Elspeth bit off the rest of her words.

"What price this time?" Tamsin's voice was harsher than she wanted it to be. Still. There was always a price for these sorts of things, and there were precious few things she had left to pay it with anymore.

"With the right papers you could teach, or maybe enter service? A lady's maid? You could make a better life at one of the big houses."

"I'll buy my own papers once I get the sovereign to pay for it," Tamsin said. "I'll get there eventually."

"But..." Elspeth fell silent when she saw Tamsin's face. "Just, stay safe Tamsin."

"I will." Under the cover of her skirts Tamsin crossed her fingers. "I'll bring these back in a few days."

She hadn't quite lied to Elspeth. It was easier to get back into the Narrows than it was to leave it. The Bluecoat at the gate gave her basket a perfunctory toss for contraband and waved her through. The old king had walled in the Narrows in her grandmother's time, at least that was what Lacey told her, just after his daughter's murder and the purge of the blood mages. The purge was one part of Aradwyn history that Tamsin never forgot.

It wasn't that the Narrows were a true prison, Kingsgate gaol served that purpose, but renting a room in the Merchants' Ring was a silver crown a day, and a day's labour paid considerably less. And all of that depended on having the correct papers, up to date, with the king's warrant embossed into linen paper. Expensive, short term, and nearly impossible to forge since the crown changed them frequently to prevent just that.

No, the king kept the Narrows folk hidden away and left them to their own devices, unless it was tax time, with a whole battalion of soldiers to keep the peace. The tension simmered after this last storm, when the clean water lines had frozen again, leaving only snow melt, fouled as that was from the tannery and the coal fires. Tamsin prayed for something to change before it boiled over.

The basket's frayed edge dug into her hips. Perhaps the next time something shredded in her tub it could pad the basket edge. Of course, a shredded shirt meant less pennies earned for the washing. The inside of her head had turned into a tally book in the last two years, and every copper penny had to be spun out finer than a silk thread, lasting as long as she could make it. Each step echoed with a familiar litany: three silver pennies earned with this week's washing. A silver penny for bread for the week and soap, that left two to save for rent, for shoe wax, for rushlights, thread, and a new needle. And while she was dreaming of new needles, maybe a proper pelisse to break the wind, or a new basket.

"Miss, I need you."

Tamsin yelped and jumped back. She dropped the basket and shirts spilled out across the muddy track. Careless.

The man who'd spoken had seen better days. One of his brown eyes was blackened and his boots and britches were covered in a thick layer of mud and goddesses knew what else. He must have read the alarm in her face, because he spread his hands out wide in front of him, like he was approaching a spooked horse. And wasn't that a flattering comparison.

Tamsin bent down and stuffed the laundry back in sloppily. One of the shirts had ended up near his begrimed boots. He picked it up gingerly.

"I didn't mean to scare you," he said. He held it out to her.

The streets were less crowded at this hour. The water was shut off till morning and the labourers wouldn't be heading out to drink their wages for another hour or so. A few children pelted through the muddy streets flinging shards of snow and ice at each other. At least someone was enjoying the slush. He wasn't holding himself like a threat, but that didn't make him safe.

"Miss?" he said.

She held the basket out between them and he dropped the shirt inside.

"Thank you." She bobbed her head down. "I'll bid you good day sir." For all his filth, he didn't have the look of a Narrows man. His coat was tailored too close to his frame. And was that a cravat drooping out of his mud-crusted collar? How'd a kingsringer like that end up in this part of the Narrows? The brothels by the docks were more his scene.

"Sorry to intrude. Good day miss." His frown was absent of malice, but Tamsin took a step away anyway. He stood there, a strange mixture of calm and confusion on his face. After a moment, she walked on. At the end of the street she glanced back, and he was walking towards the group of children, who whooped and lobbed slush at him before darting away.

That was odd. Still, nothing good ever came from getting involved with strangers. The muddy twilight was starting to fade into true night. Her legs ached and her feet had reached the pins and needles level of chill. The cook carts along the street began calling out their dinner wares, all fish. Her stomach growled. Could she spare a copper penny? The thought of a hot meal made her mouth water. Winter had thinned her savings more than she was comfortable with. After, she decided. She didn't need grease or sauce spilling on the shirts to make her job harder. But the dress was a windfall. Surely it would be all right to splurge a tiny bit.

Baker's shop was in the Grainery. There weren't any grain silos here anymore, not since the mill had found a fairer berth across the river in Kirkswald, but the name stuck like pine sap. Under the remains of the old mill, the shop was squeezed in between a dry goods shop and another tenement house, hung heavily with fading laundry and rain collectors.

Tamsin rented out the tiny rise room alongside the great chimney. Deep shelves lined all the walls, but Tamsin had knocked a few down to make a rough bed and table. Baker had added a workaday door to the outside and latches to both doors. She wouldn't trust them to hold against a determined effort, but it let her avoid disturbing Baker's dough every time she had to fetch water or empty a piss pot.

Her stool and a washtub occupied most of the remaining floor space. That was it, a four-by-eight-foot space that was almost all her own. Luxury and poverty all in one. She emptied her basket out onto the tally marks inscribed on her worktable. One gold sovereign. She earned fifteen silver pennies a month. After rent, food, and necessities she could usually save two silver pennies a month. Twenty-four of them made up a silver crown, and twenty crowns made up a sovereign. It was an impossible sum. Her stomach growled. Tamsin traced the tally marks. Barley water and day-old bread would keep her fed another day.

The shirts and linens went into the water with a good helping of lye soap. She left them to soak while the last of the light faded away. The dress was another story. The wine stain covered the bodice and continued onto the skirt.

"She was probably angling for a better costume," Tamsin muttered. Talking to herself was another habit she'd picked up here. She pulled a clay jar down from the shelf and mixed a handful of powder with water and daubed the paste into the grey wool fibres. Outside, the church bells rang an unharmonic hour chime. Someone rapped on the inner door. Tamsin pushed her basket out of the way and drew up the bar.

Baker was standing outside twisting his apron into knots. His thick, red face was lined with more worry than usual.

"Miss Tam, if you have a moment?" he said.

"Of course. What's wrong? Are the children ill?" Logan's lungs again? Something cold pushed its way under her ribs.

That snapped him out his tongue-tied state. "No, no, no one's hurt. I just need rent." He pushed imaginary hairs back from the top of his bald head.

It felt as if someone was kneeling on her breastbone, and she choked on the yeasty air. "I don't have it yet. I've still got another week and a half!" She counted on those days. Why was he asking early? He'd never done that before.

Something flashed over his face before it settled into a careful placidity. "When can you get it to me?"

"I've got six now," she said. She had six and a handful of the copper pennies. Her stomach chose that moment to growl again, louder this time. She flushed. "I can have the last four by the end of the week, I've got a job from Emirya I just picked up today." She paused. "Why do you need it so early?"

"It's none of your concern." As soon as the words came out of his mouth she could see regret settle in the lines of his face.

Snapping wasn't like Baker. Her anxiety cranked up another notch.

"I'll take what you have now. But I need the rest..." he hesitated clearly weighing her chances. "I'll need it tomorrow night latest."

Her heart sank. Even washing everything in cold water, she'd never be able to dry them, iron, and collect from Elspeth in time. This would set her back weeks. Baker was still waiting for her answer.

"I—" she hesitated. If she told him it was impossible, would he set her out on the street tonight? Were six silver pennies too much to gamble on a miracle? But this was a home, and she could not go back to squatting in the ruins, waiting for the Bluecoats to roust everyone out again once a sevenday. "Give me a minute to get the coins." She shut the door in his face.

He'd understand. That was another rule particular to the Narrows, never let anyone know where you stashed your coins. She climbed up on the bed and reached up to the raw pine beams. Her fingers found the hollow knot and plucked the rag bundle out. She sorted the silver pennies, from the larger copper ones. Three of them were from the old king's reign, his profile still scowling two years after his death. The young king's face was both haughty and wan. She slid the few copper coins back in the bundle. It wasn't enough copper to make up a full silver penny's weight and if things went sour, she'd need them.

She placed the remaining coins carefully back in the hidey-hole before she climbed back down and opened the door. Baker was twisting his apron again. If anything, he looked more uncomfortable than before.

"Thank you, Miss Tam." He stood there just staring at her. Tamsin considered shutting the door in his face again. How much ill will would that earn her? Still, Baker had played fair with her, more than fair, till now. After an uncomfortable minute, he cleared his throat.

"The missus, she's got a load of charity loaves bound for the Goddess Point Temple in the pantry. If you need it."

Tamsin flushed even harder than before. She hadn't had the charity loaves since she moved in here. They were hard, brown flour things, more sawdust than wheat. It filled your belly, for a short while, but a steady diet of them left you with the running shits. It was most of what she ate at Kingsgate.

"Thank you," she said after her own awkward pause. "If I need it."

He let her keep that lie and stumped back up the stairs where Missus Baker and the children were no doubt waiting.

She waited at the door until she couldn't hear his footsteps anymore. Cheeks still aflame, she fetched one of the charity loaves back to her room.

Tamsin poured water into her cup and soaked the bread in it. Softened, she could just manage to choke it down. She started beating the laundry around the tub. She could hang them to dry at first light and iron them damp in the afternoon. It still wouldn't be fast enough. Maybe she could ask around and see if anyone had an odd job or two while they dried, but a four-penny a day job was rare and often dangerous dock work or worse.

There were the scripters. The interest they took from each loan was a cancer though. She shook her head. She'd only be able to keep the room for a couple more weeks that way. Besides, she'd nothing to put up for collateral. Her wash tub? Her wool blanket? Herself?

The thought made her shiver. Ever since the gaol, ever since they'd opened the gate and let her out into the Narrows, she'd vigorously protected her independence.

Maybe she could ask Lacey for a loan? But Lacey had enough to worry about. Every penny Lacey and her brother Frank earned had the hanging threat looming over them. Every penny was a pound of contraband rowed over Kyrin river in the dead of night. And nothing turned friends against each other faster than putting money between them.

Tamsin alternated her scrubbing with bites of the bitter, brown bread.

Chapter Two

Thud. Tamsin opened her eyes, heart pounding. Still dark. Her gut said it was not far past midnight. With a pang, she recalled a walnut clock that had sat on the parlour mantel at home. Polishing its curved sides had been her job as a child.

Her hand reached along the mattress and wrapped around the too-smooth grip on her laundry beater. The pounding on her door came again.

"Tamsin? Please wake up!" Lacey's voice was low but frantic.

Tamsin slowly relaxed her grip. What in the five hells could Lacey want here, at this hour?

She pulled her blanket around her. Baker's ovens were still cold. Lacey's knocking was getting louder. She muttered a curse and stumbled over to the door. If Lacey woke Baker's family, there would be hells to pay.

"Lacey, what in the…" Tamsin trailed off. Lacey wasn't alone. She was holding a lantern out in front of her and from its light Tamsin could see both Lacey and her brother Frank with another man leaning heavily over their shoulders. Tamsin glanced up the street. It was empty.

"He's hurt," Lacey said.

Tamsin stepped back and let them in.

Lacey was a small woman, a few years into her twenties. She shared Frank's dark hair, grey eyes, and tawny skin tone. Frank towered over his sister, all morose rough edges to her quick lightness.

It took them both to support the man through the door. Support was a generous term. The man was out cold, and Frank was sweating with exertion. Her room was suddenly brimful. Tamsin couldn't move without touching someone else's skin. She shuddered. How long had it been?

Tamsin swept the dress off the table and onto a shelf. "Lay him out there, I'll see what I can do. What happened?"

Lacey hung her lantern up on the rafter nail and opened all of its shades. The shadows swung wildly as it settled into a rocking arc.

Frank laid the man out on the table, trying for gentleness. Not that it mattered. Their friend had a worrying bonelessness. Tamsin bent over the man's face. It was caked with mud and blood.

"Bring me my kit," she said, pointing to a bundle on the highest shelf. Frank settled himself on the bed out of the way.

Lacey handed it down. "We were bringing in a shipment." Three years ago, Tamsin would have paled at the idea of befriending smugglers, but Lacey was not what she had expected. She was optimistic, amiable, and best of all, she was resourceful and willing to share.

It was Lacey who showed her the markets for used goods down here, where to buy bread, turnips, and apples for less than the upmarket stalls charged, and Lacey who made the connection with Elspeth, when the Bakers had offered her the room. It was worth losing a little sleep to help her.

"He was out at the Wharf after dark," Lacey said.

Tamsin winced.

"We saw the Runners working him over," Lacey said. "I figured they'd just take his purse, but they kept saying what a piece of luck it was to find him and didn't stop once he was down." Somehow, even having seen the very worst the Narrows contained, Lacey still managed to be disappointed when the world wasn't kind. It was another reason Tamsin would do almost anything, including bleed for her. She wasn't the only one. Lacey had a web of people, from underworld criminals to gentle Baker and his family, willing to help keep her optimism from burning out.

Frank rubbed his forehead. "Another one of her strays," he said, with a pointed look at Tamsin. Frank still treated her with suspicion. Two years in the Narrows didn't make her one of them, not yet.

Tamsin rolled her eyes. Waiting for Frank's good opinion was like waiting for someone from her old life to come looking for her down here. She wouldn't hold her breath over either.

She turned her attention back to the patient. His breathing was steady. She found his pulse just under his jaw, strong and even. Her shoulders relaxed a little. Those were good signs. Where her fingers met his skin, there was a charge, like a spark after working with wool in winter. Her fingers tingled and she pulled away. She knew that feeling. Magic. The kind that could bring the Bluecoats to her door. She fought an urge to scratch her shoulder blade.

"He's alive." What was someone magic-touched doing down here? Neither Frank nor Lacey seemed to have noticed. Of course, they didn't have the touch. She needed to stay calm. *If you don't react, they will never know.*

His coat was soaked through and slimy with mud. Tamsin unbuttoned it gingerly, avoiding contact with his skin as much as possible. Beneath he wore a waistcoat, brocaded silk unless her fingers betrayed her. How long had it been since she touched silk? Focus. It marked him as a pigeon ripe for plucking.

She didn't see any wounds under the coat, although it clung to his shoulders. She'd need help to remove it. She shifted back to his head.

There was a lump on his temple and Tamsin felt the contusion gently. Nothing felt fractured. He was unnaturally still under her fingers. She started wiping the mud away from the wound. It only took a moment before she recognized him. The man from the street corner. Something curled in her ribs, something not quite guilt.

"I saw him too," she said. "In the Grainery just before the dinner bells. It must have been four hours ago. Something wasn't quite right— he seemed drunk or something." Lacey's expression didn't change. She could feel Frank's eyes burning holes into her back. He thought this was her fault.

"He didn't smell like gin to me," Lacey said. "Or move like a poppy fiend."

Tamsin gave her a short nod. His skin was pale, not flushed with alcohol or opiates. Under the street sludge there was a faint odour of charred herbs, incense and something more.

There was a new lump purpling over his left temple, and he sported a fresh cut to his lip along with the older one and his black eye. She cleaned them off as gently as she could.

She ran her hands through his mud-matted hair. Under all the muck it was some light shade, the light, damp and dirt concealed the true hue. There was an odd spongy swelling at the back of his head. That wasn't good.

Tamsin lifted each of his eyelids in turn. The pupils didn't move.

"The Runners cracked his head something fierce," she said at last. "I don't think they planned for him to walk away. It's a good thing for him that you brought him in. If he'd stayed out in that all night, he'd have frozen."

"Will he wake up?" Lacey asked.

"I don't know," Tamsin said. "He might. Sometimes, with rest, people just wake up." Sometimes, but not always. Her mother's lessons about head injuries came flooding back.

She began wrestling him out of the jacket. Lacey came over to help and, between the two of them, they pulled the coat free. Tamsin dumped it on the floor. Something in the pockets made a muffled metallic thump when it hit the boards. He hadn't been robbed.

"Are you sure you should be undressing him?" Frank asked.

Tamsin spared him an annoyed look as she unbuttoned the man's waistcoat. "He's been in a fight of some sort, judging from the cuts on his knuckles. I need to be sure his ribs are sound, and he hasn't been stabbed somewhere important."

"Is there an unimportant place to be stabbed?" he muttered. Tamsin ignored him.

Tamsin ran her hands down the man's sides. Whoever he was, he kept in rather better condition than his fancy dress would imply. There was a good amount of muscle on his chest and arms, and the plump tautness of well-fed flesh. Nothing bled or was broken. She bit her lip with frustration; figuring out what was wrong was much easier if her patient could talk to her.

His shirt was soaked through. Beneath the muslin, she could see a curious oval depression on his right shoulder. An old scar.

"What did he do when they set in on him?" Tamsin asked. That scar looked like a bullet wound.

"He fought," Frank said. "He fought hard enough I thought he might scare them off, but there were at least five Runners. He knocked one guy down, but a couple had belaying pins. Lacey and I were able to scare them off."

"Can we leave him here for the night?" Lacey asked. "We still have ... work to do." She cast a furtive glance at Frank as she spoke. Tamsin swallowed. A stranger here? Someone magic-touched? That was treading perilously close to the line where favours, even for Lacey, fell short.

Frank cut in. "You've done too much already. We'll leave him in the old mill. It's out of the wind, and if he doesn't wake up..."

If he didn't wake up no one would bother with another body in the mill's wreckage. It wouldn't lead back to them. For a moment, Tamsin was tempted. If he was mixed up with magic –scratch that, there were no if's, he was mixed up with magic. The questions were how much, and would it get her hanged? Tamsin opened her mouth to agree with Frank. The words died on her lips when she saw the pain on Lacey's face.

"I'll do my best," Tamsin said.

"You'll save him, you always do." Lacey leaned in and gave Tamsin a peck on her cheek. It had taken her six months not to flinch at the casual way Lacey touched people. It wasn't precisely that she minded, some days Tamsin was starved for company and touch, despite the close quarters, but it still felt alien to her.

"Before you go..." Tamsin's cheeks burned. "Baker needs my rent tomorrow, well today now, and I ... I'm short."

Lacey gave her a slow nod and carefully didn't ask how short. Damn it, they had to be in tight times too between the storms and the crackdown at the Wharf half a month ago. Tamsin turned back to her patient and started wiping the grime away from the cuts on his knuckles.

"I have a silver penny on me, will that help?"

Behind Lacey, Frank grumbled.

Tamsin nodded cheeks still burning. "Thank you," she mumbled as Lacey pulled the coin out of some hidden pocket. "This brings me closer." Charging money for healing, what would her mother have said? She covered her discomfort by raiding the last of her herb stocks and mashing the cloves of garlic into a paste. She soaked the man's cravat and spread the paste over the lump on his head, covering the mess with the cravat. It ought to bring the swelling down, at least a little.

"Never mind all that," Lacey said. She set the coin on the table. "You'll pull him through. I've never understood why you don't hang your shingle here as a healer."

"Head injuries are tricky. I'll do my best, but it will all depend on how he goes through the night," Tamsin evaded. Lacey didn't know about the magic. She thought Tamsin's cures were only herbs and stitches. "Do you know blood magic, like your mother?" was the third question Lacey had asked her, after her name and if she was hungry. When the witch brand was still raw and weeping on her shoulder. Her "no" was the only lie Tamsin had told her so far.

"I'll come back in the morning to check on you both. Do you want to leave him on your table?"

Tamsin weighed her options. "No, he can't stay there." The silver penny reflected the lantern light reproachfully. Tamsin stuffed it in her pocket. "Can you help me move him to the bed? I should probably stand watch in case he has a fit," she said.

Frank caught the man's shoulders and, mostly gently, hauled him over to the bed. Lacey grabbed his boots and pulled them off. They set him on his side, with his coat rolled up as a pillow.

"You're a kind soul," Lacey told Tamsin, squeezing her hand. She slipped a fresh bar of lye soap onto Tamsin's worktable.

Tamsin gave her a weak smile. They left, taking the lantern with them.

Tamsin settled herself on the stool with her cudgel laid across her knees, and her blanket tucked around her. It felt like Lacey had taken all of Tamsin's energy with her when she left. She put her head down on the table.

The oven wall was radiating heat now. Baker must have started the fires. Outside, the church bell sounded the second hour. Lacey's penny made paying rent possible now if she finished the shirts tomorrow. She could make it.

Chapter Three

The screech of the oven doors woke her. Tamsin lifted her head and rubbed the sleep sand from her eyes. If Baker was setting the loaves in to bake, it must be dawn. She'd slept through the bells. Did the man still live?

She pushed the window open and blinked as the room's dimness brightened. The man had not moved in the night. Tamsin shrugged out of her blanket and checked his breathing. It was still steady and even; his heartbeat was the same. She peeled back an eyelid. No change since last night. That wasn't good.

She shook his shoulder gently, then harder. Whatever residue of magic that he'd touched had faded from him in the night.

Tamsin stood up and pulled out a large jug at the very back of her shelves. She hauled it to the bed and shoved the neck under his nose before she removed the cork. The stench set her own eyes to watering, despite the arm's length.

Piss rendered into ammonia. If this didn't wake him, nothing short of a miracle would. And miracles were dangerous. She waited until she was sure he'd inhaled at least once, then she corked it again. Nothing. She shoved the ammonia bottle out of the way.

"You need to wake up now," she said.

He remained still. She knew wishing wasn't going to fix this. Still, exhaust the practical remedies first. And then…

What did she remember about head injuries? The brain could bruise, like flesh, she remembered that, and sometimes it bled.

Was he worth the risk? Would he remember her magic when he woke up? If he woke up.

She could just hear her mother's voice now sharp with disapproval. *"Tamsin Saer, I did not raise my daughter to ignore those in need. Try."*

"He's a rich kingsringer. He doesn't weigh the same as one of the charity cases in the village mother," she muttered. *And anyways, you're dead*, she finished silently. She scrubbed her eyes.

She sat gingerly on the edge of the bed, the cudgel propped up on her knee. It didn't take much effort to roll him onto his back. The swelling from last night had gone down a little under the garlic poultice, but being this close to a stranger made her skin crawl. She slid her hands to his temples.

Her heart was racing. Calm, she needed to be calm for this. Tamsin took in a deep breath and held it. Then she exhaled and let the magic out.

After so long it was like relearning to walk, or push the spinet keys after an injury. Her mind stretched and strained with the activity. She was acutely mindful of the warmth of his skin under her fingertips. His cheeks were rough with stubble where the heels of her hand cupped them.

Somewhere in the middle of the night his lip had split again. She bent over and slowly spread her lips over the cut, a gross parody of a kiss. Copper and salt slid over her tongue and brought with it a keen awareness of him. It wasn't enough. She stretched her mind further through the bond and with a sort of click, she wasn't in her own body anymore.

The first thing she noticed was their pain. Their head felt like it was underwater, their right knee was sprained and throbbing, everything ached and there was a sting of freshly opened cuts on their face and hands. Too much information pulsed its way through her. For a moment his injuries asphyxiated her. Tamsin pulled back until she could feel where her body ended and his began. *Sloppy*. Mother would have had sharp words for anyone who jumped too quickly into a healing.

Smaller bruises and contusions dappled his body, and an old scar twinged at his shoulder. Irritating, but irrelevant to what she needed to do. She pushed all that pain away and sharpened her focus down to just his skull.

Something was wrong there. It wasn't just the blow to the temple, or the hidden injury under his hair. His mind was like nothing she had ever felt before, like wood sanded too far into the grain.

It was another compression that kept him unconscious. The back part of his brain was bleeding slowly, and under enormous pressure. She threaded a thin bit of her magic through his veins and stopped the trickle of blood. That was the easy part. Then she drained the fluids away, absorbing them into his own flesh. Outside of his head, she was dimly aware that his nose was bleeding over her lips, or maybe it was her own. She was going too fast.

As the pressure lessened, she felt his mind start to stir. She used a third wisp of magic to put him into a true sleep. If he woke up and interrupted her now, it could make her lose all the threads and the resulting snap could be lethal to both of them. This third thread was almost too much for her. Her mind was as taut as the warp on a loom, keeping the blood draining evenly. Too fast was almost as bad as too slow here.

While the pressure abated, she checked his other injuries. The man's temple injury wasn't damaging, swelled skin mostly. It would heal in a few days. But the shape of his mind was disquieting. In a deep healing like this she should feel more of the temperament of the person's head she was skittering around in. Here there was nothing.

Was it the magic she'd smelled last night? She shifted a little deeper. Whatever caused it was outside of the magics she knew. At the corner of her awareness, she could see a grey fog sliding in around her. She was spending too much of her energy too fast.

Tamsin pulled her magic back. Slowly her heart started beating its own rhythm again. She could feel the stool beneath her and hear the sounds of people walking down the street outside. The salt flavour left her tongue. Then she was back looking down on him, blood drying around her chin.

He was still asleep. She pushed herself up from the stool and the room tilted. She clutched the wall until it settled into a less dizzying wobble.

Food. She needed something to eat after that, something sweet would be best. Her mind filled with images of jam-filled tarts and honeyed rolls still warm. The aroma from Baker's oven was overwhelming. She pulled a few of the dried mint leaves down from the stalk on the ceiling and chewed. It helped, a little. She managed to wet a rag down and wipe the blood off her face.

The man's colour had improved a little. His face, under the grime was kind-featured, with a strong chin and sharp cheeks. She reached over and gingerly daubed at the blood drying under his nose. He was going to live. She tried to celebrate that, but everything was still exhaustion and hunger. Still, Lacey would be pleased.

Should she let him rest a little longer? Her stomach growled again. No. No, there was not enough time. She pushed the exhaustion back with practiced effort. That was a loan with interests higher than the scripters charged. She'd need food soon. She held the ammonia pot under his nose again.

He coughed once and his eyes fluttered open. They were red-brown, like polished cherry wood. He started to give her a sleep-muzzy smile that froze mid action. He touched the re-opened split on his lip with his tongue.

"Where am I?" he rasped.

"You're in the Narrows. Some men attacked you." Tamsin kept her answers short. The less he knew the less he could tell the Bluecoats someday.

He frowned. One hand reached up to explore the wounds on his head. "I—" His lips were dry and cracked and he tried to wet them with his tongue.

"Just a moment. Let me get you some water," Tamsin said. Her pitcher was almost empty. She measured out a generous half for him.

His hands wrapped around hers on the tin cup. They were calloused and warm. More calloused than she expected. She pulled back quickly, and some water sloshed over onto his chest and the bed.

"I'm sorry." She found the scrap of rag and daubed at the spill on the mattress while he drank.

"It's all right." His voice was stronger now. "I needed to wash up. Thank you. How did I get here?" he asked.

"Someone found you and brought you to me."

"I don't remember." His eyes were darting back and forth, taking in the room. It must seem shabby and strange to a man who wore silk brocade. Sometimes it still felt strange to her.

"After a shock people forget things," she said. "You were unconscious when they brought you here."

"No." The man pushed the blanket back and swung his legs over the edge of the bed, wincing. The poultice fell off his head and the scent of old garlic was sour and heavy in the air.

"Careful of your knee," Tamsin said.

He reached out and seized her wrist. "You misunderstand me, Miss. I don't know who I am."

Tamsin froze when he grabbed her. The man must have read her fear. He released her instantly. She stepped out of reach.

"You don't remember anything?" It sounded like something out of a poorly written play or a penny novel.

"I remember a few things," the man said. "I remember dirt streets, daylight, and children throwing snow, and a fountain with no water. But I didn't know my name then, and no one I spoke to knew it either."

This was a level of complication that Tamsin hadn't counted on. Her heart sped up. The blood magic she'd sensed before? Had someone used magic on him?

"Hold out your hands."

He looked at her oddly but complied. She turned them, palms up and traced the callouses there, over the centre of each index finger and one on the inside of the middle finger. His sleeve lacings had come loose, and she pulled it up. Along his forearm was a shallow straight line of scabbing, at least a day old. Purple oval bruises marked his arm at the elbow and wrist. She wrapped her hand around them, fitting her fingers into the impressions, and ignoring the feel of his skin under hers. Someone had held his arm as they cut.

"Do you remember anything before that?" Tamsin asked slowly. He didn't know about the magic. How had it been done? She'd seen blood magic used to heal; she knew that the very properties that let it heal could be used to harm. But memories?

"I don't know." He scrubbed his forehead, wincing as his fingers found the lumps. "I remember fish, the smell of them."

Yesterday had been Fishday. They would have been unloading the catch throughout the night before. Tamsin sank back on her stool. What sort of mess had Lacey left her?

"I don't know what to do," she said at last.

"I understand." He seemed calm, outwardly at least. His eyes were following her movements a touch too quickly, and his fingers were worrying the hem of his shirt. He was hiding his fear with practiced ease.

"Why were you down here in the first place?" Tamsin asked. "Anyone with half a brain can tell you're a kingsringer, probably landed by the togs on you."

"Togs?"

He didn't know Narrows slang. If he'd come down here for something underhanded, he was naïve or foolish. Was that why he'd been set on?

"Clothes, togs are clothing," she said.

"And what is a kingsringer?" he asked. There was an edge of frustration to his question.

"The King's Ring is where rich people live. As opposed to the Narrows or the Merchants' Ring. Are you sure you don't remember anything else?"

"You seem familiar to me."

Tamsin felt her cheeks warm. "I saw you yesterday briefly. You startled me on my way home." He remembered that? What must he think of her not helping him?

"It must have been before the men attacked you," she said, pushing on to safer grounds. Relatively safer. "You were brought here in the night."

Would anyone *want* to shed their own memories like this? Was there a rogue blood mage wandering the Narrows? That sent a chill down her spine. She needed to focus on smaller, answerable questions first.

"Have you checked your pockets?" Tamsin asked.

"I checked yesterday. I didn't have the forethought to leave myself a note explaining everything." He sounded wry.

"No 'in case found wandering the streets deliver to this address'?" Tamsin asked lightly. "How unprepared." They both smiled at the small jokes. Tamsin's eyes slid away first. He didn't carry work papers everywhere, another indication of his higher station.

The man passed her his coat. Tamsin started checking pockets while he did the same with his waistcoat.

He had half a dozen gold sovereigns tucked into his inner coat pocket. She remembered the sound the coat had made when she'd dropped it last night. There was at least another sovereign's weight in silver crowns and mixed pennies spilled out across the bed from his own search. For one moment, she was tempted as never before. Just one of those sovereigns would fix so many of her problems.

And create ten times as many. Theft was a hanging crime. *Any* crime she committed with the king's brand burned into her shoulder, was a hanging crime. Better homeless than dead. Homeless she could improve on. "Here," she said. She shoved the coins at him a little too fast.

"Thank you. The engravings on these are quite lovely."

A few of the copper pennies slipped out of his hand and landed on the floor. He didn't notice. Tamsin twitched. After a moment she bent and retrieved them.

"You need to take better care of these."

The man held up one with the new king's face in fine relief on the face of a silver crown. "I like the ones like this. He looks kind."

Kind wasn't how Tamsin would describe the sharp planes of King Reginald's face.

"This is a lot of money," she said instead. "How you managed not to be robbed is beyond me."

"Wasn't I though? The men who attacked me, were they looking for this?"

Tamsin paused. Were they? They'd have had ample opportunity to take his coins, when he was attacked. Perhaps he'd carried more money than a dozen sovereigns? Or perhaps money was not what they were looking for. Tamsin turned back to his coat.

The last pocket turned out a silver snuff box. It fit in the hollow of her hand, aged silver with a shield crest enamelled in royal blue on the top. There was a message engraved under its lid.

"R. C. For luck. M. E."

Instead of snuff, the box held small pastilles that smelled like violets.

He had produced a gold watch from his waistcoat, with a carved malachite fob and heavy gold watch chain, and a wad of paper scraps. They traded.

The papers proved to be gambling notes torn from scraps of other papers and badly crushed. Drunken gambling notes by the state of some of the signatures. They were signed Fox, the Earl, and Piggy, and addressed to Captain, the Damn Captain, and a few variations. She ran the sums up as she went. If all of these notes were real… Her hands shook. No wonder a dozen sovereigns didn't faze him.

"You shouldn't lose these either." Her hands shook as she passed the notes over. "They call you Captain. Is that familiar?"

He hesitated before shaking his head. "I don't know. It fits without being familiar, if that makes any sense at all."

"Perhaps you were a real captain?" Tamsin said. Her voice caught on the word captain. The pieces clicked into place, his calloused hands, the bullet wound in his shoulder, the crest on the snuff box enamelled in royal blue. He was a Bluecoat. Her arm reached behind and rolled the cudgel into her hand.

He was studying her face with an unnerving intensity. "You don't like that." It wasn't a question. He had the knack of reading people it seemed. No wonder he had that stack of gambling notes.

She forced her shoulders to relax and release the cudgel. He hadn't offered any threat to her. Sometimes the younger sons of the gentry would do a round of military service. Usually, it was some sort of honorarium, their parents bought them a commission and rank enough to make a suitable enough trade. It didn't make him a threat. She hoped.

To cover the lull Tamsin turned her attention to his watch. The cover was engraved in a diamond pattern, with tiny blue stones set where the corners met. She opened the case and examined the front and back interiors. Unmarked. The fob was carved into a rearing horse over a cross of wheat sheaves. Nothing she was familiar with. Another dead end. She turned it over.

"Sometimes people engrave the inside of watch cases," Tamsin said. Her father had a watch engraved on the inside. She used to cajole him into showing it to them after dinner, so she could read the inscription. "I could try to pry if off and look."

The man shrugged. "I didn't know that. Go ahead."

The back pried off easily once she was able to get the edge of her clasp knife under its rim. The inside of the back was engraved with a lock of flaxen hair braided and fastened under the rim.

"To my Rhys, with love—Mother."

Tamsin brought it over to the bed and showed him.

"Rhys." He drew the vowel out and rolled the name across his tongue. "Rhys. That could be right. Thank you."

"It's only a first name," Tamsin demurred. "It's not enough to figure out where you lived, or who your family is."

Rhys shrugged. "It's more than I knew a few minutes ago."

She pressed Rhys's watch pieces back together until the case clicked back into place.

"You don't want to lose this." She set the watch on the edge of her bed. She was reluctant to touch his hand again, even accidentally. In this space, with his secrets starting to be spread out between them, even the brush of palm to palm felt as intimate as a kiss. He was arranging the coins intently into small piles along the edge of the bed where her mattress didn't quite fit the frame. Too intently. He'd noticed the distance she had placed between them. He wasn't pushing at it though; he was letting her set the tone, she realized.

"What else do you remember about being attacked?"

He shook his head. "When they came up to me, I asked them if they knew me. They laughed at that. Someone swung a club at me. I remember knocking it out of his hand, and someone knocked my knee."

"What was the first thing you remember?"

He closed his eyes and his hand tapped on his thigh. "Fish. There were buildings all around me, bare-board construction, and muddy streets."

That could be almost any part of the Wharf. Lacey or Frank knew the area enough that they might pull enough details out of him to find out where precisely he'd started from. Did she want to look though? There was a blood mage out there with enough power to strip memories, and if it had happened over a day ago, and he still felt like magic when she saw him, the mage had to be strong. Stronger than her?

"I should wrap up your knee and see if you can stand on it."

"Next best thing to walking," Rhys said. He shifted around on the bed, wincing as his legs swung over the edge.

Her kit was still on the table from the night before. She unrolled the bit of canvas and started rummaging through it. If there was any white willow bark left, it might help with the pain. Arnica would help too, but she knew she didn't have that, at two pennies a dram. Damn her tally book. At the bottom she found two thin lint covered branches.

"Chew on this," she said, handing him the willow branches and pulling a length of stained wool out of her kit.

He eyed it.

"It dulls pain."

His expression was dubious, but he tried a piece. His face scrunched up.

"This is awful!"

"All the best medicines are," she quoted without thinking. She bit her lips. For a moment her mother's shade hung in the room again. He didn't notice. "Let me wrap up your knee. It might hold your weight then."

He nodded, his mouth still consumed with the effort of chewing. She handed him the bowl.

"You can spit it out when the bitter taste stops."

He stretched his leg out when she asked. His stockings were black with soot and mud. She peeled the right one down and unlaced the cuff of his breeches.

It was odd, touching the calf of a stranger. The side of his knee was a sickly yellow-green in the centre, edging off to purple. She had to work to get the pant cuff high enough to wrap the wool strip around. He finally spat the bark out into the bowl and helped her.

"Is it too tight?" she asked when she was done.

"No, it's fine." His face said otherwise. She loosened it a little.

"If you can walk when the willow bark starts working, I can lead you to the gate. It's a bit of a walk, but we can take things slowly. Once you are there you can ask the Bluecoats at the gate to get you home."

And then this whole mess would be done with. It would leave the blood mage on the loose, but that wasn't her problem. Let the Bluecoats hunt them down, if they were able. If the Bluecoats were going to start a hunt down here, it was best she had nothing to do with it. Her spell traces had faded. No one would ever know.

Someone pounded on the outside door, interrupting her thoughts. "Tamsin!"

Tamsin unlatched the door for Lacey.

Lacey pushed her a full step back into the room. Lacey hadn't slept and her fine dark hair was abandoning her braid by the handful. She pushed the door shut behind her. Her face was panicked.

"Tamsin, they're here!"

Chapter Four

The blood drained out of Tamsin's face. "The Bluecoats are here?"
Did they know?

"No," Lacey said. "The Runners, the same crowd of toughs that beat that man last night." Lacey looked over at Rhys still in the bed, propped up by the blanket. He waved.

Tamsin barred the door. That would buy her a bit to think. Everything around her dropped into a quick clarity she'd only felt a few times before, all of them as she feared for her life.

"They don't know he's here, do they?" Tamsin asked. Fear was crowding the calm on Rhys's face.

Lacey shook her head. "No, I don't think so. They're going door to door working out from the wharf offering a reward to find him, but I heard them saying that they didn't need him alive to make their wage."

Tamsin bit off a curse. The room was so small. "Whoever you pissed off has money then, a lot of it to hire all of the Runners. And you're all over mud, where—"

"We have to do something. They were just down the street when I got here," Lacey said. "Would Baker help?"

"No time, and it's better to keep him out of this. The children." Tamsin ran through scenarios in her head. She couldn't chance Baker or his family seeing Rhys in their shop, and Rhys couldn't walk far.

"Right, Rhys, under the bed," Tamsin ordered. "Lacey, help me."

"That's the first place they'd look," Lacey argued. She moved to help, despite her protests.

For his part, Rhys didn't hesitate. Together the women pulled Rhys onto his feet. His face grew pale and pulled in with pain when he had to put weight on the knee, but he didn't cry out. There was just enough room between the floorboards and the straw tick for him to fit. She shoved his boots and coat under too.

"Try not to make any noise and keep your eyes closed," Tamsin said. She flipped the mattress over. No blood or mud on this side. "Lacey into the bed. You are going to be very ill." She shook the blanket back onto the bed and let it trail over and brush the ground. There wasn't much light in the room already and the blanket deepened the shadows under there.

"If you say so." Still, Lacey climbed under the blanket and lay back.

"Just try to look like you have a fever." Tamsin tossed the last of the water jug onto Lacey's face.

Lacey sputtered and looked like she was about to argue. Someone pounded at the door.

Lacey gave one wide-eyed glance at Tamsin and lay back on the pillow. Her hair was damp now and the heat of the room from the ovens had made both of them red in the face.

Tamsin took a deep breath and opened the door.

The man standing outside was shorter than she expected. Limp, dark hair fell across his eyes, small blue tattoos covered the back of his hands and wrists. A dockhand, former, by the state of him. His left boot bulged oddly around the ankle. She guessed a dock injury had brought him to the Runners.

"What do ya want?" she said before he could open his mouth. If she could keep him off balance she could keep control of the conversation. Lacey had taught her that.

"I'm lookin' for a man," he said.

From the bed, Lacey groaned and coughed.

Tamsin didn't have to pretend to be exhausted.

"Careful. The coughing fever's here." She leaned back so he could see the whole of the small room.

His eyes rested on Lacey in the bed, and he stepped back.

"A man," he repeated. "Cut up with a bruise on his head. Yeller hair, brown eyes and wearing a silk waistcoat. I heard tell you do some healing down here. His wife is looking for him."

Tamsin let scorn drip in her voice. "I nurse some," she waved her hand towards Lacey in the bed. Lacey coughed. "I've me hands full with her." She snorted. Oh, let her accent not be too off here.

"You're the laundress. The one who helps the sick around these parts," the Runner repeated.

Tamsin nodded. "I am. S'what I'm doin' here. She's been coughing blood all night."

He took a bigger step back. He was definitely favouring his left leg.

"Just the two of you here then?"

"D'ya see anyone else? Where'd I put em in this place?" Indignation, but just enough. Too much was suspicious, but a little bit could keep them off-balance.

The tough narrowed his eyes and loomed. He was enjoying this hunt, taking power away from people in their own homes. Tamsin didn't give ground, though her shoulders twitched with the effort. Lacey gave another groan, a touch too energetically. Tiny mistakes, but tiny mistakes could tip a mark onto their lies. Sweat slid down Tamsin's forehead and into her eyes.

"There's a sov in it to anyone who brings him to us, or the news that brings us to him. That man's dangerous," he said. "I can check for you. Make sure a bit of a thing like you isn't troubled by anything." He tried to squeeze past her into the room.

He sensed something was off here. He needed to see greed, she guessed. Greed he'd understand.

"A whole sov?" She licked her lips and leaned forward in the door frame. Her skin crawled with his closeness.

Lacey shifted on the mattress. Under the bed, Rhys smothered a cough. Lacey's eyes went wide. She started coughing as loud as she could and writhing under the blanket.

"What was that you said she had?" the man asked.

"Some sort of lung ailment. Nasty fever with it. Went to her chest. Not sure if she'll make it through the night," Tamsin said. "About that sov?"

"Is it catching?" He shifted away from Tamsin.

Tamsin shook her head. If he needed to see a lie let him catch one here. "I don't figure." Tamsin faked her own cough in his direction. "Just a bit of a tickle in my throat. Is it cold in here?" She shivered.

He took a step back from her. Good.

"It's hotter than the third hell in here woman. And the sov's only if you bring him to us."

She sighed. "That's a shame. For a sovereign I'd sell my mother."

"Right." The man turned and left.

Tamsin latched the door.

Lacey sat up and held one hand up. "Wait," she whispered. "If they are clever, they'll knock again hoping to catch you in a lie. If they really know the game, they'll use more than one man to do it. It's always harder keeping lies straight between two people."

Outside Tamsin could hear people knocking on Baker's door. Baker's voice carried through the walls.

"I'm the only man here and there's no silk anything in sight. Now piss off."

There was a little more grumbling and then Baker slammed something down. From the echoing it was probably one of the oak peels he used for the oven.

Tamsin kept her eye to the door crack. There were four of them canvassing her street. They were entering each house alone. Whoever was hiring these people clearly didn't know his game or he was hiring fools. Maybe a little of both. They had to be moneyed then, but new to the way things worked in the Narrows. It took about ten minutes more and the men left the street.

As soon as Tamsin gave the all-clear, Lacey hopped out of bed. She poked her head under. "I didn't smother you, did I?"

Rhys slid his head out slowly. A thick layer of dust clung to his hair and nose. He opened his mouth to speak, and violent sneezes shook his body.

Tamsin couldn't help herself. Laughter bubbled up in her belly and spilled over until she was shaking. It was that or scream. She felt tense as a fresh-wound watch spring. Lacey joined in after a beat.

"If you could see your hair," Lacey choked out.

Rhys gave them a pained look. He tried to speak, but another fit of coughing choked out his words.

Tamsin bit her lip, but giggles still escaped around the edges.

She reached down and grabbed his stretched-out hand. His hand was just as warm and calloused as her own. He slid out in a flurry of dust balls that set all three to coughing again.

"It's good to see you in the daylight," Lacey said. "When we aren't trying to hide you from ruffians."

"Have we met?" Rhys asked. He pushed himself up to a seated position. Hope was palpable on his face.

"I brought you here. Well, I had help. Didn't Tamsin tell you?"

His face fell.

Tamsin winced. He'd thought Lacey might hold better answers than what Tamsin had given him. "I wasn't sure how much credit you wanted for the rescue," Tamsin said.

Lacey gave Rhys a dazzling smile. "All of it when he's that pretty."

Tamsin looked away.

"He's rich too," she said lightly. "Rhys, meet Lacey. Lacey, Rhys. Now do you know anything about why those men were looking for him?"

"Not a clue on why," Lacey said. "But everyone in the Narrows knows, or soon will, that there's a fat reward for a blond kingsringer who's been in a fight recently."

"And you are sure they were going to hurt him?"

"That's what they said. Someone's been hiring everyone even a little shady at the Drunk Duck and the Barrel to find him. But none of the Bluecoats are involved."

Tamsin cursed. "We need to get him out of here. Is he wanted by the law?"

Lacey shrugged. "Not that I heard. Who in the sixth hell did you piss off?" she asked Rhys.

"I don't know," Rhys said.

"How do you not know something like that?"

"I'm assuming it's a long story, but I don't remember any of it," Rhys said.

"But you just told me your name," Lacey said.

"We found my name on my watch, well, Tamsin found it," he said. "Unless it isn't my watch…"

"What is he talking about?" Lacey asked Tamsin.

"Let's assume it's your watch unless we learn differently. At least this way you have a name," Tamsin said to Rhys. To Lacey she evaded. "I think it was the blow to his head. When he woke up, he remembered yesterday but nothing before that."

"He got his head injury last night though," Lacey said. "I saw it happen."

"Yes, well you can't always tell how a blow to the head will addle someone," Tamsin said.

Lacey seemed to accept that. "What else do you know about him?"

"He gambles, and he's good at it," Tamsin said. "Or you hold your wine better than your friends do, Rhys. You ride a lot. It left callouses on your index fingers. You were shot, at least a year ago. You're probably a younger son or untitled, especially if you were in the military."

"Well then," Lacey said. "You have been learning."

"I've paid attention," Tamsin said, shrugging.

"Well, you made things easy for me. I'll ask around and see if I can figure out who is doing the looking and why," Lacey said. "Can't leave a rescue half done."

"Thank you. You might be able to check the army register book," Tamsin said. "They keep a copy at the barracks."

Lacey looked away. "I don't think that would work."

Tamsin's face went hot. "Oh, of course. I'm sorry."

Lacey waved it away.

"Why can't you check the registry?" Rhys asked.

Lacey squared her shoulders and looked him straight in the eye. "I can't read." Her gaze was a challenge. *Laugh, I dare you.*

"Oh." He digested that. "I can read."

Lacey rolled her eyes. "'Course you can, you're from the King's Ring. All of them read up there and eat beef on Fishday and plum puddings with breakfast."

"Tamsin reads," he said.

"I let my friends keep their secrets," Lacey said. Tamsin shuffled the wet shirts around, time to change the subject.

"You know if the fellows looking for him were clever, they'd set men at the gates. And if anyone saw you and Frank last night—" Tamsin said.

"Don't you worry about us. We covered our tracks. But Rhys can't go out on the street until things calm down."

"That shouldn't be hard to manage." Rhys said. He patted the bandages encasing his knee.

"That's all right then. In a few days, they'll run out of money or get sick of looking for him," Lacey said.

"But ... he can't stay here. Baker will find out. And I still need to get the washing back to Elspeth and rent is due." She was still three silver pennies short.

"Washing?" Rhys asked.

Tamsin ignored him. "Lacey, Baker is being twitchy already. He'll pop his cork if he finds out he's here."

Lacey winced. "The new tax?"

"Tax? I was in the Merchants' Ring most of yesterday. I missed that," Tamsin said.

"The king set another tax on grain, a silver penny a pound," Rhys answered.

Tamsin turned and looked at him. "How..."

"I might not remember who I am, but I can still hear. They were talking about it on the street yesterday. The collectors were coming... today I guess."

"Another tax?" Tamsin groaned. "They raised the window tax a month ago, and the lumber tax before that." She looked over at Lacey.

"That's what kings do," Lacey said.

"If it is only the money..." Rhys pulled gold coins out of his pocket.

Lacey's eyes bugged out. "Marry me now!"

"Er..." Rhys turned red all the way to the tips of his ears.

"She's joking," Tamsin said.

"Oh." He looked even more confused.

Tamsin sighed. She pulled his coat and boots out from under the bed. The mud had dried, and large chunks flaked off across her skirt. "This coat is going to need a lot of attention to be wearable again and I don't think anything will get the smell out." And honest work wouldn't get her charged with theft once this was over.

Rhys just looked at her. Lacey caught on a beat later. A gamine grin spread across her face.

Tamsin took a deep breath. "I can clean it, but... my rent is due today and I'm short." The words spilled out of her all at once. "I need a few coins to make it square, eleven silver pennies. I'll clean the coat and fetch you a bath and food and medicine as well, but you have to pay for it." Eleven pennies should count next to nothing to someone carrying that many sovereigns. It was a fair price.

Rhys shrugged and held out a handful of coins. The knot of tension in Tamsin's gut unwound. She took a deep breath, her knees weak with relief. She plucked the eleven pennies out of his hand.

"Thank you." Tamsin handed one penny back to Lacey. "I need to give these to Baker."

"Oh." Lacey frowned. "I can stay for a while, but Frank needs me again tonight."

"Two nights in a row?" Tamsin glanced at Rhys. "You usually have a few nights between..."

Lacey gave her a disarming smile. "What can I say, business is brisk. Go and give Baker his money. And spend some of this generous fellow's fine coin on some food, and maybe some new togs so Baker won't be suspicious. We'll pass him off as a cousin."

Tamsin snorted. "*Your* cousin perhaps."

She glanced at the door. Air sounded lovely. The room was stifling.

"All right. I'll be back with water soon so you can clean up."

Lacey laughed. "I think we can manage that. Can you let Frank know where I am? He should be at the usual haunt."

Tamsin nodded. She picked up her water pail and left. Despite, or perhaps because of, their brush with danger, her feet skipped. She'd made the rent. She could handle everything else.

Chapter Five

By the late morning light Tamsin could tell the fountains would be shutting off soon. Centuries ago, someone had shunted clean water from the northeast mountains down to Celdre. The aqueduct fed fountains in the King's Ring and both the lower Rings. That water was running out, so the flow in the Narrows stopped at noon. The king's father had said the Narrows folk could drink river water. But the Tannery upriver made the water brackish and acidic and turned the stomach of anyone who drank it. It yellowed any fabrics you washed in it, and the fibres would rot faster. The fish had disappeared downstream.

The top trough was already starting to flow sluggishly when she got there. Tamsin managed to squeeze her way through the crowd of people and set her bucket in one of the streams.

"You're late today," one of the women said. She had a baby tied upon her hip, sucking on the knotted end of her sling, as she filled her buckets.

"I had some men at my door asking odd questions," Tamsin said. The baby fussed and the woman turned back to him. Tamsin realized, after two years of filling her bucket next to her, she still didn't know the woman's name.

The woman rolled her eyes. "They came to my door too, waking this one. All for some kingsringer that doesn't know how to find his way home."

"The reward was rich enough," Tamsin said.

"Truth, his father must be flush to waste a sov down here."

This was a different version of the story than they'd used on Tamsin.

Were the Runners getting it wrong, or were they tailoring their story to each person? That was more sophisticated a plan then the man who'd come to her door. Tamsin pulled her full bucket out of the fountain and stepped aside.

"They told you his father? They told me it was his wife," Tamsin said.

"Who knows with quality folk." The woman snorted. "But Runner Jim, made out like it was kin and a man asking."

"True enough. I'll see you tomorrow?"

"As long as the water flows." The woman's baby took advantage of her lapse in attention and wound one grubby fist into her twisted hair and yanked. The woman winced and turned her attention back to him. Tamsin left.

It took three more trips to fill the tub, and a bucket for Rhys to clean himself with. Tamsin's arms ached and she was sweating despite the cold when she went to see Baker. He was at the dough again.

He didn't look up when she came into the shop. His eldest daughter Anne was at the counter. She was scarcely at the age to let her skirts down, but today she'd twisted her dark hair into a haphazard knot like her mother wore.

"Tam!" she squealed. "I practiced that dance you showed me. I think I have it now."

She pirouetted her way around the counter and started flailing her feet in a tolerable imitation of a quadrille.

"It looks good," Tamsin said. "I've brought my rent," she told Baker.

Baker looked up at that. Something passed over his face, and Tamsin wasn't sure if it was relief or irritation. She set the coins on the counter. "How'd you get these?" he asked. He made no move to collect them.

Without an audience, Anne stopped dancing and went back to her stool.

Tamsin swallowed. It was hard lying to Baker. She respected him.

"Lacey brought a patient," she said. True enough. "He'll be staying for a day or two. He paid."

Suspicion clouded his face. "Him?"

Baker was smart, he'd made the connection with the Runners who had been by earlier. She had to stick close to the truth here.

"He fell on ship, hurt his leg, and he needs a couple days off of it."

"Nothing that will bring trouble here?" That wasn't really a question. Tamsin kept her voice light.

"I shouldn't think so. He's her cousin, John Greene."

Once upon a time lying had been harder. She missed that.

Baker seemed satisfied with her answer. Anne tucked the coins away and that was that.

Tamsin opened her mouth to ask him about the men searching for Rhys. She closed it, words unsaid. Reminding him wouldn't help anything. She judged him not to be the kind of man who would sell out Rhys, but if Lacey was correct about the new taxes, fear changed people as fast as anything Tamsin had ever seen.

She turned to leave. Her eyes fell on the shelves of bread in the window. They were full, too full for the mid-morning rush to be past. She looked back but Baker was already elbow deep in the next day's dough.

*

Tamsin stopped next at the ragman's shop. Bernard was an acquaintance of Lacey and Frank's set. He was a fence, a broker of all the news in the Narrows, and he was old enough to be her father. Both his shirt, and the open waistcoat he wore over it, were grease-marked and rank.

"What do you have for me today, little Tam?" he said. His voice was always a little too jovial. He looked at her as if he was weighing the bits of clothes she wore, and marking her worth down on the register he kept beside his chair.

"Errands today," Tamsin said. "Lacey asked me to find something to fit Frank for a surprise."

He spread his hands out wide. A few crumbs from his last meal slid down into the pile of clothing in front of him.

"I'm sure I have sommat that would fit. And at a special rate for dear old friends."

Bernard caught more coin from fencing goods than he did from the rags he sold. Sometimes that meant his prices were lower than the other rag and bone shops. Sometimes.

His shop was nothing more than a string of rough tables heaped high with clothing. The air was mildewed and clammy. His windows had long since been boarded shut to avoid the tax. There was no order to the heaps of clothing. She dug through the furthest pile from him. Skirts, stays, and stockings spilled over onto the floor, to join the other discards.

Bernard just watched her.

It was unnerving, his eyes on her back. She found a shirt, that might do, its cuffs frayed and patched over.

"That won't fit Frank, he's far too tall for it." Bernard's eyes narrowed.

Tamsin hesitated. It would fit Rhys, who was a couple of inches shorter than Frank, but Bernard missed nothing from his perch.

"It might hit him above the wrist, but I haven't found another, and beggars can't be choosy."

Bernard's eyes made the hair on the back of her neck rise. In the third pile she found a pair of dockman's trousers. Her nerves were scraped raw by the time she found another shirt and a moth-eaten coat that would fit either Frank or Rhys. She brought them over to Bernard.

"Four silvers."

"Four is robbery," she said.

"The price can change," he said leaning over the piles. "Have you learned anything interesting of late?"

"Interesting how?"

"Do you know what dear Frank is up to?"

"No." I wouldn't say if I did, she thought.

"Pity. I've been hearing such interesting things. Did a man come to your door looking for a rich fellow?"

She nodded.

"And do you know where this Gentry cove would be?" he asked.

"No." She kept her eyes on his face and her expression soft. Tensing the jaw, narrowing the eyes, or looking away were all typical tells for lying. She couldn't afford to let any of them drop. "If I knew, I'd have myself a fat sov and wouldn't be bargaining for these rags. One and five."

He was silent a moment. "Three then, unless you have some bit of news to trade."

Tamsin closed her eyes and ran back through the last day's events. Anything about Rhys or the hunt for him was dangerous. Bernard wouldn't be interested in the latest play at the Emirya. Lacey and Frank's business was off the table as well.

"The bread isn't selling," she said at last.

Bernard tilted his head and considered this.

"And tempers were hot at the North gate and in the market yesterday. I thought the Bluecoats might shoot someone. They had an old woman out as a spy in the lines causing trouble."

After a minute he straightened his head. "Two and five."

"I have two even." It wasn't a terrible price, but spending that much felt like a sickness in her belly.

He rolled his eyes. "Fine. But you owe me more news. See that you bring it to me, or I'll have to collect."

She bundled the clothing up in the bottom of her basket and dropped the coins into his hand.

*

She found Frank at his usual table in The Barrel. Like his sister, he hadn't slept either. He wore exhaustion well. The half-empty mug of strong tea in front of him probably had a lot to do with it. She could smell the bitter over-brewed leaves from four paces away. There was another man sitting across from him engaging in an intense conversation.

"It's not enough, we need at least double the powder in two more sevendays," the man said. He was dressed a little too well for The Barrel. A wool hat was perched, carefully out of casual view, on the seat next to him. That man screamed danger to Tamsin.

"I'm the one taking the risk here," Frank said. He leaned forward and caught sight of Tamsin waiting.

"We'll finish this in a moment." Frank took a long swig from the mug and pushed back his chair.

The pieces fell into place for her. The stranger's coat was a coachman's coat, the livery colours recently picked off, with the wool unfaded in stripes around the arms and capes. The coat didn't fit the man, but his shirt, waistcoat and fawn-coloured leather breaches beneath it were cut to the quick. On his hands were pale indentations, where he'd removed rings.

Frank wasn't smiling as he came towards her.

"Where's Lacey?" he asked.

"Hello, to you too. We're *all* doing well, thank you for asking," Tamsin shot back. Frank didn't change his expression.

"Lacey sent me to tell you that she's staying at my place for the day." Tamsin shifted her weight a bit until her back was to the tables. Frank adjusted unconsciously with her.

Frank cursed. "Tell her I need her, now. If she mucks things up..." his eyes darted around the patrons. There were empty seats this morning, but not too many of them. The day's catch had to be a light one.

"Have you heard anything?"

He grunted. "No. I'll send word if I do but tell her to hurry." His eyes darted back to the table.

"Frank," she pitched her voice as low as she thought he'd be able to hear, "That man isn't what he seems, he's shamming that livery."

His mouth formed a thin hard line. "It's nothing to you."

Fine. She'd tried. She could tell Lacey at home. "Where should she meet you?" Tamsin asked.

"Lacey'll know," he said, turning his back on her. He went back to his seat and glared at Tamsin till she left.

Friendly person that Frank.

Chapter Six

The sun was dipping below the buildings by the time Tamsin returned home. Almost an hour until the dinner bell's chimes she guessed. Lacey's laughter stopped her before she knocked at the door. Rhys said something, too quiet for Tamsin to make out the words. Lacey's reply carried clearly through the clapboard walls.

"Don't worry about Tamsin not liking you, she's just slow to warm up," Lacey said.

Tamsin knocked before Lacey could explain any more.

Lacey's eyeball appeared at the door crack. Tamsin could hear the wood-on-wood scrape of the bar being drawn back, then the door swung open.

"You need to keep your voices down," Tamsin said. "I heard you from the street, Lacey. Baker might suspect something."

Lacey shrugged. "I haven't used names. Baker knows you have a patient?"

There was a puddle of water around the bucket from where Rhys had washed. That was a lot of wasted water. He was sitting on the bed, shirtless, with her blanket wrapped around his waist. His hair was damp and tousled. She carefully avoided both of their eyes until her temper cooled.

"Frank is looking for you. He sounded upset," Tamsin said.

Lacey rolled her eyes. "Frank always sounds angry; how could you tell the difference?"

Tamsin hesitated. "Look, I don't want to muddle in your business ...

but are you two all right? He seemed more tightly wound than usual. And he was talking to a kingsringer trying to hide his nice clothes, badly."

The smile slid off Lacey's face. "We're fine," she lied.

After so long of an acquaintance, Tamsin knew Lacey's tells. It was subtle but Lacey's eyes shifted down every time she lied to Tamsin. "Things are just busy, but we'll be able to put something away after this. Maybe even buy a place," Lacey said.

Tamsin's heart sank. "Lacey, this isn't about... I mean you don't think Frank would..." her eyes slid over to Rhys.

"No! This is someone else, from before this whole mess." Lacey's arms stretched wide to include Rhys and the chaos of Tamsin's room.

Tamsin was only partly mollified.

"If you need help..."

"I'll ask, but I need to get back to Frank," Lacey said. Rhys was watching the conversation closely. How much was he understanding?

"I'm serious Lacey, after all you've done for me, I'd be glad to," Tamsin said.

"Careful or I'll take you up on that." Lacey smiled as she backed out the door.

"Wait don't you want ... food?" Tamsin said to her back. Lacey waved and kept on walking down the street. Tamsin set the basket down on her now-cluttered workbench.

"Was everything quiet while I was gone?" She focused on laying everything out and avoided Rhys altogether.

"No one else stopped in," Rhys answered. "That smells delicious."

"Physicker's orders, a hot meal with meat," she said. "It helps the bones knit and your blood come back."

"That seems like an order I daren't countermand."

She turned to see if he was serious. Half a smile hovered around his lips. The charm he must use at the gaming tables fairly oozed out of him. He didn't seem to know he was doing it.

"I've got an herbal draught that might help. You had enough coins that I could buy it already steeped." She waved the small bottle between them like a ward. "It should help your knee as well." She just needed to keep things formal between them. It should only be one more day and he could go.

"I put myself entirely in your hands, milady." He half bowed still seated.

"I brought you clothing too. You'll fit in better if you don't look too flush," she said all at once. The blankets had shifted a bare inch down when he moved. She could feel her whole face burning red.

He felt his cheeks. "Flush?"

"I mean rich. Here, get yourself dressed." She threw the clothing onto the bed and turned her back.

Behind her she could hear him struggle. He suppressed a curse, probably when he was putting on the trousers. But that was an image she was *not* going to think about. Instead, she mopped the puddle. There was less than a quarter of the water left in the bucket. They'd wasted that much on the bath. Well of course he wouldn't think of such things. Still, she was surprised at Lacey.

"There we go," Rhys said at last. She turned. The clothing wasn't new. Sweat stained the shirt already and the jacket hung ludicrously low on his shoulders.

"Lacey filled the pitcher for you before I cleaned up," he added. "I hope there is enough left for you. Carrying enough water to fill your tub must take you all day."

Tamsin bit her lip. She'd misjudged him, at least a little.

"You look the part of a Narrows rat," she said instead. "Another couple of days of not shaving and no one would look at you twice down here."

"Thank you, I think? Were you able to find out anything else?"

Tamsin sighed. "Nothing very helpful. The people searching for you have gone all over the Narrows, but they had more than one story."

"Oh?"

"Well, the ones here talked about you being dangerous, your wife, and talked about a reward. The ones a few blocks over talked about your father looking for you," she hesitated. "Lacey could have gotten it wrong."

"Is that likely?" he asked. When she mentioned a father, his eyes lit up. She felt his family hopes keenly.

"I don't think so," she said. He tried to mask his disappointment. "Lacey is pretty good at picking out those sorts of things, and she spends her time at the—at a place where they hire men like the ones who were hunting for you. It's more likely that the other men were lying so they could get better information."

For a moment he looked so lost. She wanted to reach out, but instead she held out the medicine. "One swallow of this now and another at night bells."

He obliged. "Oh, that's vile." His face screwed up in a grimace.

Despite everything, she smiled at the look on his face. "It's more willow bark and arnica, plus the alcohol is a home-brew. It's hard to get liquor down here, but it's the best thing for this sort of concoction. We improvise."

"I'm impressed by anyone's fortitude if they can manage enough of this to get drunk."

"Desperate times," Tamsin quipped. She handed him dinner.

They ate in silence. Rhys abandoned any sign of table manners after the first bite. He scrambled after the crumbs and licked the grease from his fingers. He probably hadn't eaten since he'd awoken yesterday, Tamsin realized.

Afterwards, she stowed the rest of the food and set about straightening up the room and returning her healing kit to the top shelf.

She fetched her cudgel and stirred the shirts again to beat the soap out. They could be dry by morning if she worked hard enough. She might be able to take them back to Elspeth tomorrow afternoon. Every little bit of savings would help her leave.

"You don't like to be still, do you?" Rhys said.

"When would I have time to be still? I need to clean off the bed. Are you able to get up?"

Rhys didn't mention her silence when she turned around and reached out her hand to him. His grip on her forearm was stone strong this time. Together they got him moved over to her stool. Tamsin began shaking out the bedding and brushing the mud from the mattress.

"Can I help?" Rhys asked. "I don't know what to do right now, but I feel awfully in the way."

Tamsin gave him a measuring glance. "You could beat the washing. I want to get this lot back to the theatre tomorrow. Careful of the water though, it will sting if it gets into your cuts."

"I think I can manage that."

It took a little more shuffling but at last Rhys was arranged in the corner with the tub, carefully agitating the shirts through the water. If she had a copper tub, or even an iron one to sit over a fire she could do less actual scrubbing. That is if she had the money for wood to burn, for the bars of hard soap, money that was not going towards getting her out of here.

Maybe something showed on her face. "How did you come to Celdre?" Rhys asked.

"This isn't your business." She smoothed the blanket back over the straw tick mattress.

"Oh, I'm sorry. Lacey said you were from Woburn. I thought... I mean... we've talked about me a lot today." He swirled the shirts around in the tub.

"It's not something I want to talk about." To cover the awkwardness, Tamsin made up the bed again. She wiped down the shelves and table and used her fingers to sweep the dried mud floor into a heap. She was almost done when her fingers brushed up against a wad of paper, in the shadows under her bed. That hadn't been there before. She slid on her belly until she could reach it.

Uncrumpled, it proved to be the lined page of a ledger book. Tamsin smoothed it out over her lap.

"Did you find something you lost?" Rhys asked.

Tamsin shook her head. Could it be something from Lacey? She took it over to the light. The writing was tiny. She didn't recognize the words written there; they weren't in Aradwyn or Cyprycian. Tamsin weighed the likelihood that Lacey or Frank would be carrying around a ledger that couldn't read. This had to be something from Rhys.

"Does this mean anything to you?" she asked. "It must have come from your things."

He bent over the paper. "It's a tally of silk and cotton fabric imports. Their weights, the ships they came in on, the sale prices."

"What language is that?" Tamsin asked.

Rhys looked up from the papers with a puzzled look on his face. "I... I don't know which language it is. It is different from the watch or the other papers, isn't it? That is a little disconcerting. Can you read it?"

Tamsin shook her head.

Rhys frowned and read the ledger page again. "Hmm, that's odd."

"What?"

"You charged me a fair price of eleven silver pennies to clean my boots and coat, buy me clothing and heal me?"

"Yes, it's very fair. The big laundries charge crowns."

"And silk is expensive, isn't it?"

"Very," Tamsin said.

"So, is silk supposed to sell for three silver pennies a bale?"

"No, it isn't." Tamsin set the cleaning rag on the floor. "Three silver pennies?"

"Yes, and there is one here that is only a few copper pennies for five bales."

"Does it mention an address?" she asked.

"It mentions a place called Ampré."

"That's in Orness," Tamsin said. "But what does it mean? A code?"

"Orness?"

"Orness is a country southeast of Aradwyn, between us and the mainland. They control most of the silk trade, at least the legal silk trade."

Rhys digested that bit of information.

"If I ever go through this kind of misadventure again, I'll remember to write myself a note before I start," he said at last. "Maybe I should keep one on my person at all times now. Although it would be fairly short at the moment."

"My name is Rhys C. Help me find home?" she suggested.

"Return to Miss Tamsin? Payment on delivery?" he suggested.

Tamsin snorted. "I'd need more coins for that." She couldn't help smiling though. There was beginning to be an ease to speaking with him that reminded her of when she first met Lacey. Her eyes fell on the snuff box he was turning over in his hand. Bluecoat. That stripped most of her smile away.

"I'm all done, you can go back to the bed." She didn't offer him her hand this time.

"Ah." His face showed that he caught her mood. He set the cudgel down and limped back to the bed. He was moving easier, between the bandage and the medicine. She stopped herself reaching out to help him. She needed to keep some distance. Rhys wasn't going to be here for long.

"I wonder if you'll remember all the Kingsringer manners once you go back?"

"There are different sets of manners?"

"You're the first gentry man that I've seen eat with his fingers," Tamsin said. That wasn't completely true. She remembered sneaking a pudding out of the kitchen with Thomas, his skin the same warm brown shade as her own. The pudding was nearly too hot to hold, still wrapped in yellowed muslin. It had burned their fingers as they picked the spongy thing apart in the garden, and raspberry juice had run down his face like blood. The memory sent a chill through her and she shuddered. The silence spun out between them as fine as silk thread.

To cover her emotions, she spread his coat over her worktable. She took up her brush and started scrubbing at the dried mud crusting the fibres. It would never look new again, but it might pass muster for a country hunt eventually. A small shabby one.

"In the King's Ring, you'll bow when you meet a lady on the street," Tamsin said, not looking up from her work. "And you'll have three different forks at each meal and ices after supper or at an assembly." And candles, she missed candlelight, down here in the gloom. After dinner mother would light three candles by the fire and the four of them would take turns reading stories aloud to each other.

"Ices aren't something you have here?" Rhys asked. His eyes held no guile or mockery.

"No, we don't," Tamsin said with a bitterness she wasn't expecting. Ices were a treat she missed, especially in summer when Baker's oven broiled the room.

"How do you know about all that?" Rhys asked.

Tamsin opened her mouth and closed it a couple of times. "I grew up not here," she said at last.

"Somewhere with ices?"

"Yes."

"So, you were a kingsringer?"

She laughed bitterly. "No, my father was in trade. It doesn't matter. I'm not that person anymore."

"But you are sure I am a kingsringer, not a tradesman?"

"Belike. You wear the clothes, have the city accent. And you gamble with more money than I'd see in ten years."

"You don't like that about me?"

Tamsin shrugged. "It's nothing to me," she lied. "It's your life. Do what you will with it."

"I see," Rhys said. His face was looking masked again.

"Look, someone has to be searching for you," Tamsin said. "Someone not trying to kill you. If we can find out who, we can get them to sneak you out of here. Or they can bring a whole army of guards or a carriage with them, and I don't have to think of it again."

"I... I didn't realize I was causing that much trouble for you."

"Well, I'd wear my second-best dress to lie to Runners. If I had one." Tamsin sighed. The lack of sleep was catching up to her. "I'm sorry. You paid me, and it helped me out of a tight spot, but you don't belong here."

The brush raised a cloud of dust around her workbench. That added to her irritation, and she worked the brush harder.

Rhys's coughing broke the silence. She put the brush down.

"Sorry, I didn't think. Well, I thought let's not put this outside in case someone comes by looking for a fine coat." Her lips twisted into not quite a smile.

"Why are you here?" he asked.

Of course he would ask that. Everyone who spent any time with her down here did after a while.

"What is it to you?" she said at last. Her voice was weary. Deflect. Idle curiosity didn't usually press past that.

"You've spent the whole day talking about everyone else but you."

"I have not."

"Things that I know about you; you live behind a bakery, you were short of coin, and you do laundry for wages. You aren't from here, and you had money once from your father in trade. And you hold a lot of fear for Bluecoats."

"That's everything," she said, faking lightness in her voice.

"You know everything about me that I know, literally. Hells, you named me."

"I have more questions than answers there."

The exasperated look he gave her made her shift awkwardly on the stool.

"I don't know you." Tamsin set the brush down.

His smile was sardonic. "What a coincidence, I don't know me either."

She crossed over to the tub and started wringing the shirts out.

"My father made furniture." Slosh went the lye-filled water back into the tub. That was a bit of an understatement. The desks and chairs made in his shop had graced the halls of lords of both business and land. Perhaps they still did. He hadn't ended up in Kingsgate with her and her mother. He also hadn't been there to take her home when Tamsin was released. It was easier not to think of him.

"My mother was Cyprycian." Slosh. She'd met Tamsin's father when he'd travelled to Cyprycia looking for hardwoods. Something about her father's smile had lured her mother into travelling half the world back with him as his wife.

"Three years ago, I ... came here, to the city." Slosh. Escorted by half a score of Bluecoats, paraded through the streets with her mother while people stared and jeered.

Her forearms ached with the familiar work. There was a puddle of water forming around her feet. She no longer cared.

"Why do you hate the Bluecoats?" Rhys pressed.

Because they killed my mother, Tamsin thought. She wrung another stream of water from the twisted shirt in her hands. Because they kept me locked away in that cell for a year, waiting to see if I would show some sign of magic every time they dunked me. Because even though I lived, they won.

"They hung my mother," she said at last. For all she knew Lacey had already told him that part of the tale. Besides, it had been in every paper.

Along her shoulder blade the brand itched. The water along the floor had seeped into her shoe toes and soaked her stockings. In the edges of her vision, she watched as he worked through that information. If he had more questions he didn't ask them.

"I'm sorry."

"So am I." She fished another shirt out of the tub.

They spent the rest of the day in a stubborn silence. Tamsin hung the clean shirts around the room turning it into a maze of tiny spaces she could pretend were private.

Night Bells came and she passed out medicine and food as brusquely as she could, avoiding his eyes.

"I'm sorry I pressed you," Rhys said.

She shrugged it away. "You should be able to walk tomorrow." Outside the sun was dipping down below the buildings.

"Tamsin, you've been kind. If I am what you think I am, perhaps I can help you."

She snorted. "Help." Her voice dripped bitterness. "You say that. I'm quite sure you believe it. But it doesn't work that way down here."

He opened his mouth.

"No," she said. "When I first came to be here, *someone* offered to sponsor me so I could leave the Narrows. If you get banished into the Narrows, you need papers to leave. Did you know that? And that a respectable citizen has to wager money that you will behave and follow all the inane laws that they keep upcity?"

He shook his head.

She was twisting apart the meat roll in her hand. She put it down in her lap and gathered up the crumbs. For once she wasn't hungry.

"He wanted something from me of course. I even gave it to him." She spread her hands wide. "And I lived happily ever after, far away from his promises."

Once she had thought that truth was something always good and light. The Narrows had honed truth into another weapon to be used. And if it kept him a little farther away, so much the better.

His eyes had a pitying look.

"Don't. You aren't allowed to look at me that way. I'm not dead. I have this, and now that I do, I'm not going to let anyone, not even some kingsringer, take it away. I did a job, I got paid, that's all."

"I don't know the right thing to say here," Rhys said at last.

"There isn't one."

"I see." He processed that thought for a moment. "What do people usually say when things like this happen?"

"To your kind? You talk about the weather, the state of the roads, anything without consequence. Narrows folk you'd say something about how we deserve being down here. Bad choices made by bad breeding, usually."

The pause after that threatened to go on forever.

"Well, a beautiful woman rescued me from dying in the streets, two of them actually. I suppose that is enough of a story for one day."

Tamsin acknowledged that with a tight nod. She was going to ignore him calling her beautiful.

"Would you prefer the bed tonight?" Rhys asked.

"You are still hurt, and you paid for it." Tamsin handed him another dose of the arnica as the evening bells chimed.

He shrugged. "It's your home."

"I'll manage another night." She adjusted the shirts until they made a clammy tent around the workbench.

In the dark, she could hear Rhys moving on the bed. Outside there were still people on the street, despite the hour. Tamsin double checked the door latches. There was an odd roar coming from the Wharf. It sounded angry.

"Do you think someone really is looking for me? Someone not trying to kill me, that is," Rhys said as she made her way back to the workbench.

"It makes the most sense." Tamsin rested her head on her arms and yawned. "Even if you don't have family, you'd have to have a valet, or live somewhere. If nothing else, they'll put a warrant out on you to collect your debts. But people like you have families, friends. They'll look for you."

"Why was I down here?"

Tamsin shrugged before realizing he couldn't see her. "I can't think of a good reason. There are bedfellows and gaming in the Merchant Ring, and you could afford their prices. If you were after opiates, well you have coin enough to buy them there too and you don't show any of the signs."

"Signs?"

"Down here if you see someone sweating in all weather, if their hands are stained brown, their pupils are too small, or they are shaking... you just stay out of their way. They have a smell too, like fruit that's just starting to go off. You didn't smell like that."

"What does that tell you?" Rhys pressed.

"Tell me? Why do you keep asking me about these things? I'm the last person who would know."

"You seem to be putting the pieces together just fine so far. Besides, who else do I have to ask?"

Tamsin hesitated. "If it wasn't opium or companionship ... it could be the thrill, but you wouldn't have been alone... Unless you were ... are a fool."

"You think I was with someone, and they left me here?"

"No." She struggled to find the right words. "The alarm should have been raised immediately. And why would they not search for you plainly without the lies? I think you came down here alone." And found a blood mage, she finished silently. Was it terrible luck or something else?

He didn't feel like a mage himself. Beyond that small spark when she first touched him, his mind hadn't had the ... texture was the only word she could think of. Her mother had it, and Thomas once he'd caught up to her lessons. She squeezed her eyes shut. She wouldn't think of them now.

"Will my memories come back?" he asked.

"I—I don't know. It's possible." If she was right, and someone had done this with magic, it went beyond the healings her mother had taught her. Rhys could wake up with his memories tomorrow, or they could be gone for good.

"What will you do if they don't come back?" she asked.

"I don't know."

In the darkness, she could hear fear lying underneath those three words.

"Tamsin, if they don't come back... could I stay here?"

Chapter Seven

Tamsin opened her mouth. The words died on her lips. What could she say? Staying here wasn't safe, though for him or her she couldn't say.

Boom. The glass bottles on her shelf rattled together then tipped over. She heard the mattress rustle as Rhys sat up. Thank the gods, a distraction.

"What was that?" he said.

"The cannons at Kingsgate," she replied. "It's been a few years since they fired them though, at the coronation."

Outside from the street, someone screamed. Tamsin threw the blanket off and pushed through the clammy shirts to the door.

"L'me through!" someone yelled. Lacey. Three times in less than a day, and good things didn't come in threes for Tamsin. She opened the door and peered out into the alley.

Lacey shook off the people trying to hold her back. In the early moonlight her face was too pale. Something dark soaked her sleeve and trailed down one leg of her breaches. She clutched her side.

"Frank," she gasped. "Riot at the wharf."

"You're hurt!" Tamsin reached for Lacey's arm. Lacey pulled away.

"Frank's shot," Lacey said.

Tamsin glanced back inside. Rhys was at the door, her kit in his hands.

"Let's go," he said.

She opened her mouth to argue and switched paths mid word. If Lacey was hurt too, another set of hands, not in shock, would help.

"Can your knee make it?" Tamsin said. The arnica and willow should be helping the swelling, but it had to be painful for him to move.

"We'll find out," Rhys said.

Lacey was running on nerves alone. She led them through the streets at a pace just faster than Rhys could manage. His mouth was set in a thin line of pain. At least with two days of beard growth and the new clothing, he seemed unexceptional. Tamsin hoped that, and the darkening streets, would keep them safe.

The streets were crowded. They were heading towards the roar, the riot, Tamsin supposed. Although it had lost most of its volume after the cannon blast.

"Was he hit at the riot?" Tamsin asked. "Is this about the grain prices?"

Lacey only gestured at them to hurry. Rhys took a hold of Tamsin's shawl after the second time the crowd pulled them apart.

Lacey led them back to a set of rooms not far from the docks. There was a heavy smell of old fish and yeast hanging in the air. Her door had a brass lock. It made a heavy thunk as she turned the key. Inside someone groaned.

Tamsin pushed her way past Lacey into the room. A pair of oil lamps sat on the table, their flames set too high, a pile of splintery crates were pushed against one wall. Her focus narrowed to one point, Frank.

He was curled up on the floor between two sailcloth hammocks. His left pant leg was soaked in blood. At some point he'd belted a pad of cloth over the wound, and he was pulling the end of the belt tight with white-knuckled intensity. Sweat beads stood out on his forehead.

Tamsin knelt next to him. When she touched his hand, it was cold.

"It's all right now Frank," she said. "Let me see it."

Gently she peeled his fingers off the belt.

There was so much blood. His pant leg was pasted to his skin, and it left a sticky pool under him. There hadn't been so much since ... her mind shied away from the comparison. This was not the time to think those thoughts.

She smelled smoke, black acrid smoke. She was choking on it, her throat already raw from screaming.

No. There was no smoke here. Tamsin took a deep breath.

Lacey sank down on the bench. Rhys limped over and handed Tamsin her kit. Slowly she cut away Frank's pant leg and picked at the bandage. The cloth pad was stuck to his leg. Frank keened when she tried to peel it back. It was an animal sound, higher than she imagined him capable of. Her stomach heaved.

Someone else was screaming in the room, shrill enough to pierce the ringing in her ears. More than one someone, she realized. She blinked her eyes. They were wet and heavy with tears. When had she started crying?

Concentrate. Stay in this moment, Tamsin thought. Her eyes focused on Lacey's terrified face. You can't let him die.

Lacey's slender fingers were fluttering arrhythmically across her knee. "I need water," Tamsin said.

Lacey stared at her. It was Rhys who brought the bucket over. Tamsin cupped her hands and let the water spill over the cloth pad until she could work it free. It soaked her skirts where she knelt.

She was running across the room, shoving furniture out of her way. She sank down next to something, someone. Her knees ached where they had hit the floorboards. The rose muslin was turning warm and crimson under her knees. Hot, wet, and cloying.

Rhys touched her arm and she jumped. The smell of blood and black powder was exactly the same. Frank.

Beneath the makeshift bandage was a ragged hole on the outside of Frank's thigh where the ball had entered. She felt along the back of his leg. The wound didn't go all the way through. Her stomach sank. The ball was still in there.

The wound was still bleeding, enough to be alarming. She pressed the cloth down again. She needed a minute to think, plan.

"Tom! Thomas!" She couldn't hear her own voice with all the chaos. Only the movement of her lips let her know she had spoken the words out loud. Behind her was a bass rumble of orders that didn't register.

Her hands were hot and sticky. All she could feel was the blood slowly cooling on her flesh. This time her brain wouldn't let her push the memories away. She closed her eyes.

She scrambled at his jacket. Blood welled up between her fingers, hot and sticky. There was too much. She had to stop it. He had to stop it. She looked around. Mother. Mother could help.

Tom gasped. That was the only sound she could hear; gasping over and over until someone's hands seized her shoulders and dragged her away. His gasping had stopped.

"Thomas!" Tamsin screamed.

"Tamsin!" It was Rhys's hand on her shoulder. Tamsin shoved him away. She wrapped her arms around herself, shaking.

"Tamsin." This time he didn't touch her. "Tamsin, you have to hold it together. Frank needs you." Rhys's other hand was holding pressure on the wound.

She inhaled, again. Slowly she nodded. Thomas wasn't here. That hurt too. Her eyes were wet. She hadn't realized she'd wept.

"He, it's bad." Her voice was shaky. "I'll try ... but..." She took a deep breath to steady her hands. Frank just nodded. Pain had eaten into his eyes and carved new lines down around his mouth.

"Lacey?" Frank said.

 Lacey made her way over. The force that had carried her to Tamsin was fading. She stumbled the few steps to Frank's side. Tears had turned her complexion blotchy and raw. Frank reached out a hand, still wet with blood.

"I ... I can't." Lacey shook her head and stumbled back.

"Lacey!" Frank said again.

Rhys caught her when she stumbled.

"Lacey, it will be all right. Tamsin is here now." Rhys's faith in her felt misplaced. How could she fix this without using magic?

Lacey let him hold her shoulders. At last, she nodded and reached over to hold Frank's hand.

Tamsin pulled her knife out. "Put the water bucket right here." Rhys moved it closer. Tamsin laid out her kit. She washed her hands and the knife blade, once, then again, with the new bar of lye soap.

"This will be painful. I need to get the ball out. I think it's come to rest against the bone. Rhys, Lacey, can you keep him still?" After prompting Lacey sat on his unhurt leg. Tamsin straddled the wounded leg. Rhys took Frank in a bear hug, pinning his arms down.

"A'fore you cut." Frank spoke through teeth clenched around a bit of kindling Rhys had found. Tamsin nodded and helped him spit it out.

"Lacey, if this goes bad, get out. Trenton'll make you the papers to leave Celdre." That took most of his breath and Frank leaned back against Rhys and waved his hand like a bloody king at court.

Lacey glared. She seemed to come back to herself. "Fuck that. You got us into this mess, you are damn sure going to help me finish it."

Frank managed something close to a smile. He bit back down on the kindling.

Tamsin slid her fingers under the belt and worked it up on his thigh. Blood spilled out but slower. She handed the end to Lacey to hold tight. Frank was still calm. Tamsin picked up the knife.

Cutting his flesh alternated between dispassionately easy, and the worst thing she had ever done. Blood spilled over her hands and made everything warm and slimy. The blood link hovered just at the edges of her awareness. Another distraction. She took a deep breath. Tamsin reached her first two fingers into the wound and felt for something not muscle or bone.

It took a few minutes. She tuned out Frank's screams, but it was a mercy when he passed out. Rhys took the belt from Lacey and let her cradle Frank's head.

Tamsin found the ball at last, distorted but intact, buried in the layers of muscle. She cast it away to skitter off into some dark corner of the room. She pulled out her curved needle and linen thread. Rhys winced.

"This is the smallest needle I could afford," she said. She started drawing the wound closed.

"Silk thread would be better," he said. And how did he know that? The wound on his shoulder perhaps? Still, no time for it now.

Lacey answered before Tamsin could. "No silk to be had in this quarter." She kept her eyes away from Tamsin's needle.

Tamsin was sweating by the time she laid the last stitch. She pulled the belt away and waited. Blood slowly trickled back into the flesh. It welled up around the stitches and the flesh started to stretch and bulge. Fuck. The musket ball had hit something that wasn't clotting. She pulled the belt tight again.

"Tamsin, tell me the truth. He's going to die. Isn't he?" Lacey's voice broke on the last word. Her face was already wet with tears.

Tamsin inhaled. "Lacey, do you trust me?"

Lacey nodded slowly.

"Both of you, wait outside."

Rhys looked confused, but he took Lacey's hand and helped her up.

As soon as Tamsin heard the door shut behind them, she opened herself up to the blood link that had been humming around her. Twice, twice in as many days. She was just asking to be caught. But Lacey. Tamsin would do anything to pay back the smallest of what Lacey had done for her.

Her brother Thomas's ghost hung like a spectre in the room. Not this time. She let go of the belt. It was easier to connect with Frank, there was so much blood, but Frank's mind was aware in a way Rhys's had not been. On some level he would know what she had done when he woke. She'd deal with it later.

Something was still bleeding deep inside the wound. If she had been honest with herself, she'd known that before she loosened the belt the first time. He was a breath away from bleeding out. She reached across the link, her hands sliding inside the stiches, spinning the threads of magic tighter and tighter into the wound. Clot damn you, clot.

When she opened her eyes, the bleeding was done. Frank was breathing, shallow and quick, but even. Tamsin raised her hands, still slimed with blood up to the wrists. She plunged them into the bucket and tried to wash the feel of someone else off her. Her skirt was blood sodden, and it twisted around her legs as she rose. She made it to the chamber pot before vomiting.

"You can come back," she said after she'd emptied her stomach. It took her two times before she could make her voice loud enough to carry through the door. It trembled in a way that she would be worried about if she wasn't so damn tired. She hadn't realized how much this would take out of her. Two healings in as many days. There was a grey fog hovering at the edge of her eyes. She pressed it back again, but it took more effort this time.

Rhys came in holding Lacey. He had her coat off and draped over her, but her head lolled.

"Is she all right?" Tamsin asked. She should be more alarmed. But she was so tired. Everything sounded like she was talking underwater.

He grunted and set her down on the pile of crates near the door.

"Arm's cut, not serious," Rhys said. He slid down the wall next to her, wincing.

"Tamsin's walking wounded," Tamsin joked. "I think Frank'll make it through the night."

"You're a brilliant doctor," Rhys said.

Tamsin shrugged. If she denied it, he might guess that it wasn't her skill with the needle keeping Frank alive.

"Let me see her," she said instead.

Tamsin made it over to the crates. Lacey had caught a knife blade to her forearm, several times. The slashes had already started to scab over. Tamsin wrapped the arm, but Lacey didn't wake up.

"Shit. I fouled the water bucket. Frank needs to drink something."

Rhys nodded. He hauled himself back upright and limped to the cupboard.

"I don't see anything," he said after a brief rummage.

Tamsin sighed and pushed herself up on her feet. All she wanted to do was rest her head on the table and close her eyes.

"I still have a coin or two, I'll buy something from the pub," she said. "I can go."

"No, on your leg? You could scarcely walk here. Besides, what if someone recognized you? This is near where those men jumped you. I'll manage." She took a step, and the world swam. Rhys caught her before she hit the floor. His hand rested warm against the hollow of her back.

"You can't go anywhere, you're exhausted."

"I suppose you getting killed will help immensely," Tamsin said, with all the dryness she could muster. "Lay off. I'll be fine in a moment." She pushed his arms away.

"I could just run to a pump?"

"It doesn't run this late, they shut the water off at noon."

"Oh."

"The Barrel will sell me something." She took an experimental step. It went better than before. "Stay here and keep them safe for me please, Rhys."

Rhys's mouth made a thin line, but he nodded.

Once out in the night air, Tamsin regretted her decision. The Barrel was the closest, but the three blocks seemed to go on forever. She shuffled down the street, one hand on the wall.

The Barrel was brimful. If the Bluecoats were trying to keep people inside, this was the place to be. Tamsin elbowed her way through the press to the counter. Bill of the Barrel was a round chested man with skin a few shades darker than her own. He ignored her until she slapped four copper pennies onto the pitted wooden bar.

"We're out of rum," he said.

"I need broth," she corrected. Gods, she was covered in blood. What must he think? Still a glance around the room showed her there were other walking wounded.

He eyed the coins and weighed it against her dishevelled appearance a few moments more, then jerked his thumb towards the back of the place.

"Ask for Sara, she'll give you your pennies worth." He tucked the coins into the till and went back to drawing out beers.

Tamsin pushed her way to the kitchen.

Sara proved to be Bill's daughter, and she measured the broth exactly out to four pennies worth, minus the cost of the bottles. Tamsin leaned against the hearth while Sara worked. The warmth felt amazing, and she caught herself nodding off on the hearth stone.

"D'ya think this is an inn?" Sara woke her with a rude poke to Tamsin's side. "Take your things and get out!"

Tamsin obeyed. The bottles were warm against her chest as she pushed back through the crowd towards the door.

"How hard can it be to find a soft rich fellow who's been hurt?" The man speaking was loud enough to cut through even the crowd's din. Tamsin froze. "I haven't been paying you good coin to come back empty handed!"

Rhys, they were talking about Rhys. She ducked into the fringes around another man's accounting of the riot to listen.

"How hard can it be to find someone in silk?" The man scolded. "His waistcoat alone had thirty sovereigns of silk stitching on it. Have you checked the clothing markets?" He had to be someone who knew Rhys or had seen him without his coat to guess that value.

The man's next words were swallowed by a wave of laughter from the crowd around her.

"And I said to that Bluecoat, 'you and what army's going to make me move?' That's when the whole lot of them came down the street."

She looked for the man who had been speaking. He was in a corner of the bar, surrounded by men and women with runner tattoos staining their wrists. The man's clothing was not precisely out of place here, but it was fresh from a dry-goods shop. His shirt still had the creases from where someone had plucked it from the shelf, passable, but not perfect in his subterfuge, yet he clearly had coin to throw at problems though, else he'd have used the economy of a ragman's shop to blend in better.

The laughter around her died down, and more of his conversation came to her ear.

"My supply of crowns depends on your success," the man said. Tamsin tried to memorize his face. Middle aged, and with a hardness to his features that spoke of a physical life, but well fed. Hunting the clothing stores, that was smart. A thread of fear slid through her. Would Bernard remember her? Could they trace her through that purchase? Surely not, she couldn't be the only person to buy a set of men's clothing yesterday. Rich and smart; what had Rhys done to merit such an enemy?

"We can break some heads. That might help if someone is hiding him from ya, Marcus," one of the men around him said.

Marcus shrugged. "The only important thing is that we find him. Those idiots never should have left before finishing the job. Are the gates covered?"

The group Tamsin was hiding in started to break up. With a start, she realized the story was over. She let herself get pulled away with the crowd.

Marcus. At least she had a face to put to the search now.

*

Rhys opened the door at her first knock. He'd cleaned up a little. Lacey was sprawled in a hammock snoring. Frank had been shifted slightly until he was out of the puddle of blood and wrapped in a blanket.

"Is he—" Tamsin started to say.

Rhys cut her off. "He's breathing and the swelling is almost gone." He took the bottles from her and set them on the table. "Sit down. You look greyer than Frank."

"I'll be all right," Tamsin said. Still, she allowed him to guide her to a seat. Not standing was wonderful. She wanted to never stand again. After a minute, she tried to push herself back upright.

"What does he need?" Rhys asked. He gently pushed her back down on the bench. She handed him one of the brown glass bottles, still warm to the touch.

"Broth. He needs to drink as much as we can get into him for the next little while."

"I'll manage it," Rhys said. "I'm not sure what you did, but it's enough. Your turn to rest. You've been running nonstop all day."

"Just for a minute." She sank her head onto her hands. "I just need to put my head down."

"Of course," he whispered. He had a nice voice, low and sweet. Her eyes closed.

*

Tamsin woke sometime later. The lamps had burned down low.

"Frank? Lacey?" she asked. Her tongue was thick with sleep.

"Fine. Frank's had a cupful of broth already. It's your turn now." Rhys reached under her shoulders and helped her onto her feet.

She stumbled across the room, and he helped her clamber into the other hammock. It smelled like salt and unwashed shirts.

*

This time the afternoon sunlight streaming in through the window cut high up in the wall, woke her for good. She sat up and the bed swayed, ropes creaking.

Rhys was sitting on the floor next to Frank, his head nodding down on his chest. He'd left the bad knee straight on the floor. Even from here she could see it was still swollen under the bandages. Last night must have been painful. The other hammock gave a jerk, and someone snorted.

"Whass'it?" Lacey poked her head over the side. Tamsin had always admired the way Lacey seemed to always look tidy even when the water was shut off or she'd been up all night. Now she was in a state, her hair was matted out in wild directions, and soot and dried blood were caked on her face. Tamsin climbed out of the hammock carefully. Not carefully enough evidently. Her skirt got caught up beneath her and she hopped the first few steps to the floor. Rhys lifted his head and peered blearily at her. She crossed over and laid a hand along Frank's jaw. His heart was still beating. She let out a breath and sank to the ground.

"His colour is good," she said.

Lacey swung out of her own hammock adroitly. She moved over and touched Frank's shoulder. All the morning fog was gone now.

"Tamsin, what did you do? I … I thought he was going to bleed out." Relief crossed her face followed by a slow fear. "Tamsin?"

Tamsin shook her head. "I can't tell you, Lacey." She watched as understanding slowly filled Lacey's face. Lacey edged her body away, half an inch but it was enough.

"Would you like me to check your arm? I bandaged it last night…" Tamsin trailed off as Lacey looked slowly from her arm to Tamsin. Terror was etched in every line of her face.

"Just bandaged," Tamsin said quickly. "I'd never hurt you, or Frank."

Lacey's eyes were as unforgiving as stone. She knew. Tamsin got to her feet. Rhys had gathered her kit together and left it on the table sometime in the night.

"You need to make sure he keeps drinking things, broth, water … not beer." She rushed to get the words out. "He needs clear things. And watch it to see if the wound goes feverish or it gets red or green pus or blackish. That's corruption, and it's hard to fix if it gets on. Willow bark if you have it. You, you know where to find me." The last words she whispered. She carefully avoided looking into Lacey's face.

Tamsin picked up her kit and headed towards the door, shoulders slumped. She didn't look until a, by now familiar, inhalation of suppressed pain sounded behind her.

Rhys joined her at the door.

"You don't have to come," she said quietly. "Lacey could find your home."

"Lacey is a good person, but I trust you."

Tamsin nodded, and together they started the painful journey home.

Chapter Eight

Every morning at the Wharf a crowd assembled dockside, in the hope of picking up a day's work. Most of the Narrows' able bodied, and a few who were not, showed up. Tamsin had tried the work. They'd laughed at her hands, still soft even after a year in gaol, and passed her over for someone else every time.

It paid well, dock work, but the jobs ebbed and rose with the river level. There were never enough jobs to go around, and they left their workers broken early, pressed under the weight of a hundred thousand crates and nets of fish.

The press of the crowd jostled Tamsin and Rhys. After they had to jump aside for one of the freight wagons, Rhys reached out and grabbed her hand.

"I don't want to lose you," was all he said. There were more missing cobblestones here than there were actual stones. Tamsin knew of whole hearths made of the scavenged stones.

Of all the places in the Narrows, the Wharf was where Tamsin was the least comfortable. The streets were wider here to accommodate the wagons that hauled goods up to the Merchants' Ring. During the daylight hours the Bluecoats patrolled the streets openly in clusters of four or five, rifles gleaming. And the docks were nearer to the gaol than Baker's shop.

"Just stay close to me." Tamsin didn't pull her hand away though. The front of her dress was dark with dried blood. It was attracting some notice on the street.

"What is that?" Rhys pointed at the line snaking its way around the block and around the corner.

Tamsin pushed his arm down.

"Never point. People notice other people pointing."

Rhys looked confused. She slipped her hand out of his and hooked it into the crock of his elbow instead. It made him walk a little closer, his hip brushing hers. She tilted her head up and whispered in his ear.

"It's the dock line. They're looking for work. And it happens every day but Se'enday, so don't stare. You're supposed to live down here; you have to act it."

"Does that mean no questions?" he asked.

"No pointing, questions asked quietly, and try to relax. Tell yourself that this is what happens every day," Tamsin said. "It's familiar."

"That might help if I had a frame of reference for familiar."

"Just act like I do."

Tamsin steered them through the crowd, keeping Rhys right at her side. His gait started off faltering, but as they walked, he moved easier. That was a good sign. Another day and he'd be walking normally, she judged.

"Why was Lacey upset?" he asked. Softly this time.

Of course he'd ask. She steered them off the street and behind one of the stalls selling sprats. They weren't fresh, and their fishy odour clung to her throat.

"I can't talk about it, not to anyone."

He hesitated. "You didn't do anything wrong, not that I could see."

Tamsin ran through a litany of lies in her head. Which one would he believe?

"I used an herb that is dangerous," she said at last. That was close to the truth.

"How so?"

"People think it's horrible, but it worked. It healed him. But I could be in a lot of trouble if anyone knew I did it."

"Lacey won't tell anyone." There was complete confidence in his face.

Tamsin wasn't so sure. Lacey wouldn't turn her in to the Bluecoats. They'd be as like to bring Lacey to gaol with Tamsin, and Frank with them for being magic-touched. But there were other ways Lacey could rid herself of a witch down here if she set her mind to it.

Rhys must have seen some of that on her face. "You saved her brother. She'll forgive you anything once she's had a chance to calm down."

"Of course," Tamsin lied. Lacey would do no such thing. Tamsin had sworn to her, sworn up and down when Lacey had found her shivering on the streets. It was her mother that had the magic, not Tamsin. It was the first lie she'd told Lacey. It was the one Lacey would never forgive her for.

"Which herb was it?" Rhys asked.

"Come again?" She took half a step away from him. The boards of the stall were up against her back.

"The herb that you used?" When she didn't answer, he pressed the matter. "I drank the last of the draught last night. You had no herbs in your kit." His eyes never left her face.

Tamsin's heart raced. He was so close to the truth. Was he going to betray her? "You don't believe me?" Maybe she could buy some time.

Rhys met her eyes squarely. "I saw his wound. Something was badly hurt in there. At best he should have lost his leg. He didn't. I checked while you were out. Blood was flowing to all of his toes. He's going to be fine."

He'd seen bullet wounds before. She remembered the lump of knotted tissue in his shoulder. Of course he had.

"You remember something from before?" she asked. If she could distract him, maybe she could stall for time until she could figure out what he knew.

Rhys paused. "No, I still don't remember anything specific, just facts without the context of how I learned them. But I know you are lying to me. I'd like to know why."

Tamsin pressed her lips tight. Was there anything she could say here that wouldn't lead to the gallows?

"I can't."

Did he see the fear in her face? In the way her shoulders and hips were pushed against the rough stall boards, away from him? He stepped back and gave her space again.

"I'm sorry. You don't have to tell me. I've trusted your judgment so far. I trust you. I want to know, but if it would hurt you or Lacey or Frank, I don't need to know."

"And you'd let it drop? Even after you leave?" It couldn't be that simple. She searched his face. She wanted to believe him. His face, everything in his bearing was familiar to her in a way she hadn't known she missed. Still, one of her perfectly mannered neighbours back home had called the guard on her mother for healing. Someone dressed in silk and sipping ices had set in motion something that killed half of Tamsin's family. She had no reason to trust a pretty face.

"I trust you. After all, never in my memory have you steered me wrong," Rhys said.

Tamsin snorted. "It's been three days. Give it time."

"In truth though," he said, "Lacey said that when they brought me to you, they thought I was dead. I'd guess that whatever you used on Frank, you used something similar on me."

She inclined her head a fraction of an inch.

"So, I owe you for my life, as well as the answers to some of the questions about who I am," he continued.

"Lacey and Frank were more than half of it," Tamsin protested. "If they hadn't brought you to me..."

"But they did, because they trusted that you could help me. And when Frank was hurt, they trusted you again. In fact, everyone I've met has trusted you."

"Given your limited circle of acquaintances that means nearly nothing," she said, but the bitterness was gone. This was getting too close to something real. Tamsin changed the subject.

"Rhys, last night, I saw the man who was looking for you. Does the name Marcus mean anything to you?"

"Not a thing."

"He's got money behind him, all his clothes were new, and he was paying out crowns for people to go look for you. He can't keep that pace though; he'd have to be rich as the king to pay that many people a crown to look for you."

Rhys looked up the street. "Are we safe here?"

Tamsin shrugged. "It would take a king's ransom to buy another door-to-door search, and time. They mentioned hitting the clothing markets and covering the gates. We'll have to be careful getting you out of here, but where is it safer to hide than in a crowd? All this should be done in another day or so. It has to be. Then you can go home."

"Tamsin, if you have some way to heal, why are you down here? Wouldn't healing make you rich, or at least keep you from doing laundry?"

"There's nothing wrong with doing laundry!" She was surprised how much his questions stung. "You make it sound so simple. The world doesn't work simple." She stepped back. "You don't know anything about me."

His shoulders drew back at that. He bowed, some half remembered courtly gesture.

"My pardon milady. I seem to have overstepped again." This time the mockery was missing.

"When I was first here in the Narrows I waited," she said. He'd touched some wound she hadn't even realized was still there. The words bubbled out before she could think about them. "Someone would have to come to help me. Someone I used to know from back home, they'd come and bring me home again.

"Oh, life wouldn't be like before, I knew that. There are too many people dead for that. But there had to be someone who would care." Tamsin spread her hands. "No one came." Her voice shook. "Lacey taught me that the only one you can always rely on down here is yourself."

"You've done a good job of it," Rhys said.

Tamsin's mouth twisted. "I survived."

Rhys digested that.

"You let me rely on you," he said at last. "When the man came your door, you didn't choose to turn me over then."

"That was different."

"How?"

"I'd just put you back together. I wasn't going to let anyone undo all that work." She shifted away and studied the crowd on the street.

"Will Lacey forgive whatever happened?" he asked.

"I don't know."

"Whatever happens to me I won't mention the ... herb again. You have my word on it."

"Words really don't mean much down here," Tamsin said.

"I suppose honour wouldn't convince you either," he paused. "Assuming I was ... *am*, an honourable man."

She gave him a wry look.

"Truly, I owe you my life Tam. I wouldn't harm yours."

"Thank you." Her words were automatic. He certainly sounded sincere. And she was tired, tired of the lying, of the caution, of all the fear. Resignation wasn't trust, but her hand was laid on the table.

"Where should we go?" he asked when the silence had stretched out too long again.

"Home." She blinked away the last of the moisture in her eyes and turned back. Rhys had a wistful expression on his face.

"What is it?" she asked.

"Home just sounds like a lovely place."

She looked at him, and the thought of spending the rest of the day cooped up in her little room was too much. The sun was out in force, bringing a welcome thread of warmth to the street.

"Do you have your coin?" she asked.

Rhys nodded. "I wasn't sure if it was safe to leave it behind. I brought everything," He reached into his pocket and started to pull something out.

Tamsin crossed over and laid her hand on his arm.

"The next rule for today, don't show or tell anyone how much money you have on you."

Rhys nodded and drew his hand out of his pocket empty.

"And don't speak if you can help it. Your accent will give you away."

He mimed sealing his lips.

"Do you have any pennies in all that wealth?" she asked.

Rhys tilted his head and gave her an arch look. "I might or might not."

She couldn't help it. Tamsin laughed. "Very good, but if you have any small coin, I'll pick us up something to eat and drink."

"Which are the small coins? The copper ones?"

She nodded. He pulled a couple out and passed them over. Tamsin linked her arm with his again.

"It's a good thing you weren't a dandy," she said. "Your hands are nearly as rough as mine. They fit in better."

She led him back out into the crowd and through the streets to one of the taverns lining the wharf. Not the Barrel. The manager was eager for customers, and he traded Rhys's pennies for a slick, stoneware bottle still cool from the cellar and a sack of day-old buns.

Tamsin led Rhys through the streets to the wreckage of the mill. She clambered up the stairs, skipping the places where the stone had crumbled away, helping Rhys up. He was favouring his knee more by the time they reached the top. The floorboards here were suggestions littered with trash. Tamsin kept them both near the wall where a great stone ridge supported the beams the floor had sat on. A bit more scrambling and they were at the remains of the great wheel.

The wheel itself had parted from its mooring decades before. It left a pitch-blackened trunk still splintered off where it had fallen, and a wide stone window. Tamsin fetched up against the far side of the window ledge and let her legs dangle.

"I come up here when I find the time." She pulled the cork out of the bottle easily.

Rhys settled himself gingerly opposite her.

"It's high," he said.

"That's why I like it. You can see over the walls here." She took a long swig of the bottle. The wine inside was tart and bitter and went down her throat like a cold fire. She passed the bottle over to Rhys.

"See over there?" She swung her arm out wide into the open air. This was the first place she had found here that didn't feel claustrophobic.

Rhys looked, but he was keeping his body firmly inside the window.

"Over there, that bit of green? That's the park for the king. I saw his father once. He waved from inside his coach when he passed through my hometown."

Rhys took a drink and grimaced.

The wine was making her belly warm. Tamsin smiled. "I warned you, we don't get good spirits down here."

"It's..." he searched for a word. "Fresh," he settled. He chased it with one of the buns.

"Apple wine always is."

"Wouldn't that be cider?"

She shrugged and reached out for the bottle again. "I lost my friend today, I plan to drink."

"Lacey will come around, Tamsin."

"Based on your day and a half of her acquaintance?" Tamsin'd had just enough wine to be blunt. "I lied to my friend, and for all the—" she stopped herself before she said smuggling. "All the kinds of work they do, they never lied to me."

"What sort of work do they do?" Rhys asked.

Tamsin ignored that question.

"The crates in their room, do you know what they are keeping in there, Tamsin?" Rhys asked.

She shook her head. What did she care why Frank and Lacey had crates in their home? They were probably bringing work home. Wait.

"You didn't look in them?" she asked.

"When I was looking for the food."

"No, no, no, no! You can't do that. We keep secrets down here for a reason." Frank would kill him if he found out Rhys had snooped.

Rhys took a moment to consider that. "But what if the secret they were keeping was guns. Lots of them."

Tamsin took another drink. Smugglers. It made sense that Frank and Lacey would bring in guns, and gin, and anything else taxed highly or outright forbidden. But why would anyone need a lot of guns down here?

"It's their secret," she said at last. "You'd best keep it. You owe them your life." She passed him the bottle.

"Are you sure that drinking and heights are a good match?" he said. She noticed he'd drawn his legs inside.

"I'm not going to get all fall down. It's just—" she stretched her arms out again. The alcohol had burned a pleasant trail to her belly and was edging out the ache in her temples.

The sun was beating down and baked warmth into her bones the way only spring sun could do. When the breeze wasn't hitting her, it felt like spring at last.

She reached over him and pointed at a grey smudge on the horizon. "That's the high road. It goes from one end of Aradwyn to the other." Her arm brushed his. She could smell the apple wine gently on his breath.

"Have you been down it before?" he asked. He handed her one of the buns they'd bought.

"Once." She pressed her lips in a thin tight line, and he didn't push her further.

They spent a long while in silence, watching people move down on the streets and boats slide up and down the river. The bottle was more than half empty and Tamsin felt relaxed, safe, for the first-time in... a very long time.

"I don't plan to be here forever," she said.

Rhys nodded.

"There has to be a place out of the city where I can raise potatoes and carrots." She gestured away from the bulk of the city. "A village that needs a laundress who can satin stitch." The Celdre road cut a dark path southeast, through the new spring growth sprouting around the city.

"Once, long ago I wanted to come here," she said, not moving her gaze from the road. "Well, not here. There." She pointed to the wall of the King's Ring rising above them. The walls had been faced with a polished white stone, so they gleamed. The arched gateways had gilt crenellations that glowed in the low sun's light.

"It's pretty," Rhys said. A generous portion of the bottle had ended up in his belly and the tip of his nose was just a little red. It was adorable. She looked away.

"Is that where you think I came from?" he asked.

Tamsin nodded. "Most landed folk at least rent a place in the King's Ring when they come to town if they can't keep a place there year-round." The air was starting to cool as the sun swung lower into the west.

"Do you really think there is someone looking for me up there?" His foot was tucked under him, his toes curling and uncurling to a beat only he heard.

She hesitated. "There should be. If I knew for certain what you were doing down here... If you came here or if someone..."

"Someone what?"

"The Narrows is the place where people put things they'd rather not find again," she said at last. "With all the people looking for you... someone brought you here to disappear."

"It all comes back to why, doesn't it?" he asked.

"A lot of things do."

He was quiet for a moment. "Do you think I did something terrible, Tamsin?"

She looked back at him. Something dark and worried was etched into his face.

"I don't know. You don't seem terrible now. But I have no idea who you were. And if who you were, is who you are... or if that sentence can be untangled." She picked at the mortar around the stone walls.

"Is it odd that I can remember things but not people or places?" he asked. "You are the physicker."

She weighed the answer carefully before answering. Too carefully.

"It is odd. I see it on your face. Is there something else you haven't told me?" Rhys pushed himself upright against the flaking remains of the whitewashing.

"It isn't..." she said and stopped. What could she say?

"Tamsin?"

She took a deep breath. "It wasn't the head injury that caused your memories to leave. Someone did this to you deliberately."

"Who? How?"

"I don't know." She kept her eyes focused on the white stone walls. "When you came to me, you smelled..."

"I took a bath."

"No, not exactly an odour. I'm explaining it all wrong." She bit down on her lip and turned back to face him. "Rhys, you smelled like magic."

He looked puzzled. "Magic has a scent?"

"To some people, but there were herbs too. Rosemary, cloves, something else..."

Between one breath and the other it fell into place for him. "It was magic that healed Frank," he said.

She looked away.

"Why are you hiding it?"

"Because I like my neck," she said. The cloth of her dress scratched at the brand. She laced her fingers together to keep them from scratching it.

He still looked puzzled.

"The king outlawed blood magic. At least his grandfather did, and the next kings never changed the law."

"Why outlaw it?" Rhys asked. The sky was starting to darken. The sun had hit the edge of the mountains, and the light was like molten brass.

"Because it can do things like take your memories away, or worse," Tamsin said. "The way I can stop the bleeding means I could stop your blood. I could reach out and stop your heart and the worst I could get was a headache. Blood mages killed the old king's daughter. That's when they built the outer wall and killed all the blood mages, or drove them out." She flushed. She'd drunk too much.

"Can you bring my memories back?" It was barely more than a whisper.

She shook her head. "I'm not sure how it was done. All I know is how to heal. That's all we ever did. Heal."

"So, someone with magic took away my memory. It still doesn't tell me why."

"It tells you something though," Tamsin said. "They could have killed you. It would have been easier. They didn't. That means it was probably someone different than the person who is looking for you now."

He nodded slowly. "Do you know anyone else who could do this?"

"No, I'm the only one I know of anymore." She waited a beat. "I didn't do it. In case you were being too polite to ask. I know, I would think it would be me, if I were you. But I didn't. My word on that."

"Words don't really mean much down here," he quoted.

Tamsin opened her mouth and closed it. "I suppose they don't. You shouldn't say anything though. When they look for mages sometimes the Bluecoats take anyone magic-touched."

"Again, you have my word and my silence, Tamsin. I don't think you stripped my memories. I was teasing."

"Ah." Tamsin turned her face back out over the city. "Bluecoats, magic, bullet wounds... I'm quite ready for things to stop falling apart now."

"At least it can't get worse," Rhys said.

"From your mouth to the gods' ears," she replied.

They sat in silence for a while longer. The breeze gusted, and this time it brought a wave of chilly air with it. A storm was coming. Tamsin shivered.

"We need to head down. Once the sun's down this place gets dangerous. More dangerous."

Rhys corked the bottle for her. Tamsin tucked it away and they began the precarious climb back to the ground.

The dark seemed to be chasing people inside, or maybe it was the riot from the night before, or the drizzle that started once they reached the ground. They made their way back to Tamsin's place quickly. Her door was ajar.

Panic cut through the alcohol. If someone broke in, if they took her wash tub, or her blankets, she'd have to start over again from scratch. Rhys pushed ahead of her to go through the door first.

"It's all right," he said as she pushed into the room. "It's only Lacey."

Relief followed closely by fear washed over her.

"Is Frank?" Tamsin asked.

"He's fine." Lacey was holding herself rigid. She didn't look at Tamsin.

One part of the fear bled away. Frank was going to be all right. Tamsin started to put her bundles down. She stopped. Someone had rifled through her things.

The herbs had the worst of it. Their leaves were stripped from the hanging stalks and jumbled together on the top shelf. The shirts were piled, almost folded, on her bench. Everything else was a little askew.

Tamsin looked at Lacey. A crumble of mint clung to the end of her braid.

Tamsin sucked in a breath.

"I'm glad he is doing well," she said. "How did it happen? Did you both get caught up in the riot."

Lacey ignored her questions.

"I'm here about you," she said tightly, pointing at Rhys. "I found where you belong."

"How?" Tamsin started to speak, but Lacey talked over her.

"You're Rhys Carwyn, Lord Carwyn the younger. Your sister is looking for you. She's at number ten Merriton Square in the King's Ring." Lacey stood up from Tamsin's stool.

"Lacey, wait..." Tamsin said. "How did you find out? Are you sure it's real and not another trap?"

Lacey glared at her. "Elspeth. Only one kingsring fool managed to get himself lost this week. She answered my message. His sister is real and worried sick."

"Oh," Tamsin said.

Lacey shook her head and walked out of the door. Tamsin watched her until the Narrows swallowed her up.

Rhys walked over and laid a hand on her shoulder. "Are you all right?"

Tamsin eeled away from his touch. "I'm fine." She shut the door and pulled the latch tight.

"Rhys Carwyn," he said. "Carwyn."

"Does it sound familiar?" She was so tired. Thunder boomed outside and rain started sheeting down, creeping in through the cracks around the door.

"As much as anything. How do I get back home?"

Tamsin lay out on her bed. The wine seemed to have soured in her belly. She should set the buckets outside, but she was too tired to sit with them and guard them.

"It depends. If the gates aren't being watched, you could go now. But if someone is watching for you it could be a trap."

"I have a sister."

"It appears so." Tamsin put an arm over her head which had begun to ache.

"Are you sure you are all right?" Rhys asked.

"Rhys, just leave me be. For two days, I've been nothing but nursemaiding or fetching or worried. I need a minute to think." Crap. She shouldn't have said that. She was drunk, and hurt and angry.

Rhys didn't say anything more. The stool scraped outwards and there was a clatter of things being laid out on the table. She closed her eyes and let sleep come.

Chapter Nine

It was just before dawn, by the sounds of Baker starting the day's baking. Somewhere in the darkness she could hear Rhys snoring. Tamsin felt a flash of guilt. He must have slept on the floor.

Why was she feeling guilty? It was her bed. Besides, this would be his last night here if things all went to plan. They just needed to get Rhys past the first gate. Once he was in the Merchants' Ring, they could find a cab to run him home. And she'd be done with Rhys Carwyn.

There was relief in that. Relief and not regret. It had been nice to have company, and he'd made himself fairly handy in a very tight spot, but complications followed that man like a ship's wake.

But how would she get him through the gate? This Marcus was not a complete fool; he'd set watchers at the gates. It had been three days of nothing, though. Surely, they would be growing bored. Were they good enough to identify Rhys through the stubble, dirt, and ill-fitting clothing? His bruises had passed from the purple to the sallow stage, legacy of her healing no doubt. A coating of grime should hide them from all but the most minute examination. They'd have to chance it. The gates would be opening soon. But he had no work papers. She had her papers and the shirts due back to Elspeth; how could she use that?

Rhys was on the floor between her bed and the door. His old coat was wrapped around his shoulders and the new one was balled under his cheek. She watched him for a moment. Mother had a saying, "sleeping reveals a person's true face." Tamsin never agreed with that. Rhys slept like a child in a tangle of tucked up limbs making him seem smaller somehow. His face seemed plain without the layer of intelligence and tension that usually animated it. She didn't like it. It looked too much like when he had first been brought to her.

Tamsin rolled out of bed. Her stomach was violently protesting her liquid meal from the night before. Rhys stirred when she stood up. Her feet were almost in his hair, the quarters were so tight. She made it to the pitcher without stepping on him and sipped water while he rubbed the sleep sand from his eyes and stretched, his arms and legs brushing the walls.

"Good morning," he said. He smiled widely.

Great he's a morning person, Tamsin thought. She grunted and took another sip of water. With a pang, she remembered her destroyed herb stores. Mint leaves would be welcome right now.

"We need a plan to get you through the gate," she said, when her nausea subsided.

"Do you expect trouble?"

"Always."

She glanced down at her own dress. Between Frank's blood and Rhys's mud it had gone from shabby to destitute. Maybe if she soaked the stain in milk the blood would come out. But milk was dear. Rhys might not be the only one they don't let through the gate, papers or no.

The Emirya dress was still laid out on the shelf. Tamsin pulled it down and rubbed out the paste she'd set on the stain. The wine mark was still there, slightly faded. The actress had gotten her wish; the dress was ruined. Tamsin's fingers brushed the soft wool. It was dated, but there was lace at the cuffs and embroidery at the band just under the short bodice. It would do.

"I have an idea," she said. "Turn around I need to change."

*

An hour later found them back on the streets. Rhys was in his new clothing, barefoot, his boots and finery wrapped up at the bottom of her basket in her blanket. Before he'd left, she'd made him stand on the street and poured grit into his damp hair to darken the colour.

She'd scrubbed up as much as she could manage and tucked her hair up into a chignon at the base of her neck. If she kept her shawl over the wine stain, she looked respectable, if out of fashion. She'd tucked a few of Rhys's crowns in her pocket.

There was another crowd at the gates. Tamsin scrubbed the sweat from her hands and handed Rhys the basket.

"Do you remember your part?" she asked.

"I won't say a word," he promised.

She nodded and moved them into the queue. Things were moving quickly today. As they waited, she tried to scan the crowd. There had to be someone here looking for Rhys. Just to the left of the gates, near but not in the queue, Tamsin spotted her. The woman wasn't being subtle. She scanned each person going through the gate like they owed her money. Stranger still, the guards weren't running her off for loitering near the lines. Tamsin's heart sank. Had the guards been bribed?

She could feel the woman's eyes on them as they neared the gate. Tamsin forced herself not to look at her. Head up, shoulders back, just like before.

Their turn came up too quickly and not quick enough. The Bluecoat glanced over at the woman as they approached. Tamsin forced herself not to follow his gaze.

"Your name," —he paused a beat, taking in the style of her dress— "Miss, and your reason for entry today." Another beat. "Please."

"Elspeth Williams. I am returning home." She kept her shoulders back and stared the Bluecoat in the eyes.

"Home? Why are you in the Narrows at such an early hour Miss?"

"That damned laundress chit. She ruins my husband's shirts every time she touches them. I came early to settle the matter, since this lout," she waved her hand towards Rhys, "can't be trusted with such matters." She kept her shoulders back and looked the man in the eyes. Beneath the layers of wool and shawl she could feel her brand, as if it were pulsing in time with her heart.

"What part of the city are you from?" he asked.

"Larchfell Row." That was near the fashionable part of the Merchants' Ring. A woman with a manservant would not be exceptional there. Tamsin kept her eyes on the Bluecoat's face watching for signs of disbelief or trouble.

"Do you have papers for your man, miss?"

Tamsin rolled her eyes. She pulled her work papers out and fanned them out with one of the silver crowns. Paused.

"You fool!" She turned on Rhys. "You brought the housemaid's papers instead of yours." Tamsin sighed.

"I should have checked myself before we left. Though when would I have time? Anna overbrewed the tea this morning and burned the toast."

The Bluecoat glanced at the papers and handed them back. The crown disappeared.

From the corner of her eye, she noticed a child running away from the gate. Had they been spotted?

The Bluecoat walked over to Rhys and moved the first layer of shirts aside.

Rhys bobbled the basket.

"Careful, you clod!" Tamsin pitched her voice to carry over the entire street. "If you ruin another garment, you will be out on the streets." She let the shawl slide down her arm, revealing the wine stain. The Bluecoat frowned. He had shifted his weight as if he was going to block their way. Everyone at the gate was watching them.

Well, if you can't avoid notice, draw enough notice that no one could imagine that you are trying to hide. Tamsin hoped it would work. Rhys stepped back and artfully fumbled the basket again. She slapped his cheek as lightly as she dared. His eyes watered, but he hid his surprise. The Bluecoat looked amused. He waved them through.

"You best listen to your mistress. Work's scarce these days," he told Rhys as they passed. Rhys nodded, only a tiny hint of amusement evident in the twitching of his lips and set of his shoulders. He kept his eyes on the ground until they passed under the gate. Tamsin kept her nose in the air until they were out of sight.

"I'm so sorry," she told Rhys in the first alleyway they reached. She plucked the basket out of his hands. "I tried to be gentle, but it had to look real."

He rubbed his jaw. "It's all right. It worked. We're past the gate."

Tamsin smiled. They were.

*

They were two blocks away from the gate when Tamsin spotted the tail. Inwardly she cursed. Marcus was cleverer, and richer, than she had thought. He'd put eyes on both sides of the gate, a weedy man wearing a green neckerchief, tattoos poking from under his coat sleeves. There were no cabs in sight yet, just one lone wagon jostling over the cobblestones. Rhys would have to make it to one of the markets, and fast.

She reached over and grabbed Rhys's hand.

"What's wrong?" he asked.

"Someone is following us." Tamsin pulled him with her down an alley between a dejected looking toy shop and a dry goods store.

"Who is it?" Rhys craned his neck around.

"The fellow with the green neckerchief. I recognize his tattoos. He's a Runner." He seemed to have passed by their alleyway. If they were careful, they could come back out behind him. She started humming a verse from the Moon's Marriage under her breath to mark out the time. Two verses ought to be enough time for him to lose them.

"Why do you call them Runners?" Rhys asked when she stopped humming.

"It's the name they use. They're one of the gangs that work the Wharf. They're more brawlers than bungnippers though." At his blank look, Tamsin clarified. "They're more likely to mug you than pick your pocket."

She poked her head out and checked the street. It looked clear. It was only five more blocks to Paperwright Square. There should be a cab there. They just needed to make it before the Runner circled back. She pressed them onward as fast as the crowd would let them.

Behind her, Tamsin heard someone whistle, three shrill short blasts and one long trill. They'd been spotted.

She pulled Rhys into a shambling run. Around her people cursed and pushed back as she shoved their way through the crowded street.

Beside a dubious looking butcher's shop was another alley, slightly larger. Tamsin aimed them in that direction. With luck, it would empty out onto one of the other main streets.

More whistles answered the first one. How many people did he have over here? Three? Five? The alley spilled out into a small muddy courtyard with walls on each side. Damn it all, if this was the Narrow's she wouldn't have led them to a dead end.

Rhys had been limping heavily for the last hundred yards of their dash. He couldn't run forever on his knee. She hadn't heard a whistle for a few moments.

"Do you think we are clear of them?" he asked, echoing her thoughts.

"Even odds," she said between breaths. Despite his limp, Rhys didn't seem winded. "There's men in that mob that would kill for the sovereign bounty. If you pray, now's the time."

The courtyard was empty except for a few iron rings fastened into the walls and ground. She inhaled slowly and began another verse of Moon's Marriage. Three verses in and it looked like they were safe.

Three quick whistle blasts broke the silence.

"Shit!" Tamsin pushed Rhys behind her. "As soon as they pass into the courtyard, run North. You have most of the money. They won't bother with me for long, but it will buy you time. Find the nearest Bluecoat or cab and give them Merriton Square, they'll get you home." She braced her basket in front of her like a shield.

Four people jogged through the gate. Three of them were Runners. She could see blue tattoos spiralling around their wrists. Two carried cudgels, slapping the weight of them against the palms of their hands. The first fellow had a sailor's dirk between his thick fingers. The fourth man was Marcus, although dressed considerably better than she'd seen him in the Barrel. He hung back as the others moved towards them.

Mustn't get his grey gloves dirty, Tamsin thought bitterly.

The man in the green kerchief held one of the cudgels. "I told ya, she got him new togs and mussed him up a bit," he said. Sweat had pasted his shirt to his chest. Too much time drinking ale on his ass, Tamsin thought.

"I'm sorry I doubted you." Marcus scrutinized them. "Whoever your friend is Captain, she did good work. If I hadn't kept a sketch circulating at the gates, I doubt we would have caught you."

Just who was this man? Tamsin thought. He was well dressed, but his waist coat was wool and bare of decorations. Did he work for someone then? Gloves could be part of a livery. She glanced back at Rhys. If he knew this man, he showed no sign of it. She needed to distract them enough for Rhys to run. She made a quick calculation and shifted her weight to the left. In one smooth motion, she pitched the basket at the first man's head. It hit square on, and the courtyard was filled with snowy white linen.

"Are you addlepated?" she yelled at Rhys. "Run!"

The man with the dirk reached for her. She ducked away. Then the man was right in front of her, and she could spare no more attention on anything but keeping away from his knife.

She ducked back from his sloppy thrust and pulled the clasp knife out of her pocket. She slid the catch free behind a fold of her skirt. Lacey had drilled her on this move until she could manage it by touch alone. With a blade this small her tricks would only work once, but if he grabbed her, he'd regret it.

Somewhere to her right came the meaty thunk of flesh against wood. *Can't think about that now. Stay alive.*

She kept her eyes on the man's shoulders. They twitched and she ducked another tentative swipe. He didn't see her as a threat, yet.

She needed him to get closer. His blade was longer than hers with greater reach and a cross guard. He wasn't worried about slicing his fingers off. Unlike her. This fight was going to hurt.

He feinted again. His eyes shifted right, she skipped left. She kept her free arm up, the bony side facing him. He grunted when she didn't back up. His next swipe wasn't a feint. She caught it on the outside of her forearm. It parted the wool and sank into the flesh beneath.

The pain was sharp and clean. She shoved her arm away from her torso, moving his knife with it. It bit further into her flesh, but she couldn't think about that. She stepped in close enough to breathe in the ripe unwashed scent of him.

His eyes opened wider, then she shoved her small blade under his ribs and up. Her blade caught on something, and she didn't complete the thrust. He staggered back, one hand clutching his belly. Her knife twisted in her hands, and she pulled it free. Hot blood covered her hand and the handle slid in her grip.

He had her measure now, and he kept a more respectful distance between them. Blood was running down her arm and making her sleeve sticky wet. Another dress soaked in blood. She hoped this wasn't a trend. Shock was making her silly. She hoped he kept his blade clean.

Something was happening behind the knifeman. She kept her eyes on his blade. He came at her again, his longer blade jabbing towards her own ribs. She slid back. Her skirts caught between her legs. She kicked them free, and he lunged again. She let herself fall out of range and rolled away.

Elsewhere she heard another sickening thud. The knifeman's eyes darted that way, and she used the distraction to clamber to her feet.

Rhys had acquired a cudgel. Its owner was stretched out in the mud bleeding. The second man was reeling back. Rhys was covered in mud and blood. As she watched he laid the second man out flat with a vicious blow to his throat.

The knifeman looked back for help. Marcus had vanished. The knifeman bolted toward the gate, still clutching his side.

Rhys let the cudgel fall into the mud. He swayed. Tamsin hurried over to him.

"I didn't know I could do this," he said. It wasn't quite a question. He looked at his hands like they belonged to someone else.

"We don't have time for this," Tamsin said. Marcus would no doubt be back soon with reinforcements. She scooped up one of the shirts and wrapped it tight around her wound. Someone had crushed her basket in the fight. She spotted the bundle of Rhys's clothing in a corner and shook it out. She thrust his old coat and boots at him.

"Quick! You need to look important." It would be a job getting a cab to pick them up as dishevelled as they were. Still Rhys's coins could smooth the way if they could get one to stop.

Rhys was still in shock, but he stepped into the boots and followed her, pulling his old, abused coat on over the shabbier one as he limped.

"It's three blocks till Paperwright Square, if we don't find a hackney before then," she said. Rhys was still standing there. Tamsin gave him a shove and he broke out of his thoughts and followed her.

They attracted a few stares, but Tamsin glared at anyone who moved towards them.

A block away from the square she hailed her first coach. The driver glanced at her bedraggled gown and kept on going. Tamsin cursed.

"You try the next one," she told Rhys.

He shook his head, and his eyes grew a little more focused. "You're hurt!"

"It's not going to kill me, but they will. We have to keep moving."

Once they reached the square, he made one quick signal and a driver pulled up. The man gave Rhys's eclectic attire a long look.

"Had a rough night of it, sir?"

Tamsin opened the door. "You could say that." She pushed Rhys at the steps. "He needs to go to number 10 Merriton Square."

The adrenaline was fading, and she was starting to feel the cut on her arm. It was going to be harder to cross the gate this time without questions. Still, she could think of something. Rhys had grabbed onto her elbow.

"You're coming with me," he said. "That needs looked after, and you lost all the laundry. I need to cover that expense."

All of Elspeth's shirts were lying in the mud. She'd have to pay for all of them. Elspeth would probably let her have this dress out of charity since the stain had set, but the shirts were worth five crowns at least. She'd be scrubbing her knuckles raw to make that back. While she was considering, Rhys had maneuvered her to the cab door.

"Just to clean off my arm," she said. They had to have a kitchen or stable where she could clean up a little. She made to climb up on the box with the driver, but Rhys helped her up the steps and into the cab. He pulled the door shut and tapped the carriage top, like he'd done it all before. When he wasn't thinking about it, muscle memory seemed to take over. The cab's wheels gave a tortured squeal and then they were jostling down the street, each dip in the cobble stones sending a wave of fresh pain down her arm.

Chapter Ten

Tamsin had never noticed how poorly-sprung a hackney coach was. Each jolt of the wheel sent a new wave of pain through her arm. Rhys had taken the forward-facing seat, by habit she guessed. She couldn't sit next to him, that would be too close. But sitting backwards made her stomach churn. She kept pressure on her wound and concentrated on keeping breakfast in her belly. The cabman was setting a brisk pace at least, weaving through the usual traffic. As they rose up the hill, the buildings grew more and more elegant, the streets grew wider and better paved.

When they reached the gate to the upper Ring, she marvelled at how fast they were waved through. Not even a check inside the cab. The implication of money greased a lot of wheels. Although from the sound of it, not the ones on this cab.

"I don't need to stay," Tamsin said as they cleared the gate. "I just need to clean this out, and maybe set a stitch or three if it needs it. And settle up for the shirts." It felt cold in the cab, but she was still sweating. Her fingers tightened on the wound, sending a fresh wave of pain up her arm.

"Stitch yourself? How? You'd need two hands," Rhys said. "I can call a doctor."

"It's not that deep. I can manage." How would she afford a doctor? She closed her eyes. The streets felt smoother here, or maybe she was getting used to the jostling. "I doubt your sister, or whatever other family you have, will want me to stay long."

"That's stupid. You helped me. Of course, they'll want to help you." Rhys fiddled with the watch case on his knee, not meeting her eyes. "What do you think my family will be like?"

Tamsin sighed. "How would I know? Proper. Rich." Dangerous, she thought. "I can't tell you about your family."

"But you'll stay with me while I meet them?" His hands were tapping his knees. He was nervous.

Tamsin hesitated. "I don't know, Rhys. You're the Lord Carwyn if Lacey is right. Or at least a Lord Rhys if you are a younger son. I would be out of place here." Letting Rhys convince her to get into the cab had seemed like a fine plan when toughs with weapons were chasing them down the street, but the downsides were quickly coming back to her. She was a long way from home.

"I want to help," Rhys said.

"Enough coins to break my losses on the shirts, fare home, and a place to clean up is enough," Tamsin said.

"What about papers? A sponsor to help you leave the Narrows? If I am a Lord Carwyn, could I arrange that for you?"

Tamsin couldn't swallow. Leave the Narrows? Would it be safe? What price would Rhys set?

"I—" Tamsin stopped herself. She was leaning towards him. He had to see how much she wanted this.

"It wouldn't be like before, Tamsin," Rhys said. "Stay with me, help me figure this out, and let me help you leave."

Tamsin pursed her lips. No. She couldn't let her hopes rise too high again.

"Let's see what happens when we get you home."

*

The cab pulled off the cobblestone street and onto a smooth, brick drive. Tamsin glanced out the window. Number 10 Merriton Square covered the entire block. A long, well-manicured lawn filled a half-circle between the drive and the street edged with narrow even hedges and a white marble fountain.

The house was covered in more pristine, white stone. All Tamsin could think of was the time involved to wash it regularly to keep the soot and dust from marring the facing. A solid ton of carved white marble pillars held up the porte-cochere entrance, with a carved double door that towered over the cab. The driver hopped down to open the cab door, but a liveried man was already there with a set of steps.

Rhys gestured for Tamsin to exit first, but she shook her head. Best for them to see him first. He climbed out. She scooted after him, keeping him between her and the footman. She didn't like the blank expression on the man's face. Her arm gave another twinge as her feet hit the gravel. Blood was coming through the top layer of cloth.

"Does this look like home?" Tamsin whispered to Rhys.

Rhys studied the doors. "It's not familiar," he said at last.

Tamsin sighed. Whoever had pulled the memories from his mind had been thorough, which was odd. What had they been after? Had Rhys learned something he shouldn't? Stripping everything away was like carving a pigeon with a sword.

"I beg your pardon Lord Rhys," the footman interjected. "But Lord Carwyn and Lady Eira will want to see you as soon as possible. Lady Eira has been quite worried." He avoided looking at Tamsin.

Tamsin relaxed a bit. This was the right house. She turned to the footman. "Your Lord Rhys got struck in the head. He's been a bit addlepated because of it."

"Lady Eira is my sister?" Rhys asked.

The footman's demeanour shifted as if he was speaking to a child now.

"Yes, Lord Rhys, your sister," he said.

The cabman was looking awkward watching the scene. He cleared his throat. Rhys brought out a handful of coins. "Which one do I give him?" he asked Tamsin. Tamsin fished out two crowns and tossed them at the driver.

The cabman tipped his hat and set the horses away down the drive.

"Let's meet my family," Rhys said. He offered her his arm with a bow, both coats flapping open and straining over his shoulders. He looked absurd and she couldn't help laughing.

The main door opening interrupted Tamsin's laughter.

"Rhys, where in the world have you been? What happened to you?" The man at the door was a few years older than Rhys. He shared a similar structure to his pale face, but his hair was half a shade darker, and longer than Rhys's. His brother, perhaps the Lord Carwyn the footman mentioned.

The silence stretched out and at last Tamsin bobbed something between a bow and a curtsy. "Hello milord, I brought your brother back." She gave Rhys a one-armed push forward.

Rhys reached out and grabbed her hand, the unwounded one for small favors.

"Pardon me, but you do know me?" Rhys asked him.

Lord Carwyn recoiled. A look of sadness passed over his face, quickly smoothed into bland civility.

"Indeed, I do know you. I'm your elder brother, David. Why don't you both come inside, and we can discuss this further?" he said. It wasn't really a question.

The footman followed on her heels as everyone decamped through the entrance hall. Lord David Carwyn herded them into a sitting room filled with delicate sofas and chairs upholstered in white brocade. His laundry bills must be enormous. A pale young woman, a few years younger than Tamsin, sat on a sofa with a book spread over her lap. She was golden perfection, blond hair in ringlets dressed high on her head and a dress of sheer lemon muslin trimmed in deep green ribbons. This had to be the Lady Eira.

"David, you found him!" The girl rose from her seat and crossed the room.

No, she danced the length of it, Tamsin thought. Eira moved like a seed puff on the wind. She embraced Rhys without any care for his mud or her clothes. Rhys hugged her back awkwardly. He looked over his shoulder to Tamsin and nodded. This was his family, his home. Something here had to spark recognition soon. Something had to make him stop looking lost.

"Where have you been? What happened? I was so worried," Eira said when she broke off the embrace.

"I'm not sure," Rhys said. Tamsin could feel the discomfort rolling off him.

"What do you mean?" Eira asked.

Tamsin glanced at the door. The footmen had taken up positions just outside the doorway. Lord David Carwyn must be giving some sort of orders, because one of them nodded and left the room.

Rhys hesitated. He licked his lips and looked from Eira to David.

"Are you really my sister?" he asked.

"Of course. Rhys?" Eira reached out to touch his arm again.

"I… I can't remember you." Rhys looked around the room, and it was clear he was seeing it for the first time.

"What happened?" David said. His voice was tight, anger or fear?

"It's not clear," Rhys glanced at Tamsin. "Some people attacked me. I woke up in Tamsin's home and she nursed me back to health."

He neatly avoided the wandering, the second attack, Lacey and Frank, and the group of people hunting him, protecting her secrets.

"He took a blow to his head," Tamsin said.

"Thank goodness you were there to help." Eira smiled at Tamsin. "Welcome to our home, Miss–?" Tamsin noticed the front of Eira's dress had a layer of dried mud down the front from Rhys's coat.

"Saer," she said. "Tamsin Saer."

"Saer. I know I've heard that name before," David said. Was he remembering her mother? Tamsin glanced over at Rhys. He caught her distress and changed the subject.

"What happened the night I disappeared?" he asked.

"Nothing sinister," David said. "You were acting yourself when I left for the club. As far as I knew you were going to the theatre."

"The theatre?" Tamsin said. "In that jacket? Did you see him leave?"

"No," David said, with a sharp look her way. "But Rhys has never been a man of fashion."

Tamsin swallowed any other questions. She needed to find her way out of this.

"I left early because Lady Hedworth invited me to Lady Gilbert's musical," Eira said. "I didn't see you leave."

"What are you thinking Tamsin?" Rhys asked.

"I don't know," Tamsin evaded. Even under layers of mud, a day coat like what Rhys was wearing would never be appropriate for a King's Ring theatre. Was David lying, or just in error?

Eira caught the slight tension in the room and deftly steered the conversation elsewhere. "What happened to your face?" she asked Rhys. Her hand traced the cuts.

Rhys had a fresh abrasion on his cheekbone, to match the array of half healed marks from his previous fights. "A group of men set on us on the way here." Rhys said. "We had to fight our way through them."

"Both of you?" David asked.

"That's how Tamsin came to be hurt."

"Well, you have my deepest thanks, Miss Tamsin." David pulled a red leather purse out of his coat. He fished around and pulled out a silver crown. "For your help, and your silence." A single crown? Lord David was cheap.

"I've invited Tamsin to stay here for a while, as my guest." In the set of his shoulders, Tamsin fancied she could see an echo of the Lord Rhys who lived in this alabaster paradise. He left Eira's side and walked to

Tamsin's. He placed his hand on her shoulder. "I want to look into to sponsoring her."

David gave him a look. "Rhys, do you even know this woman?" he asked.

"She knows me," Rhys said. "The people who attacked us on the way here may still be out there. Tamsin got hurt helping me. This is the least I can do to repay her. And this is my home, isn't it?"

"Surely Miss Tamsin doesn't wish to linger here while we finish this private reunion?" David pled.

"Tamsin was injured helping me," Rhys said. "She needs food, rest, and some measure of the care she showed me. I will give it to her."

"The house isn't prepared for a guest," David demurred. The press of his lips showed what? Snobbery, Tamsin decided. Elspeth's stained dress wasn't fine enough for the Carwyn parlour, but he was trying not to show it.

"That's nonsense," Eira said. "We have plenty of space. You are very welcome, Miss Saer. Grayson," she looked over to one of the men still blocking the doorway. His livery held a measure more of gold braid than the other footmen in the room. "Have you already sent someone to Doctor Carmichael's?"

"Mr. Henry went with the carriage, Lady Eira."

"Excellent. Perhaps someone could bring some food in the meantime? And draw some baths."

David looked between Rhys and Eira, then put his coin away. "Welcome to my house, Miss Tamsin." His voice was tight.

"Well," Eira said, deflecting the conversation again, "We are grateful for your assistance, Miss Saer." Her eyes darted to David as she stressed Tamsin's surname.

"Tamsin has been a brilliant help to me," Rhys said. "When I woke up in her bed, I had no idea of my name or anything."

"Her bed?" David raised an eyebrow.

"I only have the one," Tamsin said. "Of course, I would give it to my guest." Two could play the game of manners here.

"She was able to tell me a lot about myself," Rhys pressed on.

"Indeed," David's tone was politely incredulous.

"How?" asked Eira.

"She found the engraving under my watch cover, and she predicted my occupation from my manners and calluses. A captain in the army," Rhys said.

"Cavalry," Tamsin corrected. Something about David's behaviour was bothering her, but she couldn't put her finger on what.

"That's right," Eira said.

"It's hardly a secret though," David said. "Really Rhys, we must get you looked at by a proper doctor. I'm concerned."

"Other than my memories and the odd bruise, I'm in excellent health, David," Rhys said.

"You don't seem it." David fiddled with his coin purse. "You aren't acting yourself at all."

"I'm sure Doctor Carmichael will put all our minds at ease," Eira said.

"Perhaps," David said to her. "But your safety is my paramount concern."

"What are you insinuating?" Eira asked. She'd drawn herself up to her full height.

"Miss Tamsin herself said he was addled outside," David said.

"That isn't what I meant!" Tamsin protested. Had he been listening at the door?

"Addled but not without my ears," Rhys broke in.

David had the grace to flush deeper.

"Doctor Carmichael should be here shortly," he said, and left the room.

Eira was frowning. She noticed Tamsin's scrutiny and shifted her expression back to a more pleasant one.

"Let's see about your accommodations, Miss Saer." Eira crossed to the doorway and started a low whispered conversation with the footman standing there.

"How are you doing?" Tamsin whispered to Rhys.

"I'm not sure," Rhys said. "Eira seems lovely."

"It's only the first day," Tamsin said. "And it's far better than what we left in the Grainery. But if it will cause trouble with your brother I don't have to stay. Laundresses don't usually stay as guests to lords."

"Well, we should make an exception." Rhys's smile flitted between manic and mischief. On some level, he was enjoying the household's upheaval.

"It's your family, and your home." The cut on her arm throbbed. At this moment, all she wanted to do was lie down.

Eira was watching the two of them with an odd expression on her face. "There is something you aren't telling me about how my brother was hurt," she said to Tamsin.

"Does clever run in your family?" Tamsin asked Rhys.

"Yes," Eira said. "Don't dodge the question. You didn't tell David the whole story. And that's fine. The boys have never gotten along. But you should tell me."

Tamsin glanced over at Rhys. He shrugged.

"The people who set on us today were looking specifically for your brother. Led by someone. Someone rich," Tamsin said. "They weren't the first ones to come hunting for him either."

"I was looking for him," Eira said. "After the first day, I had David send Rhys's description to all of the gates and patrols with a reward notice."

"It wasn't the Bluecoats who were looking," Tamsin said. "These men were trying to kill him, we think."

Eira grew still. "Why?"

"I don't know for sure. There was a man named Marcus who seemed to be in charge. He's working with someone with a deep purse, because his togs were nice, but not quite fine enough to buy all the toughs in the Narrows to hunt for Rhys."

Rhys was smiling, smugly.

"What?" Tamsin asked him, exasperated.

"You notice so many things," he said.

"If I didn't notice I'd be dead half a dozen times over in the last few years," Tamsin snapped.

"In that case," Eira said, "may I show you where you'll be staying Miss Saer?"

Chapter Eleven

Eira led Tamsin and Rhys back into the enormous entryway. Most of the space was in the height of the ceiling which ended some three stories above them. A gilded staircase held court over the room, carpeted with something pale pink and geometric. The rest of the floor was tiled in a pink and white stone mosaic. Lady Carwyn had a distinct taste.

Eira took a moment to confer with a footman standing at attention by the door. Whatever he said she wasn't happy with the news.

"Let's get you both settled," Eira said. "Miss Saer, may I call you Tamsin?"

"Certainly," Tamsin said. Already she could feel her affected Narrow's accent slipping away. This home was far grander than where she had grown up, but the tiny tables filled with candles, paintings on the wall, and the scent of floor wax and furniture polish caught at her memories of it. Somewhere a clock chimed the hour.

Rhys trailed along, as Eira ascended the stairs. Tamsin hesitated before she stepped on the carpet. She looked down at her mismatched shoes covered in mud. Her right one was too small, and her toes had pushed through the seam and brushed the dyed wool carpet.

"Tamsin?" Eira asked. She didn't act worried about the mud that Rhys was tracking in, but she wouldn't be cleaning it up. Tamsin shrugged, it was her house, and caught up.

After the second flight of steps Eira led them down a corridor and through a panelled door at its end. There was another stair behind the door, plainer and uncarpeted.

Eira's cheeks were red. "David gave you a room upstairs... in the nursery." She wouldn't meet Tamsin's eyes.

Tamsin shrugged. The nursery was a kinder option than the stables or the kitchen. She hadn't expected that David would allow her in one of the guest rooms. He was probably in the pantry, locking up the silver at this minute.

"Where is my room?" asked Rhys.

"It's back on the first floor, just off the first landing," Eira said. She was quiet through the next two flights of stairs.

The nursery was in the attic, complete with a row of beds set up along the roof slant. There was a fire, newly kindled on the hearth, and dusty fabric still draped over most of the furniture. Eira frowned. "I thought they were going to clear this; I'll speak to Mrs. Beauchamp." She bustled about tugging the sheets off and raising a cloud of dust.

"It's fine," Tamsin said between coughs. Her eyes watered.

Rhys had wandered over to a shelf filled with toys and cobwebs. He ran his finger along a row of painted lead soldiers.

"I think that Mrs. Beauchamp will have a bath ready soon. Would you like to borrow one of my dresses?" Eira asked, after she'd uncovered a few of the beds.

Tamsin eyed Eira. "Thank you, but I don't think they'd fit me." Tamsin was at least a hand span taller, and despite the lean years, her shoulder breadth was wider then Eira's. The bath sounded heavenly though.

Eira laughed. "You may be right. I'll speak with Mrs. Beauchamp and see what we can find for you."

"I need to tend to my arm too." Tamsin patted her bandage.

"Of course. Does it hurt a lot? I asked Mrs. Beauchamp to have things ready to tend to it," Eira said. "And Mrs. Plumtree put together a luncheon for you both. Rhys, I think David wants you downstairs to get ready for the doctor."

Tamsin caught his arm as he started to follow Eira out. "Rhys, be careful about what you say to the doctor. You don't want to give them an excuse to send you away," Tamsin said.

"David wouldn't allow that," Eira said. But she wasn't looking at Rhys when she said it. Perhaps she wanted to believe it.

"Just, be careful what you say," Tamsin insisted.

Rhys caught the second meaning. "You have nothing to worry about."

From Eira's look, she knew she'd missed something in their conversation. She plastered a polite smile over her face anyways. "Mrs.

Beauchamp will be up in a moment, to take care of everything. I told her to give you anything you might need." She tugged gently at Rhys's arm. "Rhys, Doctor Carmichael will be here soon."

After a moment, Rhys allowed Eira to lead him out of the room.

The nursery had not been used for some time. The carpet was still rolled and standing in the corner. Eira had uncovered two of the tiny narrow beds. Their mattresses sagged in the ropes. There was no bedding. Clearly a sign for Tamsin not to overstay her welcome here. Well, that was fine with her. Without Lacey, life in the Narrows would be intolerable. But if Rhys did give her papers, she could leave the city, where prices weren't so inflated, and find work. She could sew, embroider a little, and there was always laundry or scullery work. Somewhere else she could save, maybe buy her own home. Her arm was pulsing in time with her heartbeat. Maybe she could close her eyes, for a minute.

The door opened without a knock. In the door frame stood a woman, just out of middle age, with tan skin, and a white starched cap covering her mahogany hair.

"You're to come with me," she told Tamsin.

"Where?" Tamsin said. From the cut of her dress and the number of keys hanging from the woman's chatelaine, this had to be the housekeeper, Mrs. Beauchamp.

"Lady Eira said you needed cleaning. There's a bath drawn in the laundry room." Mrs. Beauchamp didn't wait for Tamsin's response. She turned on her heel and started back down the hall. Tamsin had to jog to catch up.

"I'll need to stitch my arm as well."

"So the Lady said." Mrs. Beauchamp sniffed. "I've laid out supplies for that as well." Mrs. Beauchamp brought her down all three flights of stairs then one more besides to a bustling basement kitchen.

The kitchen air was warm and humid, with the scents of bread, roasting meat, and spices. Tamsin's stomach growled. Someone was shouting near the range, and two other women were hard at work stirring and chopping on the oak table in the centre of the room. Mrs. Beauchamp led her around the chaos to a hastily cleared laundry room. The hip-height wooden tub was only half full. The room had a door. Thank the gods.

"Clean yourself up and mind you do it well. I'll be checking up after you," Beauchamp said. "I keep a clean house here."

Tamsin nodded. It was clear Mrs. Beauchamp was not happy that Tamsin was here.

"Lady Eira mentioned you were hurt. Sit down and show me," Beauchamp ordered.

"It's really all right," Tamsin said. "I can manage it by myself if you have supplies."

Mrs. Beauchamp sniffed and pointed at the chair.

Tamsin gave in and sank into the chair. Beauchamp pulled the improvised bandage off. Tamsin clamped her teeth together and didn't scream. The wound had clotted around the linen and began bleeding again, slower this time. Tamsin breathed easier when she saw it. The Runner had sliced a crescent shaped gash into the flesh of her arm, but it didn't extend into the muscle. A few stitches should close it.

Beauchamp sniffed again. "The doctor should see that; it will need stitching."

"If you have a needle and thread, I can do I myself," Tamsin said. "And willow bark and witch-hazel if you have them."

Beauchamp narrowed her eyes. "I do have them. Lady Eira was very specific to give you what you needed."

"I will be fine on my own. I'm not here to steal the silver." Pain and relief made her imprudent.

Mrs. Beauchamp's lips tightened.

"Very well, then. Someone will bring you clothing and the things you require shortly." She left, shutting the laundry door behind her.

Tamsin wet the corner of the bathing sheet and started cleaning out the wound. As she finished, a young man walked in still in the gangling age. His eyes fixed onto her cut, and he looked like he was going to be ill.

"Mrs. Beauchamp sent these for you, Miss." He offered her a bundle.

"Thank you," Tamsin said.

He swallowed and tore his gaze away.

"I'll be just outside when you are ready, Miss."

He retreated to the door and shut it.

Tamsin took a deep breath. They really didn't trust her. When she finished cleaning the cut, she threw the towel over the keyhole. The deepest part of the cut was not clotted. She reached into the fresh blood. The throb of her own heart was enough to slide into a healing trance. Her bleeding and pain eased. She reached over only half aware of the word outside and picked up the silk thread. It took three stitches, the pain carefully pushed back to the smallest corner of her mind.

Sliding into the tepid water felt amazing. Mrs. Beauchamp had left her lye soap, rather than some perfumed cake from upstairs. It burned when she got it in her wound, but Tamsin welcomed the fire. Sitting in water, her hair curling around her shoulders, Tamsin felt cleaner than she had in years.

The garments they'd brought her had to be Mrs. Beauchamp's or one of the other maids. The dress was a pale blue linen, only a little large for Tamsin, and plain. It had a pocket as well, large enough for her freshly-cleaned clasp knife. She slid the layers on almost reverently, a fresh linen shift, stays that laced the whole way up, without frays or holes, stockings, and shoes that almost fit. Heaven. She triple-checked the dress, but it covered her brand completely.

Mrs. Beauchamp pronounced her fit enough with a sniff. She handed Tamsin a wooden comb, then left her to dry by the kitchen hearth. A bell rang from the long row of them along the wall. Mrs. Beauchamp came back after a few minutes, looking stiff and disapproving.

"Lord Rhys is calling for you," she said.

Of course, he was. It was an effort to leave the sleepy warmth of the hearth. Her hair was still damp, curly and loose.

Mrs. Beauchamp led her up three flights of servant's stairs, to a corridor filled with portraits. Halfway down the hall Mrs. Beauchamp stopped near a portrait of a woman in an old-fashioned lavender gown.

"Lord Rhys is in there." Her voice was tight with disapproval.

"Thank you," Tamsin said. Mrs. Beauchamp turned to go. "Wait! Is this his bedroom?"

Mrs. Beauchamp gave her an exasperated look. "What did you think it was? The grand parlour?"

Tamsin flushed. Did Rhys realize how this would look to the staff? Her being brought to his bedroom, freshly washed, and wearing some housemaid's best dress. No wonder Mrs. Beauchamp looked upset. Wonderful. Should she explain the optics to Rhys? No. Her reputation wasn't pristine enough to worry about, whatever below-stairs might whisper about. Tamsin knocked on the door.

Rhys'd had a bath too. His hair was still damp and in disarray. He wore a shirt of muslin so fine she could see the hairs on his chest and the fresh bruises dappling his upper body. This wasn't helping anything. She could feel her flush all the way up to her ears.

"Tamsin, good. They are bringing up food in a moment." He stepped back to let her enter.

His walls were hung with a figured silk, in a misty green colour. The same silk also curtained the four-poster bed, large enough for a full family to sleep in. A fire burned at the grate, putting out enough heat to feel it across the room.

"Your dress looks nice," he said.

Tamsin pulled at the excess material around the bodice. "You're a terrible liar."

"Then that's something else we know about me." Rhys fiddled with the laces at his wrist. "How do people tie these things?"

"You'd've had a valet to do all of that for you," Tamsin pointed out.

"I suppose making clothing one can just dress themselves in is out of the question?" He poked at a cranberry-coloured waistcoat laid out on the bed with back lacing and front buttons. He started to struggle into the layers.

"I wonder where your valet is?" Tamsin asked. "He might be able to answer your questions about what you were doing down at the wharf."

"True. When they bring the food up, we can ask." He finished with the waistcoat buttons and tried to reach behind to tie the laces. His fingers kept missing. Should she help? Was it more proper to help him dress or be in a room with a half-dressed man? Rhys gave up.

"Penny for your thoughts," Rhys said.

Well, she wasn't going to tell him what she was really thinking. "I was wondering if you are the same as you were before you lost your memories?" Tamsin said instead.

Rhys looked up from pulling on a pair of clean boots.

She pressed on. "I mean, how much would having your memories back change you? Will you wake up one day with all your memories intact and be horrified at what you have been up to the last few days?" Or the promises you've made.

Understanding bloomed on his face. "Or the company I kept? I don't think I will regret offering to sponsor you, Tamsin. But who I am is something I've worried over. What if there is something so terrible, something I did, that caused all of this? Something with magic?" His face grew pensive. After a moment, he shrugged. "In this moment though, you've been nothing but a friend to me, Tamsin. Whoever I may be, I could not be the sort of man who abandons my friends."

"I'll believe it once you have your memories back."

"Perhaps they will never return," Rhys said. He took in a deep breath. "I will simply have to become myself again."

Tamsin sighed and shed her ire. "Have you found any clues here?"

"I am not sure what I should be searching for. Can you help?"

Well, she had already gone through his pockets, she could hardly start being squeamish now. She crossed the room to his clothes press and pulled the door open. The scents of sandalwood and cedar washed over her, and she couldn't help inhaling deep.

Rhys stood to the side close enough she would only have to shift her weight and she'd brush against his shoulder, and watched her face.

"What do you remember?" he asked her.

"My mother had a chest made of this, her wedding gift. She kept her wedding dress in there." Tamsin could feel the fine threads of the embroidery against her fingertips. She turned to Rhys. "Does the smell bring anything back to you?"

He reached around her and fingered the cuff of a pale green coat.

"No."

Tamsin shook the shreds of memory away and started to rummage through the clothing. There were a dozen coats in various shades and cuts, each a softer, finer wool than the last. David's words came back to her. If Rhys was not a man of fashion, she would hate to see the size of the wardrobe of a man who was. Alas every pocket in his coats were empty. The shirts, too, yielded no secrets. Tamsin ran her hands along the bottom and sides of the press and pulled the drawers out, but nothing was hidden there.

In the second clothes press she found his uniform coat wrapped away in tissue paper. The blue wool was frayed at the seams and showed signs of mending. It was covered with gold bullion and braid, and a battered Captain's brass gorget was still pinned to the collar. Captain Carwyn indeed. She shook it out of its paper wrappings and held it out to him.

Rhys frowned when he saw it. He reached over and took it out of her hands and pulled it over his half-undone waistcoat. The edges of the jacket didn't quite meet across his chest.

"Does this bring back any memories?" Her voice shattered the small bubble of stillness.

Rhys slipped it off and flipped it around. The back was patched, a swath of coarser wool covered a section as big as Tamsin's hand. He flipped it inside out and there in the pale linen lining was an ominous ruddy stain.

He flexed his shoulder absently.

"I was shot." His voice had a distant tone. "Someone got me when I was turning the men back from the charge. It knocked me out of my stirrups, but I managed to keep my seat. It took them forever to dig the ball out. By then the surgeon had broken out his good whiskey and I didn't notice it as much."

Tamsin shuddered. The image of Thomas lying so still on the floor of her house flooded back.

Rhys noticed her expression and replaced the coat in its paper nest. "I don't know when that was, or why we were there, but I remember being shot. It's odd that I would recall that, but not Eira or David."

"Perhaps because it was a very strong memory?" she said.

"Perhaps..." He let the thought trail off. "It's a good start."

She glanced at the door. How long did it take someone to walk up from the kitchen? She started rummaging through the top of his writing desk. Rhys shut the press and joined her. His hip was so close to hers that Tamsin could feel his body heat. She kept her face turned away. It wasn't fair that the first person she wanted to get close to was him. Unattainable was an understatement. A lord's second son would have been out of her reach, even back in Woburn, in her wood-panelled parlour.

Rhys's desk was cluttered with an array of papers, odd ends of wax, and crumpled drawings. One woman in particular, appeared over and over in the pictures, drawn in both charcoal and ink. She was thin, something shadowed her cheek bones in most of the drawings. Straight, dark hair clipped shorter than the fashion, and freckles dotted her nose. They were a good likeness. Rhys was talented. Tamsin handed the pile of sketches to Rhys.

"Do you remember this woman?" she asked. She sorted through the rest of the papers. There were a few bills, with the annotation "paid in full" lettered neatly in the corner. That must be Rhys's handwriting. It was different than the ledger pages. There were more gambling notes and a few letters bundled up in a blue silk ribbon. Love notes, Tamsin guessed. She set those to the side.

Rhys handed back the sketches.

"I don't... I wish I knew her face," he said, shaking his head. His voice was quieter than she'd heard it before.

"Maybe these letters will tell you." She passed him the bundle and continued sorting the contents of the desk.

Someone knocked on the door. After a moment the door opened, and a brown-haired man entered, his slight frame bent with the weight of a tray.

"Begging your pardon, sir, but here's the luncheon for you and—your friend."

Tamsin flushed.

Rhys walked over and took the tray out of the man's hands.

"Thank you very much, umm…" he trailed off hopefully.

"Lady Eira told me you were having issues remembering. I'm Henry, sir, your batman."

"Thank you, Henry." Rhys set the tray on the dressing table and picked up a fruit tart with his fingers. Henry looked amused at the breach of etiquette.

"The doctor is on his way sir," Henry said. "He was caught up by Lord Warren's gout again. He should be here in the next hour."

"Good," Rhys mumbled between bites. "These are amazing. Tamsin, you should eat."

"In a moment. Henry, do you know where R—, er Lord Rhys was going the night he went missing?" Tamsin asked instead.

Henry didn't look at her. "Sir?"

Rhys, still occupied with the tarts, waved his hand in a vague continue motion. Was Henry's dissembling a sign of loyalty to Rhys or mistrust of her?

Henry took a deep breath. "Well, you were acting not yourself for a couple of days before this, sir. Skipping out on things, and you lied to Lady Everwood to duck a dinner engagement."

"Who is Lady Everwood?" Rhys asked.

Henry's eyes shifted between them. "She's… his lordship's fiancé." He looked at Tamsin when he spoke.

Tamsin felt the blood drawing away from her face. She forced her lips into a light smile.

"My brother is engaged?" Rhys asked.

Henry looked at him open mouthed.

"No, lackwit, you are," Tamsin said. Her voice was tight. So, he was engaged. That was to be expected, engaged or married. Rich, from an old, titled family and military service; any of the great families would line up to join their house to his.

"Are you all right, Tamsin?" Rhys asked. He stepped a little closer to her.

Tamsin gave him a tin smile. "Of course." She turned to Henry. "Rhys had lied to Lady Everwood?" She kept her voice light when she said the name, but the knowledge hurt her more than she was comfortable with.

"Well, that night you didn't dress for dinner with the rest of the house. And you plum skipped out on the theatre show you were meeting Lady Everwood at afterwards. She's been very upset with you being gone. She called here every morning and stayed with Lady Eira for over an hour each time."

"Did she know I was gone?" Rhys asked.

"She knew that you were gone, but only yesterday did she ferret out of Lord David, how serious things were. They thought you might have been dead, sir," Henry said.

Rhys and Tamsin exchanged looks.

"Did he tell you anything else?" Tamsin asked.

Henry shook his head. "You said you were going to the Carolina sir. But you looked worried. More than I've ever seen you before, and here I've been with you since Port Farrole and the rout there."

Rhys and Tamsin exchanged a glance. It certainly sounded like Rhys went into the Narrows expecting trouble. Details, she needed details.

"Henry, do you know where Rhys keeps his private documents?" she asked.

Henry looked more uncomfortable.

"It's all right, Henry," Rhys said. "Miss Saer is helping me. She has saved my life twice now. You can tell her anything you would tell me."

"You kept your papers in your desk, sir." Henry eyed the opened and ransacked desk.

"Is there another place I keep things Henry? This could help me quite a lot," Rhys asked.

Henry walked over to the desk. He pulled the first drawer out of its place and pressed his fingers to the inside of the cubbyhole. At the side of the desk a small drawer popped out. Tamsin sat up straighter.

"My father used to put secret drawers in his desks. I haven't seen that mechanism before. It's done with a spring?" she said.

Henry raised his brow. Right, that really wasn't the point right now.

"I know I'm not supposed to know about it, sir. But you opened it once in my presence. I would never open it, except, well, you asked me to," Henry said.

Rhys put his hand on Henry's shoulder. "It's all right." He peered inside and pulled out three folded letters.

"Begging your pardon sir, but the doctor will be here soon, and you aren't in company order. If you could slip out of that coat, I'll set you to rights."

"Of course." Rhys handed Tamsin the letters. "Can you look at these while I get ready?"

"Of course, Lord Rhys," Tamsin said. Rhys raised an eyebrow at her formalness, but he didn't argue the point.

Rhys steered Henry to the other side of the room to finish dressing. Did he mistrust Henry? Or was he just being cautious?

The letters Rhys gave her were written in different hands. There was one in a smooth flowing script. The paper smelled floral, and it was older and showed signs of being handled a lot. Tamsin couldn't read the words, but they seemed to be in a similar language to the ledger pages Rhys had on him. She set it aside for Rhys to translate.

The other two letters were written in a bolder script. The seals had been stripped away leaving only a discoloration of burgundy wax at the bottom of each page. Both spoke of meetings and plans in carefully couched and covered tones. The dates on these letters were recent, both from within the month. Both were unsigned and without address. Tamsin sighed. At the bottom of the drawer was a crumble of dried rosemary needles twisted around a porcelain painted miniature of a green eye and the shape of a tan freckled cheek and nose.

Someone knocked at the door. All three of them jumped guiltily.

Henry brushed a bit of lint off Rhys's shoulders and crossed to the door. Tamsin dropped the letters back in the secret drawer and slid it closed.

David was outside. He took in the tableau with only a raised eyebrow.

"I'm glad to see you've cleaned the gutter stench away," he said. "Doctor Carmichael is in the downstairs parlour, waiting for you."

Rhys nodded.

David waited a moment, then vented an exasperated sigh. "We can't keep him waiting."

"Of course. Tamsin, would you like to come along?" Rhys asked. "Your arm?"

She bobbed a servant's curtsy.

"Begging your pardon, Lord Rhys, but I think I'd best go back to my room, unless you need me? I don't need to see a doctor."

Rhys caught the double meanings there. "Of course. Henry, could you bring the food up to Tamsin's room?"

"What's really going on with Lord Rhys, Miss Saer?" Henry asked when the two men were gone.

Tamsin weighed him. Her gut was calling him for loyal to Rhys.

"When he went missing, he was hit on the head. When I found him, he didn't even remember his name, and someone had a price out on his head in the Narrows." The bundle of love letters on the desk tempted her, but it wouldn't be right to read them without asking and did she want to torture herself reading his fiancé's love notes to him? Best to make a clean break of all this. She closed the top of his desk.

Henry looked alarmed.

"I think Rhys'll be all right," she reassured him. "He remembered being shot when we found his uniform jacket a bit ago." Maybe other things would come back with time?

Henry's face softened. "We were just starting out together then. It was his first command. The general commended him for that action."

"He had a good run in the cavalry then?" Tamsin asked.

"He liked it well enough. The Earl, his father, bought him a commission as a Lieutenant right out of school. The general brought him up to Captain by merit rather than buying it. We saw a good bit of action in the last war." Henry changed tactics. "Now where are you from, and what are you looking to get from him? You've got a low country accent, for all you're trying to hide it."

Tamsin'd spent quite a while purging the Woburn lilt out of her voice. He was sharp.

"I've been in the city for a few years now," Tamsin said. "The accent fades when you don't go back home."

"Nothing to go back to?" It wasn't quite a question.

"No."

"Well, the Captain won't do wrong by you. I've never met a better man."

"I never thought he would. He's offered to sponsor me out of the city."

"Well, he'll make good on that," he said cheerfully. He seemed to accept that she was working for Rhys's interests now, although she wasn't sure what had convinced him. He plucked the tray up and led them back into the hall. "Where did they stow ya?"

"The nursery."

"Oh." He glanced up and down the hall checking for eavesdroppers. "Best be careful of Lord David then. If he's put you up there, he's trying to be rid of you. That place leaks like a sieve."

"I'll remember that."

He led the way back up. Someone had been in the room, and they had left bedding and filled one of the mattresses ticks up again. Henry set the tray down on a table.

"If you need anything best ask for me or the housemaid, Kate. She came with Lady Eira. If Lord David's against you he'll set the rest of below stairs against you too, and they work for him."

Tamsin nodded. She'd started to sense that.

The fire had been built up again. A good portion of smoke was seeping back into the room. Tamsin suspected they were using green wood from the smell of it. Henry frowned when he saw it.

"The flue must be blocked." He fiddled with it until something screeched and the smoke volume dropped considerably.

"Thank you." Tamsin sat on the bed. The blankets were moth eaten, but ample.

"Henry, could you help me, or rather Lord Rhys, once more?"

"I owe my life to the captain, miss. What do you need?"

"Can you keep an ear out, discretely below stairs? In case someone else in the house knows more than they are letting on about him being missing?"

"I think that would have come out when he was first missing, Miss. But should I tell him or you?" That question was another test for her. At least it was an easy one.

"Rhys first of course, but both of us if you can manage it. I'm not keeping things from him."

"I'll let you know if anything unusual comes to light."

"Thank you," she said.

He gave her a measured nod and left.

Chapter Twelve

Rhys was engaged. But it didn't matter. She was here for the coin Rhys owed her and the papers he'd promised. He must have enough resources here to find the answers. Once he settled his debts, she could wish him well and leave.

Her stomach growled. The tray Henry had left was filled with delicate sandwiches and a pair of fruit tarts heaped high with clotted cream. That and tea, fresh black tea, sweetened with honey. It had been years since she'd had tea like this. Her mouth watered, and hunger overtook her earlier nausea. She was on her second sandwich when someone knocked.

"Come in," Tamsin said. The healing and herbs had helped, the pain in her arm was a dull ache.

A young woman entered with a bundle. Her skin had a familiar russet hue. Tamsin wondered if she was Cyprycian as well.

"I brought you a dressing gown, Miss Saer. Seeing as Mrs. Beauchamp said you had only what you wore when you came here. And walking boots, if they fit." She looked a little dubiously at Tamsin's feet. "But they mightn't. They were Mrs. Farrow's."

"Thank you, but I'm really not a Miss here. My name is Tamsin."

The maid smiled, and her posture grew less stiff. "We weren't sure, y'see. Beauchamp said you were just a servant, but servants don't stay in nurseries. But guests don't, neither. I overheard Lady Eira saying you were a guest, so "Miss" seemed safest." She gave Tamsin another easy smile.

Tamsin's shoulders relaxed. It felt almost like a conversation with Lacey. Well, the Lacey of before.

"I think it's complicated, my visit here," Tamsin said. "What's your name?"

"Catherine. Of course, there's two of us Catherines here, so since I'm the second housemaid I go by Kate."

"Do you have a minute to sit? There are some sandwiches left over from the lunch tray."

Kate grinned again. "Mrs. Plumtree heard from Beauchamp that you were skin and bones, and that Lord Rhys was looking peaked too. She said no guest here would stay that way for long."

"She sounds nice." Tamsin scanned Kate's face for any of Mrs. Beauchamp's hauteur or David's shiftiness and found neither.

"Mrs. Plumtree?" Kate said, "I suppose she is in her way. Gods help you if you interfere in her puddings though."

Tamsin laughed.

"And who is Mrs. Farrow?" Tamsin asked. There were too many people in this house. She'd never keep them all straight.

"Lady Eira's chaperone for the season, at least until Lady Carwyn can come down. But his Lordship's health isn't good."

Tamsin nodded and pressed more of the cooling tea on Kate.

They were on their second cups when a loud brass rumble sounded, and Kate jumped up.

"Oh! Mrs. Farrow will have my head!"

"What was that?" Tamsin asked.

"It's the dinner gong. I've sat up here far too long. I need to help the ladies dress." Kate gave her a sharp look over. "Are you meant to go down to dinner with them?"

Tamsin spread her hands wide. "I've no idea. If I am, they never said."

Kate gathered up the tray. "I'll drop a word to Lady Eira, and if you're meant to be there, I'll try to nip up and help you dress."

Tamsin snorted. "It'll be an easy task. I only have this dress on charity."

Kate pursed her lips. "I'll be back soon." She bustled out the door with the tray.

Dinner. With Rhys. She hadn't been to a formal dinner in years, and only the one held at the community hall. She wondered how Rhys had fared with the doctor. Even here, warm and full-bellied she was uneasy, though. She'd assumed that once Rhys was here, he would be safe. But home was not as settled as she'd hoped.

There was a knock, and Eira entered followed by Kate holding an armload of garments.

Eira had changed from her muslin day gown into something gauzy, pink, and spangled. She twirled, and the gold chains woven into her hair caught the firelight.

"I brought you dresses! Kate remembered that we still had them."

Kate laid the pile on the nursery bed. "They've been in storage for two years now," she said. "Any longer and the bugs will be at them." She shook out a burgundy gown.

"I don't know, Eira..." The dress was lovely. She reached out and brushed the fabric with her fingertips. Silk.

"Rhys asked if you could join us." Eira hesitated. "Marion is coming to dinner."

"Marion?" Behind her Kate was rearranging the dresses again and avoiding eye contact.

"Lady Everwood, my brother's fiancé." Eira watched Tamsin's face carefully.

"Ah." Tamsin kept her face still. Of course, his fiancé would want to see him now that he had been found. "I should think he'd want to see her alone."

"I think he's afraid," Eira said.

"Oh." Tamsin touched the silk again. "And his mother won't mind me wearing her old dresses?"

"They aren't from the countess; these are from Lord David's wife," Kate said.

Eira pulled a pale green dress out of the pile and held it up.

"She's abroad," she said.

There was a subtext in those two words that rang of scandal. Tamsin tucked that fact away for later digestion and turned to the dresses.

Tamsin chose the wine-coloured dress; it was cut high in the back and she slipped it on without revealing the witch brand on her shoulder. Kate made quick work basting the bodice closed, while Eira wove a ribbon through her hair.

"You look marvellous! That colour favours you far more than it did Jeanne." Eira took Tamsin's hand and tugged her towards the door.

Tamsin ran her hands down the skirt. It was a little long and the front of the bodice was pleated into a fan across her chest. The gloves Eira had lent her were tight over her forearms, but they hid the bandage.

"Are you sure Lord David won't mind me wearing his wife's clothes?" Tamsin asked.

"He won't notice," Eira said.

She pulled Tamsin down the layers of stairs until they reached the tiled floor of the entryway. Eira pushed opened a panelled door and led them back into the same parlour from this morning. Had it only been this morning? Tamsin wondered. It felt like weeks had passed.

The room froze when they entered. David stared at Tamsin. Eira was wrong. Rhys was in the back of the room with a book opened in his hands. Perched beside him was a tall woman a few years older than Tamsin. The only word Tamsin could use for her was chill. From the crisp white silk of her gown, setting off her dark skin, to the diamonds strung in her black tightly curled hair, she was a decorous presence. This must be his fiancé, Lady Marion Everwood. She was not the woman from Rhys's drawings. Interesting.

Rhys broke the moment with a smile. He shut the book and placed it carelessly back on the shelf.

"Tamsin, your dress looks nice," he said.

Tamsin gave him a slight smile. Lady Everwood hadn't taken her eyes off her. She felt like a scrap of rag before Bernard weighed it for the paper man.

Eira behind her, acted oblivious to the tension. "Sorry we were late. Three flights of stairs are so tiring." She smiled too sweetly at David. She still was unhappy with Tamsin's sleeping arrangements.

David's lips tightened. "Shall we go in?" He held out his arm to Eira and led her back out the door, to the dining room on the other side of the hall. Lady Everwood claimed Rhys's arm and followed. The fourth woman, a lady of about forty years fell in beside Tamsin. This must be Mrs. Farrow.

"This way dear," she said, her voice brittle and disapproving.

Tamsin paused at the threshold of the dining room. A footman was hastily setting out another place setting, another was carrying in a chair. David walked Eira to the foot of the table, then he moved to the head. Lady Everwood placed Rhys between herself and David. Tamsin sat across from them with Mrs. Farrow on her right, in the fresh chair.

Spread out on the table, was more silver than she had ever seen at once. She resisted the urge to touch all the glittering tableware laid out before her. Her mother had drilled these manners into her. Surely this wouldn't be too different from the dinner at the assembly halls.

Rhys was looking lost at the other end of the table. Lady Everwood leaned over and whispered something in his ear. Whatever she said, he looked surprised at her words.

The footmen were coming around now pouring red wine into the crystal flutes. Someone else was bringing around a porcelain tureen of soup and ladling it into their bowls.

It was creamy, with layers of buttery yellow and green running through it. When Tamsin lifted the spoon to her lips, it tasted of garlic, butter, and shellfish. It was the most marvellous thing she could recall eating. It was an effort to eat it slowly and not slurp, or dribble down the front of her borrowed gown.

Eira broke the silence once the soup had been removed.

"How is your mother, Marion?"

"She is as well as can be expected." Lady Everwood's voice matched her exterior, cool and even. She kept her eyes from resting on Tamsin.

"Will she be up to town soon?" Eira asked.

Lady Everwood tightened her lips. "Perhaps. It depends on what the season brings. I think she is happier at home, in familiar company, until she puts aside her mourning for father."

Tamsin kept her eyes on her plate. They were serving a roast dripping in juices. She twisted her knife between her fingers. Don't spill. Lord David and Lady Everwood seemed like they were just aching for her to make an error.

Eira turned the conversation her way. "And Tamsin, where are you from?"

David coughed.

"Woburn county," Tamsin answered.

"Oh, we have a cousin there, the Marquise of Tamswold."

"I don't believe I have met him," Tamsin said, deadpan. Tamswold was about thirty miles north of Woburn. The Marquise was a notorious gambler, who spent most of his time in Celdre.

Eira flushed. "Of course." To cover her slip, she asked "What did the doctor say Rhys?"

"I'm in good health," Rhys said. "Tamsin's poultices were very effective."

"Indeed?" Lady Everwood said. "I'm afraid I'm still not clear of your role in this whole affair."

Tamsin felt her cheeks warm.

"I know some herbcraft," she said. "When Rhys was injured one of my neighbours brought him to me and I did what I could."

"How badly was he hurt?" Lady Everwood asked.

Tamsin glanced at Rhys.

"A serious blow to my head that caused the—gaps in my memory."

Tamsin bit the insides of her cheeks. Gaps. More like a gaping chasm.

"Still, Doctor Carmichael said to rest and not to exert yourself," David said. "Indeed, I question the wisdom of this dinner. You could have had a tray sent up."

"I'm not an invalid, David." Rhys's words had the ring of repetition. "I disagree with his conclusions. None of my earlier exercises have harmed me. And I don't wish to return to the country."

David moved the dregs of soup around the bottom of his bowl. "I'm only concerned about your health," he said, not looking at Rhys.

"I can guard my own health," Rhys said. "Besides, we haven't finished our investigations here."

"Investigations?" Lady Everwood asked.

Eira locked eyes with David. "Did you not tell her everything?"

David pushed more soup. "Doctor Carmichael was very clear…"

"The gaps in my memory are more significant than David wanted me to let on," Rhys said.

"Why would you conceal this from me? We are to be married."

"For that reason," Rhys said. "David said you wouldn't want to continue our engagement if you knew, and as I didn't remember you, I considered his advice."

"You think too little of me David Carwyn," Lady Everwood said.

David gave up on his soup and waved in the next course.

"Tamsin believes we can figure out the rest of what happened. Her investigations are what brought me home," Rhys continued.

"I see." Lady Everwood sank back into her chair and looked between Rhys and Tamsin. "It appears I must thank you for your service to my future husband, Miss Saer. You have my gratitude." She looked like she'd bitten an onion raw.

"I didn't want to alarm you when Rhys went missing," David broke in, placating.

"Indeed?" Lady Everwood was back to chill.

"It was only a few days," David said. He was giving Lady Everwood an unusual amount of deference for his brother's future wife, entirely at odds with how he spoke to his family.

Lady Everwood turned to Rhys. "So, the night you stood me up at the theatre, you found yourself in the Narrows? To what business?"

"I'm still not sure. I was in a fight with someone. Tamsin thinks…"

What was he about to tell them? Tamsin tipped her wine glass over.

The burgundy liquid washed over the polished walnut surface, and everyone pushed away from the table in alarm.

"I'm so sorry," Tamsin said. She caught Rhys eye and shook her head slightly. He bit his lower lip, then nodded.

The footmen had the spill contained within moments. They brought a cloth to cover the damp spot on the floor and served the next course. Tamsin sipped her refilled cup. It was no wonder they were practiced, she thought, this wine was strong enough to go to anyone's head after half a cup, let alone the amount they were pouring out.

Have you sent a letter to your parents?" Lady Everwood asked Rhys.

Rhys looked surprised. "I should do that, shouldn't I?"

Eira broke in. "I sent a special post when you arrived so Mother and Father would know you were safe. They should have only received the news you were missing this morning; it went by the normal post route. We were sure you'd show up soon that first day."

The conversations gradually drifted away from Tamsin. She picked at her food. Her stomach had knotted up again. She shifted the shoulder of her dress a little higher.

Eira steered the conversation back to safe grounds, asking about Lady Everwood's acquaintances, and Tamsin let the conversation drift by her.

Once the dessert was removed Eira took her hand and steered her out of the room with Lady Everwood and Mrs. Farrow following. "So, the gentleman can have brandy," Eira whispered in Tamsin's ear.

"After today's events we should get brandy too," Tamsin whispered back, a little too loudly. Perhaps she hadn't been as temperate with the wine as she'd thought. Behind them Lady Everwood chuckled for the first time. "I agree."

Eira brought them back to the drawing room and directed Tamsin to the settee beside her.

"You must be gentle with Tamsin, Marion. On her way back here with Rhys she was injured helping Rhys escape a group of thieves."

"I should like to hear that story," Lady Everwood said.

Tamsin touched the bandage under her glove. "There isn't much to it. They cornered us. Rhys did most of the bravery in that battle."

"Rhys said you were heroic!" Eira turned to Lady Everwood. "She suffered a knife wound for Rhys. I'd call that heroic."

"It was stupid. Rhys has at least six inches on me and experience with fighting from the cavalry," Tamsin said. "I should have let him take the knife man and tried for one of the other two men, but I wasn't sure how his knee would hold up."

"You mean there were three of them?" Eira said leaning forward and clasping Tamsin's hand.

"How did you know Lord Rhys was in the Cavalry?" Lady Everwood asked.

Tamsin extracted her hand gently from Eira and turned towards Lady Everwood. "A lot of little things, the snuff box in his pocket, the way he cursed, the musket wound in his shoulder; it all pointed the same way."

Lady Everwood touched the tip of her fan to her chin. "You are cleverer than you appear, aren't you?"

Tamsin shrugged off the barbed compliment. "Rhys, er Lord Rhys needed help. I helped. That's all."

"And he asked you to stay here?"

"I'm his *friend*." Tamsin stressed the friend a little harder than she intended to. "I'm familiar to him, and this place" —she spread her arms wide— "is not yet." Damn that wine. It had loosened her tongue far too much.

"Ah." Lady Everwood flicked her fan opened and seemed to brush the topic aside, like you might a dead fly.

"Tell me Eira, how are your studies coming?"

Eira and Lady Everwood turned to the topics of needlework and dancing. It wasn't much longer before the door opened, and Rhys and David passed through. David was looking a little green. Rhys sat next to Lady Everwood, across from Eira.

"I think I will have to call it an evening, ladies," David said. "I'm a little under the weather." He bowed at Lady Everwood and exited the room.

"I think I am unwell as well," Tamsin said. The wine was making everything a little too bright.

Eira looked surprised. "I'm sorry we've kept you too long, especially after the day you've had."

"Yes, I've got a … headache." It wasn't even a lie. Tamsin stood up from the sofa. "Good night."

Rhys held the door open. "I'll walk you back to your room."

Tamsin shook her head hard enough that her ribbon dislodged and slid down her forehead. "I know the way, Rhys." She shoved the ribbon more or less where it started, copied David's bow, and fled.

*

Back in the nursery, Tamsin struggled to get the stitches undone on the dress. Evidently Lady Carwyn relied on her maids a lot. The mystery about David's wife puzzled her. Her dresses were out of fashion by a few years, although they seemed hardly worn.

Tamsin just managed to get the dress off, with the requisite stays and petticoats, when someone knocked. Probably Kate, to take the gown away. She'd already cleared the debris from Tamsin dressing during dinner.

Tamsin pulled a dressing gown over her shift. It was tight over her shoulders and hit her mid-calf.

"Come in."

Rhys pushed open the door. He took in the fire, burned down to the embers.

"Are you all right up here?" he asked.

Tamsin drew the edges of the gown closer together.

"You shouldn't be up here." Away from the elegance of downstairs, she could feel the easy rapport from the Narrows coming back between them. Or maybe it was the wine.

"I wanted to see if you were all right. And I remembered something." He held out a single gold coin.

Tamsin rubbed her head. That was a sovereign piece, worth four hundred and eighty of the silver pennies she scraped together for her rent. Enough to ride the mail cart anywhere in Aradwyn she wanted. To pay for the shirts. Her fingers shook as she took it from his hand.

"Thank you." She rubbed her fingers over the face engraved on its side, Prince Nicholas. It had to have been struck during the year the king's health had demanded the regency.

"Thank you, Rhys. This…" she reached out and took his hand. "This helps so much." Tears pricked at the corners of her eyes, and she blinked them back.

Rhys shuffled his feet.

"Tamsin…" he started to say. One hand made a quick move forward, as if to reach for her hand.

"What did the doctor say to you?" she interrupted, stepping back. There was nothing productive about thinking about things that couldn't be.

"About the same things you did," Rhys said. And the moment was broken. "Except he applied a great many more odoriferous pastes, bled me, and told me to drink wine."

Tamsin snorted.

"The healing properties of old grapes. Did you read that foreign letter?"

Rhys nodded. "It was someone I must have met long ago." His voice was odd. "I don't think it is relevant to what happened to me, she died. It was her final letter to me."

"Was it related to the invoice we found? They were written in the same language," she pressed.

"I can't see how," his voice was quiet now. "The invoice was about silk trade and dated a week and a half ago." Rhys thinned his lips. "The letter spoke about a time when we knew each other. Intimately. During the war. But the end of the letter is from her brother. She died three years ago."

There was something underneath his terse answers. Had he remembered something? Should she press him further? About his dead lover? No. If he said it wasn't relevant it wasn't.

"You should go back down to your fiancé, Rhys. We can talk about this tomorrow."

"Of course," His face was still pensive. "I'll speak to you then."

Once she heard his footsteps on the stairs she crawled into the bed and let herself cry.

Chapter Thirteen

Tamsin woke the next morning, early. Outside the nursery doors, she could hear the muffled sounds of the maids dressing for the day. The dress from last night's dinner was still laid out where she left it, next to the blue dress. At least no one had come in while she slept. But what now?

When things were out of control, deal with the things you can control. She could pay Elspeth back. And maybe make preparations to leave the city, if Rhys came through with sponsorship papers. A few days ago it would have felt like a bigger if.

What about Rhys's memories though? Her slim hope that familiar circumstances would jog it all loose had faded. He'd had most of the family paraded in front of him. If there was an answer, she didn't have enough of the equation to piece it together. Yet.

Orness silks didn't come into the Narrows docks often. Tamsin swallowed. There were two people who knew the Wharf, and its shipments, better than anyone, and one of them hated her.

She took a deep breath. Maybe if Lacey knew it was for Rhys? Maybe if she offered them enough coin? Maybe Lacey would forgive her?

The back stair was deserted, but when she reached the kitchen level it was bustling with breakfast preparations. Kate noticed her standing at the doorway and waved her in.

"Quick 'fore Mrs. Beauchamp sees you," Kate said. She led Tamsin around the chaos and into the mostly empty servant's hall.

Tamsin took the seat next to her. Kate passed her a cup and the pot of tea.

"Did you sleep well in the Nursery? No one was expected to be up there until Lord David... until there is an heir. But that hasn't happened yet, and it's become a clutter."

"It was fine," Tamsin assured her. "But I need to run out today. I have an errand in the mid-city that will take most of the day. I wanted to leave Rhys a note."

"I can tell him any message you like."

"Do you have a pen and paper?"

Kate looked askance. "I only just know my letters. Mrs. Beauchamp would have some in her parlour, but..."

"Let's not bother her with it. Just tell him I went out, and I'll be back as soon as I can." Tamsin wasn't sure how much the story of his missing memories had spread below stairs, but it wasn't her place to spread it further.

Tamsin looked down at her borrowed dress. "Do you know what happened to the clothes I came here in?" She didn't think Elspeth would want the dress back, but its presence would go a long way towards explaining the missing shirts.

"Oh." Kate avoided her eyes. "Mrs. Beauchamp burned them. Were you fond of it? The sleeve was torn to shreds." Kate looked stricken. "I... I could ask her if she has anything else. I know that dress is a little plain."

Tamsin ran her hands through her hair. It had taken her weeks of eating the charity loaves to save up for those used stays. "No... it's fine."

Kate smiled. "If you're going to be running about through breakfast, you'll need something to bring with you. Wait here, and I'll pack you up a meal."

"That would be wonderful, Katie."

After a few minutes of sitting alone, Mr. Henry came in carrying a familiar pair of riding boots and his polish box.

Tamsin pulled her chair up next to him. "Can you get that much horse shit off a pair of boots?" she asked.

"What are you doing in here Miss Saer?" Henry asked, keeping his eyes on the boots.

"Just Tamsin please. Kate's getting me a bit of breakfast for the road."

His face turned towards her, wary. "And where are you off to Miss Saer?"

"Following up on a hunch about Lord Rhys's time in the Narrows."

"Ah. Luck to you then." He returned to his work.

"Look after him for me please, Mr. Henry."

"Always Miss." He'd do it too. She could see it in the way his shoulders fell back when he spoke. To the ends of the Aradwyn to help his Lord, that one would go. That was a comfort, when she was gone.

Kate came back with a parcel, wrapped in clean brown paper. It was warm under Tamsin's fingers, and it smelled wonderful.

"I had cook put a bit in for lunch too, in case you don't get back in time for it."

"Thank you, Kate." Impulsively Tamsin reached over and hugged her. "I'll be back as soon as I can. Don't forget to give him my message."

The street outside the house was empty. It felt naked without the crowds, unnerving. In the Narrows, there was always someone on the streets. Tamsin hurried a little faster. The main roads had a little traffic, but the King's Ring had a hushed air, like church or the prison.

The guards barely glanced up as she passed them into the Merchant Ring. Here the streets had a familiar hum. It took her a moment to realize she wasn't being stared at this time. The blue dress marked her as respectable enough. In Glassmaker Square, she found a spot on the rim of the fountain and opened the parcel from Kate.

Inside was fresh buttered bread with a slice of cheese. Below that was a hot sausage bun and an apple, unbruised. Tamsin's mouth watered. There was so much food here. She could get used to that. But she shouldn't. That thought stole some of her appetite. She couldn't let herself get used to any of this. It was going to come to an end, and soon.

She finished the bread and cheese, and took a long drink at the fountain. Around her the shops were opening.

When Elspeth answered the back door of the Emirya she made a gratifying double take.

"Tamsin? I was worried. I thought you would have the shirts yesterday." She took in Tamsin's empty arms. "Where is the laundry? Where did you get that dress?"

"That is a long story. But I brought something to cover the costs of them." Tamsin dug into her pocket and pulled out the sovereign.

Elspeth's eyes narrowed. "You'd best come in."

*

"So, the shirts were lost, and the dress with it, although I couldn't get the wine stain out either. But this should cover the costs, and it's unlikely that this sort of thing will happen again. I try to avoid knife fights," Tamsin concluded. She pushed the sovereign across the table. It would more than cover the costs of the shirts and dress.

"You are out of my sight four days, and you manage to bring down this much trouble on you?" Elspeth shook her head. She weighed the gold coin on her palm, then she tucked it away with her other coins and left Tamsin a generous measure of silver crowns in its place.

"I wasn't about to let him die, Elspeth. He offered me sponsorship. I could go home," Tamsin said.

Elspeth counted her remaining coins. "I offered you the same four days ago. Why trust his offer? Are you sure you should be mixing it up with this kingsringer? It's chancy." When Elspeth was upset, a hint of the Narrows edged in around her more urbane vocabulary.

Tamsin swallowed her first defensive words. "Lord Rhys and I came to an agreeable price. I think he will come through." Her mind flitted to Lord David. Rhys was the younger son; would that limit the amount of sway Rhys had? No, she'd counted those gambling markers. Younger son or not, Rhys had coins enough to sponsor a hundred people out of the Narrows. Money could buy any amount of respect.

Elspeth hemmed her lips together tight, but she let the subject fall.

"Well, what are you to do next?"

Tamsin swallowed, more than just the washing debt, had brought her here. "I need you to send a message for me."

Elspeth's brows rose higher.

"To... L—Frank," Tamsin stuttered.

Elspeth reached into one of the tiny drawers and pulled out something tin bright and slender.

"Where do you want to meet?" she asked.

"The Drunk Duck." It was a bit away from Frank's usual haunts, but that would be no bad thing here. "Tell him there is money involved." Lacey she would have trusted to loyalty alone, but Frank's word was as good as copper coin.

Elspeth nodded. She went back to the hall and caught one of the lamp boys. Tamsin heard a muffled buzz of instructions, then he was gone, with a rattle of coins ringing in his pocket.

Elspeth came back in and settled herself at the work bench. "And now we wait." She rolled out a length of light-weight linen and started to cut it into lengths for a new shirt. Tamsin waxed a length of thread and started to help.

It took the boy just over an hour to return. He must have used the dock gate, and run near to the whole way. He brought back a brass button, the grooves turned green from the damp.

Elspeth tucked it away.

"What does it mean?" Tamsin asked.

"Oh, he'll see you. Not that he knows who, just that there is money involved and I vouch for you."

Tamsin's stomach wrapped itself about the lunch she'd shared with Elspeth.

"I need to go," she said.

"I'll have another load for you to wash in a week if you are still here. And mind you don't tear this one to shreds this time. We'll be short shrift until I finish his next lot of shirts, as is." Elspeth's eyes were worried.

"I'll be safe, Elspeth."

Tamsin wound her way through the layers of scenery, props, and scrims back to the alley. She started to step into the street traffic again and stopped. No one gave her a second glance when she stepped up onto the wooden sidewalk. Tamsin smoothed the front of her borrowed dress. Imagine what looks she would get if she walked down here in one of the muslin frocks Eira wore, or the silk gown from dinner. But no, that would be silly for the streets. The train would be ruined in half a block. As she was, she merged into the crowd, like a pebble in gravel. Would that un-notice hold through the gate though? The church bells rang the hour, and that decided it. Frank wouldn't wait for long. She cut through Paperwright Street and headed for the river.

*

There was no line at the dock gate, not going in. On the other side, she could see the line stretching down the street, lent length by the ox carts. The guard looked at her a bit askance, but he waved her through with a simple, "Mind where you wander off to Miss."

The warehouse district smelled of piss and fish. The streets were broader here, broad enough two wagons could pass each other. Tamsin dodged the wagons now as they plodded in from the docks. One of the drovers cursed as she ducked a little too close for his comfort. His yelling followed her the next few streets over.

*

The Drunk Duck was almost empty. Frank sat at a table in the back, and if he was surprised to see her it didn't appear on his face.

Tamsin glanced at the barkeep dozing at the counter. She decided not to wake him. She slid onto the bench opposite Frank.

"You've come on better times," was all he said.

Tamsin nodded. She noticed a walking stick beside him. "How is your leg healing?"

"I manage."

Tamsin bit her teeth down over the questions she wanted to ask. Lacey? How had he been shot? Where's and why's would just annoy him right now.

"I need information, and I have some coin." She pushed a silver penny across the table.

Frank just looked at it. "What do you need?"

She couldn't help the tiny slump her shoulders made when they relaxed. "There is a warehouse down here. It should have received an order of Orness silk recently, a sevenday ago. I need to find it."

His eyebrows quirked at that. "Find a warehouse, on the wharf? You don't ask for much."

"But how many of them trade in silk?" she asked. "It should be close to the river, and there should be clay soil nearby."

Frank exhaled and took a sip of his mug. "I know a place. It's empty now though. They moved the silk two days ago. Why do you need to see it?"

"Rhys," Tamsin said. "It could help him." Frank's face was unreadable.

He reached out and pushed the penny back to her. Her stomach sank.

"There's no coin between us now, Tamsin," he said. "You saved my life, I owe you this much at least. I can take you to the place, but I can't get you inside."

Tamsin's mind reeled. Frank, being kind. Her mind latched onto the last bit he'd said.

"What do mean you can't get me in?"

He shrugged. "Lacey is the one who is the dub-hand at a lock. They keep that place tight, even when it's empty. But there shouldn't be a guard there now."

Tamsin inhaled. "Lacey hates me."

Frank drew another draft from his mug. "She's fair to angry now. You lied to her. I understand why she feels betrayed. Besides… she likes you."

"She what?" Tamsin said. "I thought she hated me?"

"Well, there's a little of both, but Lacey half loved you from the moment she met you. She's only mad now because you lied."

"I—she's one of my dearest friends but I don't—"

"I know," Frank said. "But you're still her friend, right?"

"Of course, if she'll still have me after all this."

"Mayhap, mayhap not. I understand why you didn't tell us though. I always knew there was somewhat you were keeping back." He set the mug back on the table and heaved himself upright. "Well, best to get it over with."

"Wait, you want me to go see her now?" Tamsin rolled the penny in her hands.

Frank leaned on his stick. "By tomorrow they might have another ship come in, the place is empty now. Today is the best time, and waiting isn't going to make this easier. Lacey's like a grease fire, she flames and smokes a lot at first, but after a few days she burns herself out."

"Somehow that isn't that reassuring," Tamsin said.

For a wonder, Frank cracked a smile. He clapped her on the shoulder and started limping for the door. "Come on, see if you can keep up."

———

When they reached his door, Frank hung back. "Perhaps it's best I make sure my sister isn't smouldering before you charge in."

Tamsin nodded and waved him ahead of her. He was limping heavily on the bad leg as he went inside, but he got about better than she thought he would this soon. Perhaps her healing was getting stronger.

This was a foolish idea. She shouldn't be trying this. Lacey wasn't going to forgive her. Tamsin took a step away from the door, then back to it again. She was wavering when Frank opened the door and waved her inside. "I'll be out here." He winked at her as she passed inside.

Frank smiling, and winking. Weird.

Lacey was standing at the back of the room. It had been tidied since Tamsin's makeshift surgery, but the floorboards were stained between the hammocks. Lacey had crossed her arms over her chest. Her shoulders were set back and stiff. Tamsin looked away.

The silence stretched out between them. Too long. Tamsin cast about for something to say.

"I'm sorry I lied."

Lacey's eyes narrowed.

"I've never used the," Tamsin's voice choked over the words, "the magic to hurt anyone. I only use it when I have to. When someone is going to ... to die without it." Tamsin's eyes flitted down to the stained floor and back up to Lacey.

Lacey's face twitched. Tamsin couldn't tell if she was getting through or if Lacey was too angry to speak. Something in her impassiveness struck a spark of anger within Tamsin.

"Would you have helped me if you'd known? Do you know what I could do?" Tamsin's voice had risen higher and louder than she wanted. She took a breath. "I could ease the rheumatism in Elspeth's hands, I kept Baker's son from choking to death on his own phlegm, and your own brother from bleeding out where you are standing. I don't expect you to grovel at my feet, but you could at least not hate me for helping."

"Why would you think I hate you?" Lacey's voice was cold.

"You tossed my home." Tamsin blinked. Did that mean Lacey didn't hate her?

"I had to be sure," Lacey said.

"Sure of what? That I wasn't hiding the bones of murdered children under my mattress? You've known me for two years. Do you think that I would be capable of hurting someone like that?" Tamsin rubbed her face with her hands. "The stories aren't true Lacey. I can't control a man with a drop of his blood. I can heal. I never harmed anyone."

"You don't have a pile of puppets hidden somewhere?" Lacey asked.

Tamsin winced. The blood mage who turned the woman he loved into a prop in his puppet show was a particularly lurid, and pervasive, street show. Even the Emirya had performed a version of it.

"If I could have done something like that, then why would I have spent a year in Kingsgate Gaol?" Tamsin vented an exasperated sigh. "I can only heal if I am touching someone. And if there is blood, their blood. I don't need a lot, a drop or two, to make the connection. But I never learned to hurt people."

"Then why did they hang your mother?" Lacey asked.

Tamsin flinched back as if she'd been struck.

"I ... I don't know." Heat flashed over her face and pricked at her eyes. "My mother never hurt anyone. She helped. She delivered half the babies in the village, for all the raised eyebrows and silly scolds talking about it was beneath her station to do so. Whenever someone was sick, they called for her. Even the apothecary consulted with her when he came across a dire case. So, I don't know who told the guard that she used magic sometimes when a birth wasn't going well, or a bone wouldn't set another way. I don't know." Tamsin had her suspicions but now was not the time to dwell on that.

Tears stood in Tamsin's eyes, and she dragged her sleeve across her face.

"I didn't know that." Lacey's voice was still stiff, but it was lower now, and closer. Tamsin looked up. Lacey had closed the distance between them until she was about an arm's length away.

"Lacey, I'd lost everything. You were the first person in the Narrows who was kind to me. I was afraid I'd lose you too."

"You might have." Lacey's face twisted into something between a grimace and a smile. "The Narrows ain't a good place to advertise these sorts of things."

"Do you believe me?"

Lacey's nod wasn't as enthusiastic as Tamsin wished it would be. *Just be grateful for what you have*, she thought.

Frank knocked on the door. "If you ladies haven't managed to murder each other, we have a bit of work to do."

Chapter Fourteen

Frank led them to the docks by the least intuitive path Tamsin could discern. When she looked at Lacey to remark on it, something in her face made Tamsin pause. Both Lacey and Frank were warier than a trip to the docks would seem to warrant.

Around them were signs of the riots. A few buildings still smouldered near Kingsgate, but Frank took them wide of that. There were fewer ships in harbour than Tamsin had ever recalled seeing before. More people though, mostly dock hands pressed against each other, lining the edge of the pier, and their conversation held an angry hum.

"Has there been some news I missed?" Tamsin muttered.

Frank answered her. "The grain shipment is late coming from downriver."

Tamsin stopped mid stride. The bread tax, the late grain.

"Another riot?" The words passed through her lips before she could stop them.

Behind her Lacey made a strangled noise.

"Don't say that!" Lacey spit in the street and twisted her fingers in one of the gods' signs.

Tamsin swallowed. There should be Bluecoats everywhere if they expected a repeat of three nights ago. She didn't recall seeing any Bluecoats on the street.

Tamsin glanced around. They were still well away from people, sheltered in the lee of an alley. "Was the riot how..." her eyes went to Frank's knee.

"No," Lacey said. Her tone didn't invite further inquiry.

Frank led them to a bank of warehouses on the water's edge. The cobblestones had been removed from the streets leaving only the hard-packed river clay. The warehouse in the centre stood out from its neighbours. Its doors were new, and the chain binding those doors had only a touch of rust on it.

Frank pointed at the centre warehouse. "There was a ship last week that came up from Orness. Silk, some wines, and a few other things. We're familiar with its captain."

The waterfront warehouses must be ideal for smuggling. That explained how Frank found the silk so fast. The penny dropped for Tamsin. The crates at their home.

"Guns?" she whispered.

Lacey swallowed and looked at Frank. That glance was confirmation enough for Tamsin.

"You need to keep that to yourself," Frank said. "You're here for that kingsringer. Our business has nothing to do with that."

Tamsin gave him a tight nod. That they brought in illegal goods was not news. But guns weren't opiates or stolen coal. It was a traitor's drawn and quartering for bringing guns in.

"How do we do this?" Tamsin asked.

"You'll stay back with me," Frank said. "Lacey will go in and get the lock open. Once she is clear she'll whistle. I'll walk you down and make the door look like it's still locked tight.

"Do you know *A Roving and a Riding*? When you hear that, it's safe. We'll keep whistling that song. As long as you hear one of us, it's still safe. If the song changes, someone is coming down the street. If you hear *Lover's Lost*, they are going inside. We'll do the song four times to give you enough time to look around. Fourth time we'll open the doors, so be ready to leave."

Tamsin nodded. She waited with Frank at the corner while Lacey approached the building. Lacey walked past the doors slowly, then circled back and laid her ear flat against the wood. She pulled a string of rusted looking skeleton keys from beneath her jacket and tried a few of them, working them back and forth. On the fourth key, the lock slipped open. She fussed with the lock hasp, then walked down the street whistling.

Frank rolled his eyes. When she was out of sight at the other corner Tamsin heard the faint strains of *A Roving and a Riding*.

Tamsin swallowed down the acid anxiety that rose in her throat.

Frank nodded and they set off down the street, dodging the puddles in the muddy wheel ruts.

He slid the chain aside deftly enough Tamsin could scarcely hear its links ring. As soon as the door was open, he pushed her through, and shut her in.

She could hear the chain settling back into place. Outside Frank whistled, just off key and out of tempo. *Stick to the plan, Tamsin.*

The inside of the warehouse was a twilight haze. Just under the eaves were a set of shutters that let in a few slivers of light. Tamsin closed her eyes and took a deep breath. The air smelled like old wood smoke, and a layer of voltaic tension blanketed everything like fog. When she opened her eyes, they had adjusted a little more to the darkness. If this place had held silk, there was no sign of it now. The only thing she could see was a bank of tables running along one of the walls. No. Not tables, desks.

The floor was stone. That was odd. Perhaps it kept the dust and vermin away from the silks? It was an expensive investment for a Narrows warehouse.

She ran her fingers over the top of the first desk, well waxed with a faint scent of linseed oil. The first drawer she pulled on was locked. Damn. She tested them all.

There were a few that came open, filled with the debris of business, sand, ink, and wax shavings, nothing more.

At the last desk, a single drawer was left open. Inside she found a sheaf of quality paper and that was all. Nothing that would help Rhys. She started to push the drawer back but there was the tiniest scraping along the outside track as she pushed it in.

Outside she could hear the second repetition of A Roving and a Riding. She was still safe. Tamsin pulled the drawer completely out of the desk and reached inside. If this was a pen nib caught on the tracks, she was going to feel ridiculous. Instead, her fingers met a piece of metal that had sprung out from the side of the desk. When she pressed it back into place something on the side of the desk clicked. A panel jutted out ever so slightly. Tamsin pried it open with a fingernail.

Inside was a leather folio. Tamsin slipped off the band holding it together and held the pages up to the light. The writing was cramped, but familiar. The same language and handwriting as the ledger page Rhys had been carrying? Yes, here was the place where the page had been torn free. She had to get this to Rhys. She shoved the pages into the bodice of her dress. The empty sheaf of paper she placed into the folio and replaced it in its hiding spot.

Outside the whistling had stopped. Tamsin froze, then she slid the drawer back into place. They hadn't signalled danger yet...

And then, *Lover's Lost*. Tamsin swallowed hard. Outside she could hear boot steps and the sound of the chain rattling against the wood. This place was dim, but not enough that she could not be seen in all the emptiness. She ducked under the desk. If they didn't bring a light... But that was stupid. Why wouldn't they bring a lantern to a place they owned or worked at? She forced herself to stay as still and silent as she could.

The door opened and a new block of daylight stretched towards the bank of desks. The owner of the boots had a lantern, something with glass sides and a mirrored back. Tamsin could see a pair of gleaming leather boots with a red leather cuff. The toes were free of mud. Whoever this man was, he hadn't walked very far in them.

The man walked closer. He stopped at the second desk, and she heard a thump as the lantern was set down. Then came the brassy scrape of a key fitting into a lock. A drawer opened. There was a brief rattle of papers. A second set of boot steps came to the door, someone heavier.

Outside Frank and Lacey had both stopped whistling. Tamsin wondered if they had run off and left her.

"Y—er sir, the cab doesn't want to wait here long. Do you need more time?"

The man at the desk vented a frustrated sigh. The drawer slid shut and Tamsin heard the lock click back into place.

"Impatient clod," he said, under his breath. A bit louder he added "I have the receipts I need."

"You could always bring a coach instead of hiring, sir." The voice at the door was maddeningly familiar to Tamsin.

The booted man moved away from the desks and towards the door.

"And wouldn't that be a sight here? It's only for another week, then none of this subterfuge should be necessary."

As Tamsin watched his boots leave, her gaze was drawn to the centre of the room. The light from the door lit up a doubled metal circle set into the flagstones, with lumps of wax marking out four points along its circumference.

When the door locked, she pushed her way out and moved to the circle. Outside she heard a muffle of voices then the sound of hooves and steel-clad wheels rolling away. She bent down. If this was a ritual circle it would explain the odd electricity of the air and the anxiety she was feeling. Her eyes hadn't adjusted enough to make out what runes were chalked between the circles. This wasn't the Kristiri forms of magic that she knew. Her fingers came away coated in chalk and something dark and flaky. From the jolt it made against her skin it was blood. She tasted a bit, bitter salt and copper, and familiar. Rhys's blood? There was a familiarity, and a strangeness. Her stomach gave a halfhearted churn. Perhaps this circle had been used for more than one ritual?

Tamsin pulled out one of the pages stuffed under her bodice and gathered a bit of the dried blood onto the page, then folded it over until it made an envelope. She stuffed all of that into the dress bodice again. It pushed her skirt front out a little, but the dress was made for a larger frame than hers.

Someone rapped at the door. Tamsin froze. Were the men back?

She heard the chain links clink together and someone franticly whistling *A Roving and a Riding*. Lacey, or Frank. Tamsin stumbled to the doorway. Lacey was on the other side. Somewhere further along, Frank was whistling some other song. Lacey seized Tamsin's arm and pulled her through the doorway.

"Goddesses and gods, I thought you were made for sure," Lacey said.

"So did I." Tamsin's eyes met Lacey's and then the tension bubbled up in both women. Lacey clutched her arm, and they started giggling. Frank came back around the corner and rolled his eyes.

"Honestly, the least you can do is shut the door," he said.

Lacey choked back another round of giggles and refastened the door. She slid a piece of grey wax into the hasp before shoving the lock home. She noticed Tamsin watching her.

"It kept the lock closed but keeps it from locking. In case we need to come back."

"Good, good," Frank said. "Now let's go!"

The three of them hurried away from the warehouse. Frank kept their pace brisk, turning them this way and that until Tamsin wasn't sure where they were anymore. After two years, she knew some of the Narrows's secrets but Frank and Lacey knew nearly all of them.

"Were you able to find what you needed?" Lacey asked, when Frank finally brought them to a halt.

"I think so," Tamsin replied.

"Good," Frank said. "This would have been a hell of a risk for a waste of time."

Lacey rolled her eyes at him. "It wouldn't be a waste for Tamsin, she likes the Kingsringer."

"Lacey!" Tamsin's cheeks were hot.

"Admit it." Lacey's smile was just the tiniest bit sad. "He likes you back you know."

"He's engaged."

Lacey shrugged. "Engaged isn't married and look at all you've done for him."

Tamsin inhaled, let the breath out. "This isn't a players' show or a penny novel, he's a lord's son. I'm helping him, and he's going to help me get out of the city. To go home."

Lacey looked away. "Just, don't get hurt up there, Tam." She gave Tamsin a quick hug.

Frank was giving Tamsin another inscrutable look. He pointed north. "The Dock gate is a block up from here. Lacey, we need to go. More business to attend to. Take care of yourself Tamsin."

"Wait," Tamsin said. The gaol was so close? Despite the cool air, she began to sweat. "Was it bringing in the guns that got you shot?"

Frank froze and some of the geniality left his face.

"I told you, that doesn't concern you," he said.

Tamsin looked at Lacey. She wouldn't meet Tamsin's eyes.

"I don't know what you two are involved with," Tamsin said. "But be careful. Not every bullet wound is able to be healed."

Frank's head gave a tiny dip of acknowledgment. Lacey reached out and gave Tamsin's shoulder another squeeze, then they were gone.

Chapter Fifteen

Tamsin joined the gate queue as the sun was dipping low in the sky. Her skirt was a little sooty from the warehouse floor, but it was neat and unpatched. At last, it was her turn to enter.

"Name, occupation, and reason for entry?" the kingsman asked. He looked tired.

"Kate Little," Tamsin lied. "I'm a housemaid for the Carwyn house on Merriton Square. I came back to visit my sister."

He weighed her story. Tamsin reached into her pocket and pulled out one of the silver crowns. His tongue flicked over his lips. The coin vanished into his pockets, and he waved her on her way. She'd probably overpaid him for a maid, but it had worked. It was a long walk to Merriton Square's gravel drive.

She hesitated at the front doors. Eira and Rhys had said she was their guest. She walked up the front steps and knocked.

After a long few minutes, a single door opened, and Grant looked down at her. She saw him recognize her, then he shut the door in her face. Tamsin felt her cheeks flush. She should have known better than to use the front door. Rhys and Eira might be kind to her but that didn't make her the same as them. She turned and walked down the stairs holding her head straight with effort.

The back door was deserted, even the polished brass lamp hung outside the door was unlit. Tamsin's knocks echoed in the back courtyard. Mrs. Beauchamp answered. A smug smile tugged at her lips.

"You are no longer welcome here, Miss Saer," she said. "Goodbye."

"What? But I have something for Rhys, I mean Lord Rhys." Was Rhys having second thoughts about sponsoring her? Her hands shook.

"Your kind of services are no longer required in this household," Mrs. Beauchamp said.

"Please, I need to speak to someone. Maybe Lady Eira would see me. If you only send a message up..."

"The Lady isn't at home at the moment." Mrs. Beauchamp started to shut the door.

Tamsin slid her foot into the frame.

"Kate? Henry? I could leave a message!" she pitched her voice louder hoping someone else inside would hear. "This is important!"

Mrs. Beauchamp shoved the door hard against Tamsin's instep. Tamsin winced but kept her foot in place.

"Mr. Grant! Martin!" shouted Mrs. Beauchamp. She shoved her own foot under Tamsin's toe trying to lever it out from the doorway. Tamsin leaned forward.

"Henry! Kate!" she yelled into the house.

Grant's face appeared behind Mrs. Beauchamp. "Miss Saer, you have been told you are no longer welcome here. Martin has run for the guard, I suggest you not be here when he returns," he said.

Tamsin felt the blood drain from her cheeks. Mrs. Beauchamp took advantage of her lapse of attention and brought a broom handle down on Tamsin's toes. Tamsin jumped backwards and slipped off the stoop. She landed on her back, her feet tangled up with the shoe scrapers. The door slammed shut and the bar scraped into place.

Around the front of the house footsteps crunched in the gravel. Someone was running and fast. This place wasn't safe for her.

She scrambled to her feet and ran towards the strip of trees that bordered the row of houses along the square. She glanced behind her. Above the back door the curtains were drawn aside. They were watching to make sure she truly left. The blood flooded back to her face. Did Rhys know what was going on? He couldn't. And now she had answers for him, or at least more of the puzzle. She'd earned those sponsorship papers, by the gods. But shutting her out wasn't Rhys's way. It was Lady Everwood's though. Perhaps with David's help? Had Rhys let slip that she'd been to gaol? Or the magic?

She followed the tree line back into a small park, just off the square, complete with flagstone paths and a tiny duck pond with delicate, white-painted rowboats moored along its shore. This close to dusk, the park was almost empty. Should she head back to the Narrows, or the theatre? She could send a letter to Rhys. But the mail would be delivered to Grant or Beauchamp, to distribute to the house. Tamsin didn't care to wager that her note would reach him.

Perhaps in the morning? All she needed was one shot at Rhys to give him the papers. If he had decided not to speak to her, well then she could wash her hands of the whole thing, and she had the remains of the sovereign to set herself up someplace better.

On the far side of the duck pond, a cluster of pine trees dipped their boughs into the water. Tamsin squeezed in between their branches. In the centre was a small, clear space heaped high with pine straw. She found an almost comfortable seat against a trunk and pulled her knees up to her chin to wait till dawn. A few times a watchman swept though, his lantern swinging the shadows in long slow arcs.

When dawn came, Tamsin stretched. Every muscle in her body felt taut as an overdrawn bow. It took her a few minutes for her chilled legs to hold her weight again. She hobbled around the park, but a servant walking a half-dozen hounds sent her back in hiding. The dogs barked and a few strained their leashes towards the pine grove. Tamsin shrank back and pressed her back into the tree trunk. The groom cursed the dogs soundly and hauled them off, further along the path. Tamsin waited until the sounds of barking faded away before she crept back towards Carwyn house.

She took up a post in the tree line, just out of direct view of the house. Her arms and hair were sticky with pine sap. Tamsin clutched the papers to her chest. She waited.

The sun was nearing noon by the time the first carriage rolled out of the house towards the main road. Tamsin took a breath. She hadn't been able to see who was inside, but the only one who should turn her away was David. Two out of three wasn't the worst odds. She crossed her fingers and whispered a quick prayer for luck. As the carriage reached the end of the drive she plunged out of her hiding spot and made a mad dash towards its path.

The horses shied away from her, and the driver pulled up cursing.

"What in the hells are you doing?" he shouted.

"I need to speak with Lord Rhys or Lady Eira," she shouted back.

"Tamsin?" Eira opened the door. One of the footmen hopped off and immediately swung the step down for her. The coachman was glowering at Tamsin.

"Daft mort, you could have killed yourself and Lady Eira both," he muttered. The horses calmed under his hands. Tamsin ignored him.

"Tamsin, what happened to you? We expected you for dinner last night."

"I found something," Tamsin said. Her shoulders sagged with relief. If they'd been expecting her then Rhys didn't know she'd been turned away. He still wanted her. "But no one would let me into the house. Mrs. Beauchamp and Mr. Grant sent Martin off for the guards."

Eira frowned. The footman was looking very uncomfortable. Eira turned on him. "Martin, is this true?"

"It was Lord David's order's milady," Martin said. "He said we wasn't to let her in the house."

"I believe my calls can wait today." Eira took hold of Tamsin's free hand. "Let's go take care of this right now."

Eira didn't bother with the carriage. She towed Tamsin along in her wake, back up the gravel drive and marble steps. She didn't even wait for Martin, who was following along a few steps behind, still half-heartedly protesting. Eira was a fast walker. After Tamsin's trip through the city and her cold night, she found herself straining to match Eira's pace. Eira's grip on her arm was iron, and she'd set her jaw in a way that reminded Tamsin of Rhys.

The front door opened, and Grant started to protest. Eira didn't bother listening. She walked forwards and Grant, towering a head and a half over her, was cowed in her wake.

He joined their procession, as Eira dragged Tamsin up the stairs, and straight through Rhys's door.

"Eira, what..." Rhys trailed off when he saw Tamsin. "Good lord what happened to you, Tamsin?"

Tamsin flushed. Sap clung to her hair and face. She looked every bit as if she'd spent a night under a tree.

"Lady Eira I really must protest..." Grant interjected. Martin was absent, probably running off to get Lord David.

"David banned her from the house," Eira said, ignoring Grant.

"I see." Rhys's voice pitched lower, and he drew his words out, the same tone he'd used when they had encountered the ruffians on their way here. Grant took an involuntary step back.

There must be something about the Carwyn family, Tamsin thought. They all seem to be able to summon intimidation far beyond their physical size. Relief and absurdity washed over her in equal parts. She was inside, and Rhys still wanted to see her.

"Tamsin is my guest," Rhys continued, "and until David inherits, I have just as much right to bring a guest here as he does. Mistress Saer is to be allowed to come and go as she wishes. Now that *will* be all Grant." Rhys shut the door on a final protest from the butler.

"Are you all right?" Tamsin and Rhys echoed each other. Over at the settee Eira giggled. Tamsin noted a trace of hysteria there. Eira had been scared too.

He looked fine, physically at least. The bruises from the last few days were more green than purple now.

"I'm fine," Rhys said. "But I was concerned when you didn't come back. Kate gave me your message. We expected you well before dinner." Being home had brought out a little more of the lordly air in his manners, Tamsin noticed, he carried himself more confidently.

Tamsin swayed on her feet. The adrenalin from this morning was gone and she wanted nothing more than to just sit down and close her eyes for a while. Rhys caught her elbow and helped her sit down on the bed.

"I'm just tired. Well, cold and tired. But I found something." Tamsin yawned.

"Have you eaten?" Eira asked.

Tamsin's stomach emitted a loud gurgle at the idea of food. Eira smothered another laugh.

"I'll go and ask Henry to bring something up while you two talk." Eira slipped out the door. Rhys sat next to Tamsin on the bed. He reached out and brushed a sap stain on her cheek. Tamsin closed her eyes and held herself still. Rhys pulled away.

"What happened to you?" he asked.

"I found the place where your memories were stripped away," Tamsin said. Anything to distract from that moment. She pulled the envelope of blood out of her pocket and set it on top of the other papers.

"Frank helped me find it," she continued. "It was at a warehouse on the dock's edge that stores silk. I didn't see anything actually being stored there now though, just a bunch of desks and a ritual circle, a permanent one set into the floor." She was babbling.

"Isn't that unusual?" Rhys asked.

"Very. All the old ones were torn down. Every once in a while, you can find an old country church who just threw a rug over theirs or something, but this warehouse isn't that old. There was blood all over the circle." Tamsin yawned. "I brought some back with me. I'll need to find something else for it though, this is one of the ledger pages." She showed him the packet.

"I wasn't able to find too much more though, some kingsringer came in and was poking around. I had to hide, so I didn't see his face. His boots were worth at least ten sovereigns though. My brother always wanted a pair like those with the red leather tops." She yawned again. Exhaustion was stronger than any alcohol. "But I found these papers in one of the desks. They were in a hidden compartment, but I can't read them."

Rhys took the papers from her and paged through them, frowning. He sat next to her on the bed.

The doorknob rattled. Tamsin shoved the packet of dried blood back in her pocket.

Henry entered balancing a full tray. He flashed Tamsin a grin. "Glad to see you miss, Lord Rhys was worried."

"Did you know about all this Henry?" Rhys's voice was deceptively soft.

"No sir. I don't... spend much time being sociable downstairs anymore," Henry said. "From what I gathered she came while I was up here getting you ready for dinner." He was looking for something in Rhys's face. Whatever it was he didn't seem to find it. He set the tray down and gave them a short bow. "If that will be all, sir?"

"No, we're fine Henry." Henry nodded and left.

"He misses the old Rhys," Tamsin said.

Rhys sighed. "So, does everyone I encounter, including Lady Everwood."

Tamsin tensed and leaned away from him. "I ... I forgot about her."

Rhys looked lost in thought for a moment, then he collected himself. "I'll read through these papers."

"I wouldn't show them to anyone," Tamsin advised. "At least not yet."

He frowned. "Do you suspect something?"

Tamsin hesitated. "I don't know. But your brother wouldn't let me back in. It could be nothing, or something." She yawned. She'd been worrying this problem around so much that everything was going around in some sort of logic circle.

"I suppose an abundance of caution is best. But you, you should eat. And sleep. And anything else you need." He gave her a gentle push towards the food.

Tamsin crossed over to the table and dug in. This wasn't simple bread and cheese. Someone had heaped the tray full of bread puddings, cold roast, and tiny fruit jellies with cream. She managed to use the utensils, barely.

From the hallway, Tamsin could hear raised voices. Rhys hid the papers and the packet of blood under the coverlet.

"You had no right, Eira!" David threw open the door. He headed straight towards Tamsin. Eira was at his heels, red faced and sputtering.

"That's enough." Rhys wasn't shouting but those two words were enough to make David pause. Tamsin wasn't looking at Lord Rhys Carwyn, lordling, this was Captain Carwyn of the King's Cavalry.

"Tamsin is my guest, David. When father dies and you become Earl, you may command me in this home, until then I will entertain as I will."

"And what would Father... or Mother, say about your choice in company?" David said.

"I'll let them give me their opinions," Rhys said.

"You are flirting with scandal here. How will taking in such people affect Eira's marriage prospects? She'll lose all trace of respectability," David shouted.

This argument scored a hit with Rhys. He leaned back a degree.

"I can guard my own reputation, David," Eira said. "Besides, you made a bigger ruckus about Tamsin than Rhys did. Banning her from the house indeed. That is going to be all over Celdre now. But if anyone refuses me an invitation or offer because of this... well then, they are obviously a silly twit to begin with and I will be happy to be spared the pain of their company."

David glared at all of them. "This isn't over." He left.

Tamsin yawned again, wide enough that her jaw felt like it was splitting. She covered her mouth with both hands. "I'm sorry!" she said, only slightly muffled.

Eira laughed. "It's all right. Let me take you some place to sleep."

Chapter Sixteen

Rhys vetoed Tamsin's return to the nursery, citing David. Eira took her back to her own rooms, and vindictively ordered Mrs. Beauchamp to bring up a hot bath.

"You'll feel better when you're clean again," Eira said. Tamsin disagreed, sleep called her, but the tub was already being filled. *Don't waste the water.* She swallowed her protests.

"Will Rhys have any troubles going over David's head? Will your father object?" Tamsin asked.

Eira was pulling things out of her wardrobe. She didn't turn back to Tamsin, but her shoulders twitched. "Father always objects with Rhys. They've been quarrelling since Rhys left for the army. But Rhys is the one who opened the house for David this season. David—he's had some troubles at the tables in the last years. Until he can settle his debts, he's supposed to be staying at home, but I wanted to take in the season, so Rhys agreed to cover David's costs to open the house, but quietly."

Tamsin whistled. "So out of the brothers, the one who isn't inheriting is better off than the one who is? That's a shift."

Eira shrugged. "Rhys did well for himself. David will have a deeper fund when he inherits, but the estate takes up a lot of that money."

"You seem to know a lot about it," Tamsin said.

"Well, if things go to plan, I'll have the running of my own estate one of these days. Mother has been teaching me since I was twelve."

Tamsin muttered something noncommittal. Things were a little more complicated here than she had thought. Mrs. Beauchamp knocked on the door and announced the bath.

Eira led Tamsin through to another room papered in blue. A polished stove sat in the corner, and someone had brought a large copper tub into the centre of the room. Sweet smelling steam wafted around the room. Eira dismissed Mrs. Beauchamp and the rest of the servants.

"I'll be right outside, if you need anything Tamsin," she said.

Then Tamsin was alone.

The bath water was scalding. It soaked the last of the spring chill from her bones. Tamsin wished she could just lie back, but this was a tub fit to drown in. She scrubbed quickly and redressed in the chemise and dressing gown Eira had laid out. Neither quite fit, but no one was going to be staring at her calves when she was buried under the coverlets.

Eira knocked. "May I come in?" At Tamsin's yes, she poked her head in the door. "I need to go out. Henry and Kate will take turns staying guard to make sure you aren't bothered while you rest."

Tamsin tried to tell her she understood, but all that came out was a yawn. Eira laughed and waved her to the bedroom.

—

The light was the golden hue of late afternoon, when she woke. Tamsin checked the door. Rhys was waiting just outside, reading a book. He smiled when he saw her.

"I thought Kate or Henry would be here," she said. She pulled the dressing gown closer over her chest.

"They both had things to do. I said I could take over." He hefted the book. "I discovered one good thing about losing my memory. All of the books are new again. Eira showed me our library."

His grin was contagious.

Tamsin glanced down the hall. "Did you read the papers I brought back?"

His face grew grim. "I did. We need to talk. Why don't you get dressed and I'll ask Kate to bring tea to my room?"

Tamsin flushed. The dressing gown revealed more leg than she'd remembered. She shut the door. Someone had left her more dresses, laid out across the settee. They weren't Eira's, and they were too fine to be one of Kate or the other maid's discards. Perhaps David's mysteriously missing wife's wardrobe was being plundered again.

Tamsin picked a plaid day dress with a moderate number of flounces and dressed quickly.

Rhys had been replaced by Henry as the door guard.

"This way, Miss." He pointed towards Rhys's room.

"What happened at the house while I was away?" she asked as they walked.

"The captain was in a state, Lord David told him you'd run off and stole ten sovereigns from Mrs. Plumtree's grocer fund," Henry said. "Which is horseshit. She doesn't keep that amount of coin in the house, all the bills are managed with credit."

Tamsin rolled her eyes. "David doesn't think very far ahead, does he?"

"After that, the captain wanted to look for you, but we didn't know where to start," he continued. "He delayed dinner until cook was beside herself, and the roast dried up. Finally, Lord David made them start without him. Then the brothers got into it. It weren't what you would call a peaceable evening."

"I imagine not," Tamsin said. She almost pitied David though. Being dependent on Rhys for his pocket money must be galling.

"Mind you didn't hear this from me," Henry said.

"Of course not."

Henry opened Rhys's door for her and gave her the ghost of a wink.

Rhys stood as she came in. He had another spread of food set out.

"You keep feeding me," Tamsin said. But she smiled.

"Well, that's what you do when you bring people home. You showed me that. I have something for you." Rhys pulled a folded set of papers from his pocket. Blue and gold ribbons were curled around the whole thing.

"What is that?" she asked.

"Sponsorship papers. I had them drafted up yesterday and finalized this morning. You can leave the city now," Rhys offered them to her.

Tamsin reached her hands out and felt the heavy weight of the paper, the silk ribbons, and the heavy red wax seals. "You did it," she whispered. She was free.

"I told you I would."

Was this it then? She could leave now. But was Rhys really safe here? One thing at a time. She tucked the papers away in her dress pocket. Maybe the other papers she'd found had shed some light on what had happened to him.

"Tamsin," Rhys said, "you found out who I was, you brought me home, and you and you alone, are working to figure out why my memories are gone and how to get them back. David doesn't even seem to care that I lost them. He suggested I had some things in my past that were worth forgetting."

Tamsin's gaze fell on his shoulder and the scar she knew was there.

"He has a fraction of a point," she said. "I mean, everything I found at the warehouse seems like someone did this to you deliberately ... or that you did it to yourself." And that was an awful possibility she hadn't thought of before. That didn't explain the man at the warehouse, or Rhys's injuries, or ... she stopped that circle of thoughts. "What did you find in the papers?"

Rhys frowned again. "They don't make sense."

"What do you mean?"

"Look here." He fanned the papers across the table. Tamsin rescued the pot of chocolate from being overturned. "The shipments in and out are all wrong."

"If you say so. I can't read this language. But they matched the ledger you were carrying, so I took the chance."

Rhys pointed to a phrase at the top. "This content doesn't make any sense at all. Numbers of herds here, numbers of ducks there. The contents are regular shipments of random things, sometimes far more than could fit on a boat. I've yet to see a vessel that can carry a thousand head of cattle. But on this day, they received a single cockerel and shipped out thirty bales of grey wool."

"Is it an inventory list for a farm? I didn't see any animals there," Tamsin said. Had she stolen rubbish?

"Except that over here, they receive ten brass buttons, and three silver fans are shipped out." He threw up his hands in frustration.

"So, it's nonsense."

"I don't know," Rhys said. "It's not clear. It sounds like a replacement code, where one word means another, but I lack the context. These are tricky sorts of codes to break, if they were a letter replacement you can brute force that sort of thing."

"You can?"

Rhys looked pensive. "I suppose I can. Huh. But I don't know what they mean by cockerels and fans, except they were hiding the movement of things, as if they were—"

"Smuggling?" she asked. Her stomach sank.

"It's among the reasons I can think of to code a ledger like this," Rhys said.

"Could one of these things be the guns? What are the dates of the shipments?"

"Perhaps. The last one came in on this Firstday, two days after that I woke up at your home. There are three things recorded that day, three dozen steer, six milking ewes and forty pullets."

"Could they be different types of guns? Or..." Tamsin trailed off.

"The powder and shot to go with them," Rhys finished. He rescanned the note. "If we are reading this correctly, they must have brought in three dozen guns. The pullets could be musket balls, and six casks of powder? That's not enough powder though. I must be missing something."

"Are the guns for the army?" Tamsin asked. Her stomach twisted. Gods no. Lacey swore she didn't have anything to do with this.

Rhys ran his fingers through his hair. "Perhaps. Why would their invoices be disguised though?"

"Rhys, the guns that you saw at Frank and Lacey's..." she didn't finish the thought.

He nodded slowly. "There were about three dozen there. I didn't see any powder or shot though."

"I—I don't think they were involved in what happened to you, though."

"Neither Frank nor Lacey were among the people who attacked me."

"They work for people," Tamsin said. How much could she tell him? "They can't know all of the details of this. It has to be someone else. Besides, they don't have the amount of money needed to bring in so many guns and pay half the Narrows to find you." Was she being foolish? Frank had been shot after he'd brought Rhys to her.

"Perhaps I knew." Rhys tapped his temple.

Tamsin couldn't keep her eyes on his face. "If this was what they were trying to keep from you, they did a good job."

"What about the circle you found?" Rhys asked.

She shook her head. "Aradwyn magic uses structures like circles a lot. I've read about them, but I learned a different way. I've never used anything like that circle." Her mother had called the permanent circles that Aradwyn people had built around their magic ridiculous. She had always managed things without circles.

"Is there a way to do the spell again?" Rhys asked.

She met his eyes. "I don't know. There were other people's blood in the circle as well as yours."

"Really?" he asked. "How could you tell?"

She looked away. "It's like a discordant chord. I think most of it is your blood, but I am not certain. There are ways for you to find out, but they aren't very pleasant, especially if I am wrong."

"How unpleasant?" Rhys asked.

"Vomiting up everything you ate for the last day and feeling like your three days past drinking a cask of rum without water or rest."

Rhys weighed it. "If it will get us answers, let's try it."

"I'd need some water, and the dried blood."

Rhys nodded. "I'll lock the door."

They cleared the food from the table and Rhys fetched the packet of blood. While she'd slept, he'd moved it to a small glass bottle. Tamsin poured out her teacup and rinsed it well with water from the dressing ewer. She used the last of the water to fill the bottom of the cup and brought it back to the table. Rhys was waiting. Tamsin felt a small chill race down her spine. He trusted her so much.

She poured some of the blood into the water. It didn't want to mix and made a rust-coloured film over the surface. Even dried and several days old it was potent. She could feel the threads of the blood bond at the corners of her vision.

Tamsin closed her eyes and used one of the mind clearing exercises her mother had taught her. The bond was so close. She traced the rim of the cup with her finger. Outwardly nothing changed but her skin could feel the charge that lay heavy in the air. All the hair on her arms stood up. She handed the cup to Rhys. The moment the bloodwater hit his lips the charged feeling left the air.

He sat silent for a minute. "Is that it?"

"How do you feel?" she asked.

"The same as before. A little queasy perhaps?"

"Most of it has to be yours then, or you'd be retching. It took me years to learn how to taste someone else's blood without being ill."

"This doesn't feel like it is that dangerous," Rhys said. "I don't understand why it's banned."

"It's not that simple." Tamsin bit her lip. How much should she tell him. "There are things I can do with magic. I stopped the bleeding in Frank's leg, but I could have made it worse."

"So could any field surgeon." Rhys shrugged. "It's a tool. The axe that fells the tree can also fell a person."

"The crown does not feel the same way."

"I am not scared of you Tamsin," Rhys said.

The moment hung between them, too long.

"We need to figure out the next step," Rhys said at last. "How does what we learned help us out?"

"Well, the circle implies that what happened to you was deliberate, that whoever did this has been doing magic regularly. I wish I had my mother's books. It's been a long time since I read them, but maybe they would have something that could help." Tamsin rubbed her temples. This last spell had been easy. She missed using magic.

"There was more to the story about your brother's death wasn't there?" Rhys asked.

Tamsin looked away. "My mother, she was a healer ... and they killed her for it. Thomas, he was shot by ... by the Bluecoats when they came to bring us in."

The silence between them stretched thin as paper. "I don't understand that," Rhys said.

"I spent a year in the Kingsgate Gaol, Rhys. I spent a year there, and once a day they'd bring me to a room and tell me to confess to killing children and harming people with blood magic, and ... I lied. I told them I never used magic, that I didn't know how. I told them again and again and again."

"But you never hurt anyone?"

"No," Tamsin said. "But they didn't care about that. When I didn't confess, eventually, they let me go. They'd already hung my mother, shot my brother. All I wanted was not to be dead too. And when I was out, I looked for my father. He wasn't there. Maybe they killed him too."

"I'm sorry. Did you look for him?"

"How? I didn't have paper or the money for postage when they let me out of Kingsgate. If he wasn't there, he's either dead, or..."

"Or?" Rhys prompted after a minute.

"Or he didn't care." Or he was the one who turned her mother over to the Bluecoats. That was an awful suspicion, but he'd been working late the day the Bluecoats came. Far later than usual. And they'd been arguing, over money, over Tom, the house, so much before the arrest.

"We should clear this away." Tamsin carried the cup to the grate. The contents steamed when she added them to the fire. She spent a long moment looking at the flames.

Rhys crossed over and laid his hand on her shoulder. The moment was broken. Tamsin dusted ash and dried blood off her fingers. "I need to think on all of this. We can work out what it all means in a little while." When all the information wasn't tracing circles to nowhere in her head. She rubbed her temples.

If Rhys noticed her eyes were a bit red, he didn't let on. Downstairs the hall clock chimed four times.

"Tamsin, I have to go out tonight. Eira said I should attend a party at an old friend's home, Lord Hedworth. I've already accepted the invitation." Rhys took a deep breath. "You should come with us. It's not safe for you to be at the house without Eira or myself with you."

"Rhys, you can't bring a stranger to someone else's house!"

"Of course not. Eira spoke to him this afternoon. Lord Hedworth wants to meet you. And Marion will be there."

"That's a good reason for me not to go. Don't you like her?" Tamsin squished down a sudden flare of jealousy. She had no right to be jealous, Marion had been there first.

"Marion is lovely, but I don't know her. Every time she looks at me, she expects me to be someone else. And Tamsin, I don't know if I will ever be that man again. You said yourself, I might not get those memories back."

"What if you don't want them back?" Her heart was beating so quickly he had to be able to hear it. "I mean, something terrible happened at the warehouse. But we don't know what or who. It's the part of town where bad things happen, and bad people do them. What if you... are you sure you want to dig that part of your past up?" She stopped herself from reaching out to him by lacing her fingers together in front of her. Would he like her if he had those memories back? Would he send her on her way, and that would be it?

"I can't hide from it forever if that is the case, Tamsin," Rhys said. "These sorts of things always come out in the end."

She stayed silent.

"Come with me. Eira is coming as well. I'll rest easier if you are with me. And I've heard the Lord Hedworth has an amazing library."

Tamsin sighed. This was a mistake. "I'll go."

His smile was warmer than the fire.

Chapter Seventeen

By dusk they were ready. Eira looked like she wanted to bounce in her dancing slippers. "You look amazing," she told Tamsin.

"Mmm," Tamsin forced herself not to tug the bodice further up. The green silk wasn't precisely immodest. Everything was covered, but it cut wide across her shoulders and only just covered the shape of the brand. It was amazing how much difference a few inches of fabric could make in keeping you warm. She shivered. Kate handed her a wool cloak to wrap around her shoulders.

"Really, this is too much." Tamsin fingered the rows of braided cording sewn along the cloak's edge.

"It's Lady Carwyn's old wardrobe. I very much doubt she will be back to claim them," Eira said.

"What happened to her?" Everyone in the house kept dancing around the issue, well except for Rhys.

Eira bit her lip and glanced at the door. "It's not something we like to talk about." She swung her own cloak over her shoulders.

"I'm sorry."

"No," Eira said, "it's just, it's a scandal. She left him. She went off to Ampré in Orness, and set herself up somewhere glittering and interesting, and far away from here. Mother said David drove her away with his temper."

"Why hasn't he remarried?" Tamsin asked.

"It's too soon. She has to be gone for at least two years before he can call it abandonment," Eira said.

"Things are too complicated up here," Tamsin said. "In the Narrows, if you want to leave your husband, you just do."

Eira shrugged. She handed Tamsin a set of gloves. "You'll need these." The house gong sounded. "The carriage is here milady," Kate said. Tamsin gave Eira a panicked look.

"Oh, don't be like that. This is going to be fun." Eira took Tamsin's arm and towed her down the stairs.

Rhys was standing at the landing. His fawn breeches clung to his legs and his green silk coat looked painted onto his shoulders. He looked lovely, lovely and unobtainable. Tamsin hesitated. This was a mistake.

Rhys gave both women his warm smile and offered Tamsin and Eira each an arm. "Shall we go?"

Tamsin took a breath. "I cannot promise to dance," she said as she laid her hand on the arm.

*

Mrs. Farrow was waiting for them at the carriage. She kept her face turned away from Tamsin as they took their seats, disapproval written clearly across her face. Sensitive to her mood, the carriage ride was silent until they reached Lord Hedworth's home.

The house glittered in the darkness. Someone had hung thousands of paper lanterns from iron hooks along the gravel drive and the grounds. More of the lanterns flickered around the arched entryway, and a line of footmen waited for them, in full glittering regalia.

Tamsin shifted nervously on the steps while Rhys handed Mrs. Farrow down first from the carriage. Eira had teased Tamsin's hair into more controlled ringlets, up on the crown of her head, and wound a strand of paste pearls through it like a bandeau. Her curls tickled the back of her bare neck, like some sort of pest.

Inside, a servant relieved her of her wrap. Lady Everwood was waiting in the entry, adjusting her own coiffure. From upstairs Tamsin could hear string musicians starting to tune.

"My darling, how wonderful to see you." Lady Everwood's smile was brittle as bent tin.

Rhys smiled back at her. He took the hand she offered him and bowed over it. "It is good to see you again Lady Everwood. You remember my sister, Mrs. Farrow, and Miss Saer." His greeting was overly formal to a fiancé, but his courtly manners seemed to be returning to him.

Lady Everwood's smile thinned. "Of course." She took Rhys's arm and led him upstairs. Tamsin and the other women followed a few steps behind.

The ballroom was not even close too full.

"It's early," Eira reassured Tamsin. Tamsin shrugged. It could stay empty for all she cared. Mrs. Farrow's glance took in the whole room.

"If you will excuse me Lady Eira," Mrs. Farrow said, "I believe I will take a turn." She didn't bother waiting for a response before hastening for a door on the other side of the room.

Tamsin looked at Eira.

Eira shrugged, answering Tamsin's unspoken question. "She has a beau, but I am not supposed to know about it."

Lady Everwood steered the remaining group towards an older man in a brown velvet jacket, standing near a long table laid out with silver cups.

"Lord Hedworth," she said. She curtsied, and the man bowed in turn.

The Lord Hedworth proved to be a portly man, old enough to be Rhys's father. He had a salt and pepper beard that covered his cravat, and elaborately embroidered slippers on his feet. He greeted the party warmly.

"Lord Rhys, it's wonderful to see you again. And Lady Eira, you have grown so! Lady Everwood."

Was it her imagination or did his voice cool a tiny bit when he spoke to Lady Everwood? Lady Everwood seemed not to notice.

"And this must be your foundling, Rhys. How do you find life up here, my dear?" Lord Hedworth continued, turning his full attention to Tamsin.

"Overwhelming and expensive," Tamsin said without thinking. She flushed.

Lord Hedworth chuckled. "I like her."

"Tamsin does that to people," Rhys said. Tamsin shifted uncomfortably. Beside her Lady Everwood was all ice and anger.

"Lord Hedworth," Eira broke in, "you recall our earlier conversation?"

"Indeed, I do." Lord Hedworth lowered his voice. "Is it true m'boy?"

"That my memories start six days ago? I am afraid it is. Tamsin here saved me, twice, and brought me back home," Rhys said.

"It wasn't quite as dramatic as he tells it," Tamsin said.

"We are trying to keep this a secret." Lady Everwood's voice was tight with impatience.

Tamsin flushed. But the room was still nearly empty, the closest couple yards away.

"Well then, quite right," Lord Hedworth said. "Come in, enjoy yourselves." He waved them off into the room.

His ballroom was enormous. It easily could hold the receiving room and dining hall for Carwyn place and still have room to rattle. The carpets had been removed, and the wooden floor had been chalked in an intricate design of filigree swirls, centred around a coat of arms. The other guests were milling about the edges of the design.

Tamsin leaned into Eira. "How do you dance on that without spoiling it?"

Eira shrugged. "You don't, but the chalk helps keep you from slipping."

It seemed like a lot of work just to toss away at the end of the day, Tamsin thought. The dances at the assembly hall back home had been far more simple affairs.

A woman in a brown silk gown and lace cap broke away from a group of older ladies and joined them.

"Lady Eira, Lord Rhys, Lady Everwood, I'm glad you could attend," she said.

Eira bobbed a short bow. "We were delighted, Lady Hedworth. David sends his regrets that he was otherwise occupied." David had refused to show himself anywhere near Tamsin in public, according to Eira. He'd decided to go to his club for the night instead.

Rhys nodded on cue and bowed gracefully over Lady Hedworth's hand. He looked distracted again.

Tamsin fidgeted behind them. Lady Everwood stepped in front of her to greet Lady Hedworth first, stepping on Tamsin's toe. *No, this wasn't awkward at all*, she thought. Tamsin ran her hands down the skirts of her borrowed dress, feeling the silk move against the kid gloves Eira had loaned her. It was only five hours till midnight. She could get through this, hopefully.

"Lady Hedworth, you recall our especial friend, Miss Tamsin Saer." Eira reached back and pulled Tamsin up next to her.

Lady Hedworth was not quite as warm as her husband, but no one else seemed to see the slight hesitation before she reached out and grasped Tamsin's hand.

"Welcome to my party, Miss Saer. As you can see, it is still early days yet. I'm afraid we keep country hours even in the city. Fashionably, I suppose we ought not to have started until ten."

"Oh, but I miss being home, this brings me back to Kirkswald and the wonderful evenings spent there," Lady Everwood interjected. "This gives us a chance to breathe before the masses arrive. Poor Lord Rhys is only just recovered from his fever."

"Well then do not dance too much my dear, you know how these exertions go to the blood. I have heard there will be a crowd though," Lady Hedworth leaned her face close to Lady Everwood. "The prince requested an invitation."

"No!" Lady Everwood lifted her fan up to hide her face. "I do not suppose you could refuse him. Still, I wonder why he would come here of all places. Lord Hedworth has not softened his rhetoric in the council recently, has he?"

"No, but you know how the family is. Still, I would think the prince would rather see the latest crop of dancers down at the Carolina, then politic here. Well, I see another group arriving. Do be careful not to over-exert yourself, Lord Rhys."

Lady Everwood looked over to Rhys, but he was still staring off into space. She pursed her lips. Underneath all that brittleness, she really did care for Rhys, Tamsin realized.

"Thank you, Lady Hedworth." Lady Everwood wrapped her hand around Rhys's arm. "I'll be sure to keep Rhys safe."

Eira took Tamsin's arm and pulled her away from Rhys and Lady Everwood.

"Lady Hedworth always has the most delicious raspberry ices." Lady Eira steered them toward the silver laden table.

Tamsin glanced back over her shoulder. Lady Everwood was bringing Rhys towards a group of older men, talking seriously in the corner.

Eira followed her glance. "They've been engaged since he left for the war. Mother keeps pushing him to set a date."

"I see."

"She... Marion isn't as cold as she seems to be. She does care for him. The family has wanted this match for years. We grew up together."

"Did he ... does he care for her?" It was an effort to keep her voice steady. She knew this already, why was it upsetting her so much. She had her sponsorship papers, that was the only thing she had wanted from Rhys. That thought was as unsettling as it was untrue.

"I think so. I'm sorry Tamsin," Eira said.

Tamsin forced a lighter expression onto her face. "Tell me about this library? It's been ages since I've read a good book."

Eira was only too happy to change the subject and regale Tamsin with details of all the latest news in poetry and novels as they finished their ices. It felt like hours later, when the musicians in the other room started playing in earnest. Eira brought them back to the ballroom.

More people had filtered in, but it hardly touched the volume the hall could hold. Tamsin wondered if the prince was here yet. The company skewed older, most at least twenty or thirty years older than Rhys by her estimate.

A man crossed over to them. He was perhaps a few years past David's age, fashionably dressed in a sombre black jacket.

"May I have the honour of this dance Lady Eira?" He bowed low over Eira's hand. Eira gave Tamsin a hesitant glance. She clearly wanted this dance.

"Go on. I'll be fine." Tamsin shooed her off with her borrowed fan.

Eira smiled at her. She took the gentleman's hand, and they took their places in the short line of couples. Rhys and Lady Everwood were already in place nearer to the musicians. Tamsin took a few steps backwards until her back was against the wall. Despite Eira's insistence on dancing slippers and pinned up trains, she hadn't come here to dance. This might be dull, but it should be safe.

One of her hands reached down to feel the linen pocket she'd tied over her borrowed petticoats. Inside were her sponsorship papers and the last of the dried blood in its glass phial to keep it safe from any prying eyes back home. She watched as Lady Everwood adjusted Rhys's cravat. Such a little gesture, but one she had made before, perhaps hundreds of times. The back of Tamsin's throat was suddenly tight and painful.

The musicians sounded a long chord and the lines bobbed reverence. At the head of the line, Lady Hedworth started to call the figures. Couples down the line began to dip and weave in a language and pattern Tamsin half remembered.

"Excuse me, Miss." the man breaking her revelry was one of the older set. He had rather unfashionable whiskers covering his collar with a considerable amount of grey mixed in with the dark. "Would you do me the honour?"

"I don't know this dance," Tamsin demurred.

"Lady Hedworth always makes the first few dances simple, if you come now, we can join in on the last set."

She glanced at the glittering procession and hesitated. "I suppose."

He smiled. "Excellent. Well since we are officially considered introduced already can you reveal your name? Or is that a mystery not to be unlocked?"

He was charming. She grinned. "Tamsin Saer. I'm a guest of the Carwyns."

"Ah, I know the Earl very well indeed. Is his lordship in attendance tonight?"

"No sir. I believe he's back at his home, his country home that is, not the city one."

"Owen never did like the season."

"Begging your pardon sir, but if we are supposed to be introduced... what is your name?"

He chuckled. "Well, I'm pleased to know my reputation hasn't run completely wild here. Lord Gavin Porter, at your service."

Tamsin stopped midstride. "Porter, the minister of finance?"

"Among my other duties." The couple above them started their turn to lead the dance and Tamsin held her hand out for the gentleman above her to turn her.

"I take it you have heard of me?" Lord Porter said when they came face to face again.

"I don't think there's anyone in Celdre who hasn't," Tamsin said. His name was stamped on every single tax notice they posted in the Narrows. It was nearly a curse.

"Good lord, I hope at least some of it is favourable."

"Your tax on windows brought much harm to the Narrows."

"Oh?" his voice betrayed a pleasant scepticism, his eyes something like anger.

"Y'see they had to board up the attics and most of the upstairs windows. It isn't healthy," she pressed on. Tamsin thought of Logan's cough. Would she ever get an opportunity like this again?

"I shall certainly keep your concerns in mind," he said, in a tone that indicated the reverse. His hand pulled back until their fingers were scarcely touching.

They finished the rest of the dance in silence. Tamsin concentrated on remembering the figures. She bobbled the steps a bit, but Lord Porter didn't seem to be paying attention to her anymore. She made her final reverence with relief.

The next song was called as a reel. Tamsin backed out of the line of dancers, then Rhys was there. He took her hand and led her back to the dance floor.

"Won't Lady Everwood mind?" she asked.

"She told me it's rude to only dance with one person. I don't wish to be rude." The corners of his lips twitched trying to keep his expression solemn.

"I'm sure this is precisely what she meant." Tamsin snorted.

The musicians played the chord, and any further retort was drowned out. This time they were at the head of the line. Tamsin set, then caught his hands in a spin. She was remembering more of the steps and Rhys was a better dancer than Lord Porter. They spun and wove through the figures, his hand resting on the small of her back, then at her shoulder. After the first repetition Tamsin felt bold enough to add a flourish on their lead. The next time around Rhys spun her double. She threw back her head and laughed, hairpins and skirts be damned. It had been years since she felt so free.

Lady Everwood looked on from further down the line with a rather stuffed expression. Tamsin stumbled. Rhys's cravat had gone askew again. They finished the rest of their turn with more decorum.

When the final chord sounded, Lady Everwood met them at the edge of the floor. "Lord Rhys, perhaps you could dance with your sister?" she said. Her tone made it not really a request.

Rhys caught her mood. "Of course." He bowed to them both and went off in search of Eira.

"Miss Saer, perhaps you could take a turn with me? It's becoming overly warm in here," Lady Everwood said. That wasn't a request either.

"If you wish," Tamsin said warily. The room was warmer than it had been, but not uncomfortably so. Still, she was curious what Lady Everwood could possibly have to say to her.

Lady Everwood took her arm and steered her out of the room. There was a balcony overlooking what was surely a magnificent garden. In the dark, Tamsin could only make out the faint glow of the now-dying lanterns. Inside, the musicians were playing a pavane. They were alone on the balcony.

"What are your intentions towards my fiancé?" Lady Everwood said, breaking the silence.

Tamsin blinked. That was blunter than she expected. Still, blunt was better than the icy politeness from before.

"I don't have any intentions towards him. I helped him when he was injured, and I'm helping him now. And he is helping me out of my situation. Nothing more." Her hand reached down to the bundle of papers under her skirts. Rhys had paid his last debt to her. Nothing was keeping her anymore.

"I will be frank with you Miss Saer. I am not fond of you."

Tamsin's shoulders tensed. "I... I am sorry to hear that, Lady Everwood." Not that her opinion held much weight with Tamsin herself right now.

"I don't imagine you hold much fondness for me either. But that does not matter much. I know you admire Lord Rhys. He's a good man. For someone such as you he must seem a fairy tale dream come to life," Lady Everwood continued.

Tamsin dropped her arm. "One such as me," she repeated.

"I understand that men do stray," Lady Everwood said, ignoring the jab she had just sent at Tamsin. "I expected that Rhys might acquire companionship, from time to time. For all the manners you manage, Miss Saer, I know you are not from the gentry, whatever virtues Rhys might see in you. And he won't marry you."

"I'm not sleeping with him," Tamsin said, with more volume than she planned for. "I never imagined he would marry me." Damn it, what did these women expect from her? Tamsin knew this was no fairy tale. She hadn't expected any happy ever after. Did she? Tamsin took in a deep breath and held it. "I haven't slept with Rhys. As addled as his head has been, that would be wrong, even if I had wanted to."

"I know he's grown attached to you during his ... indisposition. We have been betrothed for quite some time," Lady Everwood continued. "It was understood before that. My family has property near the Carwyn estate. Once we are wed, the house there will enter into his family property, with us to have the use of it, of course."

"Provided I leave him alone," Tamsin finished the thought for her. Her voice had grown flat.

"You understand me perfectly then."

"Lady Everwood, with your due respect, I am not courting Lord Rhys for money or anything else. I'm his friend. I promised him I would help him figure out what happened to him. I am not preventing him from marrying you. Send me a piece of your wedding cake after the happy day."

"He's in very capable hands, Miss Saer, he doesn't require your services anymore." Lady Everwood had abandoned any pretence of examining the gardens.

"Whose hands? I haven't seen anyone else even looking for answers for him." Tamsin snorted

"Perhaps not," Lady Everwood conceded. "But you are harming him by being here. Neither Lord Rhys nor his family can afford even a small scandal at the moment. Not until Eira is settled."

"Why not?" Harming Eira was the last thing on her mind.

Lady Everwood watched her closely. "Surely you know... Lord David's wife has run off to Orness, to enjoy the ample pleasures of Ampré. Rumour has it with a lover. It hurt Eira's prospects severely. That is why Lord Rhys opened the Celdre house and arranged for Eira to have the season here to come out."

"Eira only said his wife had left." A lover? That explained David's stuffed expression every time she wore one of his wife's dresses.

Lady Everwood sniffed. "Their marriage was a disaster from the start."

"But how am I hurting Rhys?" Tamsin asked.

"The gossip. If it got out... I am marrying him regardless, but I would hate to see many of our societal connections severed because of his taste in low company."

Tamsin's cheeks burned. "Neither of them indicated..."

Lady Everwood sighed. "Eira has a good heart. She wouldn't want to harm you. Rhys wouldn't either, but the longer you are in their presence the more scandalous the gossip will be. You may harm Eira's chances of ever getting a husband. The best thing you can do is leave him alone."

"I'll ... think about it." Tamsin hadn't realized things were that dire for Eira. But then, she was attending a party where over half the men were of the age to be her father. Was there any more she could do for Rhys? If there was a magical way out of this, she didn't know it, and everything she had found had only brought them more questions. Perhaps she wasn't the person to solve this riddle.

"Thank you, Tamsin." Lady Everwood took Tamsin's arm and steered them back toward the party.

Tamsin unpinned her train as they reentered the ballroom. No more dancing for her tonight. Rhys was dancing with an older woman, in some shade of lavender dress piled deep with lace ruffles. He looked, perhaps not relaxed, but at least at home. Tamsin slipped out of the ballroom and into the hallway.

Outside the main hall, a footman pointed the way to a lady's cloak room. This early in the evening it was deserted, with only a layer of cloaks and street shoes strewn around its edges.

Perhaps the library. It had been so long since she had seen a novel. Lord Hedworth didn't precisely seem the novel type, but perhaps Lady Hedworth had a supply. Anything would be better than staying in that ballroom, watching. She slipped out into the hallway, unnoticed this time.

Chapter Eighteen

Tamsin found the Hedworths' library at last, tucked away on the first floor. It was larger than the modest library her father had kept at home.

She found a box of candles by the door and set about lighting them and placing them in the holders strewn about the room. For a moment, Tamsin tried to calculate what the cost of all these candles would be, but the Hedworths had filled at least four rooms with candles upstairs; surely a half dozen here would not be noticed.

The candlelight revealed a wealth of books. Leather and cloth bound tomes lined the walls, until you could not even see the wallpaper behind them stacked two and three deep. A second doubled set of shelves lined the interior and framed out areas for a desk, and a few comfortable-looking reading nooks. Large windows were set above the shelves, and Tamsin realized, through some trick of architecture, the room had been set out from the house so that three of its walls could hold windows. In the daylight, it must be a paradise. She set out to find a book.

Tamsin quickly realized this library was organized in a way that was not quite haphazard, but not precisely logical either. Botany books led into a series of books on cooking, which led to books on economics and on to agriculture, biology, and mythology. She followed the winding path of subjects onward until she reached the far corner of the room. Still no novels, but the range and order of subjects was fascinating. Why were the books of bird identification shelved separately from the ones on biology? Her breath caught at the next title, wedged behind a dusty copy of hymns.

"Cruor: Methods and Means."

Cruor was an old word for blood. She pulled the book out from where it rested among the medical texts, and carefully opened it on her lap. It was a leather-bound volume the thickness of her forearm, hand-written, the pages crumbled around the edges when she touched them. How long had this lain here? Did the Hedworths realize it was about kristiri, or had it been forgotten in the purge? Were they involved with the circle in the warehouse? She took a deep breath and start to read.

The book started with the simple, familiar lessons, using a blood bond to either encourage or limit blood flow to a wound. She skimmed further as the book diverged into the minutiae of remedies, combining the blood with herbs and unfamiliar powders, and the theory of healing over a distance from specially prepared blood samples. Tamsin jumped when someone opened the door.

"Tamsin?"

Her shoulders sagged. Rhys.

"How did you find me?" she asked, setting the book to the side. Dust marked the skirt of her dress, and she was sure her train must be a crumpled wreck under her.

"One of the footmen saw you sneaking out and I saw the light in here."

"Ah," she replied. "I didn't feel like dancing anymore."

"Did Marion threaten you?" Rhys asked. He came over and sat down with her on the floor among the candles and books.

"No." It hadn't been a threat. Should she tell him she was leaving? No, it could wait, the book was more important. "I found something," she said instead. She pushed the book into his hands.

Rhys read the open page, then carefully closed the book and stared at its cover.

"I thought you said this was outlawed."

"It is," Tamsin said. "I don't know how this book made it through the purge, or if Lord Hedworth knows it is here. Rhys, you don't think he could have anything to do with the ritual and the warehouse, do you? He has the financial means."

Rhys thought on that, his fingertips tracing the letters stamped into the book cover. "Eira said he was shocked when she told him about my condition," he said at last. "I don't know that either of the Hedworths have a reputation for play acting. Did you find something in there about removing memories?"

"They don't have a reputation for… Rhys, did you remember something?" Tamsin asked.

He went still. "I… I don't know how I know that."

"Maybe this means the rest of your memories will come back soon?"

"Perhaps." Rhys didn't sound optimistic. "What else is in the book?"

"It's just about healing." Tamsin took the book back.

"Kristiri works because blood retains a record, if you will, of how we are at our healthiest. When I reach across the link, I can sometimes … remind … it isn't quite the right word, but I can make things whole. In theory," she said. "In practice I haven't been able to make that reminder work. I can use the blood to slow bleeding, or sometimes to encourage things to heal faster but my mother, she was wonderful. She could do all these things I never mastered." Thomas had had their mother's gifts as well, for all that he had never wanted to study or use it. Her heart ached anew.

"So, if a man were to lose an ear, or perhaps a hand, could it be fixed?" Rhys asked.

"Theoretically, yes. His blood would know how to heal the rest of him. But practically it does not work that way. I've stopped bleeding twice, and both times I was dizzy and faint afterwards. I can only imagine what would happen trying to do something bigger, like heal a bone or seal a larger wound. If there is a way, I have not learned it."

Rhys nodded. "If blood retains memories though? Could it fix me?" he said slowly.

"But yours doesn't. Whatever was done to you, it doesn't seem to have left those memories behind." They were so close together, bent over the book. If her weight shifted, her leg would press against his. She held herself very still. Upstairs a gong sounded. Tamsin jumped, her calf resting the length of his thigh. She pulled away.

"It's almost time for supper. That's why I came to find you." Rhys climbed to his feet.

"I don't know if I should go up. I could stay here, and you can send for me when it's all over."

"Marion did threaten you." Rhys's face darkened.

"No, she didn't," Tamsin said. "But we talked. She, she wanted to know what my intentions are with you."

"Your intentions?" His face was too blank. He was hiding something.

"She wanted to be sure I wasn't stealing her future husband," Tamsin clarified. "And she's right. I need to go, Rhys. I don't think I can help you anymore. I don't even know where to go next with it all. I'm going to go back to the Narrows and then I am going to leave Celdre."

"If that is what you want to do," Rhys said. His voice was stiff and formal. "Still, you must come eat first." He reached his hand down to help her up.

Tamsin reshelved the book and accepted his hand. She brushed at the dust on her skirt, but it had settled into the lines of the fabric in odd pale-coloured splotches. They blew out the candles and headed back to the main room to rejoin the crowd waiting to enter the dining room.

*

The prince's party arrived so late that if he were anyone but himself it would have been rude, just before the doors of the dining room were opening. Some under servant had been called into action, unprepared for the occasion, because his voice stumbled over the string of names and titles involved with the party. No one else had received such a formal entrance, and the room froze.

Tamsin saw Lady Hedworth abandon the head of the dinner line to greet them. In the now-silent ballroom, Tamsin could hear the clink of China as adjustments were rapidly made to the table. At least a dozen glittering lords and ladies followed the prince. Lady Hedworth curtsied, and a beat behind her the rest of the room did as well.

"Your Highness, our home is welcome to you," she said.

Tamsin shifted to the edge of the crowd to see a little better. So, this was Prince Nicholas. He was a broad-shouldered man, somewhere between thirty and forty. A thin line of whiskers cut a sharp line along his cheekbones extending from his sideburns. He wore a coat of deep blue velvet, heavily embroidered with gold bullion, almost a parody of the uniform of the Bluecoats. He seemed oblivious to the amount of disruption going on in the next room.

He extended a hand and raised Lady Hedworth out of her curtsy with a pressed smile. "It is my pleasure to be afforded an invitation."

Next to Tamsin, Rhys had stiffened, and one hand had curled into a white knuckled fist. In the chaos of the prince's arrival, Lady Everwood and Eira had come up alongside Rhys. Lady Everwood was whispering something in his ear. His eyes were fixed on the prince.

A footman emerged from the dining room and caught Lady Hedworth's attention. She clapped her hands sharply, bringing the murmurs of conversation to a halt. "Shall we adjourn to dinner?" she said.

Tamsin noted the servants fleeing the room ahead of the guests, one footman breaking into a full run. Lady Hedworth offered her arm to the prince, and together they led the guests to dinner.

For a moment, Tamsin contemplated just sitting in the corner. She wasn't prepared for the political minefield that a friendly conversation could bring here. Eira caught up her arm and hauled her along with the crowd.

"Come on, Tamsin. If we find seats near the foot of the table, we'll be first when they pass the sweets around."

By the time they entered the dining room there were few seats left. The table stretched the length of the room with a second, slightly less appointed, table running parallel. Eira sat Tamsin between herself and a woman with an expanse of powdered silver curls and lorgnette perched on her nose, at the second table.

Rhys and Lady Everwood had managed seats at the first table, comfortably near to Lord and Lady Hedworth and the royal party. The liveried footmen began distributing the dishes and Tamsin was occupied trying to procure food. The servers didn't stop for long, merely thrusting the dish directly between the diners until the platter was emptied. The sweets and the savoury dishes were handed out haphazardly so that Tamsin's plate soon contained equal measure of puddings, jellies, and duck and very little of anything else.

"How do you manage to actually eat?" Tamsin asked Eira. "The food goes by so fast!"

Eira shrugged. "Well, no one really comes here just to eat. Besides, it is hard to dance if you indulge too much. Cook always has something waiting for me in my room when I get home."

The number of guests in the dining room quickly overheated it, and the combined smells of food and perfumes mingled into a singularly unappetizing miasma. The cacophony of voices was making her head ache. Tamsin pushed the duck around her plate without tasting it. Surely, they wouldn't dance too much longer after dinner?

Some resonance of the prince's voice managed to cut through din at the head table. Tamsin's head snapped up listening.

"I hear you have been unwell, Lord Rhys," Prince Nicholas said.

Tamsin stopped moving.

"I have, your highness. Although I am told I have greatly improved,"

Rhys replied. You had to look to see the signs of anger in his posture and face. Lady Everwood was an unreadable icy mask beside him.

Tamsin couldn't hear what Lady Everwood said to this, but Prince Nicholas smiled.

"That is good to hear, Lady Everwood. See that you keep him well and I hope to raise a glass at your wedding breakfast soon," Prince Nicholas said. He put a peculiar emphasis on the soon. Was everyone in uptown just waiting for Rhys to marry? Tamsin couldn't quite help the sour expression that crossed her face.

The couple across the table choose that moment to lean over. "Lady Eira, is that you?"

Lady Eira looked up from the young man on her left. Her expression never changed but her back was as stiff as a ramrod.

"Lady Warren, Lord Warren, it's good to see you again," Eira said.

"How is your brother?" Lady Warren said. Her hair was piled high on her head in a coil of thin brown braids topped with dyed plumes, and she wore a collet necklace of grape sized amethysts.

"We heard he has been seriously ill. He seems to have recovered well," Lord Warren cut in. Lord Warren was perhaps a bit younger than his wife. He had rings on half his fingers, stone set signets and one with a cabochon ruby surrounded by diamonds. Something about his face was familiar to Tamsin. Perhaps he'd been the man Eira had first danced with.

"He's quite recovered," Lady Eira said.

"Ah," Lady Warren said.

Tamsin tried to read into that "ah." Ever since she had found the book of blood healing everyone seemed suspicious.

"How are you enjoying your season?" Lady Warren asked.

"Very well, although my brothers tell me nothing really happens here until midsummer." Underneath the table, Eira had clenched her napkin into a ball.

Lord Warren laughed. "They are quite right. But I think the spring has a few delights for us."

His eyes flicked past Eira and lingered on Tamsin.

Eira flushed. "I beg your pardon, Lord Warren, Lady Warren, this is our friend ... our dear friend Miss Tamsin Saer."

Tamsin nodded and attempted a smile.

Lady Warren frowned. "There was a man near Woburn by the name of Saer. I commissioned a rather splendid writing desk from him last year. Are you some relation?"

Tamsin blinked. "I ... no," she lied. Her father was alive? Everything thudded to a stop. It felt like her heart was drowning out the conversation. Alive. And he hadn't come for her. The conversation moved on without her once it was clear she wasn't going to say more, then they were clearing the plates and everyone else rose to go back to the ballroom.

"Tamsin, are you well?" Eira asked.

"I ... fine," Tamsin said. Her father was alive. And he had not come for her. Rage burned away any hope she'd kept. She stood up too fast and stumbled. Eira caught her elbow.

When no one had come for her, she assumed he'd been shot, or hanged or something. But he was alive. Her stomach twisted. Had he been the one to call the guard on her mother? Did she want to find out? He was alive, and she was still alone.

"Dinner is over, we've fulfilled our social obligations. Stay here, I'll get Rhys and Mrs. Farrow, and we can go home," Eira said.

*

It was well past the midnight bells by the time everyone was found, wraps were located, and the carriage could be brought back around. Eira chattered about the dancing on the way home, but Tamsin couldn't focus. Every once in a while, she stole a glance at Rhys in the lantern light. The carriage's sway made his face half sinister in the shadows. It was the face of a stranger. It was past time to go home.

"Penny?" Rhys' words broke through her fog.

"Pardon?" Tamsin said.

"Penny for your thoughts."

"They ain't worth that," she said.

"Ah..." He left her alone for the rest of the trip.

*

The Carwyn house was still alight when they pulled up the gravel drive.

"That's odd," Eira said. "David usually stays the night at the club when he goes out, why are all the drawing room's windows lit?"

The doors opened promptly when the carriage stopped. Grant came out and held the carriage door open himself. Tamsin's unease rose. He locked the front door behind them with an ominous thunk and pocketed the key.

"Your brother asked to see you in the drawing room before you retire, Lord Rhys," Grant said, once they had handed him their cloaks and coats.

"Thank you, Grant."

Eira hesitated at the foot of the stairs. "Do you want me to go in with you?"

"No." Rhys looked at the drawing room doors and back to Eira. "You go up to bed."

Eira gave him a sleepy puzzled look. "All right. Good night to you both. I'll see you at breakfast." She ascended the staircase. Tamsin watched her go. None of this felt right. But she shared Rhys's desire to keep Eira out of any more conflicts.

David was not alone in the drawing room, three other men were with him, two wearing the royal blue of the city guard. Tamsin stumbled to a halt. Her heart raced. How had David known...? She should have left at the party. Rhys placed a gentle hand on her shoulder.

"Good evening, David, who is your company?" Rhys asked.

The man not in uniform stepped forward. "Lord Rhys, I need you to come with me."

"Where are you taking him?"

"To the Godsmark hospital," David said. "He requires a higher level of care then I can provide him here."

"No!" The Godsmark was a literal hell, the sick piled onto each other like kindling. The odds of Rhys emerging unscathed were slim.

"I don't wish to leave my home," Rhys said calmly.

David pursed his lips. "Mother and father both agree this is what is best, Rhys."

Tamsin edged closer to the door, tugging on Rhys's coat.

"You don't have the authority to send me there," Rhys said.

"There'd have to be a judge's order," Tamsin said uneasily. Rhys wasn't retreating. They didn't have the advantage in this room. She wanted more space.

"Ah and you Miss Tamsin are under arrest."

The blood drained from her face.

"On what charge?" Rhys planted his feet in front of her.

"Theft. Fraud," David said. "It remains to be seen how complicit she is in your crimes."

The Bluecoats shifted towards her as David spoke.

"Rhys hasn't committed any crimes." That she knew of. This wasn't the moment to spell that out for them though.

"He's been passing state secrets to Orness for the better part of a year," David said rubbing his palms on his thighs. Under the hostile exterior he was projecting, David was frightened.

Rhys considered this new facet of his personality and discarded it. "You are mistaken."

"Enough, just go with them. I'm trying to keep you safe little brother." This Tamsin believed. They must want Rhys alive, because neither of the Bluecoats had drawn their pistols. One guard pulled out a set of manacles. The links jangled, harmonically familiar. No. She couldn't let this happen to her again. The second guard started to walk towards her. She shifted her weight up on the balls of her feet. In front of her, Rhys's shoulders tensed. He was going to fight too.

The guardsman reached around Rhys to grab her forearm and she ducked backwards, out of the way. The ballgown's skirts hampered her movement a little but she was still more agile than a Bluecoat. She upended a white wooden end table between them.

In front of her, Rhys had exploded into action. The other Bluecoat was sprawled on his rear in the middle of what had been a delicate white chair. Shards of porcelain crunched under foot as Rhys stood back. He'd ducked into a boxer's crouch.

"You are only making this worse for yourself," David said. He advanced on Rhys. The guard chasing Tamsin stopped and started towards Rhys. He'd clearly appraised Rhys as the bigger threat.

Tamsin moved to help Rhys. Someone tackled her from behind. David. He had his arms locked around her waist, pressing her arms to her sides. She twisted and slammed her heel into his instep. He let go and she kicked his kneecap, sending him sprawling. He crawled away, wary now and she tossed her train over her arm.

Rhys had knocked one of the guards down flat, and he was bleeding from his head and his nose. Three against two now.

Rhys was grappling with the man in the suit. The other guard was trying to get to a better angle to assist his leader. Tamsin scooped up a cut-glass candy dish and brought it down on the guard's neck. He spun. David had reached the bell pull and yanked on it screaming.

The guard made a lunge and Tamsin stepped back. That was a tactical mistake. One of the chairs was behind her and she flailed backwards tipping the chair over with her in it. The guard knelt on her chest and pinned her arms.

There was a loud crash from her left. She kicked the guard's ribs.

Then one of the spindle chairs clocked the guard upside the head. He went down.

Rhys was rather the worse for wear in his exertions. The sleeves of his jacket were split at the shoulder seams and Rhys's lip was beginning to swell. He offered her a hand up. The man in the suit was also sprawled on the ground.

In the corner, David was backing away from both of them, abject fear spread all over his face.

Rhys glanced at him then turned his back on his brother. "We need to go," he said.

Someone was pounding at the door and trying to unlock it. Tamsin looked at the window. Rhys followed her glance and nodded. He shattered the panes with the remains of the chair and they both climbed out and into the night.

Chapter Nineteen

Glass crunched along with the gravel underfoot as they ran. Tamsin bundled the skirts of her borrowed dress up around her knees and concentrated on not turning her ankles. Dancing slippers were not designed for rough ground. Rhys seized her hand and pulled her toward the main road with him.

She was expecting the streets to be deserted at the late hour, but this seemed to be the time to return home, for a steady stream of coaches passed them as they ran. A few called out rude comments, their occupants clearly having hit the claret hard wherever they had come from. They kept running.

Rhys finally stopped when they were blocks away. His breathing was only slightly heavier than normal.

"All right, where are we?" he said.

"Didn't you have an idea where you were going?" Tamsin gasped. Her chest still felt tight.

"Away. Direction seemed mostly irrelevant, after all, if I didn't know where I was going there isn't any way anyone could predict it."

Tamsin shook her head and scanned the area. The houses were closer together here and, at the corner, the street even dared to produce a dress shop. They must be getting closer to the Merchants' Ring.

"I don't know this street, but if we follow it, it should lead to a bigger one, and that should take us to the gate." She smoothed her skirts back down to a respectable elevation. "Take my arm, and if anyone asks, pretend you're drunk. Do you have any money?"

Rhys checked his pockets. "I've got half a crown left."

"Left?" Tamsin asked.

"Marion told me to tip, three crowns to the cloakman, four to each footman, two to..."

"Laws, that's a lot of coin. I've got nothing on me. If we get to Midtown, I have a friend who might help us." She looked down the crowded street.

Rhys offered her his arm, and together they lurched down the street with Rhys whistling, surprisingly on key.

"What's that song?" Tamsin asked. Anything to distract her from her feet. Her left slipper's sole was beginning to peel away and flapped with every step. If they ran again, she'd have to ditch them and go barefoot.

"I don't know ... there are words to it. I almost remember it." Rhys opened his mouth and paused. "No, they're gone."

The expression on his face was familiar to her now, unsettled, frustrated, and sad.

"Rhys, your memories are going to come back," Tamsin said, with a sincerity she didn't feel. She shivered. The only part of her that felt warm was where her arm was wrapped around his. Rhys shifted out of her grip and draped his arm over her shoulders, tucking her in close to his body. His other hand chaffed her bare arms.

"We need to get you someplace out of the wind," he said. "After that, I think it's a little more pressing to find out why David is convinced I'm a traitor."

"Rhys..." Tamsin hesitated. She didn't want to believe Rhys could be guilty of something like this. Still, she had to ask. "Is it possible? We know you went to the warehouse."

"I don't know. It's still all a blank." He stopped walking. "Everything is blank, if I could remember, I could tell you, but there is just nothing!" His frustration was palpable. Tamsin backed up a step.

"I'm sorry," he said. "This isn't your fault, and you shouldn't have to bear my temper."

Tamsin was silent. If he was a traitor to the king, did she care? It wasn't like the crown had brought anything but misery to her. "I don't think you are the kind of person who would do anything to hurt people," she said at last.

"I never meant for you to get caught up in all of this. If you want to walk away from me now, I'd understand."

"I don't want to walk away from you, Rhys. But I can't to go back to the gaol either." They'd dunked her over and over in water, until her lungs had burned, trying to get a confession. It had taken her months after her release to shed the cough. She shivered again.

Rhys tucked her back under his arm. "I understand. I'm sorry I ever got you involved with this. I'll find a way to make it right."

"I think finding a way to stay alive is a better goal for the moment." Tamsin spotted an empty hackney up ahead. She wormed away from Rhys's grip and sprinted towards it waving her arms. They had to get off the streets. The Bluecoats would have men out searching for them soon.

The driver leaned down, "You in some spot of trouble miss?" He peered suspiciously at Rhys.

"We're late, very." Tamsin pulled at the door latch. "Half a crown if you can get us to the theatre district."

She felt him weighing their worth. Neither of their evening attire had made it through the scuffle intact, but she still had pearls in her hair. He hesitated.

Rhys pulled out the crown and waved it.

The driver licked his lips and gathered up the reins.

"Where are we going?" Rhys asked after she'd given the driver his directions.

"The Emirya theater. My friend can help us. I may be washing the Emirya's laundry free for a year to pay her back, but she won't turn us away." Tamsin hoped.

"And then what?"

"Home, at least for a little bit. We can plan the rest from there tomorrow."

Their driver was motivated, probably by the thought of getting home as much as their half crown. He brought them to the corner just past the Emirya faster than she expected. Rhys had the door open before the horses were fully stopped. They leapt out and Rhys dropped the coin into the driver's hand with a mumbled thanks.

The Emirya was just starting to dim the gas lights outside its facade. Tamsin hauled Rhys around to the back entrance and pounded on the door.

After a long wait the back door finally opened a crack.

"The actresses 'ave all gone home," someone barked from inside.

"I need to see Elspeth, right away," Tamsin said. "I work for her."

The man grunted. "Wait here, I'll see if she's about." The door slammed shut and Tamsin could hear the bolt being drawn.

She jigged up and down on her tattered slipper toes, trying to keep the cold at bay.

"Would she still be here at this late an hour?" Rhys asked.

"Elspeth has to check over every single thing the actors wore on stage, and most of the actresses like to swan about in their costumes to meet the patrons after the show, because Elspeth's work is nicer than a court tailor. She's always here late and early."

Rhys had his own nervous tells she realized. His eyes kept moving up and down the alley, tracking for movement as they waited, despite the quietness of the street. Leftover reactions from battle perhaps?

After a long few minutes Tamsin could hear the bolt being pulled back again. The door opened and Elspeth leaned her head out. In the dim light, she looked wrung out.

"Tamsin?" she asked. Her eyes settled on Rhys. "And your gentleman friend... What is wrong?"

"That is a long story, but I can explain inside. Are you interested in buying some clothing?" Tamsin said.

Elspeth sighed. "Come on in."

*

A short while later, all three of them were ensconced in Elspeth's sewing room, knees touching the tiny table she hauled out with tea.

"...So, we need new clothing, something that will let us move around in the Narrows without suspicion," Tamsin finished.

Elspeth's eyes flicked over to Rhys. "May I ask, why are you going back? My dear you've been trying to find a way out of the Narrows ever since you came here."

Tamsin sighed. "It's complicated. The less you know the better."

"Eloping doesn't seem so complicated to me," Elspeth said.

"I'm not eloping with Tamsin." Rhys frowned. "At least not if I understand that word right."

"It's politics Elspeth, and a heap of trouble if we're caught. Can you help us? Quietly?"

Elspeth sighed. "I think I might have something. I don't suppose you have the coin to cover it?"

Tamsin tightened her lips. "I have this dress. It's damaged, but it's silk. And Rhys's coat and things. They are all quality materials. Would that be enough to cover some rougher clothing?"

It should be. New, the dress had to have cost at least ten sovereigns and Bernard would charge at least a sovereign for it in his shop. Not that it would sell there. Elspeth closed her eyes making her own calculations.

"I'll find you something," she said. "Stay here." She pushed her way past them and out into the theatre.

"This is the woman whose shirts you ruined?" Rhys asked.

"Yes. She's a good friend. I owe her a lot."

Rhys nodded. He started to sort through his pockets, pulling out his watch and snuff box. Tamsin reached out and touched the watch.

"This feels familiar."

Rhys chuckled. "It's the first thing in days that feels familiar to me." He pushed the pile over to Tamsin and she added it all to her linen pocket.

Tamsin sat back against the worktable. "I don't know. It feels like no matter what I do, everything about this seems to shift and fall apart the minute we get anywhere with your memories." She reached up and rubbed her face. Her jaw was tender. She must have bruised it in the fight.

"I feel like we've learned a little."

"I don't know. We just— we'll get the clothing," she said, face buried in her hands. "Then we'll go back to Baker's. It should be safe, at least for a little while."

His hand reached out and rested on her shoulder. "I have complete faith in you."

Tamsin grimaced. She certainly didn't have faith in herself right now. There was no master plan after the Narrows. Unless. Perhaps Lacey could get her some more information, or…

"If Elspeth can give us the loan of a pen and paper, perhaps we can send a letter to your sister?" Tamsin said. "Maybe she can find out more about the charges David was talking about?"

"David might read her mail."

Tamsin's lips pressed tight again. "It's a possibility. Maybe we could send it to…" her mind searched for an answer. "Maybe to Kate, but she doesn't read… but she might ask Eira for help. We could make some sort of code or…" She swallowed. It wasn't going to work. And that led to the conversation she did not want to have right now. Still, it had to be done. "Rhys, about David…"

His jaw set. "I know."

"Would he have the funds to hunt for you in the Narrows?"

"I don't think so. Maybe the better question is why would he be involved?" Rhys said.

"He's the heir to a large estate and a title. Do you have something he wants or that might threaten him?" Had David really lost that much money at the gaming tables?

Rhys hesitated. "I went through the pile of gambling notes after you left. Some of them were secondary notes, it looks like I was buying up some of David's debts before I lost my memory."

"So, he owed you money? That can make people do horrible things," Tamsin said. "But accusing you of treason? Doesn't the crown seize properties when treason is involved? That wouldn't benefit him."

Rhys face creased in thought. "Could he just hate me?"

Tamsin shifted closer to him on the seat. "I—I don't know. I felt like he was protecting you back there. In a weird way. He seemed scared you would be hurt."

They both fell silent then until Elspeth came back with their new clothing.

Elspeth shooed Rhys outside her workroom to change and helped Tamsin out of the layers of ball gown, tutting and shaking her head at every pulled thread and tear.

"It might do from a distance," Elspeth said, holding it at arm's length. "Or I can pull it apart and make it over with a smaller skirt to cover the tears. The colour is lovely, although green onstage is unlucky."

"I appreciate this, Elspeth."

"Well, if you don't mind a little advice from an old friend, be careful. There is something a little odd about that man, and you and him leaving for the Narrows? Why would a kingsringer like that need to take a nice girl down to the Narrows?"

"I appreciate your concern," Tamsin said, trying to be diplomatic. "It's going to be all right though." *I hope.*

Elspeth sniffed, but she let the subject drop.

The dress Elspeth provided was a stamped cotton in a green leaf pattern. It hung a little loose on her, but that was another layer of disguise.

After a few moments, Rhys knocked on the door. When Elspeth opened it, he handed her a neatly folded pile of his clothing. He now wore a rough woollen jacket in brown and a pair of canvas sailor trews. His boots were the lone wrong note to the ensemble.

"Shoes!" Tamsin looked down at the tattered slippers she had worn.

Going barefoot through the streets wasn't something she relished.

Elspeth rolled her eyes. "Tam, when I do something, I don't stop halfway." She pulled a pair of worn leather boots from under a shelf. "If your gentleman friend would let his pant legs hang over his boots and tromp through a bit more muck, it should keep most people from noticing. These should fit you. I've been saving them for you."

Tamsin hugged her impulsively. "Thank you, Elspeth. I promise; I'll keep myself safe!"

Elspeth looked surprised but she settled into the embrace. "Well, see that you do. And I'll hold your young man to helping with that."

"Yes ma'am," Rhys said.

It took a little while longer to take Tamsin's hair down from the tightly curled mass Kate had arranged earlier, and to wash the traces of powders and paints away. Light was just starting to touch the sky when they left the theatre for the gate.

"Just let me do the talking," Tamsin said. The guards must have circulated their descriptions around by now. Elspeth had provided a scarf for Tamsin's hair, a wool cap for Rhys, and some paint to turn the stubble on his face darker and more prominent. She hoped it would be enough. David and the guards had to think they would try to leave the city, and the only way out from the Narrows was the docks. They were at the far gate. Tamsin felt like a harp string drawn too sharp.

The guards were more alert as they walked up to the line of mostly empty wagons and the occasional Riverman returning to the docks.

"What's your purpose?" The first guard asked. He had a paper he kept glancing down at as people entered.

"We've come to pick up charity loaves," Tamsin said. "The Goddess point temple plans to distribute them this morning." She wound her arm around Rhys's and tried to look pious.

The man consulted his paper again.

"Have you been up to the King's Ring this morning?" he said uncertainly.

"Laws no," Tamsin lied. "That's a hike. We live near the Butcher's on Paperwright Lane."

He glanced back at the paper, then waved them through.

Tamsin led them through the streets back to her home. The bar was still locking her door, so she brought them in through the bake shop. Baker looked the pair over.

"I was wondering what you were about these last few days, Miss

Tam." The smell of yeast and wood smoke made her stomach growl. "Is this Lacey's ... cousin?" Baker asked.

Tamsin had forgotten that lie. "Yes, and he won't be trouble." Damn. Perhaps it would have been better for Rhys to wait outside. She was so exhausted it was hard to think straight. "He just needs a place to stay for the night ... well, day now."

Baker pounded the loaf he was working deep into the wooden counter. "You best see he's not trouble."

"Has anyone come around since I was gone?" Tamsin asked.

"Lacey came by once, that's it."

Tamsin's shoulders relaxed a little. That Marcus cove and his men probably weren't still looking for Rhys. That made some sense, if they were just supposed to keep him from getting home. They'd failed at that, she thought with a touch of pride. Still, she'd best find Frank and Lacey soon.

"Thanks for keeping my things safe," Tamsin said. Baker gave her a tiny nod and waved them through the inside door.

The mice had been at the food she'd left behind. Tamsin poked a little wistfully at the half-eaten apple sitting on her shelf. Still, nothing else had been disturbed. She reached up and pulled out her stock of coins, six copper pennies, and now Rhys's silver crowns. It was more money they she'd had in months. It didn't feel like enough.

"We'll need to make some arrangements in the morning. Or, whatever time it is after we've had some sleep." Tamsin yawned. The energy that had kept her moving forward had dropped out somewhere after they'd passed into the Narrows. Her legs felt like dead weight.

"I'll take the floor again," Rhys offered. Tamsin nodded and sat down on the bed. They both settled in, and for a few moments the only sounds were shuffling cloth and Baker still pounding at the dough. Tamsin closed her eyes.

*

The sound of the noon bells woke her a few hours later. Tamsin sat up. She knew how to bring back Rhys's memories.

Capter Twenty

The streets of the Narrows had a sullen drone today and threatened rain. The riot had not been forgotten and Bluecoats were thick along the main roads and near the gates. Tamsin stuck to the back ways.

What would Rhys say when he woke up and found her note? He'd stirred a little when she'd left, but quieted when she murmured something about being right back. He'd understand, well no. He would be furious. But he would be in the way. He didn't know these streets, or how to blend into a crowd, or where the safe spots were, and if anyone was still out there hunting for him, she could be walking him into a trap. Going alone to the likely deserted warehouse was the safest way. Not that Captain Rhys would agree. But if this was a fool's quest, well, best not to get his hopes up. And she disliked the idea of Rhys anywhere near that ritual circle again.

Tamsin checked her pocket again: her tiny clasp knife, a page of the ledger to use as hopper, and the bottle with the dregs of Rhys's dried blood along with her sponsorship papers were still there. Just like the last time she had checked.

If they, whoever they were, had not cleaned the blood off the ritual circle, this would work. It all came back to his blood. As much old blood as she could scavenge. And why clean it away now? No one knew she was a mage. If Lacey's trick with the wax had held, the warehouse would look secure. Tamsin could be in and home in less than an hour with as much of the ritual blood scrapings as she could pry off the floor. The more the better. She wasn't sure how much she would need to siphon the memories back into Rhys's head. But in this case, there was no such thing as too much. Her thoughts were racing.

If it worked. None of this was certain. But the book of magic at Hord Hedworth's had pulled the pieces together for her. Rhys had had memories once, and this was the spot where his memories had been stripped. His blood now, did not contain those memories, but the blood before that, the blood he'd shed in that ritual circle, old blood, that should contain everything. It would explain the flashes of memory he'd shown last night. The half-remembered song, the dislike of the prince, the ability to dance. They could no longer wait for things to just come back. If Rhys was going to prove his innocence, he needed those memories. Prove his innocence and pay her handsomely so she could leave Celdre. Her motives were completely self-serving here, she lied to herself.

By the time Tamsin reached the doors of the warehouse she was humming with nerves. She walked past the door twice, straining her ears to see if there was any activity within. It seemed quiet.

The street outside the warehouse was deserted, and on her third circuit of the block she tested the lock. Lacey's wax was still there. With a sharp tug the lock hasp opened. Tamsin tucked the whole lock into her skirt. There was no way she could replace it in the chain without help. She would just have to work fast. She left the doors cracked a little, so a stripe of sunlight illuminated the ritual area and bent down to her work.

The blood made a rusty powder over her hands as she carefully scraped it away from the dark stains spread through the ritual circle and gathered it into her bottle. Halfway around the circle and her knees and back ached. The small bottle was about halfway full.

From the street, she heard hoof beats and cart wheels again. Her hands moved faster scooping up the blood she had already scraped and dumping it inside. She scrambled up to her feet, sealing the bottle, and slipped it in her pocket.

"The door is open, sir." It was that same half-familiar voice from the last time she had been there. That meant there were two people, at least. Tamsin's eyes darted back and forth. There wasn't any place to go. Her hiding spot from before was across the room, but this time they knew someone was there. It was only ignorance and base luck that had saved her before.

Could she bluff? If she seemed like a common thief, maybe they would just let her go with just a beating. Bruises would heal. Whatever was going on here wasn't the sort of thing you could call the Bluecoats for help. She had to play this right and hope she could get past whoever was out there and escape.

She let her shoulders fall into a tense but defeated pose. Her hands she scrubbed clean along the skirts. After a night of sleeping in it her dress still seemed too fine for a grubbing street thief, but perhaps they wouldn't notice. Oh gods, just let her luck hold and let them be foolish.

The doors scraped open, and two figures were framed in the light. Tamsin stepped back involuntarily. Maybe she could break past them once they left the doorway. One of the figures advanced, and his features solidified into Marcus, the man in the grey gloves. Those gloves were gone, and he held a coachman's whip instead.

Tamsin's eyes narrowed. He recognized her. The lies she had prepared dropped away. She'd have to run.

He didn't bother saying anything, he just kept advancing. Tamsin's feet caught up with her brain and she darted to the left around him. He moved with her, dropping the whip. Speed was the only way she was going to get out of this. If she could beat him to the door maybe, maybe she could get past the man standing there. Every breath seared her lungs.

"The guards are already on their way here!" she called out. She careened off the bank of desks and swung a wide arc around the doors.

The man at the doorway snorted. "I very much doubt anyone down here would call them," he said. His voice was familiar as well, with a more urbane accent then Marcus.

Marcus cut through her feint and stood between her and the doorway. Tamsin darted right instead. She just needed a moment, if he fell, or slowed. The man at the door was slighter. She could knock him down. If Marcus got his hands on her she'd be done. Marcus stumbled as she cut the turn quickly, his hands just missing her skirts.

The other man was still at the doorway and now she could see him casually pointing a pistol at her belly. Her heart pounded and each breath was a knife sharp pain in her side. She stumbled and Marcus clamped one hand down onto her arm and spun her into the bank of desks again.

Her head hit the edge. She stumbled again, blinking away a sudden searing light from behind her eyes.

She managed another few steps away, but capture was a forgone conclusion. Marcus had some sort of cloth in his hand. This time when he caught her, he shoved it over her face and the warehouse spun. Tamsin raked at his arm with her nails, but it felt as if her hands were wrapped in cotton. She sagged to her knees. He bent over her keeping the sickly-sweet smelling cloth over her face. Her head hit the stone floor.

Chapter Twenty One

Everything was dark. Tamsin could hear a pattering of rain hitting the roof above her. Something was leaking, and a trickle of icy water had wormed its way to where she lay and soaked the front of her dress. Stone floor. She inhaled the same stale wood-smoke smell. She was still in the warehouse. Besides the rain, it was silent.

Tamsin was painfully aware of how cold she was. The stone leached her body heat away, and she was shivering. Her arms were twisted behind her unnaturally high, and her wrists and hands had pins and needles tingling along their length. They'd tied her up. She took a deep breath. Stay calm.

She tried to move her feet under her. Someone had bound her ankles as well. It took a moment, but she managed to roll to her side and out of the water's path.

Right. The next thing was getting out of these ropes and out of here. Visions of her straw-lined cell from the gaol poked at the edge of her thoughts. No. If she let that in, she'd be gibbering. Tears already made hot tracks down her face. She could find a way out of this. It wasn't Kingsgate. Not yet at least.

Scream for help? It was possible whoever had drugged her had not presumed she'd wake so soon and was still away. There was no light from the air vents above her, so she'd been unconscious for a few hours. Small logical thoughts. That was good. It kept her panic away.

She twisted her wrists. Get free. If that failed, then she could try riskier options. After a few minutes of twisting, Tamsin realized the knots weren't going to give. Her wrists were raw, but she could feel her fingers a little again.

Somewhere in the darkness a door opened. The exit was to her left then. She had to be near the ritual circle, and that was another chilling thought. She was out of options. Tamsin screamed.

"Damn it, Marcus. Stop her," someone said.

Tamsin screamed louder.

There were four people coming inside. The tallest one carried a lantern, but the light was low enough she couldn't make out his face.

The man coming towards her though, she could see him all too well. Marcus, the man from the Barrel, and the knife fight that had marked her arm. He was in disguise again, a low wool labourer's cap pulled tight to his ears. Hired muscle, she decided.

She stopped screaming before he reached her. Deep breath, she told herself. He's a loaded cannon. Don't make the other man set him off.

Marcus reached down and pulled her up to balance on her numb, bound feet. His grip made a new row of bruises along her upper arm. Tamsin kept her face still. Don't let him see the pain. Gaol's lessons came rushing back at her.

There was an art to keeping your face blank. You had to take care that you didn't clench your jaw, that's where most people go wrong. And that clenched jaw would tell them so much.

The tall man handed the lantern off to his companion. They were both well dressed, boots polished to a mirror gleam, and dark wool coats with multiple capes drooping from their shoulders.

The man holding the lantern moved it expertly. Tamsin got an impression of light hair and that was it. The tall man didn't seem to feel the same need to hide.

"So, this is our thief?" he said. He motioned and the lantern man moved away and brought back the desk chair. His hands were studded with rings. The tall man sat in it, and for the first-time Tamsin could see his face. It was angular, razor-sharp cheek bones and a squared jaw without any softness. Prince Nicholas.

"Well?" Nicholas demanded. "No defence? No mewling tale of starvation?"

Tamsin just waited. Her usual glib lies weren't coming to mind. If they thought she were a thief they'd have slit her throat already. *This man wants something from you*, she thought.

The silence stretched out between them for a dozen breaths.

"You're right, David, she is clever," Nicholas said.

David... David Carwyn? Tamsin peered into the gloom. The man by the door could be him. The build was right. But he kept silent and out of the lantern light. Damn it.

"I know that you stole papers from me three days ago, Miss Saer," Nicholas said.

"You seem to mistrust your brother quite a bit, Lord David," she guessed, ignoring the prince. She needed to strike out where she could, or they'd end up with too many advantages over her. They had so many already.

David stepped into the lantern light.

"Damn you Nicholas, can't you handle anything discreetly?"

Nicholas only smiled.

"Get down from your high horse, Carwyn," the fourth man said. "If you hadn't been so squeamish we wouldn't be in this situation. You should have let Nicholas kill Rhys."

David flinched.

"Just because some people are comfortable with fratricide..." he muttered.

"What was that Carwyn?" The man with the rings moved forward and his rings caught the light. A cabochon ruby surrounded by diamonds, Lord Warren? What in the hell had Rhys gotten himself into?

David ignored Lord Warren. "Where is Rhys?" he demanded.

"I... I don't know," Tamsin tried to sham a quiver in her voice. Marcus crushed her arm harder, and she yelped involuntarily.

"You left with him. He's clung to you like a tick to a bitch, ever since he showed back up again. So, where is he?" David raked his hand through his damp hair, setting it on end. He was nervous, she realized. Perhaps he was less invested in whatever conspiracy the others had set up. She remembered the thousands of sovereigns of debt Rhys had been buying up.

What lie would they believe? She closed her eyes.

"He left." She hung her head down and tried to bring a flush to her cheeks. "He fucked me, and when I woke up this morning he was gone. He took all the money I had saved too."

David's eyes narrowed as he considered her lie.

"He's still in the city," Nicholas said. "The guards have been looking for him all night. You too for that matter. But you could hide an army down here." His lips made a peculiar smile.

David didn't seem to appreciate his humour.

"I think she's lying," David said.

"Of course, she's lying. She's a witch child. Marcus, fetch the bucket," Nicholas ordered.

Marcus released her arm and she fell heavily back down to the ground. Her new dress was a little too large. It slid off her shoulder.

"You *are* the little viper from two years back!" Nicholas reached out and pulled the dress fabric away showing the ridged scar tissue on her shoulder. His tone was abnormally calm. "I heard your mother made a good show when I hung her. They buried the pieces at a crossroads with a stake through her heart. All except the head. That I had thrown into the sea. I miss those little perks of being Regent. Reggie's recovery was… unexpected."

Tamsin pushed herself up. Her legs were a little less dead weight after being upright. She managed to get to her knees. It wasn't enough. She wanted to launch herself across the room and claw that smirk off his face. Draw his blood and let him see what a Cyprycian witch could really do. Calm. She had to stay calm.

Marcus dropped a wooden tub on the ground in front of her. Exactly like her wash tub. It was half full already, and he brought over another few buckets to slop the water nearly to the top.

"I had the water turned back on special for this. I'm afraid Marcus doesn't have the same experience as the Kingsgate gaolers, but we'll just have to work with it," Nicholas said.

Her mind stopped. Not again. She didn't recall moving but she'd managed to push herself a few feet back from the circle of lantern light before Marcus came abreast of her.

Marcus circumvented her flailing. He caught her just under the arms and pulled her back towards the tub. She could see a faint reflection of her face, then he shoved it under the water.

—

Her nose and eyes burned. She'd lost track of how many times he'd pushed her face under the water. After a while her legs and cheeks went numb, and the world was under a watery haze.

"How much does Rhys know?" Nicolas repeated.

She sputtered. "Nothing. Neither of us know anything." It was true. A handful of invoices and a prince of the realm, smuggled guns, Rhys's memories—there were still so many possibilities.

David moved into her line of vision. "Miss Saer, my brother is a traitor to the realm. He's stolen specific documents trying to incite a revolt against the king. He's been lying to you this whole time to enlist your help."

She blinked her eyes stupidly trying to process that information through the oxygen deprivation. Could it be true? No. Rhys wasn't shamming his memory loss. He couldn't fake that over the blood bond. They still didn't realize *she* was a mage. And which one of them was the blood mage? Not David or she would have noticed at the house.

The prince nodded and Marcus grabbed the sodden knot of hair at the nape of her neck and pushed her under again.

It took longer this time for her vision to clear, and the coughing to stop.

"This isn't getting us anywhere, your highness," David said. He sounded uncomfortable. *Good*, Tamsin thought. It felt as if her brain was still underwater. Surely if Rhys was a traitor, if the king himself was searching for them both, they'd have brought her to Kingsgate instead of questioning her here. What else were they hiding? And more importantly, could she use it to get out of here?

The ropes pinning her ankles and wrists had become as waterlogged as her hair and dress. She twisted against them, and perhaps it was the way the water had numbed her limbs, but it felt as if they held a fraction more ease. If she could get a moment away, perhaps she could get loose.

"Don't lose your nerve now, Carwyn. Another week and this will be done. We just need to find your brother," Warren said.

David licked his lips. "It's just … we weren't going to hurt him. That was the point of the whole bloody ritual. If you hadn't gone back on your word…"

The prince's features screwed up in a savage grimace. "That was when you could control him. Something must have gone wrong. If your brother didn't have his memories, what is she doing here? It's a tricky piece of spell work to remove memories. Something must have gone wrong. We need him out of the picture."

"He had no knowledge of any of this when I spoke to him," David protested. "You have to let me handle this."

"I no more trust your instincts than I would a child with an open flame," Prince Nicholas replied.

Tamsin couldn't help flinching as the prince spoke. Had her actions put them in more danger? But they'd tried to kill Rhys twice already. There was clearly a separation of loyalties between the men. How could she use that?

Nicholas noticed Tamsin still kneeling above the water and nodded to Marcus. Tamsin caught in a breath before her face was forced under the water again.

She needed to pass out, she thought as her chest burned and bubbles burst around her face. Black spots danced around her vision when Marcus finally pulled her head above the water.

She kept her eyes closed and willed her body to go limp. Marcus's grip on her hair became painful. Tamsin kept her breathing even but shallow.

The rain outside had slowed to a mild patter or drops on the roof. Something scraped across the shingles above. It took all her will-power not to open her eyes. Her aborted attempt to look towards the sound was covered when Marcus shook her, one hand still firmly tangled in her hair.

"I must've held her under too long," Marcus muttered.

Prince Nicholas walked over and slapped her face. Tamsin kept her eyes closed. Behind her lids she counted the seconds until she heard him shift his weight away from her.

"Just put her over there. We can continue when she wakes up. And for gods' sake be more careful next time."

Marcus dragged her away somewhere towards the circle. She could feel the skirt of her dress catch on something in the floor and rip. Four dresses ruined in what, seven days? And how would she get the money to buy a new one now? Her brain picked the most inconsequential things to focus on. With a tiny hiccup of laughter, she realized the little things were half the reason she wasn't gibbering right now. Across the room, Marcus, David, and the prince were discussing something. Tamsin could make out a few words—water, queen, tax.

She worked her wrists against the rope. They were already raw, and warmer bits than water soaked into the fibres. Still, slowly she managed to work the ropes up to the mound of her thumb on one hand. A few more minutes.

Behind her closed eyes, she could feel someone's steps coming towards her. Her heart sank. She gave one more tug on the ropes and her wrist slipped free.

Someone placed a gentle hand on her shoulder. "Tam?"

Tamsin's eyes flew open.

"Lacey?" she whispered. "It isn't safe."

Lacey's mouth twitched up. "Of course, it isn't, you fool. That's why we came to get you," she whispered.

"We?"

Lacey had a blade out and was cutting the rope at her ankle. The three men were still deep in conversation at the other end of the warehouse. Between them and the door.

Lacey pulled Tamsin up to her feet, but Tamsin stumbled. Her feet felt like blocks of ice, shooting bolts of pain up her legs. Her calves cramped.

Lacey's lips thinned. She glanced over to the corner where a rope dangled from the ceiling. "You can't climb like this. Plan B then."

"Plan B?" Tamsin whispered.

Lacey just grinned. She put her fingers up to her lips and blew a piercing whistle.

The men turned immediately in their direction. Lacey handed Tamsin her knife and reached under her coat, pulling out a well-worn pistol.

"Lacey...?" Tamsin said.

Lacey only grinned wider.

Marcus moved in front of the prince, drawing out his own, rather better kept, pistol. David was armed as well, and Tamsin flinched back as their barrels swung in her direction.

Then the front doors exploded inward. Rhys was there, his shoulder still lowered where he had slammed through the doors. He raised a musket as he charged, sighting directly onto David.

Frank was a half-step behind him, his limp evident. His grip on his own musket was sure though, and he aimed at Marcus.

"Now dear, you know me," Lacey said. "I never do anything half-way." Her grin held an edge beneath it that belied her flippancy. "I think it's time to go now."

Rhys had moved into the room enough to herd the men back away from the doors.

The bottle! She'd had it before she'd been drugged, but she didn't feel its weight in her pocket now.

The four men seemed to be in a holding pattern. Marcus had moved the prince back, keeping his body between him and the three guns. His own pistol had settled on Rhys as the most threatening target. Warren was unarmed and was trying to crawl under the desks. David stepped away from the other men. His pistol was pointed at the floor.

"Rhys," he said. "You cannot think this will fix things."

Rhys's eyes were on the pistol Marcus held. "You hurt my friend," he said. "You hurt her, and you helped them steal something from me. I don't give a damn about fixing things now."

Tamsin cast her eyes about the room. The bottle was on a desk. She hobbled towards it. Lacey kept one hand in the small of her back, herding her towards the door.

"Lacey, I need that bottle, or else all this is for nothing," Tamsin said.

Lacey's eyes narrowed, but she nodded. The prince made a small movement towards the desk, but Frank pulled the hammer back on his musket with a snap. Warren whimpered as she got close. Lacey darted away and caught it up while Tamsin stumbled towards the doors. Her feet were waking up, and she managed the last few steps almost at a jog.

Then she was through, Lacey was beside her and Frank and Rhys backed out, muskets still at the ready. Lacey grinned again and pulled the doors shut. One was off its hinge a bit where Rhys had hit it. She slid the chain through its catches and locked it with a lock Tamsin had not seen before.

"Now let's move before they decide they can afford to shoot through walls!" Lacey said.

Rhys took the rifle from Frank and exchanged a glance with Lacey. Lacey tucked her pistol away and slid her arm under Tamsin's shoulders. "It's split time. You come with me, and we'll see the boys in a bit."

Tamsin opened her mouth, but Lacey pulled her away. Away. Away was good. The men headed off in the other direction as the first crash sounded against the warehouse doors.

Chapter Twenty Two

Tamsin's lungs were aching, and she couldn't stop coughing. Panic paced every step. No, she couldn't let it take over yet. After a while Lacey led her towards the waterfront, down an embankment, and under one of the piers. The water had made the ground soft, but only the largest waves came near their spot. Frank and Rhys were already there.

Rhys stepped forward when they appeared. He still had the musket in his hands. He stopped after that step. Tamsin twisted her hands in her skirt.

"Are you all right?" Rhys said. His voice was tight. Was he angry at her or David though?

Tamsin tried to speak and coughed instead.

Rhys pulled her into his arms. "What were you thinking?" he whispered into her hair. At his touch, some of the panic receded. Enough to breathe.

"Were you followed?" Frank broke in.

Lacey tossed her head. "Not a chance. They're probably still trying to break down the doors. That was a quality lock I wasted on those fools."

"I'm sorry," Tamsin said. Another fit of coughing wracked her shoulders. She couldn't stop shaking despite Rhys's arms around her. "I'm not hurt, really." She stepped back away from his arms. That hurt. She wrapped her own arms around herself trying to keep that warmth from leaving.

Rhys's lips compressed, but he let her lie go unchallenged.

"How did you find me?" Tamsin asked.

Lacey grinned again. "You have to blame that one," she said jerking her thumb at Rhys. "He practically beat down our door looking for you. Once he told us what your note said, we figured it out pretty quick."

Tamsin looked between them slowly. "I'm sorry, it was foolish to go alone, but that bottle—" She reached out her hand towards Lacey and Lacey handed it over. "It was worth the risk though if it can help you remember."

Rhys inhaled deeply and held the breath. "Thank you. But Tamsin, if you'd been ... harmed because of this. I wouldn't be able to forgive myself." Yes, he was mad at her, but not irrevocably.

Tamsin gave him half a smile. Surely, she could match at least a little of Lacey's bravado. "I'm not dead yet." She coughed again.

That coughing was going to need to be looked at. Horehound and honey perhaps, something to help get the water out of her lungs before it soured on her.

"Where do we go from here?" Tamsin said.

Lacey and Frank exchanged glances.

"We need to split up. We don't think our house is burned, but Tamsin, yours is. They know your name, and they will be able to find you eventually. You and Rhys can use one of our bolt holes. The woman who runs the place has hidden people before, if the money is good enough."

Tamsin's heart sank. "I don't have any money."

Rhys stepped forward. "I've got that covered."

"How?" Tamsin started to say. Another fit of coughing came over her.

"Frank pawned my watch. It's enough for a little while," Rhys said.

His watch, not the snuff box from Lady Everwood.

"And once things die down, we can get you out of the city," Lacey interrupted. "Maybe in a week."

Tamsin snorted. "Out of the city. They took my papers. I'm trapped. Again." She set her jaw tight against a fresh wave of shivers. It was cold, too cold, she told herself. Rhys shed his jacket and wrapped it around her shoulders. She flinched from his touch this time.

"We'll find a way, Tamsin. I won't leave you to hang here," Rhys said. He winced as soon as the words left his mouth.

She shivered again.

"We can't stay here," Frank said. He exchanged a look with Rhys. And what had happened while she was gone to turn them into old friends? Tamsin wondered. Things were getting detached and fuzzy. Would she ever stop shivering?

Tamsin slipped her arms into the coat sleeves. It was still warm, the sleeves hung to her fingertips. She wrapped her hands around the bottle. Through the cloudy glass, she could see a good double handful of the dried blood. Was it enough?

She offered it up in both hands to Rhys. "Here is the blood from the spell that took your memories away. Blood holds memories."

Lacey and Frank exchanged a look, and Lacey edged a little away from the bottle, like it had turned into a spider. She scrubbed her hand on the side of her trews.

Rhys looked perplexed. "You said my blood doesn't have any memories."

"Whatever they did stripped them out," Tamsin agreed. "But this is your blood from the first ritual. I think it will work."

Frank and Lacey exchanged another look.

"Carwyn, can you find your way to the room alone, or do you need one of us to guide you again?" Frank asked.

Rhys closed his eyes; his hand twitched at his side. He was mentally following a map, Tamsin realized. She hadn't realized how quickly he memorized directions.

"I can find it," Rhys said. His mouth turned up on one side. "It seems I have a good memory."

Tamsin tucked the bottle away carefully in the jacket pocket, her hand still wrapped around it.

"I'll be by tomorrow with more supplies," Lacey said.

*

Tamsin paced and coughed. The room Rhys had rented was just large enough for her to make half a dozen steps before the wall brought her up short. Pacing was better than crying, and she'd done enough of that when Rhys had left to fetch them both some food. She didn't want him to see her broken down like that. If he noticed that her eyes were red or skin flushed, he didn't mention it.

Instead, he sprawled on the floor poring over the ledger papers, again. The afternoon sun made his hair gleam like gilt. His coat was still around her shoulders as she tried to stamp the warmth back into her toes. Beneath his linen shirt, she made out the lines of his shoulder blades taunt against the fabric. It was a lovely sight, almost distracting enough. Almost. Her damp hair slapped against her cheekbones.

Rhys looked up after a minute. "What's wrong?" he asked.

"What if I get this wrong?" she said. That wasn't the whole of it, but keeping busy kept the darker things from creeping up on her. Busy was good, moving was good. She shivered again.

He set the papers aside and stood, placing his hands gently on her shoulders. Tamsin flinched. The places where Marcus had grabbed her were still sore. Rhys's hands were feather light across the bruises.

"I trust you."

"It's all very well and good for you to say that," she resumed her pacing. "But what if I remove all the memories you have right now? What if I kill you? What if you become like a child, or lose your wits or get someone else's memories? What good is there in having magic if I can't make it fix your head!" Her voice was too high. She sucked in a breath, which set off the coughing again.

"Tamsin, I trust you. You haven't led me wrong thus far. If you think this ritual will work, we do it."

Eventually she nodded.

*

They pushed all the furniture to the edges of the room. Tamsin traced a double circle carefully over the painted floorboards. Where they didn't meet flush, she broke the ends of the charred twigs she was using to fill in the cracks. It took her an hour to make both circles even and unbroken. Then she had to add the Aradwyn runes. Rhys kept her supplied with burnt twigs and otherwise stayed out of her way. She checked, then double checked, her workings. If the circle wasn't tight the magic could spill away. In Cyprycian magic she spun the energy around itself into threads. Aradwyn magic was more like controlling a flow of water, requiring barriers and gates. But Aradwyn magic was what had made this mess.

"Why are Aradwyn rituals so complicated," she grumbled.

"Well, if you get it wrong it's not like the stakes are high," Rhys said lightly. Too lightly. Under the flippancy, he was worried too.

Tamsin grunted and waggled her hand at him. "Hush you." She drew another careful rune. Her mother would be clucking her tongue at her, drawing diagrams everywhere. But this was the safest path. She hoped. It wasn't like she could go back and collect the dried blood a third time.

"Are you sure you want to do this?" Tamsin asked for the thousandth time. She sat back on her haunches. She'd tucked the torn dress up above her knees while she worked so she didn't smear the marks, warmed at last by all the work and the fire. Her hand scarcely shook as she drew.

Rhys sighed. "I know you don't want to hurt me, Tamsin. But without my memories I can't be sure if David is telling the truth or not. All I can do is guess. I can't live my whole life on a guess. I trust you." Every time he said that her stomach flopped over again.

"And if David is not lying?" she whispered.

Rhys stood up from the bed and crossed over to her. He enveloped her hands in his. "I'll have to face the consequences."

Tamsin broke away. "You see, that is why I don't think you could be a spy..." The insides of his hands were smudged with charcoal, her own hands were stained black.

"Thank you for that," Rhys said. "We'll know soon."

She took a deep breath. "I'm ready for the bottle."

In the ritual back at the warehouse they had used poppy, rosemary, and sandalwood. Rhys's coin hadn't stretched that far. Tamsin pushed aside her misgivings. She wasn't doing the same spell; everything didn't have to be exact. She hoped.

When everything was in place, she led Rhys to the centre of the circle.

"What do I have to do?" he asked.

"Stay calm, which you are doing better than I am." She scrubbed her hands down her thighs. Everything she wore was already covered in cinder and ash. "The ritual that took your memories away took a lot of your blood the first time. This one should help to heal your mind, unblock whatever it was they did. But I don't know how much blood it will take." She placed the glass bottle next to him.

"I trust you."

"Good." She placed her knife next to the bottle.

She started with an Aradwyn invocation. It was simple, too simple for this kind of spell, she fretted. Nevertheless, she could feel power start to condense around her. She took up the knife and sliced a line into the pad of her forefinger. The blood welled up fast and she dripped it carefully in between the two circles. The air became stale and still. Sweat dripped down Rhys's forehead.

She slipped the cork free from the bottle and handed Rhys the knife. His own cut to his finger was swift, and deeper than needed. Tamsin caught his blood in the bottle and slowly his dry blood absorbed the fresh. When the bottle was full Tamsin took it away. Rhys was a little pale, but he wrapped the scrap of linen she had prepared around the cut and held it tight.

She stoppered the bottle and swirled it to get all the powder absorbed. Then she dumped its contents into the cracked wash jug they'd re-purposed. The bloodbond cried out to her. This was the stage that worried her the most. If she reached across it, she could try to guide the memories back to their place. But she could also spill them out where Rhys couldn't reach them.

Still chanting she handed him the mixture of bloods thinned with water. Rhys's eyes met hers. Let it not be the last time, she prayed. Then he downed the liquids.

Air rushed into the centre of the circle blowing out the tallow lights. Rhys's face twisted and he clutched his head.

Tamsin choked between syllables of the invocation. She managed a quick gulp of air and kept going. If this was going to work, they'd know soon.

Energy flowed around her, and she tried to direct it to the channels created by the runes. Rhys was doubled over in the circle's centre now. He hadn't made a sound. The bond hovered at the edge of her consciousness and at last she surrendered to it.

Images washed over them. Horses screaming. A country garden. The woman from the drawing. A bullet struck their shoulder. Their mind rushed to make sense of them all, drowning in a glut of emotions. They couldn't breathe.

Then it stopped. Tamsin was alone kneeling just inside the circle. Rhys was face down on the floor, as still as she had ever seen him.

"Rhys!" Had she killed him? She reached over and felt for his heartbeat. It was there, quick, as if he'd been running. Tamsin rolled him over to his back, heedless of her runes and lines now. He was breathing, short and shallow. His eyes were moving around quickly underneath his eyelids, but he didn't respond to her voice.

She managed to get him laid out flat, his coat balled up under his head. After that all she could do was wait. She paced around the room, smearing the marks further. Every few moments she went back to Rhys and checked. His heart still beat.

After a few more laps she lay out next to him on the floor, and leaned her head against his chest. The ritual had taken its toll on her as well, and between the events of the last few days, even her nerves couldn't keep her eyes open. Still listening to his heartbeat, she fell asleep.

*

It was full dark when she woke. She blinked in the darkness trying to remember what had woken her. Then Rhys shifted under her, and he stroked her hair. She caught her breath. He lived.

"How do you feel?" she whispered. Her voice was hoarse.

"My head hurts." He shifted his weight beneath her. "My back isn't happy with me either," he said wryly.

"I thought about moving you, but I was afraid I'd drop you and addle your pate again." She reached up and touched his cheek. The darkness gave her more courage. "Did... Do you remember?"

He sighed. "I do."

The knots of tension in her shoulders eased out with his words. She hadn't failed.

"Was David right?" she asked.

Under her hand, she could feel his mouth twist. "Not about me," he said. "David is the traitor. David, the prince, Warren, and a few more people. It was dark that night. David and Prince Nicholas were the only ones I could recognize."

"Oh." Tamsin wrapped her arms around him. He embraced her back. She wasn't sure who tilted their head first but his lips were on hers.

His hands were feverishly warm as he traced patterns on her back. She slid his shirt off and the rest of their clothing followed. Rhys lifted her up and they moved to the bed. And for a time, she let her world start and end with his touch.

Chapter Twenty Three

Tamsin woke with Rhys's arm draped over her shoulders, her back pressed against his warm skin. It was a wonderful way to face daylight. Tamsin kept herself still for a long time. This felt right, and it felt safe in a way she hadn't experienced in years. For this moment, nothing was wrong in the world.

It couldn't last. Eventually Tamsin became aware that Rhys's breathing had changed. She sighed and shifted her weight, turning to face him on the narrow bed.

He broke the silence first. "Good morning."

Tamsin searched his face. "Do you still remember...?"

His eyes closed.

"Yes, I remember... I remember everything." His arm tightened around her.

"And you are still, you?" she asked.

"Tamsin, I don't think I ever stopped being me. I just... it got complicated." He took a long breath. "I don't regret this."

"Then I suppose the next question is, what now?"

At her question his body tensed. "I don't know. I have to stop Nicholas and my brother, if I can." He pushed a little away in the bed and sat up, letting a stream of chilly air under the blanket. Tamsin shivered. She tucked the blankets back around herself.

"I knew something was wrong before I followed David to the warehouse," Rhys said.

Tamsin just nodded. The plotting of a prince seemed a less fraught conversation than asking Captain, Lord Rhys Carwyn what he intended to do after they had slept together.

He left the bed and crossed to where their clothing lay tangled together in the midst of the ritual circle. Tamsin admired the line of his body as he bent down to pull his clothing from the pile.

"David has been acting oddly for weeks now, coming and going at odd hours, and he'd paid off some of his smaller debts all at once. It wasn't an inconsequential sum. David has little talent for the betting tables, although he doesn't care to admit that. I've been buying back his markers and settling his debts when I can find them."

"I followed him and listened to what they planned. I was too reckless. I knew I would need some proof to take to Reggie, the king. I waited until I thought they had left, and broke into the warehouse. The ledger was right there. I'd hidden a page of the ledger in my boot, and another in my pocket like they trained us on the front. Divide the evidence. But they came back again, and David and Marcus found me. They had pistols and I hadn't thought... I never thought I would stumble into something like this. They held me and the rest of them came back. They dosed me with something, and I don't remember clearly after that."

"Why were they hiding the guns?" Tamsin asked. She sat up in the bed, pulling the blanket up to her throat. "Are they planning some sort of war?"

"I thought that myself at first," Rhys said. "Especially since some of the shipments seemed to be coming from Orness. But the Orness army is still recovering from the skirmishes three years ago. I saw the damage that was done there. They would not launch a new attack so soon, not until they can rebuild their forces." His lips thinned. "My regiment, and the others that fought in that war bought us half a generation of peace, perhaps more."

"War with someone else?" Tamsin asked. "Grimreadh? They had the naval forces if I recall."

Rhys shook his head. "I don't believe they have any foreign help. Nicholas wants the throne he was promised. No one expected Reggie to survive this long, he's been consumptive since he was a boy. Although they've tried to keep that quiet in case of a coup. The irony of that."

"Queen Caroline hasn't produced an heir yet," Tamsin said. "Nicholas is already the heir."

"But if she does, if she produces any child, Nicholas is out of the succession. His father groomed him for the position. He spent two years as regent when Reggie was ill. But Reggie recovered."

"But why didn't they kill you the first time?" Tamsin shuddered. "Why come after you later?"

"David," Rhys said. "He argued with Nicholas and Warren. Said if they killed me, he'd walk away from his part."

Someone knocked on the door and they both jumped. Tamsin glanced over at her clothing, still spread over the floor. Moving quietly, Rhys handed them to her and crept to the door. The knock came again, and this time someone called through the door, "Oi, you two, I brought you breakfast."

Lacey. Tamsin exhaled.

"Hold your britches," Tamsin called back. She slid out of the bed and pulled her chemise over her head. When the cloth cleared her line of vision, she noticed Rhys looking at her. His eyes were wistful. She shrugged the short stays on and started lacing them up. Shit. The ritual circle. If Lacey saw that, it might send the relationship back to that prickly uncomfortable place again. Tamsin threw the blanket to Rhys.

"Can you wipe that away while I finish my laces?"

He nodded and smeared the already smudged lines into a less recognizable mess.

Tamsin slid her battered dress on. She needed a good hour with a needle to repair the tears in the skirt, and another day in the wash tub to remove the layers of soot and grime it had acquired yesterday. Perhaps she could start a fashion for grime.

It took another minute until the room was ready. Lacey was tapping out tiny rhythms on the door frame outside. Tamsin unbarred the door and let her in. Lacey took in the smudged floor and blanket, the single rumpled bed, and Tamsin and Rhys's state of dishevelment. Her face broke into a smirk.

"We always knew you two would figure things out someday," she said.

Tamsin winced.

"I only let you in because you said food," Tamsin grumbled.

Lacey grinned wider and handed her a basket. "Frank will be here in a bit. He was checking to be sure no one has been asking around for you two."

Tamsin nodded and brought the basket to the small table still pressed against the wall. New bread, a chunk of soap, cheese, and a bottle of watered down something. It was enough for a couple of meals. Water, they'd have to head out and collect soon. By Tamsin's judgment they should be running the Narrows water anytime now. She glanced around the room for a bucket.

Rhys shook the blanket and bits of charcoal dusted out. It would take a good amount of water and scrubbing to get that section of floor clean, but it no longer looked so ominously occult.

"Are you better today, Tam?" Lacey asked when the silence stretched out too long.

Tamsin cleared her throat. "I'm fine. We're fine." She glanced over at Rhys who was trying to pull the bed clothes into a less incriminating shape.

"Good. There hasn't been much chatter about yesterday," Lacey said "Not what I expected at least. The last time Rhys ended up tangling with folks down here they set half the street gangs out looking for him. No one is going door to door this time."

"That's a good thing," Rhys said. "Right?"

Lacey shrugged, all the teasing wiped from her face. "Frank said they're rumbling about something in the upper rings. But things down here are tense enough that I don't think that anyone would want to start a big search right now."

"Why not?" Tamsin asked. The streets had felt a little off to her yesterday.

"They didn't turn the water on two days ago. And yesterday they only let it run half the time," Lacey said.

"Why would they do that?" Tamsin said. Her stomach dropped. There had already been one riot. Why would the king risk another one?

The answer came to her between breaths. "Rhys? How much inflence does Prince Nicholas hold in the Lords' council right now?"

Rhys wasn't more than half a beat behind her. "Considerable. My brother has been acting as my father's voting proxy, and Warren has a seat. Nicholas is setting up an internal threat. If the Narrows riots, the prince would have a strong case that Reggie isn't competent to continue governing. Gods knows that he's been snapping up any bit of power that the king leaves free."

He turned to Lacey. "The guns you and your brother brought in?"

Lacey looked nervous. "I didn't make the arrangements for that, but ... one of the men from the warehouse, the one that wasn't quite so well off, he was there when we brought them in."

"Marcus," Tamsin said. "And Warren was meeting with Frank just before the last riot.

"He went by John when we dealt with him," Lacey said. "He paid well, the first few shipments. It was the last one where he tried to double-cross us."

Tamsin exhaled. "This is big. Too big for us."

Someone else knocked at the door in a pattern this time, two quick, pause, two more quick, and three slower and deliberate.

"Frank," Lacey said. She opened the door.

He'd brought a bucket of water with him. He still leaned on the stick a little, but his limp was slight. Tamsin was constantly surprised how a week had healed the wound.

"I got word back from your sister," Frank told Rhys.

Tamsin looked at Rhys. "You sent a letter to Eira?"

Rhys shrugged. "Frank was able to send a runner with a message for Kate or Henry while we were planning how to get to you."

Frank passed him a folded note.

Rhys broke the seal. Bits of red resin scattered over the bedding. He read quickly.

Lacey was in a whispered conference with Frank in the doorway. Tamsin's stomach growled. To hell with manners. She tore off part of the bread and ate.

"Frank," Tamsin said between bites, "how many guns did you smuggle in?"

Frank's expression was grim. "I've been bringing them in for the better part of three months. We set up at least two dozen caches around the Narrows per John's instructions."

"Caches for whom?" Rhys asked, looking up from his letter.

Frank shrugged. "I didn't ask. They covered a lot of ground though, so it can't be just one group that plans to use them."

"Whatever they are planning, it's happening soon," Tamsin said.

"In three days," Rhys said. "If they had changed the date, they wouldn't be quite so concerned that I knew the..." He trailed off. "They let us come here. Of course, they aren't looking down here. They are setting the Narrows to a powder keg, and when they riot again, they'll have guns. It will be a bloodbath. And since I am down here, they can blame it on me. Make me out to be the rebellion leader." His face had gone paler.

"Shit," Tamsin said.

Rhys picked up his coat from the floor.

"Eira is going to meet me in an hour or so," he said.

Tamsin moved in front of the door. "You can't go out on the streets. Especially not near the gates. They must have your description."

Rhys waved the note. "If they truly need me as a scapegoat, they can't arrest me until the riot has happened. Eira said she didn't have a large window of time to meet. David has been watching her closely. I need to speak with her."

"Oh, for the love of fools, I'll go," Lacey said. "The guards are looking for both of you. Are you sure your sister is trustworthy though?"

Tamsin gave a small nod. "Eira is loyal to Rhys."

"Whatever David has been telling her, she knows me. I trust her," Rhys said.

Lacey gave a slow nod. "You two stay here. Frank and I can go and meet her. What does she look like?"

"Blond like me, maybe a couple inches taller than you. She'll have Kate with her, one of the housemaids. Kate is darker complexioned and has the same shade of hair as Tamsin. If she wants proof that you know me, tell her the Priestess's pig." His lips twitched into a small smile.

"Priestess, pig, got it," Lacey said.

Rhys gave her a few more directions and Lacey and Frank left. Rhys barred the door after them. The silence grew heavy.

Tamsin broke it. She waved her arm at the basket. "Hungry?"

"Tamsin," Rhys said. "We should really talk about last night."

"Is this the part where you tell me it was wonderful, but…"

Rhys scrubbed his face with his hands.

"Marion," he said.

Tamsin tensed. "Of course." She looked intently into the basket. As if the contents had changed somehow.

"I don't expect anything," she said, not looking up. "It was very nice but of course you have your life to lead."

"Tamsin," his voice broke between the two syllables.

"I'm not going to do this anymore." She looked up and spread her arms wide. "You are engaged to Lady Everwood. I'm not going to pretend everything is all right."

Rhys looked like he'd been hit.

"Tamsin, I—It's complicated. Having made my pledge to her, I am honour bound not to break it." He crossed over to stand next to her. "I'm sorry. I should not have let myself be so free last night. I—feel for you too. Gods do I feel for you." He stopped and recovered the calm he had lost.

"She could jilt you," Tamsin said. Her voice was abnormally calm to her ears. She knew Lady Everwood wouldn't.

Rhys sighed. His hand moved an inch until it was touching hers, fingertip to fingertip. Tamsin froze.

"We don't give women a lot of power in the King's Ring. You surely noticed how sheltered Eira is. The power to jilt a fiancé is one of the tiny ways we give that power back. If I were to withdraw my proposal, Marion would be left with no prospects. I can't do that to her."

"That's stupid." Tamsin moved a pace away.

Rhys eyed her. "Which part?"

"All of it. You shouldn't be priest shackled to someone you don't want to, and she shouldn't have to hold that over you to be able to have some control over her life. It's all horrible." Tamsin crossed over to the window.

"Men of my class are not expected to be faithful. Women either, once they have an heir," Rhys said. He examined her face.

"Lord Rhys Carwyn, are you trying to ask me to be your mistress? I don't think Lady Everwood would allow her husband to stray with someone publicly. Is that the kind of life you want, skulking in corners?" Tamsin voice mimicked the chill tones Lady Everwood had used.

"All I know is that I don't want to walk away from this," Rhys said. "But I cannot walk away from my other obligations either. I am trying to find the path with the least harm."

"You've made your choice then, and I mine." Tamsin peered out at the street again. For this time of day, it was still oddly quiet.

He took her hands. "I am not going to just walk away without trying. I... I care for you, deeply." Tamsin pulled her hands from his grasp.

"And I am not going to keep beating my head against a stone wall." Tamsin laughed. "All this may be moot anyway. If they hang us as traitors, I doubt they will let you marry first."

Rhys looked hurt again.

His pain wasn't helping her anger. She took a deep breath. "We need to focus on now. Anything else, that will come after we survive this mess."

Rhys let the subject drop.

Chapter Twenty Four

W hen Frank and Lacey came back, Tamsin was prepared for company. She'd pulled her hair back from her face, as neatly as she was able without a looking glass and made hasty and awkward ablutions at the water bucket.

At Lacey's knock, Rhys unbarred the door, and Eira launched herself into his arms.

"I've been so worried," she said, all in a rush. "David wouldn't say anything about what happened. He wants to send me back home, but I held him off, at least for now."

Rhys stepped back into the room, still holding Eira, so Frank and Lacey could enter, followed by a bemused looking Kate.

"I'm all right," Rhys said. It was another long minute before Eira released him.

"What happened?" Eira asked.

Rhys stepped away, and into Frank. With six people inside, the room was fast overheating, and everyone was bumping shoulders.

"Maybe Lady Eira and Kate could take a seat with me on the bed?" Tamsin suggested.

Eira pursed her lips at the mention of her title, but she joined Tamsin and Kate on the bed. Lacey perched on the edge of the table.

Eira turned her focus on Tamsin. "What happened? Why is David trying to have you two arrested?"

Tamsin glanced over at Rhys, but he was still not meeting her eyes. Having his memories back had changed him, everything about him was more confident. Tamsin found herself looking for shade of the Rhys she knew in the silences and syntax he used now.

"David has gotten himself in a bit of trouble," Tamsin began.

"We can't tell you everything," Rhys broke in. "It wouldn't be safe."

Tamsin clicked her teeth together. Just the fact that Eira was here meeting with them made her involved. How would keeping the truth from her help anything? She opened her mouth to say as much but Eira beat her to it.

"Don't you dare." Eira wore the precise expression she had used to stare down Grant and David. Rhys shifted away from her, without noticing his movement. "That is the same sort of weaselly words Mother used when David's wife ran off and let me tell you, not knowing the details didn't save me from the gossip. What is going on?"

"This is a little more serious than a divorce, Eira," Rhys said.

"But she came here to help," Tamsin broke in. "If you wanted to keep her out of it then you shouldn't have asked her for help."

Rhys fell silent at that. Behind him Frank and Lacey were exchanging amused looks.

"Rhys—" Eira was distracted from her protest to know more, temporarily Tamsin was sure. "You remembered what happened to Lady Carwyn?" she asked. "Do you remember...?" She let the rest of the question dangle.

Rhys nodded. "I remember everything."

Eira turned to Tamsin. "How?"

"Herbs," Tamsin said. Too many people knew her secrets already. She shot Rhys a look and he nodded.

"Tamsin is very skilled," he said, with a touch more formality than the occasion warranted. Having his memories back had made his speech patterns more proper. Or perhaps it was the other thing. Tamsin squirmed. Maybe having Eira sit with her, here, wasn't the best plan. Best to change this line of questioning though. Tamsin circled back to their argument.

"Rhys, Eira and Kate are here now. They deserve to know," Tamsin said.

"I sent for her before I knew what all this was about," Rhys protested. He was caving though. He shifted his weight back and forth on the balls of his feet.

"If you are going to have any hope of clearing your name, they should know," Tamsin said.

"What in the sixth layer of hells have you two stepped into?" Kate asked.

Rhys put his head in his hands and groaned.

"David Carwyn is part of a conspiracy against the crown, along with the prince, and Lord Warren, at minimum. They accused Rhys of treason to try and hide their actions," Tamsin said. There. Now they all knew.

"How?" Eira asked. She was taking the news of her brother's betrayal calmly.

"Nicholas has been undermining the king's decisions in the council for a while now," Rhys said. His jaw was tight. Another bit of barrier coming up between Rhys and her. Maybe that was for the best. Right now, Tamsin could use every bit of distance she could muster between herself and Lord Rhys Carwyn.

"It's more than that though," Tamsin said. "The prince has been smuggling guns into the Narrows and causing riots with the new taxes and the water shut offs."

"Why would he do that?" Eira asked. "Wouldn't arming the people down here just get everyone hurt?"

Frank broke in. "They're not good guns, and he didn't bring in a lot of powder or shot. By my calculation, there's only about one or two shots to every gun he brought in. And the gates have the cannons. He has a couple of bought men in with the Runners. They'll set things off and get the guns handed out."

Rhys considered that information. "There are at least four regiments of infantry in the capitol right now, and the King's Lancers, a cavalry company just outside. They could quell an uprising fairly handily, especially something as uncoordinated as this. But it would be messy. High casualties."

Tamsin swallowed. "There can't be more than a handful of people in the Narrows that have ever shot a gun. They'll be slaughtered." Despite the heat of the room, she shivered. She'd healed one man. How had it led to this?

Rhys closed his eyes and nodded.

"How can we stop it?" Eira asked. She put one gloved hand over Tamsin's.

"How does a riot in the Narrows help the prince kill the king?" Kate interrupted. "Won't it just make a mess?"

"I'm not sure killing the king is his end goal," Rhys said. "He just needs to make the king look incompetent enough that Nicholas can declare a regency again. If that happens there is little chance he'd ever give up that power this time. The council's been divided over how they should be paying off the debts we incurred during the war. Reginald's opinions have been divisive. I am not sure how Nicholas plans to prevent Reginald from producing an heir though. Although Reggie hasn't so far."

The penny dropped. Tamsin'd sensed someone else's blood was in that ritual circle. At least one person, perhaps more. The queen's blood? Preventing or ending a pregnancy was such an easy thing with magic, so many things could go wrong in those early days. And the king's health…

"Rhys, you said the king has been ill?" Tamsin asked.

"He was gravely ill as a child, and two years ago his health took a bad turn, but he seemed to have come through it. But the last few months or so his cough has returned."

"I wonder…" Tamsin looked at Kate and Eira, then back to Rhys.

Rhys nodded slowly. "You could be right, they may have … other ways to harm the king or prevent the queen from conceiving."

"And David is helping the prince with all of this?" Eira asked.

Rhys nodded. "I saw it myself." He handed her the ledger pages.

"So how do we stop it?" Eira asked. Despite her even tone her hand still clutched Tamsin's. Stop it, could anyone stop this? Maybe Frank and Lacey were right and the best thing to do was leave. Leave her friends, leave however many thousand people, who had no idea a prince of the realm and a handful of kingsringers were about to turn their lives upside down?

"I'm not sure we can," Tamsin said slowly. "At this point, if the prince has been turning the water off in the Narrows, another riot is inevitable."

"*Should* we stop it?" Frank interrupted. "What has King Reginald done for us down here?"

"He fought hard against the bread tax," Rhys said, "and he tried to make the window tax more fair, by excluding shop windows and houses with under ten windows. The council overruled him on that. They have the final say to levy taxes."

"He still shuts off the water at midday," Lacey said.

"That's been going on for years now. I'm not sure if he realizes it's a problem."

"He ought to," Tamsin said.

Rhys nodded. "He should. But on one hand you have the lawful sovereign who hasn't made things worse, on the other Nicholas, who will kill hundreds of people to reach his goals. Who do you choose?"

Frank frowned.

"Is there a way to get to the water supply and turn it on ourselves? It might cool some tempers," Tamsin said.

"Unlikely. They built the Regimental headquarters overtop of the pipe controls. There are at least two infantry regiments there now at best, all four standing regiments at worst." Rhys started to pace in a tight circle in the centre of the room, right over the remains of the ritual. "If we had some sort of way to tell Reggie what his brother is scheming, he might be able to rally some support on the council to prevent a regency. If we could bring him absolute proof, he could arrest Nicholas. But I have no idea how to get a message to him," Rhys said, his pacing temporarily halted. "David has seen to that."

"Why would he listen to you?" Lacey asked.

"We grew up together," Eira said. "The doctors wanted him in the country air as a child and the crown has an estate a few miles from Carwyn."

"Even with the lies Nicholas and David have been spreading about me, he'd at least give me a chance to explain," Rhys added.

"So how do we get you to him?" Tamsin asked.

Eira closed her eyes in thought. "I can't recall any public outings on their majesties' calendar right now, but there is the ball in two days at the palace. I believe the king is planning to open the dancing, although he usually retires immediately after."

Tamsin and Rhys exchanged looks.

"Are you invited?" Tamsin asked. "Could you ask the king to meet with Rhys or bring a message?"

Eira shook her head. "David received an invitation, but I haven't been presented at court yet."

"I'm not sure I want to risk sending anyone else. There are other people besides Nicholas involved in this and we don't know their numbers," Rhys said. "Damn those accusations. If I had known before this, Lord Hedworth might have been able to gain a private audience for me, but now, with the accusations David has laid against me, I doubt he would risk it."

"He had the book," Tamsin said. "Are you sure he wasn't involved as well?"

Rhys pursed his lips. "I cannot suspect everyone. I do not want to suspect the Hedworths, but your point is fair and Prince Nicholas's appearance at the party wasn't a coincidence. He must have been checking to see what I recalled. I have to see the king in person."

"Your likeness is posted at every gate in the city," Frank pointed out. "I don't think they will let you within spitting distance of the palace, let alone the king."

"Lady Eira," Lacey broke her silence, "can you get a hold of that invitation?"

Eira nodded. "I believe so."

Lacey gave Tamsin a grin. "Trenton."

Tamsin licked her lips. "Trenton's expensive. Would he be able to make a copy in time? Or alter the original? And can we trust him with a copy of the king's personal seal?" At Rhys's confused look she added, "He's a forger."

Frank answered this time. "It'd be a couple of those gold sovereigns you keep throwing around, but he'd do it. He might even cut the rush charge for a chance at a document like that."

Eira reached around and pulled out her reticule. "I brought money." She spilled the contents out on her lap. "I raided your desk, Rhys, and brought all my pin money."

Tamsin noticed Lacey and Frank eyeing the amount of silver and gold coins spilling off Eira's lap. It would cover Trenton's fee easily. She didn't feel the same pull to the coins as she had a few days ago. Had she become inured to the Carwyns' casual wealth? Or was the gravity of their situation affecting her? Either way it didn't matter.

"Look, I don't mean to rain on your heroing," Frank said. "But why don't you just get out of here. I know a way out of the city. The bribes would be expensive, but you have the coin. We can all just leave. That is enough coin to carry the lot of us out of the country. We can set up someplace better."

Tamsin looked around the room. Lacey was nodding. Tamsin drew in a breath.

"That might be the smartest plan," she started. Rhys's face was a blank mask. "But Baker, Logan, Anne, all the people at the Barrel, all the people … can we walk away from that many people?"

Lacey wouldn't meet her eyes. Frank just looked stern.

"I don't think we can make a difference," he said at last.

"You already made a difference bringing the guns here," Tamsin said. Frank flinched.

"That isn't fair. That was business. I stopped when I figured out they weren't the right people," Frank said.

Tamsin met his gaze, and after a moment, Frank looked away.

"You don't fight fair," he said. "I'll help, but there's a limit to the amount I will stretch my neck out for strangers."

"If they planned this riot, planned to push it far enough so people get hurt," Lacey said slowly, "don't we have an obligation to stop it, Frank."

Frank glowered. "No one here is talking about stopping the riot though, you're talking about keeping the king in power. I don't care whose royal backside adorns that gods-damned throne."

"But if we get to the king, we stop the riots before they start," Tamsin said.

"If," Frank said.

"Much as I am loathe to agree with my brother," Lacey said, "he has a point. That is a big if. Things are pretty tense out there, if the water doesn't come on tomorrow, that might be enough of a spark."

Everyone went silent. If the water didn't turn on… Tamsin's mind tried to tally up how many people would die. If the Narrows rioted, the people here would die by the hundreds, thousands perhaps. Could they reduce it by ten, twenty, a hundred? *Your heart knows what's right.* This time the echoes of her mother's voice didn't hurt.

Rhys licked his lips, then he turned to his sister. "Eira, what has Lord Driscoll's schedule been for the last few days?"

Eira closed her eyes. "His daughter was at Lord Hedworth's party two nights ago; I believe he was in attendance as well. And they were invited to the king's ball, because Lila was going on about her new dress for the occasion. Between then I think that they were heading back to their estate for a few days, Lila is out of town at least. She sent out cards saying she was unavailable to calls."

Rhys's shoulders relaxed a fraction. "That's good. Lord Driscoll is the municipal minister. If he's out of town, he won't be mucking about with the supply for another couple of days at least. They have to stay subtle with this or they will tip their hand to the council and Nicholas will get nothing. He's not the only option for a regent. Queen Caroline could make her own case for it now that they are married."

"So, we have a couple of days to plan both sides of this," Tamsin said. And which impossible task to tackle first. "Let's look at the ball first. If we can't manage that, the rest is moot. An invitation alone isn't going to be enough to get us into the ball. We'll need to look the part as well, clothes and the like, and we need disguises." We. When had she decided to see this through to the end? But who else could go with Rhys and have a chance not to be recognized?

Kate pursed her lips. "I think I might have a dress that would suit Tamsin, stowed away from Lady Carwyn's trousseau."

"I ought to have the clothing I need in my wardrobe," Rhys said. "You can ask Henry to put it all together for you."

Kate and Eira exchanged glances.

"Begging your pardon, Lord Rhys," Kate said. "But your brother sacked Henry yesterday morning. He claimed he was stealing."

Rhys pressed his lips together. "I'll have to correct that."

"I can put it all together if you tell me which coat you need," Kate said. "I've cleaned your rooms every day for a year and a half now. I know where everything is."

"Elspeth," Tamsin broke in. "She could disguise us. She dyes hair and adds on whiskers and wigs all the time at the theatre. But she'll need more coin."

Eira shook the pile in her lap. "I brought nearly twenty sovereigns," she said.

"Eighteen gold sovs, and it looks like a bit more than another one in crowns, plus the other coins," Lacey said.

Everyone in the room looked at her, except Frank.

Lacey gave them a crooked grin. "We all have our talents."

"We still need to get from here to the theatre and on to the palace," Tamsin said.

"We won't be able to hire a coach here. David and the prince know we went to ground somewhere down here. And we can't just walk through the gate."

Lacey and Frank exchanged another look. "I can cover that part." Frank didn't sound enthused.

They spent the rest of the morning working out the plan, with an agreement for Kate to return the next day with supplies. When the noon bells rang, Eira and Kate left, with Lacey to guide them.

Frank and Rhys were deep in conversation at the table. Rhys had turned the tabletop into a map of the Narrows, and he and Frank were bent over it marking out places where Frank had left the guns.

"How are they planning to distribute the guns from the stashes?" Tamsin asked Frank.

"The Runners, and a couple of the toughs they've allied with will pass them out to their people when the time comes," Frank answered.

"The same people who were out looking for Rhys, six, seven days back?" Tamsin asked.

Frank grunted. "Some of them."

"They set it up well. That many caches make it hard to dismantle it quietly. Do you know if they have a specific signal to start the riot?" Rhys said.

Frank shook his head. "They didn't include me in that discussion."

"So, this could break at any time?" Tamsin said.

"Maybe," Frank said. "The night I got shot, I thought it was breaking, but they didn't go for the guns."

"Can we stop it?" Tamsin asked. Twenty thousand people lived in the Narrows, maybe more.

Rhys leaned over the impromptu map. "Stop it, no. We'd need at least a regiment of infantry to secure all the locations, or a month and a well-fortified warehouse. But we might be able to mitigate some of the damage."

"Some?" Frank asked.

"Do you have anyone you can trust? If you could take over the caches here, here, and here, you could set up and defend this area," Rhys said. "You'd only need to take the guns from one and consolidate the powder and bullets from the others.

"But that's all ruins," Tamsin said, "Hardly anyone lives there."

"That means the looters aren't likely to want to get in there," Frank pointed out. "How many people do you think we'd need to hold it?"

"Depends on if you stay at the cache location or head further in. If you can move the guns, I think you can fortify this area with about twenty people. Then if you can bring in more people you can expand into these areas to protect more people. We can't protect the buildings, but with a good defensible position, a lot of people could be safe, or safer."

Frank nodded slowly. "I think I can do that."

They spent the rest of the day sorting through plans and lists, with Frank and Lacey running messages and errands back and forth across the city. Eira's supply of coins dwindled.

That night Rhys took the floor, across the room. Tamsin slept fitfully.

*

The next morning was foggy and cool. Tamsin left their rooms at mid-morning to meet Lacey and pick up some of the fruits of yesterday's labours. The streets were filled with people; she had to fight against a crowd no matter which direction she pressed. The water was on, but the pressure was low, and the lines were long.

Tamsin kicked at the door with her toe. "Rhys, let me in."

There was a muffled scrapping as he pulled the bar away from the door. At last, the door creaked open. One of her packages slipped and threatened to send them all tumbling.

"What is all this?" he asked, backing out of the way.

She stumbled over to the bed and let everything fall.

"This and that. I was able to get a friend to do a proper work over on your boots." She pulled a newspaper-wrapped bundle out of the pile and handed it over. "Trenton grumbled about the price, but he'll have the invitations for us tomorrow. For three sovereigns, he ought to," she continued.

"We're ready then?" he said.

"Near to it. Kate should be by soon with the rest of the supplies. I thought she would have been here by now actually," Tamsin said.

"Perhaps she was delayed by the crowds?" Rhys pulled the shutter open a crack and peered outside.

"Mmmm." Tamsin laid out the rest of the parcels, gloves, pomade, feathers, everything one might need to meet a king.

Someone knocked at the door again. Tamsin stopped mid-motion and waited. They knocked again and this time Kate called out, "L— Rhys?"

Rhys unlocked the door.

Kate was flushed and out of breath. Her straw bonnet sat askew, with hair flying out in every direction.

"Kate, are you all right?" Tamsin asked. She let the dancing slippers she was holding fall back on the bed and crossed over to clasp Kate's hands in hers.

Kate looked past her at Rhys. "They have Eira."

The silence hung for a long moment after her statement. Rhys broke it.

"Who has my sister, Kate? Start at the beginning." That quiet command tone was back again.

"It's your brother, milord. Last night he told Lady Eira she was required to come to some party. She never came home," Kate said. She was out of breath. Tamsin pressed a mug of water into her hands.

Tamsin and Rhys exchanged glances. "It doesn't necessarily mean they were kidnapped," Tamsin began.

Kate shook her head. "Lord David found me this morning. We knew he was following us the first time, but we lost them by running out the back of the lace shop. But he still knew. He told me he knew Eira had been in touch and asked if I knew where you were. I lied milord. He sacked me on the spot. But before I left, he had a message for you." She passed over a much-crumpled piece of paper.

Rhys read it and his expression darkened. He handed the paper to Tamsin as soon as he was done.

"Were you followed?" Tamsin asked.

Kate shook her head. "Not here. He set Martin after me again, but that boy's a clod. I lost him before I was even out of King's Ring. I was careful the whole way here."

Tamsin cracked the shutter and looked out at the street below. There wasn't a company of Bluecoats lurking outside at least.

"Were you able to retrieve everything we needed?" Rhys asked.

Kate nodded and handed him her oversized basket.

Tamsin turned her attention to the letter.

I have taken the liberty of confining Lady E as well as your sister. They will be released upon your surrender to the king's justice, due a traitor. It was unsigned.

"Rhys, your brother didn't write this," Tamsin said. "He'd never call Eira your sister. He'd say 'our.'"

"It must Nicholas then," Rhys said. "It doesn't matter." He paced the confines of the room.

"No, it does. We know your brother is involved, and the prince. They can't be keeping prisoners at Carwyn house, Kate would know about it. So, they must be somewhere else. Does Lord Warren have much property?"

"No, he shares his town house with his father and stepmother and half-brothers. He's always complaining about the lack of space, and what will happen once he inherits."

"They would have to keep the ladies close, wouldn't they? Perhaps someplace the prince controls."

Rhys took a deep breath. "You're right. They'd need to keep them close if they mean to exchange them for my surrender."

"How much property does the prince have in town?" Tamsin asked.

Rhys was silent for a moment. "He doesn't have much. Technically he's a duke in his own right, but he's been so up to his ears in creditors that he leased the ducal properties last year. It was a huge scandal. Traditionally he'd take over one of the family properties in town but..."

"Where does he stay in town then?"

"Due to his debts and the king's health, he stays at the palace. He has his own wing."

"Could he be keeping them there?" Tamsin asked.

"Perhaps," Rhys said, "but there is a full staff there. How would he keep it quiet? I think the warehouse is a better place to check."

"But they know that we know about it," Tamsin said. "And you already staged one rescue there. I'll check it out to be sure, but it would be hard to stay inconspicuous there, especially with two ladies of the ton. Lady Everwood does not seem to be the kind of person who would go quietly, and the walls of the warehouse are thin."

"You aren't going alone." Rhys started for the door.

"Your portrait is at every gate and with every guard," Tamsin said, stepping in front of him. She pressed one hand into his chest, stopping his movement. "And they've already set half the Narrows to look for you once. Besides, Frank and Lacey will be here soon with the invitation, someone needs to meet them. I won't go in, not even if they are there. If anything is suspicious, I'll come back, and you and I can make a proper plan."

"I don't like it," Rhys said.

"How can I help?" Kate asked.

Tamsin pursed her lips. "Strength in numbers, and the prince wouldn't know your face."

Kate nodded.

"And I'm stuck here," Rhys said. He made a fist by his side.

"Not for much longer. The ball is tomorrow. We can manage this." Tamsin pulled her hand back from his chest.

"Tamsin, if anything happens to them..." Rhys said.

Them. Tamsin swallowed hard. "We won't let it."

Kate handed Rhys her basket. "I think I got everything you asked for. You'll need to hang the clothing out, and we'll need to get them to an iron."

Tamsin looked over the room. Rhys looked ready to pull the walls down.

"Rhys, stay put. We'll be back in an hour."

Rhys looked for a moment like he would argue. Then he shook his head. "Be safe, both of you."

Kate twisted her hair back up into a knot and pinned her hat straight atop it. "I'm ready."

The two women made their way out onto the streets.

*

"They weren't at the warehouse," Tamsin said as soon as Rhys opened the door. Behind him, Lacey and Frank were looking harried. Tamsin guessed that Rhys had been at them to get out in the streets and look for Eira and Lady Everwood.

"Are you sure?" Rhys asked. His voice was too controlled.

"They burned it to the ground. No one was there," Tamsin said.

"We're back at the beginning then," Rhys said. His shoulders slumped.

"Or they are at the palace," Tamsin said. "Do the prince and the king share their staff?"

Rhys frowned. "I don't think so."

"They don't," Kate said. She crossed over to the bed and pulled her hat off. "One of the scullery maids in Hedworth house has a cousin who works in the king's kitchen. She said the prince keeps his own kitchen staff, footmen, and maids for his wing. It makes a lot of mess and expense, but the prince won't change."

Rhys and Tamsin exchanged looks. "You're right then," Rhys said slowly.

Tamsin said. "Frank, do you have anyone with ears that way?"

Frank shook his head and snorted. "I've tried to stay out of the court intrigues, for all the good it did me."

"While I was convalescing, I filled in as the King's aide-de-camp," Rhys said. "I know the Palace. I should go."

"No, the King won't listen to just anyone. You get to the king. I'll get to the ladies and keep them safe, you can tell me where to look. Kate, if you don't have another place in the city, you can stay here tonight. We can use your help, and the rent is free," Tamsin said.

Kate snorted. "Well, how can I refuse an offer like that?"

Chapter Twenty Five

In the morning, Tamsin looked over the little room. Most of the debris from their stay was gone now, either smuggled to the theatre with Kate at first light or thrown away. The charcoal marks on the floor had been trodden to oblivion.

Rhys perched on the bed fiddling with an oil-cloth-wrapped package – the ledger and letters. He checked and rechecked that there were no gaps in the wrappings. Frank and Lacey were due here before the next bell. Tamsin caught herself drumming her fingers on her thigh.

"I could never stand the waiting before action either," Rhys said without looking up.

They hadn't spoken much since Kate left them. What was there to say? She had no desire to rehash their previous arguments. All she needed to do was get through tonight. One more night, then it wouldn't matter anymore. The half dozen steps between them felt like miles.

Outside, the street noises rose to a muted roar. The water hadn't come on today. There was no work to be had at the dock, and no rain to keep people off the streets. Nicholas wanted to spark a riot, and the Narrows was the tinder.

When the knock came, Tamsin opened the door.

Frank was there, his face drawn. "It's time," he said.

"Where's Lacey?" Tamsin asked.

"She'll meet us there," Frank said. It was only a minute for them to gather up their parcels and walk, Rhys in bare feet, out into the streets.

Frank brought them out through the back door. They spent the better part of an hour ducking through alleyways, climbing over fences, through the ruins, and skirting any street wide enough for a cart to pass. Even these back ways were not entirely empty. Still, no one questioned them. No one here wanted to be questioned.

Eventually they reached the wall. In older parts of the Narrows the houses were built right up on the wall, but the wall itself was made of stacked stones and whatever they'd had to hand a hundred years back. It had fallen on people's homes a few times and now they built far enough so a man could come and through and fix the trouble spots.

Frank led them through that path. Rhys's shoulders brushed the walls, but they met no one. The path spilled out into the dock area, about a warehouse's length away from the water. Between the snow and the rains, the water was nearing the high-water mark, which didn't bode well for spring. Frank led them under the pier.

Lacey was waiting for them. Her hair was wound up on top of her head and she held a woollen blanket tucked up under her chin.

"You need to undress." Tension, or the cold, made her voice tight.

"Undress?" Tamsin said.

Lacey opened the blanket, underneath she wore a pair of small breaches and nothing else. There was a bundle in her hand.

"Our way lies through the river. It's cold, but not far. The more clothing you can keep dry the faster you will warm up on the other side.

Rhys frowned, but he stripped off his coat and shirt.

Tamsin hesitated another long moment. "People drown in the river Lacey."

"I know the safe ways."

Tamsin pulled the battered gown over her head. Frank turned away.

"I've got to get to my job," he said.

"How many caches have you emptied?" Rhys asked. He'd stripped down to his small clothes.

Lacey handed Tamsin another pair of the rough sailor breaches she wore, and Tamsin slipped them on.

"We moved two of the far ones. Kari and Johnathan are working on one more and that should secure the area."

Rhys nodded. "Good luck to you."

"And to you," Frank said.

They followed Lacey out into the river. The river water was colder than the air for a long few minutes, then Tamsin's legs went numb. She balanced her bundle of clothing on her head and tried to follow Lacey's steps as closely as possible. This close to the wall, there were rocks and other debris littering the riverbed. The murky water lapped around her shoulders, sending tiny wavelets up to slap her cheeks and throat. The water came up to Lacey's chin.

As they swam further away from the shore, Tamsin had to fight against the current pulling her downstream. Her toes barely brushed the riverbed. A few paddles in the shallow end of the mill pond with Thomas had not prepared her for this. The water was bitter and burned her eyes when the waves hit her face. Rhys slipped. His bundle of clothing dipped precariously towards the surface of the water. Lacey reached out and steadied him.

"You good Carwyn?"

"Can't swim," he said spitting out the river water. "This is why didn't I join the damn Navy."

At last, they were far enough out for Lacey's taste. The shore seemed miles away. Tamsin locked her teeth together to stop them from clattering together. Shivers made ripples around her.

Lacey held up one hand for quiet. She peered over towards the shore for what felt like an eternity for Tamsin, waiting for something. At last Lacey angled them back towards the shore on the far side of the wall.

The four of them emerged from the water dripping and shaking. They were under another dock, and Lacey passed out a burlap sack to each of them to dry with. The river waters had stained their clothing yellow. The dry dress and stays felt odd against her numbed skin, but Tamsin warmed faster than she expected once she was dressed.

The Merchants' Ring was ominously quiet compared to the Narrows. Despite the early afternoon hour, most of the shops were shuttered and closed. Lacey led them this time, through more back alleys and empty courtyards until they reached the Emirya.

Elspeth met them at the door and hurried Tamsin and Rhys inside.

We have two hours before the cast shows up looking for my help," Elspeth said.

Tamsin reached over and grasped Lacey's hand. "Stay safe."

Lacey forced a smile. "I'm not the one walking into the king's house, keep yourself safe," she shot back.

"I'll catch up with you when this is done." Tamsin released her hand and let Elspeth shoo her inside.

"Thank you for your help, Elspeth," Tamsin said. "Lacey told you the stakes?"

"Yes, and of course I'd help. Prince Nicholas is always rude to my actresses. He'd make a terrible king."

Elspeth took them to an unfamiliar part of the theatre, the dressing rooms. There were buckets of water there waiting for them, and she pulled a hasty curtain across the room.

"Clean off that river muck before it rots your complexions, then I need you, young man. Tamsin, Kate will be here shortly, to help you. She's a smart girl, good hands for the work."

Tamsin smothered a smile. She recognized that tone. If Kate wasn't restored to the Carwyn household she might find herself working at the Emirya now.

Elspeth left and Tamsin ducked behind the far side of the curtain. A fresh chemise and low stays were waiting for her. She washed away the mud as fast as she could manage. The water was cool, but anything felt better than the river water.

On the other side, she could hear Rhys washing as well. He finished before her, and she heard him leave the room. She wrapped her arms around herself and shivered again. This was it. After tonight, she wouldn't see him again. She rolled the idea of a life away from Rhys around in her head. For only eight days' acquaintance he'd taken over so much of her life. Still, there was a long way to go until this was over. Best focus on the moment.

"Are you decent?" Kate's voice called out from the door.

Tamsin came back to herself with a shudder. "Almost." She finished drying off and pulled the chemise over her head.

"Ready," Tamsin said. That was a lie, but she could fake it. Kate was carrying her dress. Even in the dim lamplight of the dressing room, the white silk gleamed. Rows upon rows of glass pearls lined the front of the dress, while smaller clusters covered the skirts and rattled together. Its sleeves would hit past her wrists, covered with more pearls, hiding the bruises and abrasions on her arms.

Tamsin slipped it on over the various layers of her disguise. Kate warmed up a papillote and readied the curling papers. After half an hour a mass of small, even curls framed her face while strands of glass pearls twisted back around a knot of hair at the back of her head.

Elspeth came back in and rummaged around the room, pulling out little jars of powder. When Kate was finished with Tamsin's hair, she tucked a cloth over Tamsin's shoulders and went to work. Tamsin closed or opened her eyes as directed while the tickle of a brush traced new planes on her face. After a few minutes, Elspeth pulled back and pronounced her done. She swept the cloth back and pointed to the mirror.

Tamsin frowned. It was her under the powder and paint, but this her had a sharper line of cheekbone, lips that were a little fuller, and tiny lines around her eyes and mouth. Elspeth had added a trace of silver to her hair as well. For a moment, Tamsin saw her mother looking out of the mirror.

At the doorway, Rhys cleared his throat. He looked older too, but most remarkable was the shade of brown Elspeth had coloured his hair and the new moustache that had appeared over his lips.

His coat was king's blue, with gold piping accenting the shoulders and collar. Gold braid worked its way down the front of the coat into intricate knots.

"You look..." he swallowed whatever comment he was going to say.

Tamsin closed her eyes. One last adventure together. "It's time," she said.

*

The road to the palace was jammed tight with carriages. Tamsin lifted her train up as they dodged them and the various horsiness that had occurred along the road. "Won't someone notice we arrived on foot?" she asked. The word had broken as they travelled. Riots had broken out in the Narrows. Even this far north there was an acrid hint of smoke in the air. She hoped Frank and Lacey were someplace safe.

Beside her, Rhys was looking a little awkward under his borrowed moustache. One of his hands snaked up to itch, and Tamsin tapped it with her fan.

"Don't muss the glue," she hissed.

"They won't notice us walking," he said "Half the people here get out before they get to the door, if they want to avoid the crush that is. It takes them hours to clear this logjam. Leaving is even worse."

She relaxed a fraction. This wouldn't be the detail that would kill them. Umpteen more details to go.

They reached the stairs to the front door and joined the queue of elaborately dressed couples being checked. Tamsin tensed, but the guards at the door only gave her a cursory glance. Rhys, they spent a little more time with before they waved him inside. They mounted another set of steps and another queue at the entrance to the ballroom.

Rhys took the forged invitations out of his pocket and handed them to a footman dressed in royal blue and silver livery. The footman looked them over carefully and Tamsin's fingers twitched against her side.

After an excruciatingly long moment, he passed them back and rapped his staff once. "The honourable Sir Grant Smith and Lady Smith," he cried out.

A few eyes turned towards them, but a mere knight did not hold the crowd's attention for more than an eye blink. Tamsin exhaled.

"Where do we go now?" she asked.

He scanned the room. "There is a library not far from the ballroom. It should give you the access you need. It's too early for their majesties to open the dancing. They'll be resting until more of their guests arrive. We should have half an hour, perhaps a little more."

Tamsin rubbed her gloved hands down her skirt. "Lead on."

Rhys took her elbow and steered her through the crowd to a small staircase at the far end of the room, small compared to the one their majesties would use to enter the ballroom. This one was white marble and wide enough four people could walk abreast. It was a good thing this was the last time she planned to walk in these circles, Tamsin told herself, or eventually her sense of scale would disappear.

The library was white, like the marble floor. The bookshelves had been lacquered white and the books on the shelves were all bound in white linen or leather with embossed gold titles. The mouldings and shelf edges were overlaid with a lace of gold filigree. Real gold, Tamsin discovered. Rhys shut the doors and bolted them.

"I can see why you might hide up here," Tamsin said at last.

Rhys grinned. "It was almost always empty."

"Why?"

"Half the point to these events is to be seen. White dresses are in court fashions, white floor, white walls it makes it awfully hard to stand out here."

"Ah." Tamsin trailed a gloved finger over the book spines.

The feeling of ease passed. "Rhys, what if..."

"No. Not until this is over. We have a mission." His back went fractionally straighter, all Captain Carwyn now.

"Right, you've done this sort of thing a dozen times." Sneaking into the warehouse had been easier. Then it had only been her neck on the line. She couldn't fail Eira or Lady Everwood.

"Every sort of battle is always different," Rhys said, "and it doesn't really get easier. Except after the first few times you know you are supposed to feel sick to your stomach scared. You just work with it." He wasn't looking at her.

"Well, as long as I'm supposed to," Tamsin said. He half smiled at her quip.

"Thank you for going after them. I couldn't do this if I didn't know they were going to be safe."

Beyond the doors the music stopped.

"It's time," Rhys said. He turned his back to her.

Tamsin hauled the pearled dress over her head and shoved it in a corner. The strands of pearls in her hair pulled free and she discarded those along with the gloves and the strand of paste pearls around her neck. Underneath she wore breaches and a bundle of blue skirt belted around her waist. Unfurled, it turned into a blue woollen servant's frock and a white linen apron and cap. She dressed quickly and tucked the blue skirts up into the apron's band. Beneath the skirt lay two old-fashioned tie-on pockets. She raided their contents and pulled out the bundle of letters and ledger papers and a pair of plain brown shoes.

"Here." Tamsin thrust the bundle at him. He tucked them away in his breast pocket while she exchanged her dancing slippers for the plain ones.

"Do they make the jacket hang funny?" Rhys asked. His hand kept running down the front of the coat. He was just as nervous as she was.

"Don't you be going all peacocky on me now." Tamsin caught his hand.

"I meant, can you tell I'm carrying all of it with me?" Rhys said.

She squinted, then reached under his jacket and shifted the pages down towards his side.

"That's better."

He caught her hand as she pulled away. "Tamsin." Tomes of meaning hid behind the single word.

She stepped out of reach. "Thirty minutes," she said. "I need at least that to get Eira and Lady Everwood to the ground floor and out of the palace."

"You'll have it," Rhys said. "Do you remember the route?"

Tamsin nodded. She stepped over to the bank of windows lining the far wall. She started to undo the latch and paused.

"Lacey and Frank, do you think they are safe?" she asked. Outside there was an ominous orange glow from the south.

"As safe as we are," Rhys replied.

Tamsin nodded. "I'll bring them back to you." She swung the window open and stepped out onto the ledge.

From the open window she heard Rhys mummer, "I know."

Chapter Twenty Six

Her pockets jingled as Tamsin swung her weight out onto the snow-covered ledge. From her vantage point on the palace walls, she could see the Narrows burning. It turned the southern sky copper and gold hung with thick wet snowflakes. If you didn't know better, you might call it pretty. The wind brought her scents of smoke and a cloying tang of roasting meat. Despite the height and her precarious grip, she emptied her belly along the marble walls.

Damn the king. And damn Prince Nicholas as well. If they'd cared or listened. The Narrows had been a powder keg for so long. *Goddess, keep Lacey, Frank, and all the rest safe.*

Tamsin adjusted her grip on the windowsill and swung her legs over to the next ledge. Three more to go. It was like climbing the mill, except the ledges there were bigger, and the only life she risked there was her own. The stone was snow-slick. She pressed her body to the glass and hoped no one was planning to star gaze. Each ledge required a gut sinking step over nothing to reach, her belly pressed flat to the stone pilaster. Her toes slipped on the last jump.

Tamsin's fingers clutched the masonry joins and her leg bent forward as her weight continued tipping for the missed ledge. Her kneecap slammed on the corner, and she managed to sprawl along one arm, her knee throbbing. She clung there for a moment while her empty stomach heaved. Throwing up might knock her off her perch. Deep breaths.

When her hands stopped shaking, she reached out and slowly moved her other arm off the pilaster and onto the window ledge. She wrapped her hands around it and let her knee slide off. Now one down. There was another drop, only slightly less gut sinking. Her toes brushed the glass of the window below. She dropped until she was dangling by her fingertips, then she fell.

Her knee buckled when she landed on the window ledge. She bit her lip to muffle her scream. Her right knee didn't want to hold her weight. Tamsin leaned into the glass and pulled her clasp knife out of her pocket. The window latch was a simple hook and bar. It pried up easily. She slid one side of the window open and tumbled inside the room.

The room she entered was dark and still. She managed to shut the window behind her before she collapsed. Outside the hall was silent. No one seemed to have noticed her entrance. She slid the knife blade against her little finger and made a shallow cut. Blood welled to the surface. She stuck the finger in her mouth and let the spell take over.

Healing herself was harder than she remembered. Her blood was familiar, but everything she needed from the healing was coming from her. She'd need to eat half a roast when she was through with this night. She pushed away the bruising and swelling; fortunately the bone seemed to be whole. Tamsin was halfway through when a gong sounded, breaking her out of the trance. The king arriving to his ball.

She pulled her finger out of her mouth and stumbled to her feet. Her knee ached, but it held her weight. She settled the skirts down from her hips and scanned the room for something to make her presence more believable. The bed was stripped down to its linens, no one was expected to use it tonight. She picked up the pile of pillows and slipped out into the hall. The door opened silently, and she blessed whoever oiled all the hinges and door latches here.

The prince's rooms were down another hall, up two back stairways, and another corridor, just as Rhys had told her. The first hall was deserted. On the second stairway, she met a maid coming down with an empty tray. Tamsin kept her expression blank and nodded as she passed. The woman barely looked at her.

At the door to the last corridor, she could hear footsteps. Pacing footsteps, heavy enough to make noise despite the thick carpeting.

Tamsin hesitated. This must be it. You don't set guards unless you have something to protect or imprison. The ladies must be nearby. But the chances of her taking out the guard, who at least sounded heavier than her, and doing it quietly, were not good. She pulled a small broach watch, borrowed from Eira's jewellery box, out from under her apron. It had been thirty minutes since she'd left Rhys in the library. She needed to act now.

She only made it a step out the door before being stopped.

"Who are you?" The man looming over her was stocky and grizzled in a way no razor could manage, and utterly familiar. Marcus.

"They said you needed more pillows, sir." Tamsin bobbed a curtsy and kept her eyes down. Perhaps he wouldn't recognize the woman he'd spent so much time dunking under water. Likely not though. Plan B.

"Who said that? Damn it woman, we need dinner not goose feathers."

"Of course," she said. Her mind raced. He was annoyed but not alarmed. Nicholas must not have sent word yet. A little of the tension in her shoulders eased out.

She turned to head away from the rooms he was guarding.

"Wait a minute." He seized her shoulder. She tossed the pillows in his face and ducked. Her knee protested.

It was a poor attempt at a dodge. Marcus swatted the pillows away easily and caught her wrists. Her sleeve pulled back revealing the half-healed rope burns.

"The Cyprycian meddler. How did you get in here?" he asked.

Tamsin pressed her lips tight. He only had a few options here, most of them loud, messy, and needing more authority than she judged Prince Nicholas had given him.

"I asked you a question girl." He twisted her wrist up behind her until she was on tip toes.

"And I'm not a fool," she gasped. The scabs on her wrist ached and she bent forward. "You're mixed up in this, up to your eyeballs, and if I were you, I'd pack a bag now and leave town." When all else fails, bluff.

He narrowed his eyes at her and let her drop back to her heels. Marcus checked the stairway behind her, then pushed her ahead of him. His grip on her arm was tight. She had a brief flashback to the Bluecoats pushing her along the halls of Kingsgate. There was the same rattle of keys, but underneath her feet was carpet not stone. She blinked the memories away. This had to work. There was only one logical place to put another captive...

Which was with the captives you already had. Marcus unlocked a stout door at the end of the hall. Eira and Lady Everwood were sitting on the single bed there. They looked well, aside from a layer of dishevelment from the close quarters. Beside the bed a table and two chairs were set in the middle of the room. A deck of cards lay discarded in the middle. The women stood up when Tamsin entered. Eira's face lit up.

"Tamsin!" She took in Marcus and subsided.

Tamsin gave her a ghost of a wink. Marcus pushed her the rest of the way inside.

"No funny business," he warned. "I'll be back in a moment with tea, but there's only two cups." He glared at Tamsin.

She couldn't help it. She laughed.

"You've got three ladies up here, two of them 'Actual Ladies', and you're worried about a third cup?" Tamsin managed to choke out between the laughter.

He muttered something and stumped out of the room. Behind him the lock snapped closed.

Eira rushed to her side. "Tamsin, how did they find you? Is Rhys all right?"

"He's... he was fine. We're here to rescue you," Tamsin said. "I'm doing a fine job, aren't I?" The relief that the ladies were unharmed bubbled up into laughter again, only a little hysterical.

"Quite." Lady Everwood's voice could cut glass.

Tamsin swallowed back her nervous mirth. "Look, we do have a plan. Rhys is telling the king of Nicholas's plans right now. He says there should be enough of the council here to stop the prince." Tamsin glanced over to Lady Everwood. "You did tell her about all that, didn't you?"

"It seemed the thing to do once we were locked in here," Eira said.

"We're still locked in here!" Lady Everwood pointed out.

"Ah, but I have this." Tamsin pulled a string of keys out of her pocket.

Lady Everwood's face thawed slightly. "Is that the key to this room?"

Tamsin walked over to the door and listened. "It's the next best thing," she said. She could hear footsteps coming back down the hall. She tucked the keys back into her pocket.

The door handle rattled, and the lock turned once again. Tamsin sat down and tried to look properly cowed. It wasn't working well. Hysterical giggles kept leaking out the sides of her mouth. They were going to escape. Granted, she'd rather have rescued the ladies out without being caught first, but she'd found them. They were alive. Now all they had to do was get past one man.

Marcus set the tea tray on the edge of the table. He was watching her, cautious as a cat that one was. Well, she was used to playing a mouse.

He left and the lock snapped shut again. Tamsin held up her finger to her lips.

She walked over to the door and listened again. It was quiet. Peering out the keyhole didn't show anything—but the prince did not keep his corridors as well-lit as he could. She retrieved the keys and started fitting them into the lock one at a time and trying to work the ward back over.

"Don't you know which key it is?" Lady Everwood fretted.

"These are skeleton keys. If you work them the right way they can trip the lock, but I'm not used to them." Tamsin tried a fourth key.

"Wonderful rescue," Lady Everwood said.

"Well, your idea of screaming didn't work so well," Eira said. It sounded like a familiar argument.

"Have they been treating you well then?" Tamsin asked. She tried another key in the lock.

"Mostly," Eira said. "There was a moment when they cut my finger and made it bleed into a jar. They did the same for Marion."

Tamsin stopped trying the keys. "They did what?" Her cheeks drained.

"It was only a little cut," Eira assured her.

Tamsin closed her eyes. They'd been so busy thinking about the king and the rescue, they'd forgotten the blood. They had Rhys's blood too, if they had bothered to store it right after the ritual. Maybe hers too if they'd collected it while she had been passed out. She took a deep breath. One thing at a time. They needed to get out of here. She tried the next key. The lock caught for a second, then the ward flipped over.

Tamsin took a deep breath, but there was still no sound outside the door. She tucked the keys away and checked the hall. It was empty. Marcus must have gone to tell the prince what had happened. If Rhys hadn't convinced the king, or if Nicolas had set up some sort of contingency plan, he'd have to act on it soon.

"Come on now. Move quickly and stay quiet," Tamsin said. "We can't depend on Rhys and the king to get to you. It could take some time before they are able to secure the prince. I know the way out."

Eira took her hand. Lady Everwood closed the door behind them. Tamsin led them farther down the hall. Three flights of stairs down, then along another hall to a room on the ground floor and make a break out the window.

"I rather thought you were a sly one," said Marcus from one of the bedroom doorways. The prince really needed to stop oiling his hinges. Tamsin pushed Eira behind her.

"Run," Tamsin said.

The last time this hadn't gone well, but she didn't need to be quiet now. Tamsin reached for her knife. Marcus lunged towards her. He caught her wrist before she could open the blade, and the knife fell somewhere on the carpet.

Tamsin leaned in and locked his knee with a sharp kick. He staggered and dropped her wrist. She broke backwards. Eira had retreated farther up the hall. Tamsin had lost track of Lady Everwood. Hopefully she had stayed with Eira.

Marcus recovered. He was favouring the leg, but no more than she was. Pity that. He came at her again, this time more cautiously. Tamsin dodged, but the hall didn't leave a lot of room to manoeuvre. His foot caught her ankle, and she pitched forward, slamming her shoulder into one of the tables lining the hall. She tried to roll back to her feet, but her skirts were tangled up between her legs.

He reached down for her, blinked, staggered to one side, and keeled over. Shards of beautifully painted pottery littered the carpet, and presiding over it all was Lady Everwood.

"Well, I think that takes care of that." Lady Everwood poked his ribs with her toes. "Pity about the vase. It was Jarabon porcelain."

"Well done, Lady Everwood," Tamsin said. She sat up rubbing her shoulder. Her arm was tingling, but she could move it. The bruise tomorrow ought to be something else.

"Since you are rescuing me, I suppose it's only right that you call me by my proper name, Marion." Lady Everwood reached her hand out. Marion smiled, and Tamsin couldn't help joining her. She accepted Marion's hand and hauled herself upright.

"In that case, let's get going before you cost the king even more crockery," Tamsin said. The three flights of stairs were deserted, but at the last landing men were searching loudly. Friend or foe?

"You two stay here," Tamsin said. She straightened the cap on her head. "I'll go first. If there is a lot of commotion, go up a floor and try to make your way over to the king's side of the palace. And tell them what you know."

"Tamsin..." Eira said.

Tamsin squeezed her hand. Marion looked like she was about to protest, but she swallowed the words, and took ahold of Eira's arm and pulled her back up the stairwell out of sight.

Tamsin smoothed down the front of her dress. If the king had not believed Rhys, if the prince reacted faster than they expected... A half dozen scenarios flashed before her eyes. She walked up the hallway towards the Bluecoats.

"There she is," said one of the men. He reached out and clamped his fingers down on her upper arm. "The others can't be far." He waved his free hand forward and four men moved up the stairs.

"Run," Tamsin screamed.

Chapter Twenty Seven

Tamsin could feel the wool fabric of the servant's gown rubbing her brand raw as she was marched down the halls. The four men had quickly been joined with a half dozen others, and each of the ladies was flanked by a rifle-carrying Bluecoat. At last, they came to a set of white panelled doors edged with gold. A footman waited outside, along with another four Bluecoats. The footman opened the doors when they approached, and their escort peeled back and arranged themselves along the wall.

"Where are we?" Tamsin whispered to Eira.

Marion answered. "I believe this is King Reginald's private chambers." She craned her neck right alongside Tamsin, trying to take in the room. If they were here… did that mean Rhys had succeeded?

The king's chamber proved to be an enormous sitting room decorated in more gold and white. A single sofa in royal blue dominated the far wall, with smaller white and gilt chairs in a ring around it. Rhys occupied one of these chairs.

He'd shed his moustache and overcoat somewhere along the way. He stood as they entered the room and made half a step towards them before glancing at the man on the sofa.

King Reginald looked frailer than the image on his coins. Perhaps some of that came from his lack of formal attire. He had a brocade banyan wrapped around his shoulders and a fur coverlet spread over his knees. He nodded to Rhys, and Rhys crossed the rest of the distance to the women at a run. He wrapped his arms around Eira first.

"I am so sorry. If I knew David would do this, I never would have let you go home. Are you injured?" Rhys babbled.

Eira murmured reassurances. After a long moment, he released her and turned to Tamsin and Marion.

Marion watched his eyes. "It's true," she said. Beside her Tamsin winced.

"Eira told me, but... you have your memories back," Marion said.

Rhys nodded and reached out a hand to her, Eira still in the crook of his other arm.

Tamsin turned away.

She should be happy. They'd won. If Rhys was here, like this, his evidence must have swayed the king. It was over. At least for them. She wondered again how the Narrows fared.

King Reginald brought the room's attention back to him with a gesture.

Rhys's arms were still occupied with Eira and Marion when he turned. Tamsin hung half a step behind them. What did she have to say to the king?

The king's gesture of attention flowed into a command to sit in the chairs around him with a mere flexing of his wrist. Tamsin envied him the ease of command. They sat.

"I trust neither of you ladies has been harmed by your ordeal?" King Reginald asked, neatly excluding Tamsin.

Marion managed to imply a curtsy with a bend of her upper body and smoothing her rumbled skirts.

"The accommodations were perhaps not up to the standards I'd expect from your majesty's home. Still, we are unscathed," Marion said. Tamsin noticed she met the monarch's eyes without flinching.

King Reginald's shoulders relaxed a tiny bit. His brother was guilty of harmful blood magic, torture, and treason, but he didn't hurt ladies. Tamsin wasn't sure if she should be happy the king could find small mercies or exasperated. But perhaps he didn't know about the magic. Her eyes flitted between the king and Rhys, but they held no clues. Best to stay silent then.

Someone knocked at the door, and it swung open. A Bluecoat entered, this one with so many rows of gold braid adorning his coat the blue felt like an afterthought. "The men at the east wing report that they have your brother's valet, sir, but they have seen no sign of your brother."

"How—" Tamsin started to say. Marion and Rhys sent her the same quelling look and she fell silent. How could they let him escape?

King Reginald made another motion and the kingsman left the room. The king turned his attention to Tamsin, and she shrank back into the chair. She knew better than to speak out of turn here.

"There was some…" King Reginald said, his voice strained and his breath short. "Some confusion, when my Lord Captain here caught my attention. My brother was able to leave our presence." Tamsin noticed the king slip into more formal wording. His brother's betrayal had harmed him, more than he would let on. "He must have prepared for this. Nikky always knew every hidden place here. By the time things had settled, he was gone."

Beside Tamsin, Eira shifted in her seat. "And my brother, your majesty?"

"We have sent men to Carwyn house and the city's gates have been sealed. We shall have to hope that is enough."

Tamsin looked towards the bank of windows behind the king.

"And the Narrows?" she whispered.

King Reginald returned his attention to her.

"I have sent men there to restore order. I have turned on the water, I did not realize the council had restricted it to that extent. I realize that my brother was fanning the flames of rebellion there, but I cannot allow open and armed insurrection in my city."

Tamsin felt her jaw clench and relaxed it with an effort. "The bread tax, the window tax, on top of three years left from the last war tax," she said. "People starve there for want of a penny. People I know are dying." It was Eira who reached out and laid a hand over Tamsin's.

King Reginald's lips tightened. "In light of the favour you have done for us, I shall keep your notions to mind when this is over." His tone was stern. Tamsin closed her eyes.

A coughing fit sent Reginald leaning back on the couch again. Rhys half rose and one of the Bluecoats at the doorway sent someone outside off at a run. Tamsin sat on her fingers. Elecampane might clear the air passages, Lungwort and Lobelia to build strength in his chest. But no one asked her.

When he stopped coughing, Reginald's face was scarlet.

"Where is your physician your majesty?" Rhys asked.

Reginald shook his head. A servant entered quietly with a tray and poured him a glass of something that steamed. Reginald sipped at it until the red faded from his cheeks.

"I don't know," Reginald said. "We've sent for Carmichael."

By the end of that small speech his lips were turning blue. When he raised the glass to his lips again, it took both hands and they were trembling.

Tamsin took advantage of his distraction to lean over to Rhys. "Nicholas took blood from Eira and Marion," she whispered.

Rhys's eyes widened as he took in the implications of that.

"That night, who cast the circle?" Tamsin asked.

"The prince," Rhys whispered. He looked over at Eira and Marion, then back at the king, still struggling with his drink.

"Your Majesty," Rhys said. He hesitated for a long moment with the whole room's eyes on him. Tamsin had gone still, very still. If Rhys started speaking about the magic, he could be sending both of them to the gallows, but if the prince had the women's blood, if he had saved some of Rhys's, or collected her own? She racked her memories. Had she seen any collection vessels at the warehouse? It had been three days. If she'd bled on the ropes or floor, it would have dried weakening the connection between her and it. That was why she'd required so much fresh blood from Rhys to compensate for the weak connection of his dried blood. But stored properly, blood could be potent for months, perhaps longer. Would Nicholas attack Rhys or the ladies? And where was the Doctor Carmichael?

Reginald began to cough again, and the pieces fell together all at once. The cup tumbled from his hands and shattered on the polished marble floor. Bright bubbles of red appeared around his mouth and his eyes rolled up in the back of his head as shudders wracked his body.

"The physician..." Tamsin said. She stood up and ran to the King's side. The Bluecoats caught her shoulders and pulled her away.

"No, I can help him," she said. "It's his brother. The blood."

Out of the corner of her eye she saw a wall panel swing out, revealing a door. A well-dressed woman passed through, her eyes wild.

"Her Majesty has fallen ill!" she said.

Tamsin twisted in the men's grip.

"You must let me go to him," she said. If he died, Nicholas would inherit. And what would happen to the Narrows then?

Rhys stepped forward and put his hand on one of the Bluecoats' shoulders. "Sergeant Kilpatrick, let her go to him. She can help."

The Bluecoat looked at his fellow and stepped back. Tamsin knelt next to the couch. King Reginald had stopped convulsing, but his breath had a laboured, moist quality that she mistrusted. She touched the bubbles of blood at the corner of his mouth and brought the blood up to her own lips.

An angry snarl of threads twisted around in her mind. The anger almost covered the sense of Reginald and his air-starved struggles. Tamsin placed her fingertips on his temples, her thumbs trailing down to the blood still bubbling up around his mouth. The contact with his flesh dimmed the anger a little, but it was harder to create a bond with the king, than it had been with Frank or Rhys. Somewhere outside of all of this she could hear Rhys talking, orders being given, but that was background noise. She let it fade and focused on breathing. Their lungs burned, and she choked and gasped herself, unsure of which breath was hers and which was the king's.

Tamsin pinched herself and the pain brought enough separation that she could breathe again. The snarls twisted around her as she pulled back. The anger was stronger near the lungs, sick lungs filled with fluids, being filled.

"I need to get his head elevated more," she gasped, releasing her grip. Her lungs still burned. How long had she held that breath? Rhys and the sergeant elevated the king's upper body. It helped a little. Tamsin reached out again. If the anger was the prince, it was so deep, she couldn't block it. He bore through any defence she threw up. But perhaps she could redirect it? Her fingers brushed the blood again, painting an accidental smile on the king's cheeks, and she let herself fall back into the magic. This time she kept herself distant, observing the way the blood flowed and grew near the lungs. If she could shift it away... It felt like someone was standing on her chest. She eased under the snarl and leaned, and something shifted. Reginald's breathing eased. It was enough, but only for now. She needed to find a way to block Nicholas's attack for good.

When she looked up from the King, the room had filled. There were half a dozen Bluecoats ringed around her now, with Rhys hovering at her back. The man with the gold braid was back.

"What is happening to him?" he asked.

Tamsin lurched to her feet. "The prince is killing him," she said. The room seemed to pitch around, and Rhys reached out and held her elbow until she was steady. Healing herself and the king had pressed her up against the limits of how much magic she'd ever done at one time.

"Nicholas cast blood magic on me ten days ago," Rhys filled in. "It appears he had the foresight to gather some of his majesty's blood, and perhaps the queen's as well. I know he has Lady Everwood's and my sister's, General. He's found some place to strike back at his majesty."

The general opened his mouth and closed it twice. "What do we need to do to keep their majesties safe?" he asked Rhys.

Rhys waved a hand at Tamsin. "Listen to her."

Tamsin swallowed. This much responsibility was not what she had anticipated. Her palms were slick with sweat. "I need the queen, and anyone else whose blood the prince might have. I need a knife, a cup or bowl, and quiet." There was no way to know how long the prince would keep up his attacks. If he was someplace safe, he could keep this up for months. She'd need to cut off the blood ties he had.

The General looked between her and Rhys. Then he barked an order, and the servants ran out.

"I lay the responsibility for this directly on your shoulders Captain Carwyn."

Rhys nodded. "Tamsin won't let you down."

The lady came back into the room. "Her majesty has fainted in her dressing room," she said. She swallowed. "There is a lot of blood."

The general beckoned over his men. "Bring his Majesty with us."

He led them through another chamber, through a hall to a lavender room. The queen lay in the centre of the marble floor. Someone had placed a pillow under her head, but her hair was plastered to her brown cheeks.

Tamsin ran to her. Her finger touched the blood and she recoiled. Familiar, and yet something else.

"She's pregnant!" Tamsin said.

The general gave a small nod. "It is early," he said. "And she has lost every pregnancy she carried so far."

Tamsin touched the blood again. This time she didn't need to bring it to her lips to feel the same angry hum as before.

"I need that bowl," she said. "And lay the king near her."

A servant set down a silver washbasin next to Tamsin. Another laid out cushions and the Bluecoats set the king gently on top.

"Who should I protect first?" she asked. Her eyes darted to Rhys standing near the door.

"The queen," said the king. Somewhere along the way he'd woken up, but his voice was thin and strained.

Tamsin met his gaze. "Do I have your permission, your majesty?"

King Reginald nodded. "Witness it," he gasped. Tamsin didn't wait for the rest of the room to acknowledge his words. She bent down. Should she draw a circle? It seemed to be the Aradwyn way, but she was Cyprycian. And if the magic goes wrong, it's only the king's life on the line, and the queen, and Eira, Rhys...

"I need a knife," Tamsin said. Her knife was still somewhere in the carpeted hallways. Rhys handed her his blade. Tamsin hadn't realized he'd been carrying it. She drew the blade lightly across her wrist. She needed a lot of blood, and fast. She had to cut with care, if she severed her veins, she could lose her hand or worse. The blood welled up immediately and settled into the crevasses of the raised silver flowers along the bottom of the basin.

Rhys sucked in his breath. The air was thick around her. Did she have enough energy for this? There was maybe a cup of blood in the basin. Tamsin wrapped her apron around her wrist to stop the bleeding. Her head spun.

"What is she doing?" Marion asked. Rhys hushed her.

Tamsin didn't bother to look up. She knelt next to the queen, the knife blade still in her hand. Her skirts soaked up the pool of blood around the queen's head. The bond was eager this time. Tamsin reached over and lifted the woman's wrist. She didn't stir. Beneath Tamsin's fingers the queen's pulse was a faint flutter. Tamsin slid the blade along the woman's palm, carefully. Fresh blood rose up and Tamsin brought the cut to her lips. This third healing was like pushing a needle through three layers of sail. Tamsin gasped for air underneath the shroud Nicholas had laid over the queen. She quelled the woman's bleeding, but Nicholas was trying another attack. Tamsin lowered the queen's hand into the basin of blood. She wrapped the essence of her vital fluid around the queen's until slowly the blood changed, minutely. Some of Tamsin's strength flowed into the queen, and the grey of her cheeks faded. The queen stirred.

"You did it?" Eira whispered.

Tamsin looked up, her eyes heavy.

"She'll live," Tamsin said.

Rhys sighed. His eyes grew wide, and he stumbled forward. Marion and Eira caught him before he tumbled to the marble floor. A faint line of blood flowed from the corner of his eye down his cheek.

Tamsin stood too fast. The room spun about her.

"Rhys!" she cried.

Rhys reached up and clutched her hand. "Take care of Reggie," he gasped. Marion and Eira eased him to the floor. Tamsin glanced between him and the king. The king was breathing still. Nicholas seemed to have moved on from his assault. The Bluecoats standing at the door were staring at her, hands on the polished rifles resting on their shoulders.

Reginald met her eyes. He shook his head and pointed to the queen and Rhys.

"You've helped me enough. Keep them safe," Reginald said.

Rhys had stopped moving. Next to him Eira swayed. Her nose had begun to bleed. There was no time. Tamsin cut Rhys's palm and shoved it into the pool of blood, then Eira's, then Marion's. There was scarcely enough blood. She pressed her hand on top of the others and pushed. Her wrist had started bleeding freely again. Bands of slick, sick energy twisted around Eira and Rhys. Tamsin could feel the threads starting to wrap around Marion. She clawed them away, twisting her own essence to change their blood and prevent the attacks from finding purchase.

She'd let go of the others' hands. Eira was calling something. The threads wrapped around Tamsin, trying to find purchase. Nicholas had never tried to use his magic on another blood mage before. How could he? Tamsin was the last in Aradwyn. She was dimly aware of people moving around her, sounds being made. But inside she wove her own line of defence against the prince.

Suddenly one of his threads spun out into nothing. Then another. Another. She was alone. Rhys was breathing, Marion and Eira were safe, Tamsin reached for the queen, slumbering but still protected. Someone was shouting. The king? Her mother called her name. The room went dark.

Chapter Twenty Eight

Tamsin stretched her feet under smooth, soft sheets, and touched a warm wrapped something that was keeping her toes delightfully toasty. The weight of blankets pressed down on her back. This was lovely, lovely enough that things like where's and when's could wait, and she wanted nothing more than to give back into the pillows and sleep again.

Alas, her bladder reminded her of the true reason she'd woken. Reluctantly she pushed back the covers and groped for a bedside table or something that might have a rush light or candle. Instead, she found thick cloth. She moved that aside and cold air and light entered her cocoon. Afternoon light. It had been near to midnight when they had gone into the dressing room. Was she still at the palace?

A girl dressed in black was sitting just outside the bed curtains. She put aside her sewing and stood when she saw Tamsin.

"How are you feeling Miss Saer?" she asked. She knew Tamsin's name.

"Rested. Where is Rhys? And... um... the privy?"

"Lord Rhys and his sister are staying in rooms closer to her majesty. And the facilities are this way." The woman pointed to a small door. Tamsin nodded and hurried towards them.

Someone had redressed her. The bedraggled maid's dress and breeches were gone. The nightdress she wore was soft wool trimmed with lace. A swirling C and R were embroidered on the breast.

Would they dress her in fancy clothes if they meant to execute her for witchcraft? Perhaps not, but she couldn't shake her unease. What had happened after she fainted?

When she returned, the girl in black had gone. In her place was a platter piled high with food, and fresh clothing, a dress of black wool and her own, clean and pressed, under layers. The dress showed signs of hasty alteration, but it fit. Tamsin changed into the warmer layers quickly. The fire burned high, but the windows let in a terrible draft. Carwyn house had been snugger. She picked a piece of toast out of the tray, but her stomach was still queasy. Someone had bandaged her wrist and tended to the half-healed cut on her arm.

The maid knocked on the door and opened it without waiting for an answer. Tamsin put the last of the toast down on the tray and scrubbed at the crumbs along her front.

"If you will follow me," she said.

Tamsin twisted her hands in her skirt. "Of course." She tried to sound casual. The maid didn't seem to notice either way. She led Tamsin through a short hall, up a flight of stairs, and through some panelled double doors. Rhys waited with Eira and Marion in the same room she had met the king in last night. Last night. It felt longer and not long enough. The furniture had been altered, and now the room contained a polished wood table with matching chairs lining each side. Lots of chairs, more than would be needed for the four of them.

Queen Caroline entered from the back. She wore an open robe of thick black wool over her white day dress. Perhaps a concession to the drafts. She sat at the head of the table and waved her hands at the four of them. "Please, be seated."

Tamsin kept a careful chair's distance between herself and Rhys. Where was the king? She tried to tamp down her anxiety.

Queen Caroline addressed the Bluecoats hovering at the doors. "You may leave us."

When the last door was shut, she sagged back against the chair. Her dark attire made the circles under her eyes look like bruises. "His majesty died this morning," she said.

"What? How?" Rhys said. Shock followed pain on his face. Tamsin wanted to reach out to him. Instead, Marion rested one of her hands over his wrist. He didn't acknowledge it.

"He'd been ill for such a long time," Caroline said. "We hoped..." she trailed off and Tamsin saw the gravity of the queen's situation press her frame inwards, then her shoulders straightened. "My husband's brother, and living heir, is a traitor. He cannot inherit." Her hand rested on her belly. "If this child lives, they will inherit the Aradwyn crown. We must secure that future."

Rhys looked small. Was he remembering his king, or the boy he'd played with as a child?

"I live to serve."

"I'll need your support on the council," Queen Caroline said. "Nicholas may still have allies there. I need to set up a regency council, and I mean to sit at its head. Will you help me protect your king's child Lord Rhys?"

"I have no seat on the council," Rhys said. "But I believe Lord Hedworth will support your claim. Lord Porter will be swayed with assurances that you do not intend to disrupt his oversight of the budget. The army general, Duke Evans can be swayed to your side. He never liked how fond Nicholas was of playing a general. That will make a start."

"Don't forget Lord Driscoll. His wife mentioned that Nicholas slighted him in his home at their last invitation. He should be open to a new alliance," Marion said.

"Thank you, Lord Rhys, Lady Everwood. That brings me to the first order of business today. Lord Rhys, Lady Eira, your brother David's actions mark him as a traitor to the realm. Do either of you have any evidence that might mitigate his actions?"

Eira shook her head. Rhys glanced at Tamsin.

"Your Majesty, I believe the prince may have had some kind of hold over him financially. Miss Saer observed David and Prince Nicholas arguing about the prince's actions. David argued that they should stop immediately," Rhys said.

Queen Caroline turned her gaze to Tamsin again. That was a little strong. David's actions had seemed to her to be motivated more by fear than a moral obligation that he was wrong. She realized the room was staring at her. She nodded hastily. "That's true."

"Was David caught?" Eira whispered. Her eyes were red rimmed.

"He was found trying to flee the city. We shall hold the formal trial soon," Queen Caroline said. "In light of this information I will recommend sparing your brother from the gallows." Eira covered her mouth. Rhys gave a small nod. He had known, Tamsin realized. He had known this whole time that acting to stop Nicholas would most likely be sending his brother to his death.

"He is still guilty of acting against the crown. We may not sentence his person without a trial," Queen Caroline said, "but his title is under our purview. Lord Rhys, I know you did not expect this, but I name you my new Lord Carwyn and declare that you shall supersede David's claim to the remaining Carwyn titles and lands. David has been acting as your father's proxy? Now you are. That will give you a place on my council."

Rhys looked sad. "I never aspired to the Earl's coronet," he said softly. "But I will accept it in trust for my family."

"Lady Eira," the queen continued, "I understand you have also had a not insignificant role in all of this. I would raise you to the order of the Quartered Rose and grant to you an annuity, in addition to what your brother will share from his estate, of ten thousand pounds."

Eira looked stunned. Her hands wrung together on the polished tabletop. After a moment, she managed a quiet, "Thank you."

"Lady Everwood, you were caused great harm as well. The crown owes you a boon and we can discuss how that will be paid out soon."

Marion bowed. "Thank you, your majesty," she said. Her voice was cool and even, but her eyes watched Tamsin.

"At last, Miss Saer." Queen Caroline paused and swallowed hard before continuing. "As I understand it, you require a great deal of credit, in saving my life and uncovering this plot."

Tamsin braced. They had to know that she had been in Kingsgate by now. They'd watched her cast magic. Was the permission of a dead king enough to keep her from the gallows?

"You have done our house a favour I cannot forget," Queen Caroline said. "I grant to you the lands of Freiton Manor, formerly in my brother-in-law's possession. To hold those lands, you will need a title. I suppose a knighthood would be the most suitable."

Tamsin looked at Eira. She nodded enthusiastically.

"What does that mean?" Tamsin said. She had wanted to leave the Narrows, was this it?

"We will have to dispense with most of your investment ceremony," Caroline was explaining. "The court will be in high mourning..." She stopped and Tamsin watched her recompose herself. She was new to Aradwyn and alone now. The moment passed. "There are some incomes that come with the property for you," Caroline continued, "Freiton is traditionally a crown property, so it will be entailed back to our family, but you are granted its possession and incomes for your lifetime."

"Where?" Tamsin whispered. This was all happening so fast.

"About half a day's travel north near Grosmont," Rhys supplied.

"But I didn't... I mean, thank you your majesty." A crown manor with incomes was not what she had imagined when she dreamed of leaving the Narrows.

"It's not entirely a favour." Caroline ran her hand over her belly. "Miss Saer, you are a healer, are you not?"

Tamsin didn't trust herself to say yes out loud.

"This child must survive," the queen said. "I require your services. I have lost three pregnancies since I was married. I cannot lose this one. You will make this happen." The queen's eyes would not release Tamsin's.

"To do so might break the laws of Aradwyn. Laws that have been in place since your husband's grandfather banned my kind."

"Laws can be rewritten Miss Saer," the queen said. "I have never understood this conceit of the Aradwyn to ban the healing with the harm. Bring my child into this world alive and you will want for nothing ever again."

"I believe that Nicholas was behind your other miscarriages," Tamsin said slowly. "I found your blood in a ritual circle in the Narrows."

Queen Caroline closed her eyes. "Is it likely to happen again?" she asked at last.

Tamsin swallowed. "What I did earlier should protect you, as long as they are not able to get any more of your blood. How far along are you?"

"Nearing my third full month."

"Most of the risk should be behind you soon," Tamsin said. "You will need to take some precautions to be sure that Nicholas, or any allies left behind, cannot get to you again."

The queen pressed her lips tight. "I have a few ideas on that score myself. Lady Warren has already been dismissed from my company to join her husband under house arrest. I shall need you to attend the birth of course. Are you able to check the health of the child now? Our cruors from home could determine that from a prick of a thumb."

Tamsin met Rhys eyes. He nodded.

"Do you have a needle your majesty?" she asked.

The queen unfastened a jet broach that had held the front of her over gown closed. She pricked the pad of her pinkie and offered the drop of blood to Tamsin.

Tamsin smeared the drop on her finger and brought it to her lips. This wasn't the heady bond she had shared with Rhys, or Frank, or even the king. Tamsin sensed weakness with the queen, she was overtired and drained from the events of last night. But under that was a healthy sense of growing life, small but steady.

"The child still lives. You need to rest and rebuild your strength. Eat strengthening things, red meat, beef broth and milk. If all goes well with the birth, your child should survive."

The queen sat back against her chair.

"Thank you, Miss Saer. We shall require you to make yourself available to us at regular intervals."

"I am at your disposal," Tamsin murmured.

Beside Rhys, Marion looked ill. Perhaps she didn't like the sight of blood.

"What happened in the Narrows?" Tamsin asked when the silence seemed to grow too heavy.

"There was heavy fighting around the docks," Rhys said. "A lot of the Grainery burned."

"Baker?" Tamsin asked.

Rhys shook his head. "I don't know yet. We can..." he stopped and looked between the Queen and Marion. "I'll look into it," he finished.

"And the water, the taxes?" Tamsin asked the queen.

"I have already increased the flow of water to the Narrows, Dame Saer. As for the rest, the taxation matter goes before the council. Without my brother-in-law's disrupting influence more reasonable minds may prevail. I shall exert what influence I can towards it once the succession has been secured."

"I have some ideas on that, your majesty," Rhys said. "We should call Lord Hedworth immediately. As for Lords Dalton and Porter—"

"Thank you, Lord Carwyn, we can continue this conversation shortly. Do the rest of you have any further questions before I must turn my attention to governing?" the queen said.

"Have they found the prince, your majesty?" Marion asked. "I will rest easier knowing you have brought him into custody."

Queen Caroline shook her head. "Not yet. Nicholas is not in the palace, but he has not been found in the city thus far. I have sent out messengers and sent extra men to the gate. Every door in Aradwyn is closed to him now, and the borders are on alert. I don't believe that he's left Celdre. Lord and Lady Warren have been confined along with David Carwyn and Doctor Carmichael. His bodyman Marcus was able to escape after his initial capture, but it's only a matter of time till we find them."

There was a deep irony to Nicholas being the hunted now.

"Dame Saer," Caroline went on, "I will require you to avail yourself of my hospitality for a few more days before you may inspect your new estate. Lord Carwyn, come with me to the council now to inform them of the king's death. Lady Eira, Lady Everwood, I know you have much to attend to." The queen lifted her hand and the table rose, Tamsin only half a beat behind the rest.

A maid tugged on Tamsin's sleeve. "If you will come this way, Miss, her majesty has brought in her modiste to assist with your new wardrobe."

Tamsin glanced at the others, but Rhys was occupied speaking with the queen. Eira smiled at her, but a footman had claimed her attention and was slowly herding them away.

Tamsin followed the maid.

*

The rest of the afternoon was taken up with proddings, pins, and an array of black and grey silks spread over every surface of the borrowed bedchamber.

By the time evening fell, Tamsin was left alone again. The court had entered full mourning, a maid told her bearing a heavy tray. Tamsin only nodded. The room was beginning to feel like a prison.

"Could I go out?" she asked.

The maid seemed unfazed. "Of course, would you like a carriage brought around for morning calling hours?" she asked.

"What about now?" Tamsin said. The windows of her room faced away from the Narrows; she hadn't seen the damage yet.

"The coachmen will not be available until the morning, Miss," the maid said. Despite Tamsin's efforts she'd stayed aloof.

"The morning then."

Tamsin picked a bit at the tray, but she still wasn't hungry. She woke the next morning before the sun, her body still on a schedule to match Baker's ovens. The maid found her dressed and waiting.

The palace carriage was impressive. The four bay horses pulling it were well matched, the royal seal stencilled on every door, with velvet upholstery on the seats.

"Where to, Dame Saer?" the driver asked.

"Can you take me to the Narrows?" she asked.

The driver hesitated. "The Council blocked the gates," he said. "No vehicles allowed unless they are helping to clear the streets."

Tamsin closed her eyes. She should have expected that. And what was her plan? Drive through in a royal carriage wearing a cloak and gown worth twenty sovs? She'd start another riot. New plan.

"The Emirya Theatre, please," she said.

With the royal seal on the carriage, passing through the gates was swifter than she had ever experienced. The entire trip took less than a quarter hour. Word of the king's death had reached the city. Black crepe draped every surface in the king's Ring and the Merchants' Ring had decked itself out with bands of black on every arm and vendors hawking black ribbons on every street corner.

The carriage stopped at the front door and a footman hurried to pull down the step and assist her out.

"I expect I will be occupied for at least an hour," Tamsin said. She hesitated before adding, "Will you be back?"

The driver's face was blank. "Her Majesty has placed the carriage entirely at your disposal today, Dame Saer. We will wait until you require us again."

Tamsin flushed. Of course, that is how it worked for gentry. And now she was one, even more than she had been before Kingsgate.

She eschewed the front door and went around to the back again. At this hour, the only ones here would be the stagehands and backstage staff. The stagehand who answered her knock seemed confused at her new attire, but he led her to Elspeth's workshop easy enough.

"Tamsin!" Elspeth threw the shirt she was sewing onto the table and embraced her. "We've been worried." She'd added black mourning ribbons above the row of pins on her sleeve.

Tamsin held herself still under the embrace. Lacey and Frank?

"We?" she asked.

Elspeth smiled. She turned to the stagehand that had brought Tamsin and asked, "Can you ask Kate to step around?"

"Kate is here?" Tamsin asked. Not Lacey. She swallowed her anxiety. Frank and Lacey had to be all right. They had to.

"I hired her on to help," Elspeth said. Kate came in carrying a load of fresh shirts.

"Is Lady Eira safe?" Kate asked.

"She is. She is at the palace right now. Lord Car— er, David Carwyn has been captured. Rhys is Lord Carwyn now, and if you want it, your place at Carwyn house is probably yours again," Tamsin said.

Kate exchanged looks with Elspeth. "I will have to think about it. The theatre is very different from being a housemaid. I might like this better. There's less treason and intrigue for certain."

Tamsin snorted.

"Have you any news about Frank and Lacey, or Baker, or the Narrows?" Tamsin asked Elspeth.

Elspeth pursed her lips. "Lacey came by yesterday morning. She said Frank made it through. Baker's shop was spared the fires."

Tamsin's mouth went dry. Thank the gods they were safe. "I need to see them." She thought of the carriage and driver waiting for her in the front. "Elspeth, how do you feel about a little misdirection?"

Ten minutes later Tamsin and Kate walked arm and arm through the streets, Tamsin in yet another borrowed dress. Elspeth had laughed away Tamsin's offer to trade the figured silk mourning dress from the palace for the plain wool one she wore now. "Just try to return this one without blood on it," she'd said, only half joking. "But if you do, I suppose I will be able to find the Lady of Freiton house to settle her bills."

Tamsin and Kate passed through the lower gates with alacrity, although there were more Bluecoats milling about than Tamsin could recall. They kept to the Merchants' side of the gate though, and once again they didn't seem to be keeping people out. Not that many people were looking for passage in or out today.

As she stepped through the gate tunnel Tamsin's breath caught in her chest. Even at the edge, the Narrow's was shockingly altered.

The fountain basin was cracked, yet the water was still running at this hour and streaming a muddy trail through the streets. After years of water being hoarded, Tamsin was shaken by the waste. The gates themselves were bent, one hinge free from the stone, and the walls were charred to almost chest height.

Buildings were gone. The tenements near the Drunk Duck still smouldered, blackened timbers reaching up to the new patch of sky. There was a stench, charred and cloying, hanging over everything. Tamsin's eyes watered.

"How could…" She couldn't finish that question.

"His shop stands," Kate said, "but the fires were very near to it. Lacey said something about smoke and the youngest's chest being weak. I don't think he is getting on well."

Logan. "I need to see him first," Tamsin decided.

It was difficult navigating streets where the landmarks were so altered, but they found their way at last. Her little room at the back had been broken into, her things spread across the floor, broken or missing altogether.

She took in the chaos and laughed. Tears streamed down her cheeks and the laughter took on a hysterical lilt.

"It took me six months to pay Lacey back for the tub," she said. Six months of sawdust suppers and a dress so thin she'd stuffed straw under it to keep warm. "I suppose the manor will have a washtub."

"More than one, likely," Kate said. "Tamsin, about Freiton."

"Yes?" Tamsin poked around the rafters, but her tiny stash of coins was gone.

"It's just I've heard things. It's not exactly a gift you know."

Tamsin hopped down from the remains of her bed. "What do you mean?"

"One of the chambermaids knew a footman who worked there for a while. It's old, falling-down old. She said they were constantly trying to keep it up before it crumbled away, and the lands around it aren't very good for farming. It cost the prince a good sum to keep it up."

Tamsin swallowed. Well, she hadn't really thought that the queen was giving her a huge fortune. After life down here, how bad could it be?

"Well, I'm sure I'll make it work," Tamsin said at last.

Baker's shop had been ransacked as well; the only thing that seemed unharmed was the great stone oven. Tamsin rapped on the door frame; the door was gone.

It was Anne who peeked her head down the stair. She squeaked when she saw Tamsin and they heard her small footsteps slapping the stair treads as she ran back upstairs. There was a mummer of voices upstairs, and then the footfalls down were heavier.

Baker's face was wary when he stepped onto the landing.

"I didn't expect to see your face here," he said.

"They told me Logan... can I help?" Tamsin said.

"There've been all sorts of stories floating around about you, Miss Tam," Baker said. He still hadn't moved from the landing.

"Some of them might be true, but I can help your son."

Baker just looked at her. Behind her Tamsin could feel Kate shift her weight in the uncomfortable silence. Finally, he nodded and stepped aside.

It had been over a year since Tamsin had climbed these stairs. One of the littles had scored the wall with something sharp in a wavering mark up the entire length of the stairs. Baker stopped them at the top landing. He left Tamsin's sight for a moment, and she could hear a muffled conversation, then he appeared again and motioned them forward.

Logan was laid out on the large bed. His siblings pressed their backs on the wall furthest away from her. Tamsin squeezed her lips together, but she shouldn't be surprised they were wary now. Mrs. Baker was sitting next to Logan, holding his small shoulders still against another coughing fit. Her face was crossed with fresh lines.

"You said he needed fresh air, winter before last," she said. Her voice was thin and tired. "But there was nowhere to go, and all the smoke…" she trailed off.

"It wasn't your fault," Tamsin said. "May I?" She reached out and took the boy's small hands in her own. The queen had not said anything about healing others, but surely she would allow Tamsin to fix what the king's neglect and Tamsin's own failures had wrought?

There was fluid in Logan's lungs. The way his chest shook with every breath told her that. She straightened her spine. "I need to prick his finger." Baker didn't meet her eyes, but Mrs. Baker pulled a wooden needle case from the string of oddments dangling from her chatelaine. She handed the needle to Tamsin and held Logan's smallest finger still.

Tamsin's hands shook but she gave the flesh a sharp jab and touched the small bead of blood that welled up when he jerked away. Her eyes closed and she dropped into a, now familiar, trance.

This time she kept him at a safer distance. She felt the tissues of his lungs tight with scarring from the old coughs and consumptions. She reached across the blood bond, willing the flesh to ease, the fluid to absorb back into the slackening tissue. She could feel the moment when his breath started to steady.

It took a few more minutes for her to find her way back to herself. Logan was asleep, but a flush of pink edged his lips and fingers again.

Mrs. Baker was watching Logan's face intently. After a few minutes passed without a coughing fit some of the tension drained from her body.

"I cannot promise this won't happen again. He needs clear air, and when he is recovered, he should exert himself slowly to build back his strength, but he is breathing better and the cough should subside in a few more days," Tamsin said.

Anne stepped forward. "Someone broke into your room, Miss Tam. They broke your things."

"It's all right. I think I have another place to live now," Tamsin told her.

Mrs. Baker pressed her hand. "Thank you," she said. "You will always have a place here."

Tamsin ducked her head.

They headed back out onto the streets.

*

Lacey and Frank's room was smouldering. Tamsin watched as people pushed around the ruins looking for scraps. Every once in a while, someone would expose some embers to the air and flames would flare up again to be beaten back with sodden rags and dirt.

"Maybe they will be at one of the taverns?" Tamsin asked.

The damage here was far greater than it had been near Baker's. After a half block Tamsin gave up. Ahead the streets were blocked with rubble. In places the fire still burned unchecked.

They found Lacey and Frank at last in the ruins of the old mill. The place teamed with people. Tamsin and Kate were challenged at the perimeter by a scarred dockworker Tamsin had seen around the Drunk Duck. He carried one of the smuggled muskets, but he left it resting on his shoulder.

"Whatcha need here?" he called.

"I'm looking for my friends," Tamsin called. Even with his relaxed stance, she kept a few paces between them.

"Names?"

"Lacey and Frank Green. They had a little place by the docks," Tamsin said.

"Tamsin?" Lacey poked her head out of the mill. A pistol was thrust through her belt and her face was grey from soot. She limped heavily.

"What happened?" Tamsin said. "Elspeth said you were all right." She pushed through the debris to embrace Lacey.

Lacey shrugged. "We had a bit of a disagreement with the Runners last night. They were harder hit in terms of supplies than we were. Frank managed to empty the ammo stores of five of the stashes. We've been guarding them here. Along with the food stores."

"Is Frank all right?" Tamsin asked.

Lacey shrugged. "He took another bullet, to the arm this time. The barber looked at it and sewed it up. He said Frank'd heal."

Inside the mill there were thirty or more people. Most held muskets across their laps while they tended to children or the injured. Someone had set up a cookfire and some sort of cauldron dangled over the embers.

"What is all this?" Tamsin asked.

"We expanded the plan," Lacey said. "Frank told a few people, and I told a few, and before we knew it, we had a hundred here before the riots broke. We couldn't save everything, but we held this ground. We lost ten people though, mostly last night. The Runners aren't very happy with us right now."

Lacey led Kate and Tamsin over to where Frank lay propped up against a stack of crates speaking to two armed women. Those were gun crates Tamsin realized. A bandage was wrapped around his upper arm and shoulder.

"Make sure the barricade at the south entrance is braced. We don't want the Runners flanking us again," he said.

The two women nodded, shouldered their muskets, and left.

"Well, if it isn't my favourite healer." Frank's voice was a little slurred.

"Getting hurt without calling me?" Tamsin reached down and started unwrapping the bandage.

"It missed the bone," Frank said. "You should be looking after this one," he pointed to Lacey, "she took a tumble last night when one of the stairs broke."

"There's no rule that says I can't do both," Tamsin said as she poked the flesh around the stitches. Frank winced. "Your barber does good work." It was well sewn and there was no sign of rot around the wound. Beside her, Kate looked a little green.

"If you don't mind," Kate said, "I'll see if I can help with the children until the doctoring is done." She joined the circle of children playing some sort of chasing game near the cleared-out centre of the ruins.

"How did our kingsringer fare up in the palace? Did he make it with his head still attached?" Frank asked between her examinations.

"In part. Have you heard the news?" Tamsin asked as she rewrapped the bandage.

Frank shook his head.

"The king is dead, by his brother's ... actions," Tamsin said. There were too many ears around them to mention the magic. Still Frank and Lacey could read between the lines. "The queen is leading a regency council now. She disinherited Rhys's brother, so Rhys is the Earl's heir now. They gave me a house, and a title too."

Lacey snorted. "I figured you'd land on your feet someday."

"Maybe, you two could come with me?" Tamsin said.

"Did Rhys tell them who brought the guns over?" Lacey asked.

"No, he left that out. But they haven't caught the prince yet. I don't know who else knows."

"The prince's right-hand man and that Warren fellow knew our faces but not our names," Frank said.

Tamsin winced. "Lord Warren's in custody now," she said. "He'll talk eventually."

Frank and Lacey exchanged looks. "Between this and the Runner's coming after us..." Lacey said.

Frank sighed. "You're right, you should go."

Lacey glared. "We should go."

The siblings locked eyes, then Frank waved his uninjured hand. "Fine, fine."

"Will they look for you out of the city?" Tamsin asked. "How will you get out?"

Lacey shrugged. "They might, but a whole lot of people didn't make it. There's a good chance that they'll count us among that. Especially if they have the men planning the whole revolt."

Frank pointed. "And Trenton's over there. He brought his whole family once the cannons went off, and they all made it through alive. I think he can find us some papers to get out of the city."

"I can use your help at the estate then. Kate said the place has some issues," Tamsin said.

"Are you offering us the run of some Kingsringer house?" Lacey smiled. "Sounds like fun."

Chapter Twenty Nine

After her day-long excursion to the Narrows, the palace strongly suggested that Tamsin remain in the palace until the queen released her. At the week's end, Tamsin knelt before the queen's regency court on a blue velvet cushion, wearing a new black silk gown and received a sword tap to each shoulder. Then it was over, and newly knighted, she was dismissed.

The next morning Tamsin found her bags packed with her wardrobe. And waiting by the door when the breakfast tray arrived.

"Your escort will be here shortly, Dame Saer," said the maid. The Queen had dismissed all of the servants in the prince's employment and the ones in the rest of the household had been questioned thoroughly.

"My escort?" Tamsin asked. She'd had no visitors since her excursion to the Narrows and the staff were all very precise and distant in their manners. The isolation had felt like a different kind of gaol cell. She wondered what Rhys and Eira had been doing at Merriton Square.

"To your new estate," the maid said, deliberately misunderstanding the question. "Her Majesty feels that it is time you inspect your property." The maid handed Tamsin a folio of papers. "She asked me to give this to you with her regards."

"Thank you," Tamsin said automatically. She flipped the folio open. It was stuffed with pages filled with narrow script, dripping with seals. Some of the paper was crumbling along the edges with age.

The maid led her through the halls down to the entryway. Tamsin's new trunk was already there.

It was not too long before a curricle pulled up, just large enough for two. A footman caught the reins as the driver swung down and another loaded her trunk on the back.

"Rhys," Tamsin breathed.

Rhys bowed, perfect, correct, and distant. Tamsin could feel everyone's eyes on them as she returned his bow.

"Dame Saer," he said. "I requested the honour of escorting you to your new home." He offered her his hand and helped her climb to the seat. He settled beside her, his elbow brushing her own. The groom released the horses, and they left the palace behind.

After so many years of planning, her passage through the gate was rote, routine. There was a moment of conversation, a glancing at the papers Rhys had brought along, and they were on their way, crossing the Kyrin River on a grey stone bridge.

Rhys broke the silence first.

"I hope you don't mind. I didn't want you to make this journey alone."

"Ah." She didn't mention that Frank and Lacey were en route to meet her at the house. Rhys reached into his waistcoat and flipped open his watch.

"You got it back!"

"Indeed. The shop that Frank pawned it at was in the Merchants' Ring. I sent Henry down to buy it back last week."

"I'm glad that it and Henry have come back to you," she said, keeping her eyes on the countryside.

"And..." Rhys paused. The silence stretched out, until at last Tamsin turned to look at Rhys. "Tamsin," he shifted again. "Tamsin, something is wrong."

"Lots of things are wrong, Rhys."

"Well yes, that too. But Tamsin, I didn't remember everything."

She whipped her head around and the bonnet the maid insisted Tamsin wear, twisted in front of her face. Tamsin shoved it off her head to dangle by its ribbons down her back.

"What? You said you remembered!"

"I did, I do... but not all of it," Rhys said. "I remember Eira, David, the plot, my home ... but I've found there are gaps. Significant ones, and Eira and Marion have noticed."

"Why didn't you tell me before?" Tamsin said.

"I didn't realize. Not 'til I was alone with Marion, and..." he trailed off again.

"And what?" Tamsin prompted.

"I don't recall courting her, or things we did as children," he said. "I remember her, but only in relation to others. Never alone."

Tamsin twisted her hands in her skirts.

"The warehouse burnt, Rhys. Once after you rescued me, and again in the riots. I don't think I can bring those memories back. I'm sorry."

"I know," he said. "It's only that Marion wants me to be whole, to forget any of this ever happened."

Tamsin snorted. "Because of all of this, she'll be a countess someday. She shouldn't be so hasty about a few memories." As soon as the words had left her mouth, she regretted them.

Rhys's hands had tightened on the reins.

"I'm sorry," Tamsin said. "Marion didn't deserve that." She swallowed. "This is harder than I thought."

"I know," Rhys was the one not making eye contact now. "You must understand, I left Marion once."

"What?"

"I broke off our engagement. That was in the other letter. I met a woman during the war, and... I was going to return to Orness and bring her back here after the war. But she died, a fever of some sort, and Marion was still waiting. But now she keeps looking for the Rhys she knew, and I am not sure if I will be that again."

"Everyone changes," Tamsin said. She certainly had. "You'll find a way to change together."

"No, I don't think we will."

"Rhys, marriages have been—"

He interrupted her. "Marion asked me if I wish to be released from our engagement last night."

Under the warm spring sun, Tamsin felt cold.

"What do you want?" she finally whispered.

Rhys hesitated, too long. She broke in before he could say his polite words. Of course he would want to marry Marion.

"You needn't feel any obligation to me, Lord Carwyn," she said, her voice cold and even.

Rhys shifted beside her. "I see," he said.

They rode along in silence for a while, until they stopped at an inn about midday for lunch and made banal conversations over salt-cured ham and lemonade. Was this how their relationship would play out? Not quite strangers, but too close to be friends. Colleagues of a sort with her new position at the court, always a careful arm's length away.

A few hours after their lunch, Rhys turned the curricle off the main road. This road was little more than two hard packed wheel ruts between the grass.

"It's not been well travelled," Tamsin observed. Trees overhung the road, just starting to bud.

"I don't think so," Rhys replied. He hesitated. "It was never one of the more prized crown properties." He consulted the sheaf of paper maps and directions from the folio. The horses took advantage of his lapse in concentration to slow to a walk and pick at the weeds along the path. Tamsin didn't mind the delay.

"What will all this entail?" she asked after the silence threatened to stretch out again.

"Well, you should have a housekeeper who will know how the house itself is run, and a property manager for the tenants. Between the two of them, you ought to be well set. They work for you though, so if they aren't managing things well, you can always find someone else."

"They'll expect me to follow high kingsringer manners," Tamsin said.

He shrugged. "It's your house, and you are in the country. You could dine at a picnic every night and their duty is only to ask you what sort of cheese to bring out with the wine."

"This will be so odd."

"You can do it. After all, what's managing one house when you've saved a queen, gotten back the memories of a madman, foiled an evil prince, and fought ruffians?" Rhys said.

She gave him a small, crooked smile. "To be fair, I dealt with ruffians regularly even before you came into my life."

"Truth." He turned his attention from the horses to give her one of his lightning smiles. Her own smile faded.

The road took an abrupt turn, and there it was. Freiton Manor might be considered a small estate, but the stone facade boasted an arched entryway and dozens of gleaming glass windows. Tamsin cast an anxious look over to Rhys.

"You'll do fine," he said.

Someone must have been watching for them, because as they came to a halt the doors opened and a parade of people came out. Someone ran in from the stable and took the reins from Rhys. Someone else offered her a hand down. Tamsin took it, aware of all the eyes on her. A man wearing a light blue livery stepped up.

"Dame Saer, I am Jones, the households steward. Welcome to

Freiton," he said. He wore a powdered wig that had seen better days. His whole ensemble had seen better days. The coat strained to meet across his belly. The black band on his arm was noticeably newer fabric.

"Pleased to meet you, Jones." Rhys's presence was a warm strength behind her. She almost turned back to look. But he was leaving soon. He had his own life to get on with, his own estates to manage.

"Could you introduce me to the rest of my new household?" she asked.

"Certainly, Dame Saer." Jones listed off a dozen other names. Tamsin nodded.

Jones noticed her lost expression and waved her inside. "We have refreshments waiting for you in the drawing room." The line of people relaxed a little as she entered the house. Tamsin could hear faint whispers from the entryway. This was going to be a change for everyone.

She could see signs of the disrepair. The wood floors were clean but worn, and all the furnishings were chipped or marred. There were water stains around the mantle.

"Do you like it?" Rhys asked.

Tamsin looked around. "I never imagined something like this," she said truthfully.

"You deserve anything in the world," he said. "If Her Majesty hadn't provided for you, I would have."

"Rhys, I didn't help you for money, or a title, or a house..." she trailed off. That was trending disturbingly close to the truth that she couldn't say aloud.

"I know. But you deserve them anyway," he said. The housekeeper came in with a tea tray and set it on one of the tiny tables.

Tamsin smiled and turned down her offer to pour. Rhys sat across from her at one of the dark wood chairs, very proper and formal. She poured the tea out and passed him a cup. His fingertips brushed hers as he took it, and she looked away.

"Tamsin," he said.

"Sugar?" she asked.

He put the cup down.

"Tamsin look at me, you've hardly looked at me this whole journey."

She pushed herself up and walked over to the window. "I'm sorry. I just... you are leaving."

"I am, but Tamsin, there is a question I wanted to ask you before I go."

She turned, and he was there beside her. One finger reached out and traced the path of her curls on her cheek.

"I accepted Marion's offer. We are not engaged. I want to see who this Rhys is now; with the memories I have. And I want to see if this Rhys can build a life with you?"

Tamsin closed her eyes. All she wanted to do was let herself lean forward and close that gap between them.

"Rhys, there would be a terrible scandal. With David, can you afford another one? And Eira…"

"Tamsin, look at me."

She opened her eyes and looked up into the deep brown depths of his. "Over these last weeks, you've been my rock. You have been the source of laughter, hope, the person I think about first when I wake and dream about at night. I love you. Will you spend your life with me?"

"I…" She wanted to say yes. But those worries kept the words from her lips. Surely, he didn't know her well enough, didn't know what he was getting into… Rhys kept looking at her.

"Are you sure?" she whispered.

"I am. I can't think of anyone I would rather have beside me than you." He took her hands, leaned down and then his lips were on hers.

"I love you too," she said. And at last, she let all the plans and worries fade away.

*

"I can't stay," he said, when everything else had been said. They had returned to the sofa, the tea forgotten.

"I know," Tamsin said.

"I need to see my parents. Eira went to them earlier and we sent a letter, but I need to tell them about David. And the Queen needs my support on the council, I need to be back in Celdre soon after."

"I understand. Frank and Lacey are on their way here. I won't be alone," she said. His fingers were intertwined with hers.

"Good. And Carwyn house would be happy to host you again when you return to town," he brought her hand up to his lips, kissing the back of her hand. He brought their hands back down to her lap. "I didn't have time to find you a ring," he said. He pulled out his watch and laid it on her palm, wrapping her fingers over it. "Will this stand as a token until I can find you something better?"

She wrapped her fingers around the metal. "I don't need better," she said. Rhys smiled and stood. "I'll be back soon and bring Eira with me. How does a summer wedding sound? Or is that too long? Surely there is someone in town." His smile was so bright she couldn't help but match it.

She laughed. "Go visit your parents. I'll see you soon."

It took a while longer for the horses to be readied after their rest, for goodbyes to be said properly, or not so properly. And then his curricle was vanishing down the lane. Tamsin watched until the sound of the horses had gone, then she turned to walk into her house. Her house. She shut the doors and surveyed the rooms.

Jones cleared his throat from the receiving room. She pocketed the watch, her fingers still tight around it.

"Dame Saer, if you would come this way," Jones said. "I have some correspondence that you should attend to, then Mrs. Jones can show you to your rooms."

Tamsin touched the figured moulding around the door frame. Chipped paint and all, this was hers now, bought in blood. And through blood and fire she had escaped the Narrows for good.

Acknowledgement

The first thanks go to my husband, who supported me throughout this long journey and never once suggested I stop writing. To my children, Darian and Nigel, you're half the reason I finished this. I love the three of them more than words can say.

To Trent, for giving me the first half of the puzzle. And Ian for listening while I worked it out.

To Ellen for the constant cheerleading.

And to D.A.N.G. (Dayton Area Novel Group), the Pen Fatales ladies, my VP 21 (2017) classmates and the Jellyfish crit groups who helped me shape this book into what it is today.

And thanks to Tara Bush for making such an amazing cover. And of course, my editors, Francesca, Shona and Libby who make me appear far cleverer than I am!

9 781915 556622